I0585700

La Fontaine's
Complete *Tales in Verse*

La Fontaine's
Complete *Tales in Verse*

An Illustrated and Annotated Translation

JEAN DE LA FONTAINE

Edited and translated by
RANDOLPH PAUL RUNYON

McFarland & Company, Inc., Publishers
Jefferson, North Carolina, and London

Library of Congress Cataloguing-in-Publication Data

La Fontaine, Jean de, 1621–1695.
[Contes et nouvelles en vers. English]
La Fontaine's complete tales in verse : an illustrated and
annotated translation / Jean de La Fontaine ; edited and
translated by Randolph Paul Runyon.
p.   cm.
Includes bibliographical references and index.

ISBN 978-0-7864-4161-7
softcover : 50# alkaline paper ∞

1. La Fontaine, Jean de, 1621–1695—Translations into English.
I. Runyon, Randolph, 1947–   II. Title.
PQ1811.E4R86 2009   841'.4—dc22   2008049411

British Library cataloguing data are available

©2009 Randolph Paul Runyon. All rights reserved

*No part of this book may be reproduced or transmitted in any form
or by any means, electronic or mechanical, including photocopying
or recording, or by any information storage and retrieval system,
without permission in writing from the publisher.*

On the cover: "Let's take this fellow to the shed," illustration by
Jean Duplessis-Bertaux, 1894; (background) text of an
English translation of *Mazet of Lamporechio*

Manufactured in the United States of America

*McFarland & Company, Inc., Publishers
Box 611, Jefferson, North Carolina 28640
www.mcfarlandpub.com*

ACKNOWLEDGMENTS

I would like to express my gratitude to Ms. Juanita Schrodt, Secretary of the Department of French and Italian at Miami University, for her invaluable assistance in preparing this book, including scanning the more than a hundred illustrations from which these were chosen. I am grateful to Yves Le Pestipon, of the École Préparatoire of the Lycée Pierre de Fermat, Toulouse, for his expert replies to my many queries, his encouragement, and his friendship. Most of all, I want to thank my wife, Elizabeth, for having the patience to listen to my reading aloud each of these poems in their various versions and for making suggestions to improve them.

TABLE OF CONTENTS

BOOK FOUR

THE UNCOLLECTED TALES

PREFACE

It may come as a surprise to learn that Jean de La Fontaine wrote these poems. His *Tales in Verse* are not for children. No tortoises, hares or foxes inhabit their precincts, but husbands and wives, nuns and friars, ingénues and roués, all ruled by the unstoppable power of lust. The *Tales* are delicately sensual and yet, like Chaucer's, delightfully wicked. In 1675, at the request of Louis XIV, the lieutenant de police forbade the sale of one of their installments and ordered all copies to be seized, claiming they contained indiscreet and unseemly language and that reading them would corrupt public morals and inspire libertinage. The first claim was false and the second at least questionable. There are in fact no unseemly words in the *Tales*; La Fontaine went to amusing lengths to suggest certain things without actually saying them, in verse that provides food for the mind as well as the senses. In a preface he made the reasonable claim that a far greater danger lay in the sweet melancholy induced by certain novels to make their readers want to fall in love; better to warn them of wily tricks than to set them up to be seduced. The *Tales* are a veritable catalog of recipes for deception, though it is sometimes the women who outwit the men. On the other hand, maybe the lieutenant de police was not entirely wrong: in Laclos's *Dangerous Liaisons* Madame Merteuil warms up with a couple of the *Tales* before entertaining a lover.

The *Tales* themselves proved about as irrepressible as the lust that propels their characters. La Fontaine disavowed them to win election to the prestigious French Academy at the age of 63, but then published five more the following year. On his deathbed, he appeared to yield to his confessor's insistence that he renounce them to win admittance to heaven, making a public declaration that he was sorry he had "had the misfortune of composing a book of infamous Tales" and claiming to agree that they were "abominable." Nevertheless another one found its way into print the year after his death.

The *Tales* were as important to La Fontaine as his *Fables*, and like them they have their moral lessons: Don't be naive. Watch out for hypocrites. Seize the moment. Don't let artificial constraints (like marriage) get in your way. Money is a lover's best friend.

Some of the *Fables* (such as "The Young Widow" and "The Husband, the Wife, and the Thief") could as easily have been published as *Tales*. "The Ephesian Matron" and "Belphegor" were published as both. La Fontaine kept going back and forth between the two forms of narration, publishing his first two books of *Tales* between 1664 and 1666, his first six books of *Fables* in 1668, the third and fourth books of *Tales* between 1671 and 1674, five more books of *Fables* in 1678–79, seven tales in 1682–85, and his last book of *Fables* in 1694. Each genre complements and justifies the other. We can fully appreciate neither La Fontaine nor the *Fables* without knowing the *Tales*.

The *Tales in Verse* are a treasury of wit and adventure, and yet for readers who cannot read French they must rank among the best-kept secrets of world literature—for they have never before appeared, in their entirety, in English. Six of the tales are translated here for the first time: "In the Court of Love," "Mars and Venus Making Love," The Ballad of the Books," "The Quarrel between a Beauty's Mouth and Eyes," "Clymene," and "Convincing Kate"; in addition, the prologue to "Belphegor" is for the first time rendered in verse.

In his preface to the first book, La Fontaine asked his readers to help him decide whether to write future ones in regular verse forms (such as uniformly ten-syllable lines) or in the variable line lengths found in most of his *Fables*. In this translation I have done something like both; though unlike him, I have throughout adopted the rigorously rhyming couplets that seem to me ideally suited to English comic verse (except when in "Clymene" I use the rhyme schemes of the poetic forms in which the muses engage). When I vary the meter, I tend to keep the same number of beats within each couplet, though what is iambic or trochaic in one might be dactylic or anapestic in the next.

In the commentary accompanying the GF Flammarion edition of the *Fables*, Yves Le Pestipon wrote,

> Although scholars have not said much about this capital point, it seems clear that La Fontaine deeply meditated and thought out the arrangement of his works.... The Fables are organized ... like a stream that keeps turning back on itself.... As they follow each other they form a network resembling a fertile labyrinth.... The reader can find instruction and pleasure in folding each fable over the ones that surround it. Little by little, the wealth of La Fontaine's meditation comes into view through precisions, corrections, displacements, inverted figures.... "The Cicada and the Ant" gains by being read through "The Fox and the Crow," which itself does by being read through "The Frog Who Would Be as Big as an Ox," which "The Two Mules" in turn makes more interesting (36).

Le Pestipon draws out many connections between sequential fables. Others who have examined aspects of La Fontaine's ordering of the *Fables* include Patrick Dandrey, Richard Danner, Nathan Gross, Herman Lindner, David Lee Rubin, and Maya Slater. None of them, though, have seen the significance of this sequential structure for the whole collection with as much clarity and in as much detail as he.

I too read the *Fables* in that perspective in my book *In La Fontaine's Labyrinth*, where I found that 80 percent of the 239 sequential pairs of fables shared a verbal link (while all had either a verbal or a situational link), and that 23 percent of them were linked by a word or combination of words that appeared nowhere else in the *Fables*. The figures for the *Tales* are actually higher. Of the 61 tales in the four books that La Fontaine published as organized collections, 93 percent are paired by verbal links, and 75 percent of them by words or expressions that appear in no other tale. All of them display at least a situational parallel. In my notes to this translation I outline the more salient of these connections, including those that appear to exist between the pairs formed by the remaining eight tales that La Fontaine published, though not all in the same collection.

I list in the notes as well the known sources for the tales. Twenty-one come from Boccaccio (including three that also appeared in Chaucer's *Canterbury Tales*); ten from the fifteenth-century French collection known as the *Cent Nouvelles Nouvelles*; three from Ariosto's *Orlando Furioso*; two each from Machiavelli, Marguerite de Navarre's *Heptameron*, and Rabelais; six from ancient Greek and Roman sources. In nearly every instance, La Fontaine departed from his source, when he had one, in the direction of a neighboring tale — that is, by changing or adding a detail to make a tale more like the one before or after it in the sequence.

Although his *Fables* were illustrated when they first appeared, La Fontaine's *Tales* were not. But his racy plots soon inspired editors to hire artists to visualize them, beginning in 1685 with Romain de Hooge, and continuing with Charles-Nicolas Cochin in 1743, and the celebrated *Fermiers généraux* edition of 1762 with illustrations by Charles Eisen (1720–1778), some of which I have included here. I include as well illustrations by Jean-Honoré Fragonard (1732–1806), together with some by artists less well known: Jean Duplessis-Bertaux (1747–1820?), Camille Roqueplan (1802–1855), Janet-Lange (1815–1872), and a certain Laville on whom I could find no information. The Eisen and Fragonard illustrations come from an edition by Jules Tallandier, Paris, of the *Contes et nouvelles en vers* bearing neither date nor copyright (but printed in 1925–26); the Duplessis-Bertaux from an 1894 edition published in Paris by A. Le Vasseur; the Roqueplan, Janet-Lange, and Laville illustrations from *Contes et nouvelles de La Fontaine* published in Paris in 1838 by Ernest Bourdin.

BOOK ONE

1. "Jocondo"

Long ago in Lombardy there reigned a king
  so fair
That half the ladies pined for him—the rest
  were in despair
Because they could not hope to match the
  beauty of his face.
One day as he was gazing at his own
  reflected grace
He said out loud, "I bet there is no mortal to
  be found
Quite so gifted with the charms in which I
  so abound.
On this wager—prince's honor!—I would
  even deign
To stake the finest province to be found in
  my domain.
If such a one exists and I should have the
  chance to meet him
He'd have no reason to complain, so well I
  swear I'd treat him."
Hearing this, a gentleman from Rome ap-
  proached and said,
"If your curiosity by beauty, Sire, is led,
The course to take, I would suggest, is emi-
  nently clear:
Your Majesty should order for my brother to
  appear.
Concerning things that women like I know a
  thing or two.
And I know, your Majesty, that he will surely
  do.
In matters of the couch
He really is no slouch.
With all the women you've in tow
You're going to need some help, you know.
No doubt you're doing all you can
But it's too much for just one man."

Astolfo (for that was the name of Lom-
  bardy's fair king)
Replied, "I am intrigued. Indeed, he might
  be just the thing.
Send for him and then we shall discover
If all the ladies want him for a lover.
We'll let the connoisseurs—or -seuses—
  decide,
By their own decision we'll abide."
To Jocondo's house the Roman came
(For that was the handsome brother's name).
In the country, far from worldly strife,
Jocondo lived, along with his new wife.
Happily? I cannot say.
Though she did youthful charms display:
Delicate, lovely of limb.
His happiness was up to him.
His brother came, and made his plea—
As it turned out, successfully.
What convinced Jocondo in the end
Was that it would be good to be the friend
Of a king as likable as strong.
His wife's objections were both loud and
  long;
Nor were her lamentations very brief:
She seemed indeed to glory in her grief.
The way she had of bidding him goodbye
Would bring a tear to almost any eye.
"Are you so cruel deep in your cold heart
That from my constant love you would
  depart,
Preferring to seek favors at the court?
Don't you know those favors' lives are short,
Dependent on the fancy of a king?
Those receiving them with fear will cling
To the hope he'll not take them away;
But favors seldom last more than a day."

All that you will find if you go there
Is dread, uncertainty, and then despair.
If you're getting tired of me,
Think of the tranquility
Pervading this sweet solitude
Where no worry can intrude.
At night the murmurs of the streams
Favor sleep and pleasant dreams.
How can you leave these fields and trees,
Fertile valleys, birds and bees?
How in fact can you leave me?
But at my love you laugh, I see.
You cruel man, then leave this place.
Go show off your pretty face.
I will die: I hope I may,
Sometime soon—perhaps today."
The tale I fear does not allow
For us to know exactly how
It was Jocondo got away
Nor what he found to do or say.
On this I will not write a verse
For fear of making it sound worse.
I'll simply say he couldn't speak
Because his grief made him too weak.
(Should you happen to be in a difficult spot
It's a move I find more useful than not.)
Seeing he was about to go
She many kisses did bestow
Together with a parting gift:
"Don't lose this bracelet," she sniffed.
"Keep it always on your wrist;
I want to be sure I am missed.
I wove the trinket from my hair;
My portrait too is tied on there."
I'm sure you must be thinking
Since in grief she was sinking
That in an hour at most
She'd give up the ghost;
But that's not how the game is played.
He left, then saw he had mislaid
The bracelet—left it behind.
He must return, that gift to find.
He galloped back for this mistake,
Not sure what excuse to make.
He opened the door: no one there.
None to hear him climb the stair.
He went to her room and saw stretched atop
  her
An oafish valet—how very improper!

The lovers were sleeping, in passion were
  curled.
He imagined dispatching them to the next
  world;
There they could sleep as long as they like.
Yet he held back, and no blow did strike.
A very wise move, for in such affairs
Publicity brings its own raft of cares.
By prudence or pity, that course did he take,
Yet had to be careful neither to wake
For then his honor would require
That the both of them expire.
He whispered, "Live, and feel remorse."
Then descended the stairs and mounted his
  horse.
But wending his way, he kept giving voice
To grief at the insult implied by her choice.
"If he'd been a good-looking, presentable
  fellow
Then maybe about it I'd feel more mellow.
But that she should select a boorish valet
Fills my poor heart and soul with dismay.
Love must be blind, even demonic,
Making match-ups that moronic;
The god of Love does it for fun
Perhaps this time some bet's been won."
That day's unpleasant recollection
Ruined Jocondo's fine complexion.
With hollow eyes and pallid brow
His beauty was but a memory now.
At court, in his depression
He made a bad impression.
When the ladies beheld him they said,
"We can't tell if he's live or he's dead.
Is this the famous Narcissus
We're all supposed to want to come kiss us?
The fellow has jaundice!
Someone has conned us.
Seeing this ghost we're shocked and aghast;
He looks like he's come from a forty-day
  fast.
Whatever he's got, we don't want to get it.
If you call *this* handsome, then just forget it."
The king was delighted, the Roman
  dismayed:
What was the reason for this masquerade?
His brother would not explain to him why.
Nevertheless, the experienced eye
Could tell that in Jocondo's face

"An oafish valet—how very improper!" (Duplessis-Bertaux).

There was beauty, there was grace.
It just needed filling out;
He was too sad to eat, no doubt.
But Cupid took pity, because this meant
Fewer vows, less incense sent
In his direction by his fans.
Reversing course, the god made plans
To give Jocondo consolation
Through that which had caused his frustra-
   tion.
One day in the palace Jocondo was walking;
Through a thin wooden wall he could hear
   someone talking.
He could only presume
It was some hidden room.
This is what he heard,
Transcribed word for word,
As he stood there with no one in sight:

"My dearest, try as I might
I cannot awaken your lust.
I fail to see why you must
Find it more fun to play cards with the pages
Than come when I call. It really enrages
Me awfully, dear. I sent word with the maid
But you wouldn't come till the hand was all
   played.
You don't care what I want, is what this im-
   plies."
You can imagine Jocondo's surprise
Hearing these words as he stood in the hall.
To find out some more, he crept to the wall.
Through cracks in the woodwork Jocondo
   unseen
Peered slyly within and beheld ... the queen!
The voice had been hers and to make
   matters worse

The beloved with whom he had heard her
　　converse,
Her Adonis, her ungrateful, card-playing
　　swain,
The one who had broken her poor heart in
　　twain,
Who, bored in her presence, from ennui
　　would fidget,
Was, as it happened, her husband's own
　　midget.
His dwarf, his vertically-challenged retainer,
Whose stature gave status as king's
　　entertainer.
To the maid aforementioned the queen
　　would entrust
The key to the room where she sated her
　　lust;
That the maid let it fall to the floor quite by
　　chance,
Did not escape Jocondo's keen glance.
He made good use of the room's isolation,
Finding there ways to derive consolation,
Because, he reflected, "It's really quite plain,
There's now no reason for me to complain.
My wife's taste in lovers loses its sting
If something like this can be done to the
　　king."
His health was quickly restored,
And soon he was widely adored
By those beauties who once had disdained
　　him
In those days when his grief had constrained
　　him
To wander the palace with sad, downcast
　　eye.
Now they would trail in his wake with a sigh.
Every lady at court
Would gladly disport
If given the chance
With the man whose bold glance
Made even the prude
Want to do something lewd.
Astolfo began to discover
He was losing demand as a lover
As many of those he would bed
Would opt for Jocondo instead.
But the king didn't mind
Because he could find,
Thanks to his new-found colleague,

Relief from the strain of fatigue.
Yet the knowledge Jocondo had gained
Of the queen's taste in lovers remained
A problem that he had to solve.
Should he, as a good friend, resolve
To tell the king what he knew?
He felt that he had to be true,
That he ought to be loyal.
But that's hard with a royal.
Though he didn't wish to offend,
The zeal that he felt for his friend—
A king who had been such a prince—
Meant that, although he might wince,
The truth must be told to the king.
Here's how he handled the thing:
To forestall a royal reproach
He went for a gentle approach.
Before touching the delicate mystery
Of the room, he taught him some history:
"There've been many a king and a caesar
Whose wife knew that what would most
　　please her
She never could find
While remaining confined
To her matrimonial vow.
But rather than starting a row
Those majesties took it in stride.
They found it no stain on their pride.
For it happens to all,
The great and the small,
And even," he said, "to me."
He told how, in *flagrant délit*,
He'd discovered his wife with a clod.
"So you oughtn't to think it too odd
If your queen should decide to cavort
With a fellow uncommonly short."
"Not my dwarf!" wailed the king. "How
　　uncouth!
No doubt you are speaking the truth.
But it's hard to imagine she'd fall for that elf.
I feel I must go there and see for myself."
So he saw with his eyes and heard with his
　　ears
Things that would drive any husband to
　　tears.
But, bearing up bravely, he said to his friend,
"I have thought of a way by which to
　　transcend
The misfortune we equally share.

The first round is lost, I'm aware.
But vengeance is sweet, and here's how to get
    it.
I propose that we leave this behind and
    forget it.
Let's wander the kingdom, assuming new
    names.
We'll seek out fresh partners for sex, fun and
    games.
I'll go incognito. Pretend that we're cousins.
With our looks and my gold no doubt we'll
    find dozens
Of women who will not resist.
I think we should maintain a list
Of our conquests, and rank them in order.
I bet before reaching the border
Our book would be full." So off they did go,
With register, baggage, and plenty of dough.
I'd be here all day if forced to narrate
Their triumphs with ladies of lofty estate:
The Mrs. of magistrates, aldermen, mayors
Gave in to our pair's entreaties and prayers.
Though said to have hearts that were carved
    out of ice
They melted, imagining it would be nice
To be courted and kissed
And inscribed on the list.
There are those who'll object on hearing my
    tale
That however seductive, no one could prevail
With such incredible haste.
But I swear my story is based
On the poet Ariosto,
Whose *Orlando Furioso*
Contains not a single lie.
Besides, if I had to reply
To every complaint I'd never get done.
Suffice it to say that having begun
By tasting a little of many a dish,
Love readily granting their every wish,
The king expressed the opinion,
"We are sure to extend our dominion
Over as many as we may desire,
But for the moment we ought to retire
To rest
From this quest;
The sooner the better, is best.
I have heard doctors who say
There's a price that one has to pay

For having too varied a diet.
Perhaps it is time that we quiet
This mania for variety,
Before we drop from satiety.
Let's choose some object for our lust
To share between us two in trust.
That way we can be in sync.
One's enough for both, I think."
Jocondo consented, and said that he knew
Of a woman he thought would probably do.
She was easy, and witty,
And awfully pretty,
The wife of a prominent man of the town.
But Astolfo replied, "We should aim lower
    down.
One can be fully as naughty
With women who aren't quite so haughty.
We ought to avoid the prouder flirts,
For beneath much humbler skirts
Are beauties the equal of theirs,
Who will not be putting on airs
Nor throwing jealous fits,
And threaten to call it quits.
Low wenches are more reliable,
And certainly more pliable.
You don't have to dress up and take them to
    dances.
So I would suggest that we take our chances
With one who is faithful and true
And above all, with one who is new,
A girl who needs everything taught her."
"How about the innkeeper's daughter?
She's a virgin, I swear, if ever there was.
Her dolly no doubt knows as much as she
    does."
"Then let it be her, I am resolved.
One question, however, remains to be
    solved:
Who gets to go first, will it be you or I?
The royal prerogative ought to apply."
Jocondo objected to this.
He thought it very amiss.
Given their present equality
It seemed the height of frivolity
To appeal to irrelevant laws.
Better for them to draw straws.
They continued to argue, with harsh words
    and fists
Over a thing that might not exist.

I'm referring to that which they blithely
   assumed
Was an innocent flower that had not yet
   bloomed.
In their lodgings that evening they called for
   room service.
She came at their bidding, was not at all
   nervous
When they dangled before her a most
   precious ring.
She agreed to conditions, would do anything.
The deal now concluded, they made plans
   for later
When all would be sleeping and they would
   await her.
She tiptoed in silence through hallways
   unseen,
Came into their room, and lay down
   between.
Pleasure was had that night by all three,
Jocondo especially, thinking that he
Had been the first to enjoy
What in fact had been claimed by a boy
With whom the girl was already acquainted.
Women have ways of seeming untainted.
Most men don't know this, but Solomon did.
That wisest of monarchs said three things
   were hid
From his understanding, and one of the three
Was "the way of a man with a maid," you
   see.
That's what I take Proverbs 30:19
In sacred scripture really to mean.
Things continued that way for three nights
In this fine three-way of earthly delights.
But the boyfriend was hurting from lessened
   affection
So he started to do a little detection.
He shadowed the girl, and soon he could tell
What was transpiring inside the hotel.
Between them arose a serious quarrel.
"How could you," he asked her, "be so
   immoral?"
She promised the lad once the others were
   gone
That the two sweethearts would get it back
   on.
"I can't wait, I tell you. It's driving me mad.
See me tonight, or I'll tell your dad."

"But I have contracted an obligation
And don't want to lose my just compensation.
They promised a ring, which I'd like to
   keep."
That's different," he said. "Tell me, how do
   they sleep?
"Like logs, but be as that might
I still have to lie there all night.
When one of them chooses on me to impose
The other waits quietly, sometimes will
   doze,
As long as 'the seat is taken,' they say."
"I'll show up tonight, I'll brook no delay,
Once they're both started to snore.
Don't worry, just see to the door."
She left it unlocked, just as he had said.
Her boyfriend arrived at the foot of the bed.
Somehow the two of these determined lovers
Found a way to unite beneath the bedcovers,
Though dangerously near
The king and his peer.
The boy and the girl
Gave it a whirl
While the other two thought nothing of it,
Though each for his own part did covet
What he imagined the other enjoying.
In fact it was rather annoying
To have to wait for so long
To get to the end of the song.
Yet each of them thought with alarm
His comrade might do himself harm.
The boy caught his breath and anew
Made up for lost time, then withdrew:
Once the others were slumbering
He began disencumbering
Himself from the sheet. He
Said 'bye to his sweetie,
Then left; she too thought it best
To depart, now needing a rest.
Next morning, the king, yawning, said
"My friend, you'd best stay in bed.
After last night you'll need lots of rest."
"Surely, my amorous pal, you do jest.
I am dismayed
That you had the maid
All to yourself. Was that fair?"
The dispute went on from there,
Each claiming the other'd abused
His patience. They both were confused

"Her boyfriend arrived at the foot of the bed" (Fragonard).

By what had transpired.
At last, they grew tired
Of bickering on in a fruitless dispute,
The king called her in, and she made it moot
By tearfully confessing
That last night she'd been messing
With her boyfriend instead of with them.
Her fear that they would condemn
Her two- or three-timing craft
Was groundless, because they just laughed.
They gave her the ring and many a coin,
With this the young lovers we able to join
In holy matrimony.
She went to the ceremony
A virgin, officially,
Though artificially.
Our duo's adventures were now at an end,
Each one in the register faithfully penned:
With favors bestowed
Their book overflowed,
A tribute of sorts to loose morals.
Now they could rest on their laurels,
Awards all the finer because they had cost
Just a smidgen of skill, a few fake tears lost,
Won far from dangers and war's alarms,
Safe in the comfort of feminine charms.
Generations to come their triumphs would
    know.
But now the king said, "I think we should
    go.
I've had enough of all this pursuit.
Let's head on home by the most direct route.
If our wives have been untrue
We now know quite a few
Who we can trust to falter.
The stars their courses may alter
And an age may begin in which passion's
    flame
Will only burn for love without shame.
But it seems for the present that some evil
    star
Delights in the way things now on earth are,

And on mortals has placed some dread,
    wicked curse,
Making men trick their wives, also the
    reverse.
The world is as full as it can be
Of conjurers practicing sorcery.
What we thought was tragic
Might have just been magic.
Our wives—for who can tell?—
May have been under a spell.
Perhaps what we saw was not really there.
Let us to our homes repair.
Like contented bourgeois let's spend our life
Each in the company of his own wife.
Perhaps our wives will love us now
And respect their marriage vow;
Maybe our absence has led them to ponder
And, making them jealous, of us made them
    fonder.
What Marriage has taken it may yet restore
And make our wives their spouses adore.
Perhaps in the end it will relight the spark."
His prophecy here was right on the mark.
The welcome they got was wonderfully
    warm,
Though they were scolded, just for the form.
Both were showered with kisses
From their respective Mrs.
Of the dwarf there was nothing to say,
Nor of the wretched valet.
Only dinners and dancing,
Feasts, revels enhancing
The truly joyous occasion.
The wives seemed to need no persuasion
To each do their conjugal duty,
Nor the husbands to find in their beauty
So much satisfaction
That more girlie action
On the side would be *mal à propos*.
Other wives we do not know
May be as faithful in their way
But we really cannot say.

2. *"Richard Minutolo"*

Naples has long been considered the spot
Where hanky-panky waxes hot.

It has more women who are pretty
Than any other Italian city.

The ladies there will light your flame
Even if that's not your aim.
I could cite you for example
One whose charms were more than ample,
A woman with a would-be beau
Named Richard Minutolo.
None more savvy in romance
In all of Italy or France.
He needed all his expertise,
For she was so hard to please.
Catella, who so turned him on,
As told in the *Decameron*,
Rejected all of his advances.
Richard, to improve his chances,
Thought it wisest to pretend
His broken heart was on the mend.
No more, he said, would he come calling;
He pretended he was falling
For one who would love him back.
Catella laughed, and showed a lack
Of jealousy, for after all
The one he claimed to have in thrall
Was a friend whom she held dear.
But Richard's plan did not stop here.
Catella and friends were having a chat,
With Richard there, of this and of that,
When Richard spoke up, without getting
  explicit,
Of a husband involved in something illicit.
Though the husband was not named
Catella feared the news was aimed
At her. Alarmed, she then resolved
To ask him was her spouse involved.
She drew him aside and sought to know
Of whom it was he'd spoken so.
"The love for you I once did feel
Was so strong I must reveal
The painful truth. Here's what I know:
It's Simone, of easy virtue.
I don't want this news to hurt you
But your interest is at stake.
That's the reason I must make
This painful circumstance so clear.
I know it could well appear
I'm concealing up my sleeve
Some hidden aim, but do believe
Concerning what I must impart
Your welfare's all I have at heart.
Were I still your heart's fond slave

I would not at all behave
In this true and honest way.
Things like this I would not say.
For they'd not advance my end.
Thank God that I'm just a friend.
Were I more, you would suspect
I had invented this defect
In the conduct of the man
You're married to. That's not my plan.
The naked truth you can behold.
In Janot's baths it will unfold,
In a room where he will meet
That hussy whom he finds so sweet.
A day ago I heard the news.
Money is the means to use;
Janot doubtless can be bought.
A hundred crowns will do a lot.
You should go, to be exact,
And catch your husband in the act.
The room to serve as their love nest
Will be dark, at her request.
Perhaps she wants not to be seen
Since her conscience isn't clean.
Don't try to negotiate;
Pay Janot the going rate.
Once his hands are on the loot
You can be her substitute.
He'll put you in that darkened cell,
Not to pray or fast, for well
You know it's not for monk or nun
Unless they're looking for some fun.
Don't speak—that would spoil the plot."
The gambit pleased her quite a lot.
The only thing that she did say
Was his instructions she'd obey.
"My husband and his Jezebel
Will be surprised, if all goes well,
When they tumble for this trick.
Do they take me for some hick?
I'll show them a thing or two."
To her friends she bid adieu
And hastened to await her quarry,
Confident that they'd be sorry.
Money makes the world go round,
In France as I myself have found,
Or in Italy of old,
Where this story first was told.
It's with gold that Cupid's quiver
Finds the power to deliver.

It turned out as he predicted.
Janot claimed to be afflicted
By his conscience, but did dash
To action once he saw the cash.
Richard had paid him as well;
From Satan he'd collect in hell.
Richard, first inside the room.
Made sure no light would pierce its gloom,
No holes to get in the way
Of the pleasures planned that day.
He did not have long to wait
Before Catella came, irate,
Eager to give her errant spouse
A sound reproof, that stinking louse!
But he came not, nor Simone
—Just Minutolo alone.
A distinction, though, she'd miss
When Richard began to kiss.

As for the rest, I'll let you guess.
He enjoyed that first caress.
As for her, it all occurred
With her compliance, with no word.
He took advantage; doing so,
He hoped his ecstasy'd not show;
Tried not to laugh, and did succeed.
To tell his happiness I'd need
Far abler craft than I can claim,
Two parts of it, though, I can name:
The first, that he could now possess
The one who'd made his heart obsess;
And then, that by this trick could rule
Over her who'd been so cruel.
A pious work indeed, he thought.
But she broke down in tears, distraught:
"I can't," she cried, "take any more.
I'm not who you take me for.

"The light of day revealed him to her startled eyes" (Duplessis-Bertaux).

Remove your hands, or I will bite,
And with my nails destroy your sight.
So *this* is why you stayed away,
Pretending to be sick each day.
No doubt keeping in reserve
Your energy for *her*. The nerve!
Am I less lovely than Simone?
Has she better technique shown?
Did she more love than I display?
I hope to see you hanged some day!"
Richard, hoping to appease her,
Tried to kiss and gently squeeze her,
But she fought him off too well.
"Leave me alone!" And then to yell:
"Don't dare treat me like a child.
I will not be reconciled.
Give me back my dowry, for
I'm not married any more.
Stay away and go to her
Whom I see that you prefer.
I would seem to be naive
If I were still to believe
In the sacred marriage vow.
What keeps me from sending now
For Richard, who did love me once?
He'd clobber you for this, you dunce!
And I believe I almost could."
The irony was just too good:
Richard laughed, which wasn't prudent.
"Now you snicker? How impudent!
Will you blush? Let's see your face."
Then she fled from his embrace,
To a window felt her way,
And opened it. The light of day
Revealed him to her startled eyes.
She almost fainted from surprise.
"Who could have thought you'd be so mean?
What will folks say? I will be seen
As someone one can take to bed."
"Who would know?" our Richard said.
"Janot won't spill it, as I live.
I hope you maybe could forgive
This violence and treachery.
All's fair in love and ... lechery.
I'd been forced before this scheme
To serve beneath a harsh regime;
My only recompense, your eyes.
Would you have yielded otherwise?
I think that would be long odds.

Now I'm happy, thank the gods.
You're not to blame in this affair.
Therefore why should you despair?
I know some women, I can say,
Who'd not mind being tricked this way."
His words on her had no effect;
Catella's tears just flowed unchecked,
But now so lovely she became
It rekindled his hot flame.
He took her hand. "Leave me," she said.
"You've done enough. Should I instead
Cry out to Janot and his crew?"
"That it would be mad to do.
The best is not to say a word.
If news got out of what occurred
You would fall into disgrace,
Coming to this ill-famed place:
They'd say you came some cash to earn
Rather than the truth to learn.
That's the way the world is built;
People tend to presume guilt.
If your husband should find out
We'd have to fight a duel, no doubt.
His life then would be in danger
For to combat I'm no stranger."
These thoughts must have done the job
For now Catella ceased to sob.
"There's nothing that one can do now;
Just console yourself somehow.
Might I distract you from this sadness....
But to hope for that is madness.
Though my soul did never waver
All it won was your disfavor.
But, you know, if you'd allow
The pleasure that we've shared just now
To return, we could perfect it.
Easy thing to resurrect it!
The hardest part's already done.
Why don't we just have some fun?"
So well he cajoled and preached
Catella for a hanky reached
And began to dry her eyes.
He still pressed for a reprise
In words that had a honeyed flavor
Which she found that she could savor.
Richard first got her to smile,
Then after a little while
He progressed up to a kiss.
Then after still more of this

Other favors he acquired,
Brought her to the point desired,
Happier than he'd ever been.
When love on both sides enters in
Things go better, they maintain
Who are wise in that domain.

Thus did Richard find success
Through wickedness, I must confess—
A trick that merits you be shown it.
I just wish that I had known it
When I was fruitlessly insistent
With one who was as resistant.

3. "The Cuckold, Cudgeled but Content"

No better for his trip to Rome,
A rich man's son was headed home,
Often stopping on the route:
Good wine, good lodging, and a cute
And charming chambermaid, if handy,
Were for him always just dandy.
He was in a town one day
When a lady passed his way,
Spirited and elegant;
Followed everywhere she went
By a page. He was enchanted;
His desire was strongly planted.
It wasn't virtue he had brought
From Rome, but pardons he'd there bought,
As so often is the case.
The lady's face was full of grace.
Frisky, young, with eyes so sweet,
All she needed was to meet
Someone who could be her friend
Someone like him: this thought did send
Our hero right out of his skin.
He decided to begin
By asking for some information
On her name and social station;
This the townsfolk could provide:
The village châtelaine, the bride
Of Squire Bon, whose hair was gray
(All four hairs, or so they say).
Though he was old, his high estate
For his age did compensate.
All this seemed good news indeed;
Our hero felt he would succeed.
He sent his servants on to wait
While he knocked at Squire Bon's gate.
He said he was seeking work;
There was no task he would shirk.
The Squire was pleased, thought he'd suffice
(Having asked his wife's advice)

To fill the falconer's position.
She found their new acquisition,
Our man sensed, to be quite pleasing.
But not too soon would he be seizing
His chance to declare his flame;
He knew how to play that game.
The Squire so loved his charming bride
That he never left her side
Except when, falconer in tow,
He sometimes would a-hunting go.
Though days when they'd the forests roam
The falconer'd rather stay at home,
There to take the Squire's place
And his lovely wife embrace.
The lady needed no persuasion;
They just needed the occasion.
Their wait was long, none can deny.
But Cupid would a ruse supply:
One night the lady asked her spouse,
"Which domestic in the house
Has for us the purest zeal?"
"The falconer's the one, I feel."
"It would be a big mistake,"
She said, "to trust him. He's a fake.
Just the other day, you see,
He spoke words of love to me.
I was so shocked. What could I say?
That he would act in such a way,
That such a project he'd devise,
I thought I might scratch out his eyes.
And almost did, but was restrained
By fear my honor would be stained.
In fact, so he could not deny
What he had done, I said I'd try
A rendezvous by the pear tree.
Tonight he's waiting there for me.
I said you always were about
More from love for me than doubt.

So close an eye on me you keep,
I'm only free when you're asleep.
I'd try to get away tonight
When you're sleeping very tight.
That's how things at present stand."
The flames of Squire Bon's ire were fanned.
"My dear," she said, "try to assuage
Your eminently valid rage.
Go yourself and set a trap.
I'm sure it will be a snap.
In the garden you will find
The tree in question; bear in mind
That to catch that wicked boy
You must have a clever ploy.
Go disguised: put on my skirt.
Take a stick and make him hurt.
That he deserves it will be clear
When his insolence you hear.
Strike him so hard that he'll remain
Writhing on the ground in pain.
Let this be the honor due
To a lady's wronged virtue."
The Squire memorized his part,
A willing dupe, though good at heart.
As husbands go, not all that bad;
But he, alas, would soon be had.
He did exactly as she said:
Tied her bonnet on his head,
Donned her skirt, hastened away
To where he'd await his prey.
He waited, it first seemed, in vain.
The reason I will now make plain:
Our hero'd seen that it was time
Into the lady's bed to climb.
There he took the Squire's spot;
The two warmed things up quite a lot.
The garden, though, was turning frigid,
Poor Squire Bon becoming rigid
With the cold. He clacked his teeth,
While the two inside, beneath
The warm and cozy quilts and covers
Did those things enraptured lovers
Do, in sweet delights immersed.
All this while, the Squire cursed
His servant's laziness: so late
For such a very important date!
Our hero took increased delight
In bedding one not his by right.
At last came time to bid adieu,

And go to his next rendezvous.
But not before one for the road,
With thanks for all the grace bestowed.
To the garden did he race
The angry husband now to face,
But cleverly feigned that his eyes
Were beguiled by the disguise.
"Wicked woman, you'd betray
His perfect love for you this way?
God knows I feel shame for you
And almost didn't come, it's true,
Refusing to believe your heart
Was so perverted in each part
That to this you could descend.
Well now I see you need a friend.
I'll be that friend, I can assure you;
Of this sin I hope to cure you.
I came to this assignation
Just to make examination
To see if you deserved his trust.
Don't think you can tempt my lust.
I'm a sinner, I confess,
But prize your honor nonetheless.
I'll not commit such an outrage.
You come here saucy as a page,
But my arm will rain down blows
To make sure your husband knows."
At this the Squire was pleased to death,
With tears of joy, beneath his breath,
He said, "To God my thanks be fervent
For my chaste wife and loyal servant."
But there was still more to come:
Our hero beat him like a drum,
Cracked a shoulder, bruised a bone;
Kept it up all the way home.
The Squire now began to feel
That he could use a bit less zeal.
Yet though it was somewhat unnerving
It showed loyalty unswerving:
This consoled him for the pain.
Once in bed with her again
He told his wife all that took place.
"Not within a century's space
Could we again find such a treasure
As that servant. I'd take pleasure
Seeing that boy settle down
And find a woman in our town.
Henceforth, treat him and me as one."
"No sooner said," she said, "than done."

"Our hero beat him like a drum" (Laville).

4. "The Husband Who Heard Confession"

In the wars fought by the king
Of France he did such valor bring
That Squire Artus was made a knight.

In a high and solemn rite,
His general the knightly spur
Himself did on Artus confer.

"A gentleman, a knight, a priest..." (Janet-Lange).

Artus, thus honored, had the sense
Of enjoying precedence.
A baron of the highest class
Would be obliged to let him pass
Should he meet him on the road:
That honor was to Artus owed.
In this exalted state of mind
The Squire came back home to find
The wife he'd left by herself there
Not at all engaged in prayer,
Nor in pious works engrossed,
But feasting, dancing, playing host,
Carrying on a riotous life.
He didn't like this in his wife.
"Since the day that I left town,
Have I gained increased renown:
As cuckold, and not just as knight?
I must bring the truth to light.
Such an honor for my sake
Is twice as much as I can take."
These were his thoughts, but what to do?
The ruse he came up with was new:
On a day when priests assemble
He decided to dissemble;
Donning the garb of their profession,
He prepared to hear confession.
So that she her sins could name

His wife to this priest then came.
At first she named mere peccadilloes,
Then came acts performed on pillows,
Which are of a grander scale.
She recited in detail:
"In my bed I have received,
If such a sin can be believed,
A gentleman, a knight, a priest...."
The list begun would have increased
Except her husband broke in there:
"A priest!" he cried. "Are you aware,
Unfaithful wife, whom you address
Concerning what you now confess?"
"My spouse," she said, not fazed a bit,
Revealing she had mother wit.
"I saw you sneak yourself in here;
Your scheme to me was crystal-clear.
It's strange a man as smart as you
Could fail to grasp my clever clue:
A gentleman, and then a knight
Is what you said you were. In light
Of the robe you now have on
The conclusion must be drawn
That you are a priest today."
"Bless God! is all that I can say.
A fool I was to take amiss
Something so obvious as this."

5. "The Cobbler and His Wife"
(based on an event in Château-Thierry)

A cobbler there was—we'll call him Blaise—
With a pretty wife, and clever ways.
The two of them had money woes;
They asked a merchant (not, God knows,
The brightest crayon in the box),
To replenish their lost stocks,
If from him they might obtain,
On trust, a quantity of grain.
He said yes, because he thought
The wife, whom he found very hot,
Would to his desire fall prey,
Since he knew they couldn't pay.
When time came to pay the loan
He found the wife at home alone
And said to her, "Now don't you fret.

You've what it takes to pay the debt.
Your beauty has an ample store;
Just give me what I'm longing for.
"We'll see," she said, and went to Blaise,
Who said, "That's great, because it plays
Into our hands. Let's do this right.
Tell him to come back here tonight,
That I'm away (although I'll hide
Right here). Insist that he provide
The IOU or the deal is off.
When he gives it, you're to cough.
Do it loud and do it twice
For safety's sake; that should suffice
To warn me that you've sprung the trap.
To forestall some chance mishap

"Insist that he provide the IOU" (Fragonard).

I'll spring out from where I'm hid."
This is precisely what she did.
Their plan went off without a snag.
Later Blaise would proudly brag
So much about his cunning ruse
Their neighbors came to air their views.
"Should've coughed after, not before:
Then you'd have enjoyed it more,"
Said a rich man of the town
Eyeing her both up and down.

"Three would have been satisfied.
Do that the next time that it's tried.
But say no word of what you do
(We'll keep that just between us two)."
"Sir, do you think in such a feat
That we could with your wives compete?"
(His spouse and others' were nearby
When she gave her tart reply.)
"Yours does, I'm sure, exactly so
But all are not so sly, you know."

6. "Bosom Buddies"

Alcibiade and Axioch:
Each a vigorous, charming bloke,
Randy and gallant as they come,
Were each of them the other's chum.

Being friends, they thought it best
To lay their eggs in the same nest.
But one of them did this so well
The woman gave birth to a mademoiselle

"I'll chance the risk of sin in this" (Duplessis-Bertaux).

Who was so pretty each claimed the honor
Of having fathered the child upon her.
Years passed. When the grown-up daughter
Could practice the lessons her mother had
   taught her,
Each wanted to take the girl to bed

And name the other the dad instead.
"Your spitting image—you can't deny it."
"No," came the reply. "I just don't buy it.
Besides, she's such a luscious miss
I'll chance the risk of sin in this."

7. "The Glutton"

At supper a gourmand
Decided to command
For the bill of fare
That the cook prepare
For him an entire sturgeon.
It made his stomach burgeon.
He ate all but the head,
Fell ill; his servants sped

To fetch the nearest surgeon:
"Come quick! He'll die of sturgeon!"
The best the physician could manage
In order to lessen the damage
Was to give him a high colonic.
"Although it's acute, not chronic,"
Said the doc, "I fear you will die."
Sniffed a friend, with a tear in his eye,

"You might as well bring me the head" (Duplessis-Bertaux).

"I think you should make out your will."
"But I've not," he replied, "had my fill.

And since I soon will be dead
You might as well bring me the head."

8. "A Model Nun"

Sister Jeanne, although a nun,
Gave birth to a little one,
But since then no longer errs,
Always fasting, saying prayers.
In this she does not resemble
Nuns who at the gate assemble.

To them the abbess said one day,
"Live like Sister Jeanne, I pray.
Flee the world and all its fun.
That's the way to be a nun."
Said they, "We'll live as you prefer
Once we've done as much as her."

9. "Provincial Justice"

Two lawyers refusing to budge,
So puzzled a provincial judge

He couldn't make tail or head
Of what either one of them said.

"He pinched two straws differently sized" (Duplessis-Bertaux).

"Once we've done as much as her" (attributed to Fragonard).

A remedy he then devised:
He pinched two straws differently sized
With his fingers and asked them to choose;
One of them now had to lose.
(For pinching was this judge renowned.)
The defendant with triumph was crowned
And happily went on his way

Feeling like king for a day,
For he'd won the trial by straw.
"An abuse," complained some, "of the law!"
The judge replied, "Don't make a fuss.
The law has ever been thus.
Some judges decide without cause
Without even trying the straws."

10. "The Peasant Who Angered His Lord"

A peasant once provoked his lord,
Who could the trifle have ignored
But his lordship was severe;
The price the serf would pay was dear.
Such behavior in my view
In lords, alas, is nothing new.
The poor peasant he harangued:
"You knave," he said, "you'll end up hanged.
Get accustomed to that thought;
It tends to happen with your lot.
To show how gentle I can be
You can choose your misery.
None will lead to your demise.
In your choice try to be wise.
Of the options, which is worst,
I leave to you; here is the first:
Lots of garlic you would eat:
Thirty cloves, each taken neat.
Without a pause, without a break;
No water for your thirst to slake.
I'm not sure that I would pick
Thirty wallops from a stick,
But that's what's in store for you
With selection number two.
Now we come to number three,
Which you'd pick if you were me.
All you'd have to do is pay
A hundred crowns to me today."
The peasant now began to think:
"Thirty cloves, no drop to drink!
That would surely make me sick.
Though thirty wallops from that stick
Would likely put my life in peril.
A hundred crowns! I'm over a barrel.
That's the worst choice of the three."
The peasant fell down on one knee:
"Have mercy for the love of God!"

"He dares to speak to me, the clod?
Bring a rope. Let's hang him now!"
The peasant had to choose somehow.
He chose the cloves. The lord directed
That the strongest be selected.
One by one he made the count,
Making sure of the amount.
Then he put them on a plate
For the victim. When he ate
The first (and largest), he was flustered,
Like a cat discovering mustard
Someone's put into its meal,
Making it lose all appeal.
He dared not touch it with his tongue
Out of fear it would be stung.
The master laughed, but yet made sure
He would take the entire cure.
Watching all that he was doing,
That he not swallow without chewing.
One he ate, and then a second;
At the third he thought hell beckoned.
When he'd twelve consumed entire
He had to gasp, "My throat's on fire!
Give me something, please, to drink."
The lord said, "I begin to think
You might be a smidgen dry.
Wine is good with meals, so try
This fine vintage. Drink your fill.
But realize that now you will
Have to choose the thirty blows
Or the payment." "Sir, might those
Cloves of garlic that I've eaten
Lessen how much I'll be beaten?
For I know I can't afford
To pay you that much cash, my lord."
"No. You'll get all thirty blows.
The garlic cloves won't count." He chose

To fortify himself with wine.
The first blow landed on his spine.
At the next he prayed, "Sweet Jesus,
They are beating the bejesus

Out of me, your humble servant.
Grant me patience, is my fervent
Prayer. The third came crashing down.
He gnashed his teeth, and leapt around;

"You can choose your misery" (Janet-Lange).

At the fourth, a foul grimace;
At the fifth, screamed—still to face
The other twenty-five to come.
Would he make it or succumb?
Such a cruel thing as this
Was never seen. They didn't miss,
Those two strong men with heavy sticks
Making sure the thirty licks
Rained down with equal weight and force.
The peasant yelled till he was hoarse.
"Have mercy!" to his lord he cried.
But the blows intensified.
The cruel master who had picked him
For this treatment eyed his victim,
Judging blows with steely gaze.
"My forbearance does amaze,"
He thought; the peasant thought he'd die.
At twenty, he began to cry,
"For God's sake stop, for I can't take it."
"Well then, you'll just have to make it
Up to me in crowns: cash, please.
I knew when push came to squeeze
You'd object but you would pay.
If you need to, then you may
Ask a friend to lend you some.

As it's but a paltry sum
The interest won't, I think, be high."
The peasant, daring not reply,
Ran home to open up his stash;
Then he came back with the cash.
"These are all the coins I own,"
The peasant said, with bitter groan.
The cruel lord called for the scales.
The man stood by and bit his nails;
Sweat pouring down, he shed a tear
To see his fortune disappear.
One's master one must not offend:
On this truth you may depend.
For an offense, however slight,
Can never then be put to right.
As this peasant's story shows:
Humiliated, as God knows,
His throat was tortured and inflamed,
Then he had his shoulder maimed,
Next his savings all depleted:
The punishment for him repeated
In three very painful ways.
In the end you see he pays
In full, without a sou's reduction.
Let that be to you instruction.

11. "In the Court of Love"

The Court of Love's in session now.
Lovers wronged it will allow
To come before it and acquaint
The judges with their sad complaint.
On Cythera, Love's sacred isle,
A case is now called up for trial.
A lover claims a certain beauty
Has to him been far too snooty,
Though he had, at his great cost,
In a cause, alas, now lost,
Arranged for serenades,
Concerts and promenades,
Dinners, dances, and soirees,
In the hope that these displays
Would soften her, but got no kiss,
Not even a smile;
Hence the trial.
He argued, in short,
Before the august court,

That she be arraigned,
And, he hoped, constrained,
To love him in return.
Now her lawyer's turn:
"It is," he said, "for beauty's sake
That she is obliged to take
These regretted measures.
The undoubted treasures
That comprise her body's charm
Would incur unwelcome harm
Were she to relent
And to him consent.
Her cruelty he must endure
For the sake of her allure.
Else the god of Love would suffer:
Without her charms he'd find it tougher
For the shafts he shoots to stick;
No help she'd be to him if sick.
That god's invested in her soul's repose.

I'd even go so far as to propose
She treat all her suitors to this torment,
Making thousands sigh yet none content.
Let her take pleasure in her beauty sleep,
Which will her loveliness unblemished keep,
And thus increase the tributes she supplies
To Love's domain: her suitors' tears and
    sighs.
The lawsuit is an unwelcome distraction;
Fine the litigant for this infraction.
I conclude, in short,
Throw him out of court."
The state's attorney came down on her side;

The disappointed lover was denied.
To her home in peace she could return
With permission to be cruel and spurn:
When lovers woo, it's at their own expense.
But some there were that day who took of-
    fense.
Suitors did not with the Court concur;
With them the judgment kicked up quite a
    stir:
Consider all the jewels she's now got!
To accept a gift is to be bought.
But so it is and so it's ever been:
The tyrant that is Love will always win.

12. "Vulcan's Revenge"

Gélaste, showing Acante a tapestry depicting
    Mars and Venus making love, speaks:
You have doubtless read before
How Mars, the noble god of War,
Wounded by a golden shaft,
Fell victim to sly Cupid's craft.
When he encamped before the fort
At Cythera, the siege was short.
Venus soon came to the gate,
Seeking to negotiate.
Though on the field of battle the war god
    had won the day,
He thought it only right at this meeting to
    display
Strict observance of the forms,
All the well-established norms
Of the ancient art of wooing.
His advantage thus pursuing,
He sought
To dot
His I's and cross his T's.
In an attempt to please,
And play the role of charmer,
He donned his finest armor.
Look in that corner over there:
His face bears not the warrior's glare
But with a sense of style
He shows a winning smile
His shield glows with a flame
That puts the sun to shame.

Clothes, they say, can make the man—or
    god—
Even victors need a chic façade.
He soon won her heart.
Perhaps he did impart
Some sense of his desire,
Of how he was on fire
For her myriad charms.
Unless of war's alarms
He spoke instead:
Of combats led,
Of palisades
And cannonades,
Of ballistics,
Statistics,
Of battles won and lost.
Although this could exhaust
The patience of his hearer,
She found him all the dearer
For it.
The more it
Excited her
The more his talk delighted her.
See how in this deserted spot
She shows the warrior what's she got
By way of physical attraction.
It sure is some distraction
For this martial fellow.
He's starting to turn mellow
From those lengthy kisses.

I don't think he misses
His warrior pursuits.
Armor, shield and boots
Lie abandoned on the grass.
Love requires a different class
Of weapons: tears and sighs.
They're what win the prize.
While Mars and Venus were having such fun,
Phoebus Apollo, god of the sun,
For Venus burned with desire.
In his breast there smoldered more fire
Than ever appeared round his head
When through the heavens he sped.
He was handsome, as well as quite charming
But wrote poetry, which was alarming.
Although he was very prolific
His poems were too scientific.
To make matters worse
In addition to verse
He was also a sort of physician.
But was foundering in his ambition
To win the goddess's hand
Because, you must understand,
Such knowledge, sadly, often wrecks
One's chances with the fairer sex.
Between the man of war and that of science
The former is the one who'll win compliance
From the woman he would bed.
So she preferred sir Mars instead.
Phoebus Apollo hated to lose;
He decided to tell her husband the news.
Vulcan he brought to a neighboring wood
To see for himself how it was things stood
There the two of them could view
What the lovers loved to do.
If you look over there you will find
The poor man going out of his mind.
His hammer, the sign of his trade,
Falls to earth, as he stands there betrayed.
Though another one pounds in his brain
As he puzzles out how to obtain
The revenge he wants to effect.
Now look over here and reflect
On the quarreling and on the strife
Back at home as he beats on his wife.
But on closer inspection
There's also this section:
Venus is here less distressed.
She's at home receiving a guest.

It's Mars who's come by to court her,
With no spouse around to thwart her.
Just coquettes and beaux,
Ribbons and bows,
Flirtation and games,
Gallants and dames,
Good humor and wit:
All that is fit
For such an affair.
That's what I see there...
But wait! Ye gods, it's her spouse!
He's throwing guests out of the house.
Yet what does he gain by making such noise?
Once two such hearts have tasted Love's joys
They'll go to the ends of the earth
Rather than suffer a dearth
Of the expression
Of their affection.
In this image you will behold
The storied lovers each other enfold.
They would have been no more strongly car-
    ried
Away by passion had they been married.
Over there the trio of Graces
By the sad tears on their faces
Show Vulcan's sent them packing
Because he found them lacking
In the ingenuity
To halt the promiscuity
Of his unfaithful bride.
But who could ever provide
Enough dragons to police
Such a golden fleece?
Most of all he blames the imp with arrows:
Cupid, Venus' son, a.k.a. Eros.
Holding him answerable for her spree,
He'd lock him up and lose the key.
That's not all. Having lost all restraint,
He goes to Olympus to lodge a complaint.
The very thing he ought to keep quiet
He blabs all over, running riot.
Jupiter, not exactly the model
Of fidelity, since apt to coddle
Women who are not named Juno,
Replies to Vulcan, "Listen, you know,
This is all just in your head.
The thing that you should really dread
Is jealousy—the worst of pains,
But of which one least complains.

So what's the husband up to now?
He has to get revenge somehow.
He'll forge a net of steel with his smithy tools.
The idea came from Momus, the mocking
    god of fools.
It would make a really good show,
If the husband were to throw
It over the lovers asleep.
Then all the gods could come peep.
Vulcan goes to it hammer and tong.
One link to another: it doesn't take long.
The Furies then prepare the bed,
The pair are gently to it led.
From his forge he takes the mesh he's ham-
    mered there
And stealthily envelops the enamored pair.
Venus and Mars awaken
To find that they've been taken
Prisoner, with no way out.
Clubfoot Vulcan stumbles about
To his fury giving vent.

In the meantime he has sent
For all the gods, both high and low,
To see this entertaining show.
They'll be glad they were alerted
For they're sure to be diverted.

*This poem has remained unfinished for secret
reasons; unfortunately, what is missing is the most
important part. I mean the comments made by the
gods, and even the goddesses, on such a funny turn
of events. Once I return to the concept and the
character of this piece, I will bring it to comple-
tion. However, as the plan of this collection was
made at various stops and starts, I was put in
mind of a ballad that might yet find a place among
these stories, since it contains one in a way. I therefore leave it as well as the rest to the judgment of
the public. If it is found to be out of place, and if
there is anything wrong with that, I beg the reader
to excuse this along with all my other mistakes.*

13. "The Ballad of the Books"

At Cloris's house the other day I got sweet
    Allison
To talk about some novels. She was going on
    and on
About the tastes of readers now. One of her
    complaints
Is no one any more will read the pious *Lives
    of Saints.*
Things have come to such a pass that what is
    highly prized
Are literary works the most immoral yet
    devised,
Namely novels. Urfé's, like some verses that
    are current,
Should all be gathered in one place, she said,
    and then be burnt.
"That's fine for you," said Cloris, "who have
    passed the age of fifty.
But for someone young like me, *Astrée* is
    pretty nifty.
It always has a place in my boudoir because,
    you see,
Books about erotic love are just my cup of tea."

I think that Cloris could have made her
    point with more finesse.
Though Urfé's novel is of course an exquisite
    success.
Long ago I was a fan when I was but a lad.
Now my beard is gray but the same pleasure
    can be had.
And so with prudish Allison I almost had a
    quarrel.
I said that if one looked, one would find
    lessons that were moral.
"But what's the point," she said, "in
    conducting such a search?
Is it likely to encourage folks to go to
    church?
Liars who spin fictions I most utterly
    detest.
Better far to read the truth; I'll do without
    the rest.
And I'll not endure it when a woman says to
    me:
'Books about erotic love are just my cup of
    tea.'"

Allison pronounced these words with such
    ferocity
That I believed she surely had religiosity.
But from her pocket fell a list prepared for
    her confession.
Unknown to her, I picked it up, and found
    she'd one obsession:
"I've read *Orlando Furioso* many times al-
    ready.
And every time I start to feel a little bit un-
    steady
When reading of Angelica when she is fast
    asleep
And toward her supine body the old hermit
    starts to creep.
I'll daydream of such silly things sometimes
    an entire day.
And so despite the censure I admit that I
    must say:
'Books about erotic love are just my cup of
    tea.'"

Aha! I thought, sweet Allison, so you read
    novels too!
The hermit's sneaky stratagem's a favorite
    with you!
You bear a striking likeness, with your mor-
    alizing air,
To *Amadis*'s heroine, so oft engaged in
    prayer.
That hypocrite, the story runs, supped 'ere
    grace was said,
As Oriana, passion-bit, did take her love to
    bed
And for that indiscretion paid—for unwed,
    she gave birth.

Many a girl has doubtless found this tale a
    source of mirth.
The Pope's condemned it, Cloris, as I think
    you might have guessed.
Among the books that one can read, I'll
    name to you the best
(Books about erotic love are just my cup of
    tea):

"*Clitiphon*, the oldest that we have, by
    Achilles Tatius,
Though Heliodore's *Ethiopian Tale* is more
    racy and salacious.
Ariane, from our own time, is quite full of
    invention;
I've read *Polexander* forty times with rapt at-
    tention.
Cleopatra and *Cassandra* are chock-full of ac-
    tion,
And Scudéry's *Map of the Heart* gives me
    much satisfaction.
Even the oldest you shouldn't spurn,
There's always something new to learn.
Percival from the Middle Ages
Can make you really turn the pages.
In my pleasure reading I will mix it
With Cervantes' ravishing *Don Quixote*.
Books about erotic love are just my cup of tea."
                        Envoi
You can't read Boccaccio in Rome without
    permission.
There are others like it in their style of com-
    position;
Some are good, some not. But you will, I
    hope, agree
Books about erotic love are just our cup of tea.

BOOK TWO

1. "The Ear-Maker"

Guillaume, a merchant, had to travel one
   day;
His wife stayed at home, with a child on the
   way.
A back country girl, her name was Alice.
She was youthful, naive, unsuspecting of
   malice.
André, a neighbor, would often come
   calling;
It was obvious why: he found her
   enthralling.
What André desired he could always attain.
He never did cast his love-net in vain.
Of all the birds that he could attract
Rare was the one who escaped him intact.
Alice, they say, for her part
Was never accused of being too smart.
Nor had she knowledge of the ruses
That on the naive Love uses.
So with her husband out of town
André thought he'd come around.
He stared at her, said nothing of her beauty,
But told her that Guillaume had failed his
   duty.
"I frankly am astonished!
Your spouse should be admonished
For going off to kingdom come
And leaving work at home undone.
From your coloration I can say it's very clear
That the child you're carrying is going to
   lack an ear.
I've so often seen it happen in this sort of
   case."
"Good God! Will it be born with but one ear
   to its face?
Do you know a cure? Is there something you
   can do?"

"There is, which I'd not undertake for any-
   one but you.
For others' plight my pity does not normally
   extend
Except when it's your husband, whom I
   count a bosom friend.
For his sake I think I'd even sacrifice my life;
So I'm pleased to offer some assistance to his
   wife.
I think it best if we proceed
With all necessary speed."
"All I ask is that you aim
At making both ears just the same."
"Have no fear upon that score.
Though it could prove to be a chore.
It sure will take a lot of work."
"There's no task that I would shirk
To ensure the child's well formed."
"I think it's time now that we warmed
To the task." To bed they went,
And to the tender task they bent.
She may have been naive, but still
She did the work with diligent will.
André too did persevere,
Toiling to produce an ear:
Now a tendon, now a fold,
Now an eardrum, now a lobe.
Material and labor mattered not:
They are some things that just cannot be
   bought.
"Tomorrow, we will add the final touch."
"Thank you," Alice said, "so very much.
In this world I have at least one friend."
Faithful André came again to lend
Assistance at the same hour the next day;
He was not the sort to laze away
At bed when there was labor to be done.

33

"Let's finish," he said, "what we have begun."
"I was just about to send you word to hurry
    along
Let's get to work and go upstairs to bed
    where we belong."
So up they went, and worked so hard that
    she began to wonder
If they'd overshot the mark and made a
    major blunder.
The baby, she feared,
Might become over-eared,
Having, that is. more than two.
"Don't worry," he said. I've thought it all
    through.
In all my years of doing this I've never made
    a slip."
Soon after this the absent husband came
    back from his trip.
As he caressed his darling wife he was a bit
    surprised
When she began to talk of ears and then
    when she chastised
Him for having left undone
The work that he'd begun,
But which by inattention could have been
    hopelessly marred
Had not André volunteered his help in that
    regard.
"You should go and thank our neighbor
For the free gift of his labor."
He wondered how his wife could be so
    dumb.
How could she to a trick like that succumb?
Of all the dirty low-down lying stunts!
He made her tell the story more than once.
The more he heard, the more his anger
    spread.
He saw a dagger lying by the bed
And thought that with it he would slay his
    wife
But then decided he would spare her life.
Her naiveté and innocence
Reduced, he saw, the guilt of her offense.
"Alas, my dear," she asked him through her
    tears,
"Is it quite so bad as it appears?
I gave away no cash nor merchandise
And of myself there's still lots to suffice
For all your needs, as André said

When we were at work in bed,
Bringing this our dear child to perfection,
As you'd see if you made close inspection.
You can kill me if I lie."
Calmed somewhat by this reply,
He said, "O.K., the matter's closed.
I know the thing that he proposed
You thought it was but right to do it.
There's no reason to pursue it.
I'd just like to make this clear:
Make sure tomorrow André's here
So that I can catch that snake.
Listen though: for your own sake
Let no word of this be said
Or you'll likely turn up dead.
Make André think I've left again.
You'll find a way to entertain
Your guest, but leave the infant's ear alone.
I'm sure by now that it is fully grown."
She fulfilled his order to the letter
Since she was aware that she had better.
Simple though she was, I will submit
That fear gives even animals some wit.
André came; heard Guillaume on the stair.
Now he had to hide himself—but where?
The only spot he found was by the bed,
Between it and the wall, so there he fled.
Guillaume knocked; she opened. With her
    hand
She silently gave him to understand
Where André hid. Guillaume had come well
    armed;
By even four Andrés he'd not be harmed.
But instead he went to find
Some friends for what he had in mind.
Something less than killing,
Though equally fulfilling.
He'd thought of cutting off an ear,
Or some other part more dear
(A penalty inflicted by the Turks—
They say that every nation has its quirks).
To his wife he did these thoughts confide,
In a whisper, taking her outside,
And leaving André locked inside the room,
Thinking that he had escaped his doom.
Relieved, since of the danger unaware,
André assumed the delicate affair
Was to the husband still unknown.
Upon reflection, though, Guillaume

"Not far from André, who could see it all" (Eisen).

Another plan of action spun:
It would be a lot more fun,
And more easily kept quiet.
So he figured he would try it.
"Tell his wife the sordid tale,"
He told his wife. "Spare no detail.
And be very sure to say
She must come here right away.
Tell her that the case is grave.
Only she that part can save
Which ear-makers tend to lose
When they another's wife abuse.
The thought alone will inspire dread
And make the hair stand on your head.
Say your spouse will do the deed
Unless she comes with utmost speed.
Since no guilt on her is laid
There's a chance she could persuade
Me, though angry, to be kind,
Maybe even change my mind
And the punishment commute
Or maybe in some way dilute.
If in this errand you succeed,
I will pardon *your* misdeed."
With joy did Alice hurry there.
André's wife came up the stair
All out of breath, but couldn't find
Her husband, thought he was confined.
As she trembled in alarm
She felt a hand upon her arm.
Guillaume sat her on a chair.
"Madame," he said, "do not despair.
Ingratitude's the mother of all vice.
Therefore, I have thought it would be nice
To do for André what he's done for me.

That would be poetic justice, see?
Since he was kind enough to make an ear
For my infant, then it would appear
That the best way I could pay him back
Would be to make up for a certain lack
In *his* children. Everybody knows
They tend to be deficient in the nose.
The fault, you see, is doubtless in the mold,
Which I'm good at fixing, I've been told.
I think we should proceed without delay
To see to its repair this very day."
As he said these words, he grabbed her tight,
Threw her on the bed with all his might
Not far from André, who saw it all
From his spot between the bed and wall.
With patience she accepted it quite well,
Thanking God the retribution fell
On her, not him, in its severity.
For her spouse she had such charity!
Guillaume was so consumed with raging ire
It appeared that he might never tire
Of paying back his neighbor André's trouble
At a rate that was much more than double.
Vengeance, as they say, is very sweet;
Exacting it like this made it complete.
Since it was his honor here at stake
This method of revenge was best to take.
André took it in, but didn't stir.
He judged it like a perfect connoisseur,
Thanking God it hadn't turned out worse.
To lose an ear he'd not have been averse;
But to lose much less was quite a coup.
Less I say, for thinking of the two
I'd rather cuckold's horns display
Than give an ear up, any day.

2. "The Catalonian Friars"

Now I think it would be fun
To tell you of the toiling done
By the Catalonian Brothers,
A different order from the others.
In the place of their abode
Such fervent charity they showed
That many a wife was made content,
Thinking she'd be to heaven sent.
Wives could go to paradise

By following the friars' advice
To pay the monks a certain tithe.
Every woman, plump or lithe,
Came with regularity
To do this work of charity.
These events appear to date
From an age when women's state
Was benighted; they occurred
When women could not read God's Word.

A swarm of friars had descended
On a town, which they found splendid
Since they had great appetites
And it was chock-full of delights:
Many pretty girls, but few
Young men there to spoil the view;
Their husbands were advanced in years.
The Brothers, hardy pioneers,
Established there a monastery.
Wives of that town did not tarry,
But came for the worthy goal
Of saving their immortal soul.
When their faith had passed the test
They heard a deeper truth expressed
By plainspoken Friar André.
This is what he had to say:
"If there's one thing that can block
Your salvation, little flock,
It's when wives for husbands save
More than they already gave.
Spouses this excess don't need,
Given that what might exceed
What is strictly necessary
Could go to our monastery.
Considering all you have got,
Had you given us a thought?
Our order's rules, you might object,
Would compel us to reject
The works of marriage. This is true.
And yet, we still must think of you.
Ingratitude's the sin most grievous;
That's why God told Satan, 'Leave us!'
And threw him into deepest hell.
So, you see, you would do well
To take your superfluity
And with assiduity,
In gratitude for heaven's grace,
Present it to us in this place,
Tithing to us monks a tittle
Of that which costs you so little.
Our right to this is uncontested.
It has been by popes attested.
And by Scripture: Prophets, Psalms,
Epistles, Gospel. Not as alms
But as a tithe, duly acquired.
Three times monthly you're required
To bring the excess of your love,
And save your place in realms above.
The burden is immense this work imposes

But monastic life's no bed of roses.
We're used to taking pains down here below.
There's something else, however, you should
   know:
You should hide the good you do within,
Somewhere between your nightshirt and
   your skin.
Say nothing to your spouse or any other,"
Declared the eloquently preaching Brother.
"May these words of Saint Paul make an im-
   pression:
'Faith, charity, but most of all discretion.'"
André's eloquence soon won the day;
The women fancied what he had to say.
Solomon the King in all his glory
Spoke not as well as André in this story.
The golden tongue of this eloquent friar
Inspired the hearts of the attentive choir
Of wives who soon put into execution
The message carried by his elocution.
To perform this work each had such thirst
That they argued over who'd go first.
Many a wife discovered to her sorrow
That she had been postponed till the mor-
   row.
Hard pressed to accommodate the crowd
To necessity the Brothers bowed
And organized a system of some rigor
To preserve their monkish manly vigor.
"Take it easy. You'll still get your turn,"
They assured the wives who rushed to earn
Points to cash in for the afterlife.
There were monks who had more than one
   wife
On their hands, and some had ten or more.
One friar had to service a full score;
Frisky, perky, full of vim,
Young ones gave themselves to him.
Some wives had such zeal to pay
That they went there twice a day.
Five or six months did elapse;
Some monks thought they would collapse
From the strain, and had the notion,
In the face of such devotion,
Of extending credit to their clients.
But, scrupulous, the wives showed self-re-
   liance
And wouldn't take a loan when they could
   pay

Out of pocket, as it were, today.
And to hold back would be wrong
On what to friars did belong.
They were definitely set
Against acquiring debt.
Far from wanting to finance
Some tried to pay in advance.
The Brothers were most expeditious
With the ones they found delicious.
These fell not into arrears
While those more advanced in years
Were sent to pay their sacred duty
To those whose taste for women's beauty
Was less refined.
I mean that kind
Of friar known as lay.
The system put in play
Was an authentic rarity:

A model of true charity.
One fine evening very late
A wife was passing by the gate
Of that same monastic house
In a carriage with her spouse.
As this point along the road
She thought to pay the tithe she owed.
"My God," she said, "there's something I
    must do.
Some business with a monk—I'll soon be
    through."
"Business of what kind?
Have you lost your mind?
It's midnight now," her husband said.
"The monks are surely all in bed.
If some sin's got you distressed,
Tomorrow it can be confessed."
"The hour doesn't matter; I must go."

"Faith, charity, but most of all discretion" (Duplessis-Bertaux).

"Hard pressed to accommodate the crowd" (Janet-Lange).

"Yes it does, and I am saying no.
What sin is pressing on your mind
That you a friar now must find?
Until tomorrow let it be.
That will be quite fine with me."
"I've done no wrong. You're quite unjust,"
She said. "The reason that I must
Go now is I have to pay
And cannot wait another day.
For if I don't pay now, you see,
God knows when he'll have time for me."
"What do you mean, you have to pay?
Pay what?" he asked, with some dismay.
"The tithes that to the friars go.
You mean to say that you don't know?"
"I know I find that it's bizarre
How charitable you wives are
To the monks, always donating.
In fact, it's downright aggravating.
What's this tithe, may I find out?"
"Oh he's a sly one, I don't doubt,
To demand that I explain.
All right then, I'll make it plain,
To stave off further acrimony:
The tithe on works of matrimony."
"What works?" the puzzled husband said.
"The sort of thing we do in bed.
I'm surprised you didn't know.
I should have paid an hour ago
But thanks to you
My bill's past due.
Yet I had been until today
Always the very first to pay."
At this his heart began to sink,
He had no idea what to think.
To learn the truth, he thought it best
For her to think he was distressed
By the secrecy alone.
For nothing else she'd need atone.
Engaging her in gentle chat,
Turning her this way and that,
He learned at last that many others
Paid their tithes unto the Brothers.
By that he was somewhat consoled.
"Indeed," she said, "they're all enrolled.
"Your sister tithes to Friar Aubry,
The Judge's wife to Father Faubry.
Her Majesty Guillaume requires,
Among the studliest of friars.

Brother Girard receives my share;
I was about to take it there."
What she recounted gave him pause.
He feared the damage tongues can cause!
Upon reflection he decided
He would secretly confide it
First to his Majesty the Prince,
But needed proof that would convince.
What better proof in this regard
Than from the mouth of Friar Girard?
He had him come, then pulled a knife,
In the presence of his wife,
Held the dagger to his throat,
Made him tell all note for note.
Then he had him tied up well
And went to the Prince to tell
The somber truth; then city hall,
To ring the tocsin bell to call
All the citizens to gather.
They were worked into a lather.
(The friars, though, were not aware
Of the tumult in the air.)
"Vengeance!" was the townsmen's cry.
That monkish vermin had to die.
The only question left was how.
One said they should go right now
And massacre the hypocrites.
Another said, burn them to bits;
Pile up flaming logs around
And raze their abbey to the ground.
Another said, "What ought to happen,
We should in their habits wrap 'em
And throw 'em in the river so
That the whole world now would know
How we deal with such perversion."
Each man offered his own version
Of a fate suitably grim,
According to his private whim.
After speeches full of fustian
They decided on combustion.
It would be a lovely fire.
There they'd perish, every friar.
Out of respect for holy ground
A less sacred place was found.
His barn a townsman sacrificed;
For the purpose it sufficed.
When the monks were locked inside
Husbands leaped about outside,
Dancing to a beating drum,

Celebrating martyrdom.
The band of Brothers now were doomed:
The towering flames quickly consumed
Each friar and father, robe and hood;
The husbands saw that it was good.
All of the monastic host

Died like piglets at a roast.
As for the women, I know not;
Poor Girard, the first one caught,
Although the manner is unknown
Doubtless met his fate alone.

3. "The Cradle"

By the road from Florence down to Rome
An innkeeper made his humble home.
He was not a man inclined to boast
Of having fancy customers to host.
The inn was not exactly of the best;
In fact, it rarely even lodged a guest.
At just thirty years of age, no more,
His wife had charms a man could not ignore.
There were, in addition to the mother,
An adolescent girl and infant brother.
Pinuccio, a lad of higher class,
Had cast his eyes upon the pretty lass.
He found her very full of grace
Gentle, sweet and fair of face.
He was so ensnared
That he soon declared
His love. Nor was she shy.
Thus they could get by
Without the sighing
And the dying
That for others is *de rigueur*.
Not only did Pinuccio dig her
But she him, for this fetching lass
Never cared for boys of her own class.
Her taste was too refined
For suitors of that kind.
Many had tried to claim
Colette (which was her name)
In marriage, but those guys
Lost; for she had eyes
Only for our hero,
Young Pinuccio.
The only fly in the ointment:
They could seldom fix an appointment
To do those things that lovers do:
Converse, make goo-goo eyes, pitch woo.
Her parents kept a careful guard,
Which made such meetings very hard

For the boy and girl to manage.
Though this seeming disadvantage
Made their passion all the hotter.
If you want to save your daughter,
Parents, don't restrain her;
It's really a no-brainer.
For love will find a way
No matter what you say.
The same thing goes for wives.
In secret's where love thrives.
It was a dark and foggy night
When our hero had the bright
Idea to pretend,
Together with a friend,
To seek a place for two to stay.
He claimed they'd traveled quite a way.
"We're full up," the landlord said.
"At this late hour, we've not a bed.
Besides, for gents of means like you
A dump like this would never do."
"Have you no cranny in reserve?
Anything at all would serve."
"All that's left is where *we* sleep—
An extra bed in which we keep
The occasional random extra guest.
It's surely not the comfiest
But if you two a bed can share
I guess that we could put you there."
"We accept. That will be fine.
Now if you please we'd like to dine."
After supper they were led
Up the staircase to their bed.
Colette had told him to take care
To mark how beds were laid out there.
The host and wife slept near the door.
There was a cradle on the floor
Close by them; on the other side,
The bed our two guests occupied.

A cot was made up for Colette.
The cradle, we must not forget,
Was closer to the host's bed than the one
Where slept Pinuccio and friend. The fun
To come before the evening reached its end
Would come from a misjudgment by the
  friend
Concerning this minute detail
(Without which we would have no tale).
At midnight, with the parents both asleep,
Our lovers had their rendezvous to keep.
Her boyfriend waited till twelve chimes had
  sounded.
Then from his bed with eagerness he
  bounded.
Noiselessly he went straight to her cot.
Was Colette asleep? I would swear not.
From him she learned a game that some-
  times tires,
But far more than it bores, when one desires.
After a while, they took some rest,
But soon again the two caressed.
While things in the cot
Were heavy and hot,
Pinuccio's friend got up from his bed
To deal with a matter I'd best leave unsaid.
He wanted to exit the room, but the door
Was blocked by the cradle placed on the
  floor.
So he moved it, but on his return he forgot
To put the thing back in the very same spot.
The place where he put it was right by his bed,
It ought to have been by the parents' instead.
He fell back asleep. Then something went
  boom
When it fell down in a neighboring room.
The wife was awakened, it made such a clat-
  ter;
She got up to see what could be the matter.
The wrongly placed cradle led her to make,
When she returned, a fateful mistake.
"By all that's holy!" she said to herself, as she
  carefully groped her way.
"I almost lay down in our customers' bed.
  That would have been hell to pay.
I'm wearing no more than my nightshirt, my
  flesh is all on display.
God be praised, the cradle is here to keep me
  from going astray."

Saying these words, she laid herself down
  right next to Pinuccio's friend.
He was no fool, and seized the occasion this
  offered, and so did pretend
That he was her amorous husband but he
  pretended a little too well.
More than a little in fact, for something was
  different, she could tell.
"What's got into that man," she thought, "to
  make him impassioned like this?
Most of the time the only affection he shows
  is a husbandly kiss.
You'd think he was twenty years old again,
  but like I always say,
Take what God offers because there may not
  come another day."
She'd barely thought these words to herself
  before he was at it once more;
The woman was really voluptuous, as I re-
  member I had said before.
Meanwhile Colette, beginning to fear that
  her father would soon be awake
Sent Pinuccio back to his bed, when the
  dawn was beginning to break.
As it happened, because of the cradle Pinuc-
  cio went to a different bed
Than the one he had left, and so he lay down
  right next to the father instead.
As soon as he got there he started to speak in
  a whisper of his recent fun.
(Too-happy people always commit some
  mistake by which they're undone.)
"Friend," he said, "the only thing that I can
  say is Wow!
I'm sorry that Heaven cannot send you the
  exact same joy right now.
Those ample breasts, that luscious skin:
An anatomy just made for sin.
A tasty dish fit for a king—
And I've not told you everything.
I've been with other girls; she's got them
  beat.
Once was not enough—had to repeat.
Six times at least, I kid you not.
Man, that girl is really hot."
The father muttered some words that
  showed his confusion.
His wife, in bed with the friend, still had the
  illusion

"Laughing, each rose from his or her bed" (Eisen).

The friend was her husband, because she
    whispering said,
"You shouldn't have let them stay; they argue
    in bed."
The innkeeper sat bolt-upright, rage in his
    eye:
"So that's why you're here!" he said. "Your
    tale was a lie!
I'm supposed to be pleased when you mock
    my daughter and me?
You think, fine Monsieur that you are, you'll
    get off scot-free?
We raise up daughters, our dear treasure,
Just so you can take your pleasure?
To you it's nothing but a game—
To us, it's dishonor and shame.
Leave my house right now.
I'll deal with you somehow,
Or else I'll know the reason why.
And you, my daughter, you shall die."
Pinuccio now was scared to death,
He had no pulse, no voice, no breath.
A hush descended on the room;
Colette trembled for her doom.
Though it was dark, the wife could see
That she was living dangerously,
Holding the wolf by the ears, as it were,
Unable to speak, unable to stir.

Only the friend could now recall
The cradle had been at the root of it all.
To Pinuccio he said,
"You know that wine goes to your head.
When you drink you're up all night
Thrashing about, high as a kite;
Walking in your sleep, you feel
Everything you dream is real.
And everything you feel you say.
Come back to bed; it's almost day."
Taking a cue from his cleverer friend
Pinuccio started to pretend
To be a sleep-walker
As well as sleep-talker.
This fooled the host, now satisfied.
The wife thought it was time she tried
Some cleverness of her own.
"Colette's not been alone,"
She said, having snuck to her cot.
"And the reason I say she's not:
I've been with her all this time.
There's no way that such a crime
Could have been committed, you see.
In fact, she's done no worse than me.
That somnambulist had us beguiled."
"I believe it," her husband said, and smiled.
Laughing, each rose from his or her bed.
They all had their reasons, best left unsaid.

4. "The Muleteer"

I often think of Lombard kings in conjuring
    up a story.
The one that I will tell you now enjoys the
    timeless glory
Of having first appeared in print in Boccac-
    cio's collection,
His name was Agiluf, and for his queen he'd
    much affection.
As well he should, for Teudelinga's beauty
    was renowned.
On top of that, it's thanks to her that Agiluf
    was crowned.
She was the childless widow of the king
    who'd reigned before;
Becoming king through marriage is a perk
    hard to ignore.

But Cupid has a way of interfering in one's
    life.
He shot his arrow blindly, consequently this
    king's wife
Became the object of the lust of one of his
    muleteers.
This stable hand, however, was more hand-
    some than his peers,
And smarter, too, because he tried to get rid
    of his lust.
But try as he might, he couldn't, and a man
    must do what he must.
So he figured out a way to get his heart's de-
    sire.
At times like these the god of Love sure
    knows how to inspire.

With his help the dullest mind can learn
more in a day
Than a bachelor of arts in ten years could
display.
To declare his love to her would certainly not
do,
And yet he had to sleep with her; that at
least he knew.
If the king were to find out he'd surely wind
up dead.
But he didn't care, as long as he got in her
bed.
The King and Queen of Lombardy both
slept in different rooms
As all kings and queens may do, I think that
one assumes.
According to a longstanding tradition,
If to her bed the king desired admission
A shirt and cloak were all he wore
When he knocked upon her door.
The serving-maid would take his light;
She would vanish in the night
When she blew out the candle.
Our muleteer thought he could handle
A disguise of that sort, and play the king
And no one would suspect a thing.
Taking the monarch's place
He was careful to cover his face.
The maid was much too asleep
To do anything other than keep
To her normal course of action,
To his relief and satisfaction.
The only thing to fear
Was that the king appear.
But more likely than not he'd refrain
For he needed to rest from the strain
Of having been hunting all day.
Not a word did the muleteer say

"Whoever it was, don't do it again" (Duplessis-Bertaux).

As he entered the room, willing and able,
Perfumed to hide any hint of the stable,
And lay down by Teudelinga's side.
Another detail I should provide
(Sorry I didn't do it before),
Is whenever the king was feeling sore
At heart about the state of his realm
Or some other problem would overwhelm
Him, he'd take his pleasure without a word.
She wasn't surprised when this occurred,
Being accustomed to it by now.
So in silence it was our hero could plow
Ahead. And did so not only one time
But several. He was, after all, in his prime.
But King Agiluf was definitely not,
Which provoked in the queen the following
    thought:
"Is Agiluf thinking of something upsetting?
Is his anger the reason that I am now getting
A much larger measure
Of physical pleasure
Than the usual dose?
Maybe he's just morose."
Justice is always Heaven's aim.
Not everyone's talents are the same.
To kings is given the gift to command;
The lawyers, the gift to understand
The ins and outs of disputation.
But muleteers have a reputation
For talent in other inning and outing.
There can be no reason for doubting
This proved true for Agiluf's queen.
In silence our hero left unseen
Before the break of dawn.
But he had barely gone
Before the king that very night
Came to demand his royal right.
This was quite a surprise.
She couldn't believe her eyes.
"For heaven's sake," she said.
"You had just left my bed.
I know that for me you are hot

But this is rather a lot.
I'm seized with fear and alarm:
Overdoing it might do you harm."
The king was not dumb.
And so he kept mum,
But left for the stable directly.
Because he'd concluded correctly
A muleteer was to blame.
In the dark, they all looked the same:
All sleeping—but one, pretending to be.
The king checked each pulse, diligently,
Figuring one could be found
That would so rapidly pound
Its owner's the one he'd like to see dead
For venturing into the queen's royal bed.
The strategy worked like a charm.
He soon discovered the arm
Whose trembling wrist
Could not resist
Revealing the culprit's deep fears.
Agiluf reached for some shears
(Available there
For cutting horse hair)
And trimmed from his forehead a patch
By which the next day he could match
The criminal with the crime.
Once he'd left, wasting no time,
Our hero, taking the shears,
Cropped from all muleteers
An identical lock of hair.
He accomplished this task with such care
That the king when he came the next day
To his deep and utter dismay
Discovered not one but sixteen
Servants who'd slept with the queen—
To judge, that is, from appearance.
Thanks to his bold interference
With the plan the king had devised
Our hero his guilt had disguised.
King Agiluf then declared to the men:
"Whoever it was, don't do it again."

5. "The Saint Julian Prayer"

Many faithfully rely
On prayers and magic formulae.

I just laugh, for I know better
Than to trust in word or letter.

Though if a girl you want to woo
Sweet words will do the trick for you.
They work a charm on any heart.
And in the tale I'll now impart
One of those prayers I just pooh-poohed
Actually did someone some good.
Saint Julian's Prayer is how it's known,
And its magic power is shown,
As you'll see, from what befell
Renaud d'Aste. It worked so well,
Could he not this prayer recite
He'd have passed a miserable night
And lost all of his money too:
It's amazing what this prayer can do.
Renaud was traveling far from home,
Heading to Château-Guillaume.
He met three strangers on the route.
They humbly gave him their salute.
Good folk, and modest, to his mind;
In all the kingdom, hard to find
Three so decent men as these, who
Said, "If you think it would please you,
We could you to our number add."
Renaud no suspicions had.
"Join our company today
For this portion of the way.
An honor it would be for sure
For us, and you'd be more secure.
Bandits abound throughout the land
It is hard to understand
Why the king cannot contrive
To rid us of them; yet the evil thrive,
And the road will always have its dangers."
So he joined up with these strangers.
As they went, the three would chat
Of many things, of this and that;
Above all, magic words and prayers
They claimed to help in some affairs,
Warding off high wind and lightning,
Wolves, and other ills as frightening.
Parasites and pests and bugs.
Physicians' remedies and drugs
Were not as good against disease
Afflicting horse and man as these.
The other three kept up this chatter;
Renaud, though, stayed out of the matter.
Then they brought their talk to bear
On if there were some charm or prayer
That he had known to serve him well.

If so, would he be pleased to tell
The gathered company about it.
"It's not that I wish to tout it,
But in fact there is a prayer
That I've found beyond compare.
I live simply, antique style
And so it's just once in a while
That I've need of such a thing.
It's only when I'm traveling.
I never lack for a good night's stay
Wherever I lodge upon my way.
I pray in Saint Julian's name
And I truthfully can claim
It never has been known to fail.
One time it did not avail
But that's because I didn't say it.
Now I never fail to pray it
Every time I take a trip."
With a sneer upon his lip,
"I hope," one said, "that for your sake
You said it today. Let's make
A wager and let's let it be
On whether it'll be you or me
Who lodges best on this cold night."
By now the wind began to bite,
It was getting dark, no inn in sight.
"But maybe you've said the very same
   prayer,"
Renaud objected. "By God I swear,"
Said the other, "it's not my style
To call on saints. Let's give it a trial.
But if you win, I promise to pray
On future travels the Saint Julian way."
"I accept, on condition you stay at an inn
And have no one else to take you in,
For I've no friends along the way
With whom this evening I could stay."
"Understood. Now I suppose
It's your horse and all your clothes
That you're betting against my purse."
Things now took a turn for the worse
When he added, with some glee,
"I'm sure to win, as you'll soon see."
It dawned on Renaud that he was dealing
With a man whose trade was stealing.
If things continued on this course
He was about to lose his horse.
As they passed beside a wood
A change came in the other's mood.

"Get off your horse. I now suggest
You put your prayer to the test.
Perhaps it'll help you find a bed."
Aste had to do just as he said.
They took his horse, his purse, his hat,
His pants, his cloak, and worse than that,
His boots. "Enjoy your walk!" they said,
As the robbers quickly fled.
With no pants about his knees,
Muddy and wet, he was starting to freeze.
Despite Saint Julian, things looked bleak,
For shelter still was far to seek.
His only hope amid these woes:
The valise with all his clothes.
The valet who had it might come soon;
That really would be opportune.
He'd left the servant back somewhere,
Having a horseshoe to repair.
But what Renaud didn't know
Was that his man would never show.
From far off he'd seen what passed
With the thieves, and took off fast.
For Château-Guillaume he set his course,
Cutting through fields, spurring his horse;
He reached an inn within the city
And by a fire was sitting pretty,
Ordering the best wine in the inn,
Leaving his master in mud to his chin.
That master, frozen to the bone
His valet's whereabouts unknown,
Trudging along in indignation,
Was obliged to walk to his destination.
It's strange what outcomes fate imposes:
Criminals loll on beds of roses
While virtuous devotees of prayer
Are beset by terrible care.
Whatever gives the fates most pleasure:
It's all or nothing; no half-measure,
As we shall see with Renaud.
Plodding along in the wind and the snow.
He arrived at the city but it was too late;
An hour before, they'd closed the gate.
To the foot of the city wall he drew.
In some small way his luck came through,
For in one place the roof extended,
Where there was a house appended.
Seeking shelter from exposure,
He was glad of this enclosure.
Since good luck will come in twos

He also found some straw to use.
He spread it out and then he said,
"God be praised, I have a bed."
All this time, the cold assailed him;
His defective shelter failed him.
It was more than he could bear;
He gave over to despair.
Through chattering teeth he made a moan,
Which served to make his presence known
Inside the house built in the wall,
Which I mentioned, you'll recall.
His moans were heard by a chambermaid
Who would come to give him aid—
Her mistress, a widow full of grace
Kept by the governor of that place.
The governor was a marquis
Who wishd his mistress none to see
Nor himself annoyed, distracted
From the business they transacted,
So used a door within the wall,
And no one ever knew at all,
Nor did his servants he apprise.
That comes to me as a surprise,
For tranquil pleasures aren't the sort
In which marquis like to disport.
They tend to value pleasures more
When there are those who can keep score.
Luckily for our Renaud,
That poor Job caught in the snow,
Her lover would have come that night
For his diversion and delight,
But in the end had been unable.
There was supper on the table,
Appetizing preparations,
Aphrodisiac libations,
Perfumed baths, soft mattress spread
On a deep inviting bed,
Wine beside it: all the arms
In Cupid's armory of charms;
Every cannon, every gun
By which his battles all are won
Not the Cupid of love's pining
But the one always designing
Clever tactics to employ,
The god of lovers who enjoy
Those pleasures in which they engage.
Word was delivered by a page
That the marquis could not come.
She did not to grief succumb,

For already they'd agreed
That's the way they would proceed.
It was lucky for Renaud
That it should have turned out so.
The maid, who was tender-hearted,
Heard his moan and then imparted
Right away the information:
"Madame, I hear the desperation
Of a sufferer outside.
Do you think we could provide
Some assistance to this man?
I'd like to help him if we can.
He may die; the cold's severe.
Could we give him shelter here?"
"We could keep him in the garret,"
Said her mistress. "Go prepare it.
Put some clean straw on the floor
For him to sleep on; though before
You shut our visitor in there,
Give him the food we didn't eat."
Thus did Renaud death defeat.
He thanked the maid; the help she gave
Saved him from a certain grave.
He told her how he'd lost his horse.
As he spoke, he gained in force
And confidence. The maid could see
He was a man of high degree.
Tall, well built, a cut above,
No novice in the art of love,
Despite his youth. (Although Renaud
Felt embarrassed by his woe.
It was unpleasant being viewed
When one is dirty and half-nude.)
The maid gave him a rave review:
"He's tall, good-looking—sexy, too."
She was perceptive and astute.
Her mistress said, "Find him a suit
Among the clothes my husband wore."
The maid had told her one thing more:
His surname bore the particle:
He was the genuine article
(For the "de" in "Renaud d'Aste"
Was the telltale mark of caste).
At this, the widow now declared,
"Give him the hot bath you prepared
For me." He thought this very nice;
One didn't have to ask him twice.
Freshly cleaned up and perfumed,
Newly clothed and freshly groomed,

Renaud d'Aste made his appearance
And with absolute adherence
To the rules of fine behavior
Paid his respects to his kind savior.
This formerly disheveled guest
Dined with more than normal zest
On the marquis's fine repast.
The widow did not eat, just cast
Her eyes on one whom she desired.
Already in that way inspired
Perhaps by thoughts of the marquis
Or there was something she could see
In his looks that touched her heart.
But right now in every part,
On every side she was assailed
By Love, who in the end prevailed.
"Who'd tell," she thought, "were I to yield?
I'm sure the marquis plays the field;
If he hasn't yet, he will.
This one as nicely fits the bill.
Man for man and sin for sin,
I'd hate to say 'It might have been.'"
Renaud was not too naive
To see the gift he could receive.
Saint Julian's hospitality
Was soon to be reality.
After dessert, the servants departed.
The two were alone; time to get started.
What she wore was most enticing,
A decolletage sufficing
To suggest splendors half-hidden
That would perhaps not be forbidden.
Given what he saw, her guest
Could imagine all the rest.
Young and sweet; without a doubt,
She was very well filled out.
She had charms that would attach you
Were you Plato or a statue.
D'Aste did not know what to say.
So she helped him out this way:
"The more that I look at you
The more I think of one I knew.
By your air and noble bearing,
And the clothes that you are wearing,
You recall my spouse, now dead,
Whom I loved so much," she said.
"That's quite an honor. But now who
Could I in turn compare to you?
No one I have ever known

Had the sweetness you have shown
Nor the beauty I behold.
Though I nearly died from cold,
Now my state is just as dire,
For I'm burning with a fire
And I don't know which is worse."
She showed she was not averse
To receiving further praise
By pretending now to raise
Objections to his adulation.
He then made enumeration
Of each lovely attribute,
With descriptions most minute
That would have been more detailed
Were it not that some were veiled.
Those beauties that he could not see
He said he wished that she would free
From their undeserved confinement.
Then he could with more refinement

Carry out the dear assignment
Of describing her delights.
Though that would take a thousand nights
And this one might be better spent.
She smiled, and he knew what that meant.
Time to stop this silly chatter
And go straight into the matter;
Time to strike: the iron was hot.
She resisted, yet resisted not.
They fondled a while, and then they kissed;
I don't think I could ever list
All the many things they did.
Some must indeed from view be hid.
But nevertheless it may be said
When they found their way to bed
There was more than billing and cooing.
These two knew what they were doing.
Each mishap it had been his fate
To meet with was kissed off the slate.

"They took his horse, his purse, his hat" (Duplessis-Bertaux).

"Here's for the road, here's for the theft,
Here's for the cold, when you'd no clothes
  left,"
She said, each time with a loving embrace,
And did each memory efface.
Renaud in the end acquired
That gift by every man desired.
Then, sweet words and kisses again,
With tasty tidbits and champagne.
Rather than put him in the bed in the attic
She made room in hers, and he was ecstatic.
I don't know what they did there
But do know the amorous pair
Agreed to continue in the future to meet.
Because of the marquis, they'd be discreet.
Not only her favors did she disperse
But was equally liberal with her purse.
He took just enough to pay the inn,
Where he found his valet sleeping in.
He gave the man some merited blows
Then went to his suitcase and put on new
  clothes.
News came by which he was enraptured:
The three robbers had been captured.
Straight to the judge he beat a track
Hoping to get his money back.
That much diligence requires
Since what the court of law acquires
It hardly ever will let go,
And it always has been so.
It is like the Lion's lair:
Those who enter must despair

Of seeing daylight any more;
It's a strictly one-way door.
The verdict at the trial came down,
Gallows erected in the town.
Just before the three were hanged
One of them the crowd harangued,
Repentantly speaking for the three;
His pious contrition was good to see.
Who can now doubt Saint Julian's Prayer?
Look at the four whom you see there.
Who would have thought those three thieves
Accosting Renaud as they laughed up their
  sleeves
And later rejoicing over the loot
As they capered and danced and went off on
  a toot,
Would later be dancing a different dance?
No doubt you would have thought: fat
  chance.
Remember the traveler looking so glum,
Deprived of his clothes, about to succumb
To a lonely death in the freezing cold?
Nevertheless, as events would unfold,
A beautiful woman fell into his hands,
Worthy of meeting a prelate's demands.
He got back his money, his baggage, his
  horse,
Thanks be to God, and Saint Julian of
  course,
Plus some fine hospitality
Thrown in for good measure, totally free.

6 "The Servant Girl Found Guiltless"

Boccaccio's not my only stock of lore.
I sometimes draw upon another store.
It is true, of course,
That he's my biggest source.
But for a varied diet
One must sometimes buy at
A different grocer.
Some are closer
To home. I can enhance
My tales with two from France:
The ancient *Cent Nouvelles Nouvelles*;
And for the one I now will tell,

Heptameron by Marguerite,
Queen of Navarre, a book replete
With tales delightful and most charming.
One has this phrase I find disarming:
An expression, I believe,
As rare as it's sweetly naive.
The phrase is "That was me."
Soon I think you'll see
All that it can mean.
Before I set the scene
I must first admit
That sometimes I will fit

Into the stories I adapt
Something of my own, yet apt.
A license you could call poetic,
But crucial to my own aesthetic.
Could it I not exercise
No more tales would I devise.
A man once had a pretty chamber-maid;
He taught her how the game of love is
   played.
This girl could decorate a bed all right,
And, succulent, excite the appetite.
Early one day, he left his wife in bed
And went to find the chamber-maid instead.
She was busy making a bouquet
In the garden, for his wife's birthday.
He flattered her bouquet-arranging talent,
Then tried a gesture that he meant as gal-
   lant,
To impose himself upon the maid—

That is, his hand upon her breast was laid.
She tried to fight him off in self-defense,
But not in such a way to give offense.
In this she did exactly as she ought,
For in these matters she had been well
   taught.
She picked up the flowers she had amassed,
And teasingly at him the blooms she cast.
He stole a kiss from her as his riposte.
By now the two of them were all engrossed
In a hot and heavy mortal struggle.
He attempted to secure a snuggle;
In fighting back the chamber-maid pre-
   tended
Her honor was at stake, but was upended.
On the grass the two achieved their aims,
Having first warmed up with fun and games.
The problem, though, about this charming
   scene

"On them the next-door neighbor had been spying" (Duplessis-Bertaux).

Is that, alas, it did not pass unseen.
On them the next-door neighbor had been
 spying;
She did not find what they did edifying.
The husband saw the spy, I don't know how.
"I'm afraid," he said, "there's trouble now.
She has a wicked tongue and she will use it.
But I think I know how to confuse it.
Don't worry, I can take care of this mess."
He ran to get his wife, and made her dress;
In the garden made her pick some flowers,
Repeating to the utmost of his powers
All the things that he'd done with the maid.
The same erotic games again were played:
Flowers once more thrown, and breasts dis-
 played.
His wife discovered she liked this diversion,
Not knowing that it was a second version.
She wound up in just the same position,
And the grass left in the same condition.
After dinner the poor woman went
To see the neighbor, who was quite intent
On informing her of all she knew.
"You know, my dear, I think if I were you,"
The neighbor said, a scowl upon her brow,
"I would kick that hussy out right now.
I would send her back from whence she
 came.
To think she has the nerve to dress the same
As one of us. I know whereof I speak,
And I know from whom she gets that cheek.
You better find a remedy and soon.
It certainly was very opportune
That this morning I just chanced to be
At my window (don't know why) to see
Your husband at the garden gate appear,
And then that hussy. They began, I fear,
To throw some flowers at each other's head."

The wife broke in. "That was me," she said.
"But listen to the rest of my tale.
Pay attention to the next detail.
They plucked a kind of flower that's called a
 kiss."
"I don't know why you're so keen on this.
That again was me you took for her."
"Something even worse did next occur:
From the game of flowers they passed to
 breasts.
After several make-believe protests
She let him caress them with his hand."
"That was me. But I don't understand.
Can't your husband do the same to you?"
"Then she tumbled back upon the grass,
Although she did no damage to her...
Why are you laughing? Is this cause for
 glee?"
"Of course it is. Because that girl was me."
"A petticoat upon the grass did lay."
"And that petticoat was mine, I say."
"No offense, but can you tell me who
Had on the petticoat, the girl or you?
Because your husband then went all the
 way."
"That was me. What else can I say?
Your head's so hard it must be made of
 wood."
"That's enough. I've done all that I could.
I still think my eyesight's pretty good
And would have sworn it was the maid I
 spied
Playing with your husband there outside.
But never mind. Just keep your Jezebel."
"Keep her? I should say. She's served me
 well."
"She has served you well? I must agree.
Better than you know, it's clear to me."

7. "The Three Wives' Wager"

Three wives one day, with good wine filled,
Got to bragging how each was skilled
In putting things over her lawfully wedded.
Each at the moment was happily bedded
By somebody else, unknown to her spouse;
Two were the masters in their own house.

Said one, "My husband's a total prince.
There's been no better before or since.
Don't need his say-so to have my fun.
With this block I could make a smarter one.
I don't have to rise that early each day
To make him believe whatever I say."

"If I'd one like that, I'd give him away,"
Another one said. "Because there's no pleas-
ure
For me unless I feel the pressure
That comes from the fear of getting caught.
He
Would take all the fun out of being naughty.
Yours you can lead if you want by the nose,
Blind to all your peccadilloes.
Thank God, with mine you must carefully
pick
The time and the place; he's hard to trick.
But don't imagine that cramps my style;
It just makes the game worthwhile.
Love's the sweeter for both involved
When there's a problem to be solved.
You may boast of your luck with husbands
and beaux,
But I'd never trade mine for any of those."
The third wife brought them to agree
That Cupid views with unmixed glee
Docile husbands who've no clue
What their spouses are up to,
Yet desires that some slight effort
Be required. All three were expert,
But each thought she was the best.
"Then why," asked one, "not have a test?
Talk is nice but what of deeds?
Let's see which one best succeeds
In tricking with a trick that's new.
The worst will pay the other two."
Each promised, when the deed was done
To tell all. To see who won,
They'd ask a friend if she could judge it.
They each promised not to fudge it.
She whose spouse kept closest eye
Loved a handsome, younger guy—
Fresh-complected, beardless chin—
By which he would be taken in.
Always being under guard
She had found it very hard
Finding how she could enjoy
Her delightful little toy—
The passion in their loving hearts
Assuaged only in fits and starts—
Always thinking of a ruse,
Looking for a house to use.
So she decides to give the boy a chamber-
maid's disguise.

He appears before her spouse and for the job
applies,
Lowering his eyes with a shy and girlish
glance—
And the husband cannot wait to get into her
pants.
Finding her to be just exactly what he
sought,
He hires the girl to be a chambermaid right
on the spot.
For the first few days her new employer
thinks it wise
Every time the two cross paths to turn away
his eyes.
But soon he starts to work upon the maid.
Gifts are given, promises are made.
She pretends at last that she'll give in
Luckily for him, the maid's a live-in,
So in the house she always spends the night.
You can well imagine his delight
When she tells him that his wife is sick
(Though of course it's just part of the trick),
And that tonight his wife will sleep alone.
To the maid he makes his wishes known.
He's in her bed, and while she is undressing
In there comes the wife, who starts express-
ing
Her pretended righteous indignation
For his having made this assignation.
"I see that you've grown tired of my home
cooking
And so you've now decided to start looking
For a little extra on the side?
If I'd only known I would have tried
To have some tasty young ones always near
Just for you, but this sweet one, I fear,
Is destined to enjoy a different fate.
You'll have to look elsewhere to fill your
plate.
As for you, you little floozy,
I will beat you black and bruisy.
So it's *my* food you fancy for your fare?
That's OK with me. Not that I care:
I can find what I want when I want it.
Men find me attractive and I flaunt it.
I'm not to be tossed out, at least not yet.
What I want I sure know how to get.
But as for the matter now at hand,
I know a good solution: I command

"You sleep with me" (artist unknown).

You sleep with me to keep you out of trou-
ble.
Come on, let's go. Quick-step and on the
double!
Your clothes and things you'll gather up to-
morrow.
You've caused me such a peck of pain and
sorrow
That otherwise I would send you away
Except I fear what might the neighbors say.
And this way I'll keep an eye on you;
Night and day I'll know just what you do."
At these words, the chambermaid appears
To be abashed, and sheds one or two tears,
Picks up her baggage and without delay
Departs, having another role to play:
By night a lover, chambermaid by day,
Performing household duties, either way.
The husband after this just feels relief
That his wife did not give him more grief.
He sleeps alone; meanwhile the loving pair
Lose no time pursuing their affair.
Knowing every moment is to treasure,
They neglect no chance to take their pleas-
ure,
For time is short and ever onward presses.
Thus ends the first of the three wives' suc-
cesses.

The wife whose husband was apt to believe
All she said when she planned to deceive
Is the author of the next endeavor,
Which you'll see was really rather clever.
The couple sat beneath a pear tree's shade;
A valet stood nearby by whom each maid
In the household was madly obsessed.
Good looks and quick wit the man pos-
sessed.
The wife said, "I would like to taste a pear.
Guillot, go and shake one down from there."
Guillot the valet quickly climbs the tree,
From where he pretends that he can see
The two below embracing, rubs his eyes
To express his shock and his surprise
At the shameful goings-on below.
"Please, sir," he says, "you really ought to go
Somewhere else instead of on the grass
To do that sort of thing. It's much too crass.
With your servants you ought not to trifle

By presenting them with such an eyeful.
If not them, at least yourself respect
Enough not to allow desire unchecked
To govern your behavior. Why so hasty?
Liberties in private are more tasty.
Even summer nights are not too short
For a wife and husband to cavort.
Why choose this place to make love to your
spouse?
There are many fine rooms in your house."
"What can he be going on about?"
Asks the wife. "He's dreaming, I don't doubt.
Come down from that tree, Guillot
And you'll see it isn't so."
He descends. The husband now inquires,
"Are we acting out shameful desires?"
"Not now." "Not now?" "Sir, you may have
me flayed
Alive, but all the same just now you played
A kissing game with Madam on the grass."
The wife cuts in, "Stop giving us that sass.
Or you'll get some blows in retribution."
"For madmen," says her spouse, "the best so-
lution
Is to put them under lock and key."
"Is it crazy to see what I see?"
"And what," she asks, "was that again?
Try this time to make it plain."
"I saw that you and he cavorted
On the grass, as I reported.
The two of you were making love.
That's what I saw from above,
Unless this tree's beneath some spell."
"Charmed, you claim?" She says. "Oh,
swell!"
Says her husband, "Now I see
I will have to climb that tree
To learn the truth." So up the tree he goes.
Soon the two below are in the throes
Of passion. When he sees their fond em-
braces
The husband screams and down the tree he
races.
He almost breaks his neck
In his haste to check
The alarming progress
Of their sexual congress.
But he's too late to stop their fun.
The damage is already done.

"This pear tree is enchanted" (artist unknown).

"How could you," he cries,
"Right beneath my eyes?"
"How could I what?"
"B … B … B … But …
"Was he not caressing you?
It took place within plain view."
"Caressing me? You must be dreaming.
"Things cannot be what they're seeming."
"Am I mad or going blind?"
"You must think I've lost my mind
If you imagine I could do
A trick like that in front of you.
Aren't there enough hours in the day
If I wanted to, to play?"
"'I don't know what else to say.
That tree must be abusing me.
Let me try again and see."
Up the tree he goes once more,
And things happen as before.
Guillot again makes his advance
And she joins him in the dance.
The husband sees it all take place
But this time takes it with good grace.
Slowly he descends the tree.
"No other causes do I see
Than that this pear tree is enchanted."
"It should never have been planted,"
Says the wife. "It must be burnt,
For making folks see things that weren't.
Have it cut down on the double.
Then it will cause no more trouble."
Guillot gets men for this task;
One of them then dares to ask
What perhaps it might have been,
What horrid crime or grievous sin
This poor pear tree could commit
That such a punishment be fit.
Says the wife, "Do not inquire.
Just throw the damn thing in the fire."

Now that the second tale we've heard,
Let's continue to the third.
At a good friend's house this wife would
    play,
Enjoying new adventures every day.
She had a lover in her neighborhood
Who told her that he wished they really
    could
Spend a night together, for a pleasure

That's limited does not give full measure.
"You're on," she said. "But why not make it
    two?
It's not too much to ask, and I can do
What I have to do to get my spouse—
So we can have our fun—out of the house."
No sooner said than done, though it was
    tough;
Good thing that this wife was smart enough.
The problem was, he always stayed at home.
He didn't see why one should go to Rome
To seek a pardon when one could just buy
One locally that's sure to satisfy.
She by contrast showed fervor and zeal
For pilgrimages, which had their appeal,
Since more than once they'd served her as a
    cover
For an assignation with a lover.
She needed, for this contest, something hard:
It was lucky he kept such close guard.
That evening to her toe she tied some
    thread;
All the way past the front door it led.
By Henri her husband she lay down,
Making sure that when he moved around
As he tossed and turned that night in bed
He would not neglect to feel the thread.
Indeed he did; it gave him food for thought.
Awake, Henri pretended he was not.
He left the bed at last and tiptoed out.
That she was asleep he didn't doubt.
The thread he followed out into the street
This was proof to him she was to meet
A lover who would tug upon her toe
By the handy thread so she would know
That he was there; the rendezvous she'd keep
While her trusting husband was asleep.
If it's not this, then what exactly is it?
Sir Cuckoldry is planning on a visit
Which I think I'd just as soon forego.
He armed himself, prepared to meet
Whoever should come down the street
And tug upon the tell-tale thread.
And yet meanwhile with catlike tread
A chambermaid the lover led
(Profit's to be made, servants believe,
When they plot a husband to deceive.)
Through the entrance at the back.
Now he could hop in the sack

"The thread he followed out into the street" (Duplessis-Bertaux).

With his sweetie for some bliss
That Henri would have to miss
Since he was outside keeping guard,
Making sure the door was barred.
The maid as well performed as sentry,
Keeping watch at the front entry.
As long as Henri kept his post
The two in bed could make the most
Of their time, which went till dawn.
When he came in with a yawn
She'd made sure the guy was gone.
He claimed a pounding in his head
Had made him seek another bed.
In two days she did it again,
And things went on in that same vein,
Both that time and one time more,
As Henri stood watch at the door.

Their ardor cooling, they called it a day;
Three acts sufficed for their little play.
When midnight chimed the lover fled;
One of his servants pulled on the thread.
Henri attacked him right away,
Not knowing at first it was just a valet.
By the collar he dragged him in;
Giving rise to a terrible din.
The wife came running at his yelling;
Clasping their knees, the valet was telling
How he was in love with the chambermaid;
That the thread was part of the plans *they'd*
    laid,
That to *her* toes he'd thought it tied,
Such were the means they'd already tried,
And indeed successfully so,
Not in fact that long ago.

They'd to each other pledged their troth.
The wife now waxed exceedingly wroth
(Or pretended to do so):
"So that's why upon your toe
I saw that thread the other day!
I tied mine in the same way.
It was a plan that I had hatched
To learn to whom you were attached.
So he's to be your wedded spouse?
Both of you must leave my house."
Henri showed a kinder heart:
"Wait till morning to depart."
Henri a dowry gave the maid;

The lover did his valet aid
In the same quite handsome way.
The two of them went down the marriage
    aisle,
Though they'd known each other for quite a
    while.
This is how the story ends.

Which trick was best? The trio of friends
Asked the fourth, but she replied,
"I'm sorry, but I can't decide."
The judgment is still pending
And, perhaps, unending.

8. "How Old Men Count the Days"

To me this often comes as a surprise:
The thing in marriage that one should most
    prize
Is the very item that's forgot
When a girl is made to tie the knot.
Parents only think of the amount
The groom has got; the rest just doesn't
    count.
They'll match a tender thing to some old
    coot
But take great care with horses that each suit
The other when a pair will pull a carriage.
They ought to put as much thought into
    marriage.
If oxen do not pull with equal force
A plow cannot be kept straight on its course.
How cannot the plowing done by couples,
When ill-matched, encounter the same trou-
    bles?
The story that I am about to tell
Will illustrate this problem very well.
Richard of Quinzica was too old
To make love to his wife, and so he told
His bride that such-and-such a date was
    holy
To some saint and thus it would be wholly
Wrong to desecrate that sacred day
By engaging in erotic play.
The trouble was those dates were far too
    many
And his poor wife wasn't getting any.

He thought in this way he could catch a
    break
But here he made a really big mistake.
A learned judge in Pisa, our man Richard
With his gray beard ought to have better
    pictured
His situation than to have selected
As bride the beautiful and well-connected
Bartholomea de Galandi, rather
Than someone his own age, whose great-
    grandfather
He'd not appear to be. Quinzica thought her
Just the thing for him, this pretty daughter
Of the best-placed family in the town.
But soon the word began to get around
That his kids would never lack for dads.
Some folks make a point of giving scads
Of pointers, free advice, but cannot see
Into their own affairs as brilliantly.
Quinzica thus not having what was needed
To serve his pretty wife, he then proceeded
To find good reasons why, as I've explained,
Most days were not quite right, and few re-
    mained
For doing what comes naturally to some,
But not to those whose body has become
Enfeebled by old age. He found some saints
Who though obscure had feasts that placed
    restraints
On doing work that married couples do.
In addition, Fridays were out too,

"He found some saints / Who though obscure had feasts that placed restraints" (Fragonard).

"As everybody knows," he'd often say
(I guess because Our Lord died on that day).
Saturday was wrong, he did believe,
Because it always was the Sabbath's eve.
Never on a Sunday, which was blest
Since it was the holy day of rest.
Mondays, when the week begins anew?
That wouldn't be the Christian thing to do.
The other weekdays had their own excuses:
They could all be put to better uses.
As for solemn days of obligation,
That's where Richard showed imagination.
Long before the day one must abstain,
And afterwards as well the fast maintain.
Then of course the forty days of Lent,
Plus Ember Days, Rogations, and Advent.
Each apostle and evangelist
And patron saint appeared upon his list,
Which he knew by heart, and every martyr
Had his day, which then proved a nonstarter.
When he'd used up all the saints he had
Then there were the days whose luck was
    bad.
Then it was too foggy or too hot.
Four times every year—it's not a lot—
Our learned judge regaled his better half.
But in such a tiny way that you would laugh.
Apart from this, no thing did he refuse.
But dresses, trinkets, jewels will amuse
A woman for a while, and then no longer.
Bartholomea wanted something stronger.
In summer what she liked to do the most
Was going to their villa on the coast.
It was alas about her only pleasure.
She and Richard visited their leisure
Dwelling every weekend, without fail.
Sometimes on the water they would sail,
Bringing home the fishes by the score,
Though never going far from the shore.
One day, they decided on a lark
That each would fish in his or her own bark.
They made a bet on whom it would befall
To have the luck to make the biggest haul.
There was just a small crew in each sloop.
A pirate saw the wife and with his troop
Of cutthroats came and carried her away.
In Richard he showed little interest, for
Perhaps he feared to venture near the shore,
Or thought that with the old man in the way

He'd find it harder to enjoy his prey.
He was the sort of pirate to whom treasure
Was far less motivating than was pleasure.
With honor he pursued the pirate's trade.
The game of love he masterfully played,
A trait he shared with many a buccaneer.
They pay no heed to saints or time of year
When given opportunity to sin.
Such was the case with pirate Pagamin.
Bartholomea, now the corsaire's booty,
Took upon herself the solemn duty
Of weeping tears exactly half a day.
The pirate for his part sought to allay
Her grief by giving comfort where he could.
It seems his ministrations did her good,
For when her wifely tears had all been shed
Bartholomea wound up in his bed.
The god of Love had no doubt had a hand.
Of all the pirates found on sea or land,
Though some may be, like this one, charis-
    matic,
The god of Love is ten times more piratic:
Abduction is his modus operandi.
While Bartholomea, née Galandi,
Had the wherewithal to pay her ransom,
To do so meant foregoing quite a handsome
Opportunity for breaking loose
From those restraints for which she had no
    use.
The calendar with saints' days marked in red
She gave no thought to when she was in bed
With Pagamin. However, when she dined
Some relevance to fast days she could find.
Our judge had not the slightest shred of
    doubt
That his Bartholomea would throughout
This rough ordeal remain steadfast and true,
And be returned to him as good as new,
He was sure his money would suffice
To get her back, however high the price.
He went to see the pirate to declare:
"I'll pay whatever sum you think is fair."
Pagamin replied, "I should regret it
If my reputation has lost credit.
And if so, it really isn't right.
I'd like to give your wife back if I might.
And free of charge as well, I want to stress:
I wouldn't want to add to your distress.
She for whom you've taken such due care

Will be returned again to you, I swear.
I simply need to know which one is yours.
Describe her to me; if your sketch concurs
With one of those I've taken, well and good.
To give you someone else's wife I would
Not want to do, for if I did my name
And reputation might incur some blame.
In recent days there's one as I recall
Who has brown hair, is young, and rather
    tall.
If after having seen you, this fine beauty
Says she belongs to you, then it's my duty
To hand her over, which I'll gladly do."
"You speak wisely and are generous too,"
Said Richard. "But I think it would be nice
If for your captive you would set a price.
Each must make a living from his trade.
Here's my purse. Just count and mark it paid.
Just because I'm well-known doesn't mean
That you should give me better than routine
Consideration. Trading for my wife,
Shall I be less fair? Not on my life.
As you shall see, the truth will bear me out.
That she indeed is mine you should not
    doubt.
It's not that you should take my say-so for it,
It's just that I cannot but have the horrid
Fear that when she sees me she may die
Of undiluted joy." She was nearby,
And so was quickly brought into the room.
The Judge's apprehensions of her doom
Turned out to have no basis in the least.
There's no way she seemed to want to feast
Her eyes upon her loved and long-lost mate,
For she continued in an unmoved state,
As if she didn't even know the man.
He might as well have come from Hindus-
    tan.
"I think," he said, "the little thing is shy
In front of other people; that is why
She's afraid to make her feelings known.
I'm sure she'd give a kiss were we alone."
The pirate said, "So that there is no doubt
Take her to her bedroom to find out.
This he did, and once behind the door,
He said, "My dearest, what is all this for?
Don't you recognize me? I'm the same.
Richard of Quinzica is my name."
In her frozen stare there was no change.

"Look me in the face: Do I seem strange?
If I don't appear the man I was
My belief I'd lost you is the cause.
Is there anything that you've desired
That I've not spent money and acquired?
Was there one more nicely dressed than you?
Was I not the slave of your will, too?
A slave is what you'll be if you stay here.
And what will happen to your honor, dear?"
"Whatever," she replied, "it darn well can.
Where was it when they yoked me to a man
Too decrepit to provide the thing
That gives to marriage its specific zing?
To tell the truth, I thought I was worthy
To receive delights somewhat more earthy
Than you, with all those saints' days for your
    guide,
Were able on an off-day to provide.
But Pagamin, as soon as I was captured,
Taught me things by which I am enraptured.
I've learned more things in two days about
    life
Than I did in four years as your wife.
About my coming back, just say no more.
Calendars aren't found in pirate lore.
You and my two parents merit worse:
They for only thinking of their purse,
You for having poorly estimated
Your strength for the task. But I'm elated
Because I know my pirate will provide
All I need, although he takes no pride
In keeping track of dates of fasts and saints.
His method is quite good—I've no com-
    plaints.
He could tell you what it's all about.
You don't like to hear it, but don't pout.
People will believe it anyway.
I think it's time we each went our own way.
Dresses may be nice, but aren't enough.
Girls like me are made of fleshier stuff.
I wonder if you've ever heard it said
There's more between the ankles and the
    head
Than you have ever dreamed in your theol-
    ogy.
It's really elementary biology."
At this she stopped. Quinzica didn't know
Quite what to think, but was content to go.
To stay right where she was on this occasion

Bartholomea needed no persuasion.
The poor rejected husband was so sad
That worn down by the troubles he had had
As well as by old age, he passed away
Not long after that eventful day.
The pirate took the widow for his bride,
Which worked out well because they first
    had tried

Each other out before they tied the knot.
This fine lesson should not be forgot
By gentlemen whose hair has turned to
    gray
But if they are accommodating, they
May solve the problem in another way:
By letting better lovers save the day.

9. "A Money-Minded Woman Meets Her Match"

That women always find a way
To make the men who want them pay
For love's delights is hardly news.
Ante up or they'll refuse.
And yet I think that I could show,
Despite the skill that we well know
With which those dears, the fairer gender,
Always make us men surrender,
That one of them can still be caught
And all her wiles just count for naught.
To illustrate, I'll tell the tale
Of how one man could yet prevail
Against one sure that she'd be paid.
The way the game this time was played,
He assuaged his desire
Without having to buy her
Because he used a pretty clever ruse.
Take note of this, in case you'd like to use
Some clever stratagem along this line;
Although I'm sure without it you'll do fine.
(I find that there are many men at court
Who like to do this sort of thing for sport.)
Gulfardo came so much to Gaspard's house
That he became enamored of his spouse.
Though she was young and pretty and quite
    nice,
All of that was spoiled due to one vice,
Which kept even the most ardent at bay.
It was her greed. This fault, to my dismay,
Is widespread in these times in which we
    live.
It seems there is no woman who will give
A lover what he wants unless he pays;
That's the way they all are nowadays,

Mere sighs a woman cannot understand;
To speak to her you must have cash in hand.
They love their pleasures—card games and
    fine dresses.
It's by these means that men will win ca-
    resses.
They are the arms the god of Love now uses;
It's from their store that Cupid now produces
Cuckolds, and they come in greater force
Than the Greeks came from the Trojan
    Horse.
Anyway, as I was saying,
Though he'd no intent of paying,
With her Gulfardo made a deal:
Two hundred ducats had appeal.
Where would all that cash come from?
The spouse himself would lend the sum,
Little knowing of the aim
Gulfardo had in his sly game.
Once Gaspard the sum had lent
Some pressing matter came that sent
Him unsuspecting out of town.
With all the servants gathered round,
Gulfardo gave the sum to her
And said, "Dear madam, please be sure
To note it's to your husband due,
This sum that I return to you.
I want there to be no mistake."
She found it wise that he should take
Such fine precaution to disguise
His true design from prying eyes.
Next day, because of their compact
She with Gulfardo did enact
All the well-known repertory

"Guilfardo ... asked Gaspard to please sign a receipt" (Duplessis-Bertaux).

We celebrate in song and story
Of amorous delights.
He rose to new heights
Of passion, as she gave to him good measure
For his money, with some extra pleasure
Thrown in, out of gratitude
For his business aptitude.
When Gaspard came back to his house
Gulfardo said, before his spouse
That, no longer needing what was lent,
To the wife he'd repaid every cent,
And asked Gaspard to please sign a receipt.
Though seething in her heart at this deceit,
She said that it was true,

For what else could she do?
The servants knew he had returned it.
Though she'd definitely earned it,
She could not collect it now.
What really irked her, anyhow,
Was the extra dose he'd got:
That really made her anger hot.
He later said to one and all
How he'd engineered the fall
Of this money-grasping dame.
There's no point in passing blame
Since every Frenchman is the same.
We know their game, alas, too well.
They like to call it "Kiss and Tell."

10. "You Can't Think of Everything"

A certain jealous husband slept
One eye open, and he kept
His wife from all society,
Such was his anxiety.
In a book he had recorded
Women's tricks both sly and sordid.
Poor soul, he really had no clue,
For their wiles are ever new.
He kept her captive all the same;
Hired an eagle-eyed old dame
To follow always close behind.
His book of ruses eased his mind
Since it listed every kind.
He thought if he knew in advance
What she might try, he'd have a chance.
He kept it with him like a psalter,

Hoping with it he could halt her
Escapades before they hatched.
No cuckold's horns would be attached
To his head if he succeeded
(Though more than this, I think, was
   needed).
It happened on a holy day,
That, having been to church to pray,
With her guardian, his spouse
Returning home, passed by a house
Where from a window fell a mess
That made a stain upon her dress.
Apologies were made, and she
Went inside, but soon could see
She'd have to change out of those clothes.
With this in mind, the lady chose

"From a window fell a mess / That made a stain upon her dress" (Duplessis-Bertaux).

To send her keeper home to find
Another dress; she'd stay behind.
Out of breath from all the stress,
The guardian spoke of the dress
To the husband, who said, "Look!
That's one that wasn't in my book.
For an unknown trick I fell
And that book can go to hell."
He was right: the refuse thrown

Enabled her to be alone
With a lover waiting there
And get her guard out of her hair.
It does no good to keep an eye
On women; things still go awry.
Jealous husbands, their temptations
Can't be stopped by compilations.
Since they are not worth your while,
Burn them in a great big pile.

11. "The Bumpkin in Search of His Calf"

A clod who lost his calf had gone to look
In the woods, where for a perch he took
The finest of the trees that were around
So he could listen for each little sound.
From there, across the distant plain he
    peered.
A lady and a youth below appeared.
To this spot they thought they would retire
To consummate a passionate desire.

On the grass the youth the lady laid
So that her many charms could be displayed.
"Ye gods, the things I can and cannot see!,"
He sighed, yet said not what those things
    might be.
But a voice that came down from above
Cut short these meditations on true love:
"You who see so much at just one glance,
Do you see my calf by any chance?"

12. "Hans Carvel's Ring"

Though well past the prime of life,
Hans Carvel wedded a young wife.
Along with her came crushing care,
Because, you know, it's very rare
To get the first without the second;
Perhaps on this he had not reckoned.
Babeau, the baillif's beautiful daughter,
Took to sex like a fish to water.
Hans, however, was afraid
That one day he would be betrayed.
When he was with her in bed
Edifying tales he read
Aloud from Scripture and Saints' Lives
And other books meant to teach wives
How it is they should behave
And a husband's honor save.
He hated lovers' rendezvous,
He said, and clothes that coquettes choose;
Of the tricks females devise
To look more pleasing in men's eyes
He took a disapproving view.

But what did all his preaching do
To keep her on the straight and narrow
And unharmed by Cupid's arrow?
Not a thing, to tell the truth.
Being in the flower of youth,
The kind of sermons that would please her
Couldn't come from an old geezer;
Those she'd from a lover hear
Would more likely catch her ear.
Hans Carvel was in despair;
He could die—he didn't care.
Yet one night he was consoled:
It's God's own truth, or so I'm told.
It happened after he'd been drinking,
Asleep and dreaming, he was thinking,
As he snored next to Babeau,
Satan had put a ring, just so,
On his finger. To explain
He said to Hans: "I feel your pain.
I know what you're going through;
I have sympathy for you.

"Ye gods, the things I can and cannot see!" (Eisen).

"Wear the ring and don't let go" (Duplessis-Bertaux).

Wear the ring and don't let go.
In that way, you'll always know
If Babeau is being true."
"Satan, I give thanks to you.
This will be a real life-saver!
I'm indebted for the favor.

May God return to you in kind."
Drowsy Hans woke up to find
That his finger ...
You may linger
On that thought.
Or maybe not.

13. "The Boasting Braggart Punished"

A Gascon vainly boasted he could sleep
With a certain lady—what a creep.
For this he was punished in a rather novel way.
(Slanderers are credited alas while those who
  say
Something good about someone are not at
  first believed.)

Philis was the name of the woman thus ag-
  grieved.
She wouldn't give this guy the time of day;
If he came to call, she'd slip away.
He'd shower her with flattery galore,
But she'd go run to Cloris, right next door.
Cloris's husband's name was Eurilas,

Which just happens to rhyme with Dorilas,
Which as it turns out (no small detail)
Is the Gascon's name in this our tale.
Damon's name is equally sonorous;
He both loved and was loved by this Cloris.
Philis was just happy and carefree.
It was evident for all to see
From her cheerful air of cool detachment
That Philis had no amorous attachment.
Though there were men who wanted to ca-
ress her
None knew what it would take to possess
her.
Not quite twenty, she'd already buried
A decrepit rich man she had married.
She had a gorgeous yet girlish physique.
Though at the same time a rebellious streak,
At least concerning matters of the heart,
Played in her make-up an important part.
That Dorilas was Gascon says a lot.
Men from that part of France have always
thought
More highly of themselves than they ought.
Naturally this Gascon begged and pleaded,
Importuning her for what he needed,
Making vows that he would not fulfill
(Such is the way, you know, with Gascons
still,
Whose words you must take with a grain of
salt.
I've heard that Normans also have that
fault.)
That he was in love no doubt is true;
But that he had been successful too—
That's what he desired people would say.
Deceptively she said to him one day,
"I have a favor that I'd like to ask.
It's not a very taxing type of task;
We need your help a husband to hoodwink.
You'll find it safe and effortless, I think.
We would like for you to spend the night
With Cloris's jealous spouse. She's had a
fight
With her boyfriend Damon, and they'll
need
To spend a night together to succeed
In patching up the rift that's broke her heart.
We just need for you to play the part
Of Cloris so Eurilas won't get wise.

Sensing you there, he won't realize
That she's disappeared. Now, have no fears.
He's not touched his wife in many years.
Whether he's unable to maintain
A you-know-what, I know he does abstain.
Maybe jealousy is at the root.
Anyhow, the whole question is moot.
Just snore away, and I'll reward you well."
To make her willing, he'd have gone to hell
To sleep with the Devil, if desired.
Night fell and the Gascon was attired
To look like the part, her nightcap on his
head.
He was placed in her part of the bed.
The torches were put out, the spouse
arrived;
Seized with dread, our Dorilas contrived,
Cold as ice, to become small
And not to spit or cough at all.
Far from approaching his bed-mate, instead
He nestled himself at the edge of the bed,
Holding on by the skin of his teeth.
He could have fit inside a sheath.
The other man twisted and tossed in his
troubled repose,
Stretched out his fingers and touched the tip
of the nose
Of his trembling neighbor, who shrank back
from their touch.
The worst of his worries, the thing that he
dreaded so much,
Was that some amorous whim
Might suddenly take root in him
(The husband, I mean).
A terrible scene
Then would ensue—
Dangerous, too.
There always came some new alarm:
Now a leg, now an arm,
Now the rough beard on his face
Would invade the Gascon's space.
The most terrible to tell:
By the bed there was a bell.
The husband rang; great was the din.
The Gascon shivered in his skin:
His crime would now be brought to light
To God he prayed with all his might,
Abandoning his lover's goal,
Hoping thus to save his soul.

"She showed what he'd missed: a half-covered breast" (Fragonard).

But no one came, despite the bell
(Which, of course, was just as well).
His bed-mate went back to sleep.
Philis her promise now did keep:
The door was opened before sunrise came,
But now, alas! the worst: a torch's flame
Illuminated all as bright as day.
He was certain this light would betray
That he was where he ought not to have
   been.
He begged the husband to forgive his sin,
Praying that he would not come to harm.
"I want to," said a voice replete with charm.

It was Philis, who'd been in the bed right be-
   side him,
All of that time, all those pleasures denied
   him.
She leapt from the bed and to Cloris ran
To tell of what happened to this shattered
   man,
Of all of the dangers he'd risked there that
   night,
To Cloris and Damon, mocking his fright.
So that he'd feel suicide would be best,
She showed what he'd missed: a half-covered
   breast.

14. "The Runaway Bride"

Whether truth or fiction, every tale
Gets told in different ways, this without fail.
To add a personal touch is always lawful
If the story's fictive; but it's awful
When storytellers mess around
With historic fact that's sound.
In telling what's important to posterity
One should maintain a high standard of ver-
   ity.
Alaciel's story is of a different hue;
To its source I've not always been true.
Some may disbelieve it; some may feel
That I go too far: it's no big deal.
Her renown has nothing left to lose,
So I might as well do what I choose.
In just two points do I follow my source,
Those most important to the tale, of course.
One: that there were eight who did caress
   her
Before the night her husband could possess
   her.
The other: her intended
Felt not at all offended,
Having found no doubt within the store
Of charms remaining to his lady more
Than enough to serve as compensation
For what some would think was aggravation.
However that may be,
In her travails at sea
And many sad misfortunes upon land,
She'd much to suffer, we must understand.

Though she changed her partner those eight
   times,
They ought not be counted as if crimes.
Acting with good intent, it would appear,
From gratitude, compassion, or from fear
Of something worse, she ought to be ex-
   cused.
Despite what happened, she was not refused
By her betrothed, who thought she was in-
   tact,
Even though it was a certain fact
She'd been a widow to eight different lovers.
It's hard to know the truth beneath the cov-
   ers,
And a woman knows how to deceive.
But eight times I find hard to believe.
I appeal in this to those who know
How it is these things can turn out so.

In Alexandria the Sultan Zaire
Doted on his daughter with great care.
Slightly more than his life did he love her.
No girl could possibly be ranked above her.
So good, so pretty, so friendly, so charming
Was the lass, and what was most disarming,
I'd like to add: she was accommodating.
In this regard I'm not exaggerating.
As her fame about the region spread,
King Mamolin, from Africa, was led
To love her sight unseen and ask her hand
In marriage—from her dad, you understand.

The Sultan judged his bid the most appealing,
And paid no mind to what she might be
    feeling.
The princess loved already, but who knew?
Kings' daughters are aware that it's taboo
For them to tell a soul what's on their mind.
Whatever they may feel, they keep confined
Within their heart. This causes them much
    stress;
They're made of flesh like any shepherdess.
Hispal, a young lord in the Sultan's court,
Well built, with merit, and of good report,
Was, the princess thought, rather alluring.
They were in love, and yet they were endur-
    ing
Each great pain, unable to confess
To the other what they felt, unless
It be through some shy and sidelong glance.
It was at this stage in their romance
That Zaire to Mamolin chose to award
Alaciel, who therefore had to board
A ship that would now carry her away
To the man who was her fiancé.
And yet all was not lost:
The lovers, though star-crossed,
Would be together after all,
Because the Sultan chose Hispal—
Of his passion unaware—
To take his darling daughter there.
It would seem, in retrospect,
He should have been more circumspect.
After a week of maritime travel
They met some pirates who engaged them in
    battle.
The fight was ferocious,
The carnage atrocious.
The assailants, accustomed to warfare at sea,
Knew how to massacre diligently.
Not only were they skillful, there were more
    of them to slay.
But Hispal by his valor strove to hold them
    all at bay.
Twenty pirates, though, did manage
To board the ship, to their advantage.
The Giant Grifonio at their head,
Horror and death about them spread.
Our hero was surrounded.
Yet Hispal confounded
By the force of his arm their ultimate aim

As he wielded his sword, his eyes all aflame.
But while he was dealing them blow after
    blow
The Giant went down to the cabins below,
For he heard that the girl was somewhere on
    board
And thought of the pleasures that she could
    afford.
He carried her off, but that wasn't enough,
So he picked up the box in which she kept
    stuff
Like jewels and diamonds, though also in-
    side
Were letters and love notes. I've heard it im-
    plied
That Hispal his passion at some point had
    told her
And that Alaciel had not turned a cold
    shoulder,
There not having been time for her anger to
    smolder.
The pirate had no leisure to enjoy
As it happened, his new pleasure toy.
As he carried the lass
And attempted to pass
From ship to ship, the gap between the two
Ships that had been lashed together grew.
In this delicate state
He met his fate,
For as he stood there a-straddle with his
    plunder
Hispal with his sword neatly sliced him
    asunder.
His head and his torso fell into the ocean.
He prayed the "Our Father" in his down-
    ward motion,
Renouncing Mohammed and Tarvagant
And other gods as extravagant.
His other half still stood upon its feet.
One would have laughed at his stinging de-
    feat
Had not the Sultan's daughter
Also fallen in the water.
Hispal leaped to the rescue; her dress kept
    her afloat.
But the ships drifted away, and now they had
    no boat.
They decided to head for some rocks in the
    distance.

Though to sailors a danger, these were in
     this instance
What kept the two from a watery grave.
According to some she was able to save
Her jewels and diamonds, for her precious
     box
Was attached to a rope that she pulled to the
     rocks.
And a good thing it was, for these stones of
     great cost,
Had she not done this, would have been lost.
With her on his back Hispal swam on ahead.
The first rock was reached, but now a new
     dread,
That of starvation, came to replace
Their fear of drowning, in this lonely place.
No vessel appeared on the watery plain,
And nothing to eat on the rock, not a grain.
Day came to an end, then a night passed,

As they continued their unwilling fast.
Deprived of all hope, what worsened their
     case:
Each stared into the other one's face
And though each loved and was loved in re-
     turn,
Neither one knew; both in silence did yearn.
"Hispal," she said, "we need some consola-
     tion.
Trapped as we are in this desolation,
Though it's certain we will die
It will do no good to cry.
We'd have something to gain
If we could soften the pain
Of these dreadful harms
In each other's arms.
What with one thing and another
We might as well console each other."
"But when one feels love within one's soul,

"Her precious box / Was attached to a rope that she pulled to the rocks" (Duplessis-Bertaux).

One desires more than just to console!
That is," he added, "unless you as well ...
But on that thought I know I shouldn't
     dwell.
No, madame, I'm sure it would be wrong
For you, who to another do belong,
To love—what a sad fate that would be.
I can brave both hunger and the sea,
But looking at you, I begin to fear."
She sighed a sigh, and then she shed a tear,
Then she sobbed, and then she wept some
     more.
Hispal began to discourse as before.
A kiss came out of this, but I know not
If it was awarded or was sought.
The two of them made many a pointless
     vow.
"We'll in the end be both dead anyhow.
It makes no difference once our souls are
     gone
Whether our mortal coil is preyed upon
By birds or by dread monsters from the sea;
It's all the same," he said, "it seems to me.
Therefore, all things considered, for our
     graves
We might as well decide upon the waves.
Instead of to this rock, I'm of the notion
That we should trust our fortune to the
     ocean.
The coast isn't far; the wind's on our side.
I still have some strength, and think if I
     tried,
From boulder to boulder, just pausing for
     breath,
We could make it. It beats a lingering
     death."
To this proposal she gave her accord.
So off they went, she dragging the cord
Attached to the box, he carrying his love.
Thanks to assistance from Heaven above,
The rocks as rest stops, Neptune and the
     breeze,
Though famished and weak, they ap-
     proached by degrees
The coast. From rock to rock they hopped;
And only very briefly stopped
At nine boulders more,
Before reaching the shore,
With the box, so they'd for nothing lack.

Why, you may ask, do I keep coming back
To this box? Why always returning?
Is its importance all that burning?
Yes, I say. Just see if I'm wrong.
Do you think our duo would last very long
Without the jewels hidden there?
Lovers cannot live on air
Nor survive on love alone.
There was many a costly stone
Stored within that treasure chest.
Some he sold, and pawned the rest.
He purchased a house where they could re-
     side,
A lovely château perched on the seaside
It came complete with woods and park.
In the woods so deep and dark
The two spent many a pleasant hour.
All this could happen because of the power
Of the treasures that that box contained:
So you see how everything is enchained.
And should you want to ask me why
I insist upon the box—that's my reply.
Within these woods there was a certain cave,
Dark and silent, to which nature gave
All that was needed for passion to flourish.
Within its confines, lovers could nourish
A spark of lust into a burning flame;
Nature put it there for just that aim.
Our two lovers were walking one day,
When Cupid, that scamp, guided their way
Toward that very solitary spot.
Hispal, as they walked, conveyed a lot
About his feelings. Partly by his sighs
And partly by his words did he apprise
Alaciel of the love he felt for her.
She trembled as she listened, quite unsure
What it was she really ought to do.
"We're abandoned by the world, we two,"
He said, "and we can do just what we please.
Who would ever know? We ought to seize
This opportunity to scale the heights
Of passion, and partake of love's delights.
Who stands in our way? There's none who
     knows
Whether we're alive, I should suppose.
Perhaps back home someone has told the tale
That we were swallowed up by some huge
     whale.
The choice, my dear, is yours: either grant

Your lover his fond wish, or if you can't,
Then tell him that he must take you away
To the land where Mamolin holds sway.
But why do that, when you could be so nice
To the man who's saved your bacon twice?
He has desires he wants you to assuage.
Don't you think that we have reached the
    stage
When it's time that you cease to resist
And we make up ground that we have
    missed?"
Hispal's words displayed such tender charm
He'd have made cold marble to turn warm.
As he gave this speech, to love inviting,
She seemed on the tree trunks to be writing
With her hairpin, while her thoughts were
    turning
Into something more like ardent yearning.
The solitary spot was hid from view;
He would be discreet, this she well knew.
She continued to reject him, but her heart
Was not in it. Springtime played a part:
The season in full bloom, who can resist
When there is such beauty in our midst?
Young hearts cannot keep their longings hid-
    den
When on all sides they're so strongly bidden.
How many have we seen who thus are led
Step by step until they land in bed,
Who at the start had never quite decided
That they would ever to that point be
    guided?
The god of Love will bring such things to
    pass
To even the most unsuspecting lass.
She'll begin by taking off a glove,
But in the end give up, because of Love,
The thing that once it's lost will not return.
And when it's gone, she might not even
    learn,
On most occasions, so at least I've heard,
How it was the loss in fact occurred.
At the cavern's entrance, he proposed
That they enter. Though she was disposed
To do as he desired, yet she declined.
But all he'd done for her now came to mind:
Her honor he had saved, and what is more,
Her life. Perhaps what he was asking for
She really ought to give him in the end.

"It's better," Hispal said, "to make a friend
By giving your possession to him than
To keep it safe until there comes a man
With a savage look upon his face
Who will simply grab it with no grace,
Confiscating it with clumsy haste.
That I think would surely be a waste.
I really think you ought
To give it some more thought.
One never knows for whom one does reserve
    it,
Nor if he will actually deserve it."
She was nearly halfway there;
A rainstorm settled the affair.
They had to find a place where they'd be dry.
They chose the cavern; no need to ask why.
What happened there's not subject to pe-
    rusal,
But she did abandon her refusal.
By misfortune she was sorely tried,
In this I think she was more justified
Than many other girls whom I could name.
So let us not cast on her too much blame.
The cave was only one of many places
Where she favored Hispal with her graces.
If the trees could talk, it would be great
To hear the stories that they might relate.
By carving on the tree trunks he left word
Of the feats of love that there occurred:
"HERE DID FAINT WITH JOY
THE WORLD'S MOST HAPPY BOY;
HERE DIED A LOVER ON HIS LADY'S BREAST,
BY A THOUSAND FLAMING KISSES BLESSED,
HE GAVE A THOUSAND KISSES IN RETURN."
The park could say a lot, and one could learn
Much from the château too, if it could speak.
So much transpired, their passion reached a
    peak,
From which it started, sadly, to decline,
Until our lovers for the court did pine.
"You're so dear to me," the princess said.
"I'm quite sure that I would so much dread
For you to think I loved you any less.
But the time has come: I must confess
I feel that true love sometimes does require
Constraint and fear and unassuaged desire.
In spite of all our kissing
Those things, I think, are missing.
It seems our sojourn here

Has become a little drear.
I have a feeling of impending doom:
This charming place could one day be my
  tomb.
Hispal, help me to dispel this fear.
Board a ship and sail away from here.
Go back home so that you can report
That I'm alive to those back home at court.
Once they have discovered I'm not dead,
Don't tell them all that's happened, but in-
  stead
Say you've come back to make the prepara-
  tion
For my long-desired repatriation.
Please make sure I have a strong escort
For my voyage to my father's court,
In case we meet another pirate crew.
Do not think that this means we are
  through.
Just find a way, Hispal, to follow me
Whatever may become my destiny.
Whether in the end I'm wed or not
Please understand I'll keep you in my
  thought.
If I cannot help you in this regard
It's because they keep too close a guard."
Whether that in fact was her intent
She had to promise it for his consent.
When he was ready to get under way
To Zaire she wrote a letter to convey.
Hispal embarked, set sail, and left the coast.
When he arrived, they thought they'd seen a
  ghost.
They asked for all the news that he could
  give:
What was the princess doing? Where'd she
  live?
When he had completed his long tale
(Though not quite divulging each detail),
They sent ships the princess to retrieve.
Hispal, though, was not allowed to leave;
He had to stay behind—
Though no one could find
The least reason to suspect
Anything was not correct
In the princess's behavior.
Her new designated savior
Was a young, good-looking man.
Who decided on the plan

Of leaving half his men upon the shore
To defend the ship; the other corps
Would march right up with him to the
  château.
The princess with such beauty now did glow
That the man was smitten at first sight.
While waiting for the wind to be just right,
To waste no time he told her his desire.
But this only served to rouse her ire.
She told him where it was her duty lay.
At this point a suitor should display
A touch of wild despair
To show he has some flair.
"Such is," he said, "my bitter desperation
I pledge that I will perish of starvation"—
Or so he wished the princess to believe.
Other ways there are, of course, to leave
An unrequited lover's wretched life;
One could, for instance, do it with a knife.
But those who do that quickly find
They've little time to change their mind.
At first she laughed,
And thought him daft.
He pursued his fast,
As a whole day passed.
She did her very darndest to dissuade
The captain from this foolish escapade.
The second day, though, she began to fret:
Perhaps this really was no idle threat.
He was letting her decide
If he lived or died.
That was too much to take
And so for pity's sake
She relented—
And consented.
To be sure she cured his sadness
She performed the act with gladness,
Showing no distress
At enduring his caress.
Once the princess he'd possessed
He no longer felt depressed.
The captain wished to stay;
So he began to say
That ill winds kept them there,
And ships he must repair
Before they could return.
And then, he did just learn,
He claimed, that on the coast
There'd soon descend a host

Of pirates. His prediction
Turned out to be no fiction:
With cutlass, sword, and dirk
Buccaneers soon made quick work
Of his troops upon the strand.
The leader of this band
Had been second in command
When Grifonio had ruled
The waves, and was well schooled.
This pirate seized the château right away,
Putting those within in disarray.
The captain, weak from fasting, cursed his
    fate.
The pirate asked to princess to relate
Her adventures. Taking her aside,
His lustful interest roused, the pirate tried
To make advances, which she then rejected.
He was not astonished or dejected
For in these things he knew a thing or two.
"The best thing," he told her, "that you
    could do
Is make me a good friend on your behalf
For I am a pirate and a half.
That poor devil starved for you;
Now you will be fasting too,
Until you give yourself up to my lust.
We pirates have a sense of what is just,
So you will have no food
Till you decide you're in the mood.
Everyone gets his deserts,
There'll be no supper or desserts
Until you come across."
Having seen who was the boss,
She saw resistance would be vain.
No point in making worse her pain.
In pity for the captain she'd relented;
In pity for herself she now consented.
She tried to put her heart in this endeavor,
For after all, no torment lasts forever.
If he had been more wise, the buccaneer
Would have taken her elsewhere than here.
But wisdom in love? There's no such thing.
He was ready to begin his fling;
The château was a comfy place to stay.
But he should have left that very day,
As the wind was propitious.
But Fortune soon turned vicious.
While we're sleeping,
No watch keeping,

Fortune is awake—
Of that make no mistake!
The lord inhabiting a nearby château,
Loving the joys that life can bestow,
With no attachment to get in the way
Was always looking for new prey.
He'd heard of the princess and the praise
For her beauty and obliging ways.
All that he could think of night and day
Was how with her to get his way.
He'd friends and money, and could assemble
An army to make a rival tremble.
With two thousand under his command,
He said to them, "Now men, let's take a
    stand.
Are we so cowardly that we'd permit
A maiden to be pressured to submit?
Are we to let a pirate sate his lust?
We will definitely not, I trust.
I propose that we make it our cause
To save this maiden from that monster's
    claws.
Let every man this evening prepare arms,
But silently; let's not arouse alarms.
Under cover of the night
We will gather all our might
On the château's lawn,
To be prepared by dawn
To strike.
I like
Our chances.
Surprise enhances
The likelihood of our success.
We shall soon, I'm sure, possess
The château and all that it contains.
They will be your justly-gotten gains.
As for my share in the booty
All I covet is that beauty—
Not to sully her like this base thief
But instead to fly to her relief,
To restore her honor and possessions,
And make up for his sordid trangressions.
All the rest to you will accrue:
The horses, the baggage, the curious crew,
The foodstuffs, the wine, the munitions too.
There's just one thing that I ask:
That you take up the task
Of hanging that cursèd corsair
From the battlement, high in the air."

This oration inspired such fire in his men
That he had to speak all over again
To cool down their ardor, which grew too
    hot.
They ate little supper but drank quite a lot
By way, perhaps, of recompense.
Indeed, for the wine he spared no expense,
Attentive to keeping his men always cheer-
    ful.
In earlier battles he'd always been careful
To follow this course of action.
In drink having found satisfaction,
They picked up their ladders and swords
And silently made their way towards
The slumbering foe
In the nearby château.
At the horizon dawn started to peep—
The hour when one's slumber is at its most
    deep.
The unconscious pirates were slain in their
    sleep.
Death was so quick, they felt not a thing,
Except for their captain—for he would
    swing.
Alaciel was presented.
Because the princess had resented
The captain's behavior
And since her new savior
Seemed so polite,
Not to mention her fright
As well as surprise
Her lovely eyes,
It appears,
Shed no tears.
Some lives were spared by her merciful pleas.
She pitied the dead, attempted to ease
The passing from life of the dying.
Life in this place had been trying
For Alaciel, so without regret
She left the château, and could even forget
The last two of her lovers, some have sur-
    mised.
I for one would not be surprised.
Her neighbor's château she now did behold:
Richly appointed, and burnished with gold.
Her savior received the princess in style,
No detail neglected his guest to beguile:
A delicious repast, exquisite wine.
The gods could partake nothing more fine.

Having been a teetotaler up until now
Because as a Muslim she'd taken that vow,
Tonight was the first occasion
She had encountered the suasion
Of a drink as divine
As she discovered this wine
To be.
With glee
Did her cup
Go bottoms up.
The effect
Of unchecked
Consumption of booze
Was, sad to say, news
To innocent her.
What can occur
To one so naive
You can conceive.
The enchantment of love had bound her be-
    fore;
But what had this other poison in store?
Both things women ought to dread.
Maidservants put the princess to bed.
Soon to his sleeping guest her host was steal-
    ing.
Can one find immobile charms appealing?
A friend told me the other day
If such charms should come his way
He'd need no one else to lend him a hand.
The wine and the sleepiness worked just as
    planned.
When Bacchus' effects had worn away
She woke up and found to her dismay
That in this man's arms she had spent the
    night.
Her voice was paralyzed, frozen with fright.
She could not cry out, and by terror seized,
Let her him do with her just as he pleased;
She even let him fix a rendez-vous
When he would return again and do
What he had done now, for as he said,
"One night or a hundred spent in bed
Together makes no difference in kind;
The sin is all within the first confined."
She believed him. But at length he tired
Of her, and for fresh conquests now aspired.
He went out one night and had the bad grace
To ask a friend to take his place
In the bed with Alaciel,

But say not a word; if he did well
She'd surely accept the fait accompli.
To render this service his friend did agree,
To help a friend in his hour of need.
Things, as promised, did proceed
According to plan,
Except that our man,
When passion reached its peak
Felt he had to speak,
Unable to contain his joy.
Angry she'd been made a toy
For these two to trade,
The princess felt betrayed.
"Where does he get the right
To give me away?" Her plight
Touched the heart of the friend,
Or so he did pretend.
The fault, he said, lay with the host.
Hoping now to make the most
Of the occasion, the fellow told her,
"Don't let your righteous rage just smolder,
But avenge his scorn and your disgrace
By granting embrace upon embrace.
Requite his betrayal
In every detail
By loving me out of resentment and spite."
This she did, to his utter delight.
The host, distracted by other affairs,
Took no umbrage at all at theirs.
Five is the amount
(I've been keeping a count)
Of lovers till now she has known.
Others, I know, have been prone
To speak of the sixth in a different way
Than what it is I plan to say.
Some may conclude
That I don't include
All of the men on her list,
As if one I intentionally missed
In order not to paint her
As being of somewhat fainter
Virtue than I'd have preferred.
But I only tell what occurred.
Of the precursors her husband incurred—
I swear I'm telling it straight—
The number was no more than eight.
The host who had left in search of variety
Came back when his friend has reached his
   satiety.

The princess forgave him his impropriety
And decided to form with the two a society,
Allowing them to share her fifty-fifty.
They found this royal clemency quite nifty.
Alaciel thus passed from hand to hand;
She often found diversion 'mid the band
Of young women who her needs attended.
One of them she specially befriended.
This girl found herself cajoled
By one though gallant yet too bold.
Handsome, but vehement in his desire.
Skipping formalities, he would aim higher
From the beginning. In his choice of prey
He began with those who never display
The least interest in love, the proper and
   prim;
Those were the women who interested him.
One day in a distant part of the green,
Where he thought what he'd do would pass
   unseen,
Into a pavilion he enticed
This girl for a lovers' tryst.
Alaciel by chance was near by.
But, not knowing this, he was ready to try
Brute force to assuage his violent lust.
He had lost the gift of women's trust
Because he liked to kiss and tell,
A trait that doesn't go down too well
With the fairer sex
Because such gossip wrecks
A lady's reputation.
This caused him much frustration,
Ruining his hopes for amorous conquest,
Since from fear they thought it best
To just say no to this dangerous guy.
She might have given him a try
If she had dared.
But she wasn't prepared
To suffer what could then ensue.
He thought then what he had to do
In the pavilion was take the key
And lock her in. He didn't see
The princess outside, near at hand.
The girl could readily understand
The fix she was in, and tried to escape.
He tried to restrain her, but she cried
   "Rape!"
The princess arrived just in time
To prevent a dastardly crime,

Or at least to interrupt it.
But the would-be rapist erupted
In rage, from enormous frustration.
"By all the gods, damnation!
Before you two leave here today
One of you will have to pay.
I'll tie your hands up if I must,
But I will assuage my lust.
No help will come, I fear;
No one's around to hear.
Resistance would be vain.
Draw lots and don't complain.
One or the other will suffice;
I'll let *you* choose because I'm nice."
"Why should the princess pay for me?
She's done no wrong that I can see."
"If to her the lot should fall
It's destiny that makes the call."
The princess said, "I won't permit
This girl to be forced to submit.
I am resolved and do prefer
I be the one who shall incur
The penalty you have in mind."
Despite her efforts to be kind
Chance decided, all the same.
When lots were drawn, it was her name
That destiny however chose.
At least that's how my version goes.
The girl departed, and they vowed
Of this they'd nothing say aloud.
But the man would rather hang
Than not be able to harangue
A listener with such a story,
Which redounded to his glory.
It didn't take long to find a friend
Whose willing ear this guy could bend.
The princess began to discover
That a constant change of lover,
Can be a bit of a pain.
She would just as soon abstain.
No longer could she enjoy
Being a Helen of Troy
If it meant having to pander
To so many an Alexander.
But the god of Love was not quite through
Showing her what he could do.
One day when she was asleep
In a woodland dark and deep
A wandering knight came passing by;

Her heavenly beauty caught his eye.
He was the sort of errant knight
Who found adventure where he might,
The sort of knight whom ladies trailed
  about
On their palfreys, ladies who no doubt
Passed for chaste and pure.
(What trials to endure!)
Seeing her asleep like this,
His impulse was to steal a kiss.
The only question would be where:
From her lips or bosom bare?
He was about to sate his lust
When he remembered that he must
Obey the law of his vocation;
To chivalry he owed his station.
And yet within his soul he prayed
That Love would now come to his aid.
That he could have a love affair
With this lady was his prayer.
The princess woke up with alarm.
"Oh no," he said, "I mean no harm.
No giant nor a savage I,
But a knight. The gods on high
I thank for their inestimable grace,
That I should find within this place
What's hard to find in paradise."
After this compliment so nice
He came to the affair at hand
And gave her to understand
He was on fire
With mad desire.
(And unsurpassed
At working fast.)
He spoke in the traditional vein,
As he repeated the old refrain
About taking a vow as a knight
To do whatever he might
For the sake of the lady whom he adored
(I'll skip the details—you'd only be bored.).
She accepted his proffer
And decided to offer
Her own life story, though chose to omit
Some juicier parts, like the bit
About the six lovers. Given the dearth
Of truth, he took it for what it was worth.
She told how fate had been unfair;
He promised that he would convey her
Within a month to dad or fiancé,

Whichever one she wanted. "I should say,"
Said she, "the former. And with reason.
I think it's not quite yet the season
To pay a visit to the African coast.
What I'd like the very most,
Rather than to meet the King
Who's waiting with a wedding ring,
Should the gods in heaven let me,
Would be, I confess, to get me
Back home to my native shore."
"Have no worries on that score.
That goal you'll achieve
If you will relieve
My amorous distress.
Allow me, though, to stress
That if I died from it you'd be alone
With your chances for return all blown.
To be absolutely frank
It's me whom you'll have to thank
So I think it's not too much to ask
That you agree to do this pleasant task."
She readily consented.
Then he a list presented
Of favors she'd perform
In order to conform
To the covenant contracted.
The favors would not be exacted
All at once, but some each day
As she made her homeward way.
She climbed up on his horse behind,
Prepared to leave, not of a mind,
By her escape so much engrossed.
To bid a farewell to her host.
The two joined with his retinue
Including the knight's young nephew
And the latter's aged tutor.
(You can guess which one was cuter.)
She dismounted his horse and was given to
　　ride
A palfrey, while he walked beside,
Telling of love, and tales to court her
And to make the journey shorter.
The pact was faithfully carried out,
No dispute did ever sprout,
No quibbles or equivocations
Concerning any calculations,
Just like merchants who've long been in
　　trade.
From favor to favor their way they made

Till they reached the shore and anchor
　　weighed.
The sea was calm, so much so
The progress made was very slow.
The knight didn't mind
Because he would find
When days were added because the wind
　　ceased
The number of payments that he got in-
　　creased.
Hale and hearty, at the port of Joppa
The knight and the princess were able to
　　stop a
While and rest before resuming their journey
　　on land.
After two days they were on their way but
　　then a band
Of brigands descended.
The knight defended
His party as best he could,
But things were not looking good.
He received a mortal blow
Just as he'd fought off the foe.
Although before he expired,
He did what was required,
Telling his nephew, young and brave,
That now it was up to him to save
Princess Alaciel, although to save her
Meant he would receive whatever favor
Remained unpaid—still quite a few.
This was just fine with the young nephew,
Who, I should also relate,
Became heir to his uncle's estate.
When all of their tears had been shed
For the knight who now was dead,
His final wishes were put into play
As the company wended their way.
Things were completed in all due order,
With the last favor granted as they reached
　　the border.
The nephew there thought it best to skip
　　out,
So that his presence would not cast a doubt
On her virtue. His tutor, old and gray,
Guided her home the rest of the way.
He brought her to her dad.
I really wish I had
The eloquence to express
This father's happiness,

His transports of joy,
But I'd best employ
The strategy of the sun
Which when day is done
So quickly disappears one thinks
It's falling as it sinks.
The tutor loved to blather
As long as he could gather
An audience to give their attention.
With a remarkable gift for invention
He told her royal sire
How much he did admire
The character and life-style of his child.
(At this she doubtless smiled.)
"My lord," he said, "when Hispal left
And she was of all help bereft,
Your daughter, recalling the sage advice
That considers idleness the source of vice,
Resolved to devote herself full time
To worshipping a god folks in that clime
With high reverence adore.
I could give details galore:
His temples there the people name
'Boudoirs.' The idol they acclaim
Is one of whom I'd never heard.
He is, it seems, some kind of bird,
With feathers only on his wings.
With other nations, old age brings
Religious devotion; but with them, youth.
The young there worship him in truth.
When you know the life that she pursued
Your heart will thrill with fervent gratitude
To heaven for this child so gifted
Who men's spirits so uplifted
In the service of their god.
Some things in that land are odd:
No eunuchs there inhibit
The women, who exhibit
The utmost carefree ease
In doing what they please.
The princess from the start
Took their style to heart,
So adaptable is she.
I think that you will agree
She deserves the highest praise
For her accommodating ways."
This news delighted Zaire,
Who started to prepare
To send the bride-to-be

Far across the sea
To where her patient African awaited,
To whom her marriage would be celebrated.
She left the port
With an escort.
The retinue who had been serving
Alaciel through such unnerving
And perilous escapades
Were given accolades
And sumptuous royal presents.
Brought into the presence
Of Mamolin the king,
She made his heart go *zing*.
He could not contain his joy,
Giving orders to deploy
His cooks to make a rich repast.
Of the dangers she had passed
She the gathered guests regaled,
Though of course the princess failed
To tell the truth in all its glory,
For throughout her thrilling story
She in fact told many lies;
A tactic she considered wise.
I must confess she was inventive,
And her audience attentive.
When night descended she was led
To the matrimonial bed.
She emerged with honor intact;
The king bore witness to the fact.
Alaciel, who might have felt queasy,
Was happy, they say, to get off so easy.

This tale suggests that married men
Can be where other men have been
Yet never have a clue.
My advice to you,
Husbands, so you're not supplanted
Never take a thing for granted.
Young women, my advice to you:
Keep yourselves pure whatever you do;
Husbands like Alaciel's are few.
When you become a fiancée
Make sure there is no delay
Between that time and your wedding day.
This method prevents, to be perfectly frank,
Extracurricular hanky-pank.
Watch out for men who "just want to be
    friends":
That's just a mask for their dastardly ends.

Cupid has his sneaky ways.
Don't let a spark become a blaze.
Men who try to stake their claims
Can go elsewhere for fun and games.
But if some poor unhappy lass
Should be brought to such a pass

That she can't defend it,
She shouldn't try to mend it.
When it's too late,
Just laugh at fate.
Purity is nice, but when it's gone
One must do one's best to carry on.

15. "The Hermit Monk"

When Venus and Hypocrisy unite
The harm they do is hardly ever slight.
A man's a man, and it's my view
That when he's a monk, that's especially
    true.
If you've a pretty daughter, sister, wife
Guard them from monks and friars with your
    life.
They command some wicked magic.
The consequences can be tragic
When they get their filthy mitts
On a naive girl whose wits
Are not of the best.
You may think I jest,
But listen to the rest:

A youthful hermit monk was thought to be
    so full of grace
That in the roster of the saints they kept for
    him a place.
He wore the customary rope with knots
    around his waist
But underneath his cassock beat a heart that
    was not chaste.
A rosary six feet in length and of enormous
    size
Descended from his belt, all the better to
    disguise
His foul intent, and on the other side there
    was a bell.
Should a female pass nearby, he'd cower in
    his shell.
He'd cast his eyes upon the ground as if he
    could repent.
You wouldn't think him capable of eating
    lard in Lent.
A little village could be found within his
    neighborhood,

At whose edge a widow dwelled who did the
    best she could.
The only thing in all the world that she
    could call her own
Was her daughter—young, naive, and
    though she was full-grown
Still a virgin, though in truth, less on ac-
    count of virtue
Than from having no idea what you don't
    know can hurt you.
For savoir-faire she had no gift, although she
    was quite candid.
She had no dowry, no prospects, nor knew
    she what a man did.
Her poverty was cause enough for having no
    pursuer,
Though had she lived in Adam's time when
    people's needs were fewer
No doubt she'd not have lacked for beaux for
    then when folks got wed
No money was required, because they had no
    sheets or bed.
Those times have gone forever, now that no
    one makes the journey
To the marriage altar save they go with an
    attorney.
The hermit monk went seeking alms within
    the town one day.
He saw the girl, and to himself beneath his
    hood did say,
"That's just the thing I need to pass these
    long and lonely nights.
Some ruse I'll find to get that girl on whom
    I've set my sights."
Indeed he did, and I will tell how he
    achieved his goal.
In the women's cottage wall the hermit made
    a hole,

Through which he placed a speaking tube
one stormy night and dark.
In stentorian tones these words he spoke: "O
women, hark!"
At his voice the women quaked, not knowing
what to do.
They trembled in each other's arms, while he
began anew:
"Awake, ye creatures of the Lord—thou,
widow, and thou, maid.
I am the messenger of God sent to enlist
your aid.
Go seek the hermit Lucius" (because that
was his name).
"Depart from here tomorrow morn, but tell
no one I came.
This is the Lord's command—fear not, for I
will be your guide.
This friar is blessèd by the Lord. Thou,
widow, shall provide
Your daughter for his manly needs, a help-
meet by his side.
From their holy union will be born a saintly
Pope
Who will reform all Christendom—this is
our fervent hope."

With such great force and clarity were these
instructions said
The widow and the daughter as they hud-
dled in their bed
Must have heard quite perfectly the sense
that they conveyed.
For fifteen minutes silence reigned because
they were afraid.
The girl at last stuck out her nose from un-
derneath the sheet
She drew her mother by the arm, all inno-
cent and sweet.
"Good gracious, Mother dear," she asked,
"and must I really go?
What does a 'help-meet' do, because I'm
sure I do not know.
My cousin Anne could do a better job, of
that I'm sure.
His sermons she could better follow, and
she's more mature."
"Oh hush, you silly goose," the mother said.
"Don't be a twit.

For the lessons he intends you don't need
that much wit.
After the first or second one you'll know
much more than she."
"Is that so?" the girl replied. "Let's go imme-
diately."
"Not so fast," the mother said. "Let's not run
off half-cocked.
The Devil can take many forms. He even
could concoct
To fool us with this voice. You notice how
it's harsh and cracked?
Satan's entire family, I've heard this for a fact,
Speaks in those very tones. So we shouldn't
be so quick
To fall for what could really be some diabolic
trick.
Perhaps you didn't hear him right, because
you were afraid."
"But mother dear, I heard him clear as day,"
replied the maid.
"Well, in that case," the mother said, "what
we must do is pray."
So pray they did, as well as argue, all the
live-long day.
When night came, the voice returned; its
message cast a chill:
"Thou faithless woman, thou dost dare to
strive against God's will!
Delay no more. Go seek the monk, or thou
shalt surely die."
"Oh, mother dear," the daughter cried, "I
fear we must comply.
You see, I heard him perfectly. The message
now is clear.
We must go see the holy man, because I
greatly fear
That if we don't, and right away, your life
comes to an end.
I'd run as fast as ever I could, my mother to
defend."
"Well, we'll go," the widow said. They
started to prepare.
The girl put on her Sunday clothes, the best
she had to wear.
Her finest skirt, her silver belt, with velvet
ribbons, too.
Although she had no inkling of what she'd
be asked to do.

A young girl always seeks to please and thus
will dress the part.
And so the widow's daughter now was looking very smart.
Our sanctimonious hypocrite did keep a
careful eye.

And by a hole that he had made he hoped
that they would spy
Within his cell the goings-on: each penitential blow
With which he seemed to strike his back to
draw from flames below

"This time the monk received them" (Roqueplan).

Some poor sinner damned to hell for his un-
christian crimes.

The women thought they heard him crack
the whip some fifty times.

Although they knocked, he did not come;
instead they were regaled

With still more evidence of how he scourged
himself and flailed

(Though all was false, merely a show to mis-
lead the unwary).

At last, the length of time it took to sing a
Miserere

The hermit came and opened up, pretending
great surprise.

The widow blushed and trembled as she
started to apprise

Him of the nightly visions, while her daughter, six steps back,

Awaited the result. "This doubtless is a sneak
attack,"

He said, "from Hell itself. Besides, no
woman is allowed

Inside my holy cell. It goes against all that
I've vowed.

There is no way that any Pope could from
my loins arise."

The widow was quite sad to hear the monk
speak in this guise.

"Never from you?" she asked. "Why not?"
But no more would he say.

As they left, the daughter said, "The cause of
our dismay

Is surely all our sins." That night again the
angel came.

His voice shook all the house. And yet this
time he did proclaim:

"Go back and see the hermit, for he's had a
change of heart."

The women when the night was over got an
early start.

This time the monk received them. The
mother left, the girl remaining.

The hermit gently started her essential holy
training.

First he took her lovely arm, and then he
took a kiss.

Then passed to beauties hid from sight,
those sources of sweet bliss.

Now she was entirely nude, as if to be bap-
tised.

O suave and false dissemblers, how you keep
your aims disguised!

When he returned from morning prayer, he'd
give her so much grace

That morning sickness soon arrived, and
then to take its place

A swelling came that caused the girl to make
her waistband looser,

But no one did she tell, for fear that someone
would accuse her

Of having done some misdeed that would
make her have to leave.

The game of Love was giving her some
pleasure, I believe.

You may well ask, Where did this naive girl
get so much wit?

Why, from the game of love itself, which
yields the benefit

Of Eden's Tree of Knowledge, since they are
one and the same.

For seven entire months the little vixen hid
her shame.

She'd later say she had no idea why her waist
expanded.

When her mother heard the news, the union
was disbanded;

The girl packed her belongings; said "merci"
to her kind host.

The hermit prayed his thanks to Father, Son,
and Holy Ghost,

For the bounteous grace this humble servant
had received.

As the women left he said the child they had
conceived

Would, God willing, come to term, though
issued this advice:

"Do nothing that could harm the boy; make
every sacrifice

For his well-being, for he'll bring you great
prosperity.

As Pope, he will provide good things for
your posterity.

Only good will come to you, you'll reign and
will pronounce

Your nephews to be cardinals; your cousins,
dukes and counts.

Mansions and châteaux to you and yours will
   he deliver.
Their flow will be as constant as the water in
   the river."
After making this prediction,
He gave her his benediction.
The future Queen of Rome,
When she got back home,
Took sheer delight
All day and night
In dreaming of bishops and popes;
She had some very high hopes.
Many a knit cap

For the little chap
Did she lovingly make.
So there be no mistake
In the sex of the child to be born,
She ate two eggs every morn.
She waited in joy
For her little boy.
But what came would destroy
Dreams of châteaux and a papal tiara,
For by some kind of terrible error
Heaven brought her ...
A baby daughter.

16 . "Mazet of Lamporechio"

To take the veil does not impart
Against love's wiles a sure rampart,
Nor even the hardest one to breach.
Better than wall or fence, for each
Wife a husband good and true
Should stand guard for her virtue.
In my opinion a too apparent
Error committed by many a parent,
Which could even be a crime,
Is to think that every time
A girl, whether she wants or not,
Is put in a cloister our God ought,
Or much less will, accept the gift.
If, that is, you catch my drift.
We really ought to disabuse
Those parents of such ignorant views.
Satan knows no better source
(Unless God intervenes, of course)
Than such sad and cloistered souls
For his own nefarious goals.
One should never be so simple
As to think those clothed in wimple
Always have a guarantee
Against thoughts of impurity.
Just the opposite obtains.
In the world, a girl maintains
Her virtue when she apprehends
Exactly what a man intends.
Those girls know they should look out.
But nuns have more to worry about:
Temptation, daughter of idleness,

Always will a mind possess;
And then of course there is desire,
Which I think the nuns acquire
Because they're under such constraint.
"My daughter's a nun, therefore a saint"
Is not a logical thing to say.
Three out of four will rue the day
That they chose to take the veil
For that holy cloistered jail.
They'll bite their fingers, and do worse.
Their convent vows they all will curse,
According to the things I've heard.
Boccaccio's tale of nuns immured
Is pretty good, it seems to me.
I've rhymed it here, as you will see:

A gardener once in such a place
Thought that it was a disgrace
How nuns chattered all the day
And never even thought to pray.
Instead, they indulged in the impulse
To get dolled up in starched white wimples
And submit to the temptation
To make worldly conversation
In the parlor with a guest.
Every sin that was confessed
Was soon known by all the rest.
Each to the other passed the ball.
Eight nuns there were, though nine in all
When you count the one in charge.
Disputes among them did loom large.

Most were good-looking; all were young.
Their attractions widely sung,
Priests were always coming by.
One doesn't have to wonder why.
This ancient gardener did find
They drove him quite out of his mind.
His troubles seemed never to cease
For each one had her own caprice.
Each nun would tell him what to do,
But he didn't have a clue
How to deal with each demand.
It was more than he could stand.
He thought it time that he retired.
In those years he'd not acquired
A single sou, owned nothing more
Than the outfit which he wore.
He went back to his home town,
Was having a drink when a youth sat down
To begin a conversation
Concerning his erstwhile vocation.
The youngster made it known that he
Would not mind working there for free.
Because the nuns were so naive
He'd snap up one, he did believe,
And then another, till he'd caught
All the ones that could be got.
The gardener, though, was opposed
To what this guy—Mazet—proposed.
"I'd rather starve than go back there.
Those nuns, they all got in my hair.
They are strange, to say the least,
A very curious sort of beast.
You've no idea how I was tortured,
Working in that convent orchard,
In the garden, or the yard.
One wants it soft, another hard.
One says plant cabbage—no, plant carrots.
Don't be the sucker who inherits
My old job. Take it from me,
You don't want the agony."
"That's not the point," replied Mazet.
"Let me be your protégé.
I can be a beast of burden
But one thing I know for certain:
It won't be a month before
They'll all come begging me for more.
The reason is, I'm only twenty.
Unlike you, I still have plenty
Of my native vim and vigor.

For you see, the way I figure,
I'm the very thing they need.
You just have to intercede
So I can get in at the gate."
"OK." "Gee thanks, that would be great.
But something else just comes to mind.
I should pretend to be some kind
Of idiot mute." "That's very good.
The priest in charge most likely would
Be much less of a mind to fret
If you seemed to pose no threat."
The scheme came off just as they planned.
Mazet received his first command,
"Take a hoe to the vegetable patch."
He did his work with much dispatch,
Pretending to be a half-wit.
The nuns got quite a kick from it.
One day when Mazet was sleeping,
Or just that appearance keeping,
Two nuns came there all alone
(The rest were indoors, being prone
To fear the sun that time of day),
One crept right up to Mazet
And to her sister, whispering, said,
"Let's take this fellow to the shed."
He was a healthy-looking man.
The nun beheld him and began
To want to have him, come what may.
The god of Love had showed her a way.
The other said, "The shed? What for?"
"I don't know. Let's just explore.
I've heard that folks do things in there."
"O sweet Jesus, I declare,"
She signed herself as she exclaimed,
"To think such things I'd be ashamed.
Our rule forbids us thoughts so wild.
What if he got us both with child?
What if someone came along?
You're sure to cause us some great wrong."
"No one will see us; don't you worry,
I think you're in too great a hurry
To be alarmed before you should.
We needn't always be so good,
Or to our rules feel so beholden.
This opportunity is golden.
Our plan, my dear, is clearly sound.
In this heat, no one's around.
The shubbery's so thick it's hard
To see, but one should still keep guard

While the other's occupied
With what's going on inside.
Because he's mute he'll never tell."
"All right," she said, "I might as well.
If I go first, you'll have more leisure,
Once I'm done, to take your pleasure.
That way you needn't do it twice.
I'm only trying to be nice."
The other one, who was more honest,
Said, "To have this fine Adonis
Would not else have occurred to you.
You're shamed by your desire, it's true."
The first to go in stayed so long
The other made her move along.
By the time her turn had come
Mazet was ready to succumb.
Three times were all he could achieve;
After which, he made her leave.

Again they trod the path that led
To the convenient garden shed.
Mazet's progress now was stellar:
Sister Agnes in the cellar;
Sister Angelica he met
In the bedroom, while Colette
Took her instruction in the attic;
Others too he made ecstatic.
Soon or late he got them all.
Time now for the turn to fall
To the abbess, waiting her chance
To join in this uplifting dance.
But she claimed three times her share,
Which really wasn't very fair;
The other nuns now had to fast.
She gave Mazet, so he could last
The longer, potions to ingest;
But he now wasn't at his best.

"Let's take this fellow to the shed" (Duplessis-Bertaux).

And so with the abbess one day,
He broke his silence in this way:
"I have always heard that one good cock
Has only seven in his flock.
At least don't make me serve all nine."
"It's a miracle divine!"
She shouted. "Sisters, come rejoice.
Our fasts have given him his voice."
The eight came running, gathered around.
They met, and this arrangement found:
Mazet the gardener would remain.
The truth, if it were known, would stain
The convent's name and reputation.

He retained his situation.
The nuns kept him well fed and nourished;
In that way, their convent flourished.
Mazet did his very best;
He had helpers for the rest.
He sired miniature Mazets;
These future monks the nuns did raise.
They did in time fathers become.
To motherhood then did succumb
Their sisters, who to their regret
Did children of their own beget.
But they deserved the name of mother
More than they did any other.

BOOK THREE

1. "Brother Philip's Geese"

Women do me too much honor when my
    tales they read,
If, that is, the fairer sex do read my tales in-
    deed.
Why not? It's bad enough that in their hearts
    they castigate
The females who do silly things in stories I
    relate.
Why could not these readers simply laugh
    right up their sleeve
At the twists and turns of the fabric that I
    weave?
But if my tales are fictive, they complain they
    have no worth;
While if they're true they disapprove of my
    attempts at mirth.
Would they after all for no good reason
    throw a fit
If they heard someone express a bit of clever
    wit?
Cajoling phrases are more likely causes of
    disaster
Than my stories—they can burn a house
    down so much faster.
Ladies, make those sighing beaux get lost;
Let my book protect you at all cost.
On second thought, don't chase them out.
Can't a good life be lived without
Being locked in with the dead?
Those you thoughtlessly have said
You give your favors for a song
Have clearly got their facts all wrong.
Not that lovers whose passionate prayer
Is rewarded are that rare.
Yet neither is success
Found to excess.
What my book says on that score

Is to amuse, and nothing more.
In every way I've served the fair,
But has it got me anywhere?
Would I want to be the cause
That the teeniest faux pas
Should be laid at the feet
Of the least little sweet
One of you?
That's not true!
Let's tell tales, but make sure they're well
    told.
Critics, please, don't be too quick to scold.
Censure all you want defective lines,
But as for bold seducers' sly designs,
Do not shout, "Beware!"
I see no danger there.
Some husbands and mothers
If they had their druthers,
Would like to take the wind out of my sails
Just because I've told some wicked tales.
My book might do what I did not?
That's a very silly thought!
Ladies, if you read me there's no danger.
Yet I wish I weren't a total stranger;
I wish I could have thanked you in advance
In person, but I never had that chance.
What might I provide in recompense?
A tale that demonstrates that no defense,
No precaution taken can forestall
The power of your beauty to enthrall:
Once there was a boy within whose mind
The beauties of the dawn and spring com-
    bined
With those of fields and lovely, radiant skies,
Had at first *your* image struck his eyes,
Would have thought that all this natural
    splendor

Was surpassed by that of your fair gender.
Indeed when he beheld you that first time
The impact was immediate and sublime.
You have such a talent to amaze
That to you alone did go his gaze.
Mere palaces held no more charm for him;
Your dazzling allures did quickly dim
The sparkle of the jewels of the crown.
The boy had been raised far from any town,
In the woods his only friends were birds.
His only joy to hear their song, whose words
Were beyond his comprehension,
Though he paid them close attention,
For their gentle melody
Gave comfort in his misery.
When his mother died, the child
Had been brought into the wild
By a dad who wished his son
Would never meet with anyone.
In such a savage place
He'd see no human face.
The world was inhabited, as far as he knew,
Only by creatures who growled or flew,
Who lived and breathed but had no thought.
There were two reasons that had brought
His father to that lonely spot.
One, misanthropy; the other, fear.
Because the father'd lost his spouse so dear
The world became too much to bear.
Worn out from sorrow and despair,
When his cherished wife met her demise
The man began to fear and to despise
The rest of womankind.
He left the world behind,
And thought he'd put his life to better use
If he became a worshipful recluse;
He chose the same condition for his son.
His earthly goods he gave to those with
     none.
Fleeing the world that he reviled,
Carrying in his arms the child,
To the lonely woods he came.
Philip was the hermit's name.
The account of the world to his son he
     would render
Omitted all mention of feminine gender;
Nor did this puritanical sire
Speak of love or of desire.
A hundred things from him did he conceal,

Not from bitterness, but pious zeal.
In raising his son, he would carefully gauge
What instruction to give with regard to his
     age:
He spent many hours
Naming the flowers
And each creature alive
When the boy was aged five,
And spoke of the birds,
But along with these words
He instilled a healthy fear of the devil in the
     lad,
Saying that this fellow Satan really was quite
     bad.
At the age of ten, it was time for a chat
About heaven and hell and all of that,
But women were not yet on the scene.
When his son reached the age of fifteen,
Philip discussed the divine Creator
But thought that he'd best save for later
Certain details about His Creation
Which might lead into temptation;
Certain particulars might cause regret
In one who was supposed to be celibate.
At twenty, the father thought it good
To take the young man from the wood
On a trip to the neighboring town.
Since Philip was now so broken down
With the impediments of old age
He no longer could engage
In the beggar's trade, or barely.
He had to face the problem squarely:
When he died, how could his son
Pursue the vocation that he had begun?
The wolves in the woods were not the sort
From whom a mendicant might seek sup-
     port.
A pouch and a stick were all he possessed,
Not much to leave as a final bequest.
As he grew older he mused upon this.
Many there were who'd think it remiss
Not to give when Philip would ask.
Had he set himself that task,
He could have garnered quite a tidy sum.
All the children knew him and would come.
"Get your money ready! Brother Philip's
     here!" they'd cry.
The esteem that he enjoyed in the town was
     high.

"A bird called a goose" (Eisen).

Many devotees he had, though all of them
were male,
For in his faith as well did his misogyny pre-
vail.
When he thought his son imbued
With the doctrines that he viewed
As vital to his spiritual health
He had him meet some men of wealth
And there begin his mendicant calling.
But this father's tears were falling
As he took him to the city,
Full of things that were so pretty.
It housed the royal court,
Which was not a sort
Of thing the youth had ever seen before.
There were so many things now to explore!
"Who are they?" asked the lad.
"Those are courtiers," said his dad.
"And those are palaces and those are statues."
So many lovely sights from which to choose.
He was taking it in when he caught sight

Of some eye-catching beauties—what a de-
light!
Courtiers, palaces, statues vanished;
Every other thought was banished.
This was quite another kind of surprise.
The happy youth could not believe his eyes.
"What is that," he asked his sire,
"So lovely in its bright attire?
What is it called?"
The dad was appalled;
His reply of no use:
"A bird called a goose."
"O wonderful bird!" said the son, filled with
glee.
"Let's hear your voice. Sing, goose, for me.
The two of us should become better known.
I'd like to have you for my own.
O Father dear, I beg you please,
Could we take home one of these?
Let it come in the woods to dwell.
I'd be sure to feed it well."

2. "The Mandrake"

The story now at hand brings to the scene
The folly of a certain Florentine.
He had wed a woman who was wise,
Young and beautiful—and in the eyes
Of the Florentines who lived nearby,
Clearly worthy of another guy
Than Nicia Calfucci, such a dope—
As he showed when he expressed the hope
Of some day decorating, with a legion
Of miniature Calfuccis, his home region.
That is, he wanted to achieve paternity.
There hadn't been a saint in all eternity
To whom Signor Calfucci had not prayed.
Not only that, but he invoked the aid
Of midwives and of quacks, and even tried
To draw the powers of magic to his side.
He thought his hopes had come to a dead end
When it chanced that he made a new friend:
A youth just back from France, a Florentine.
There was no trick this fellow had not seen.
He fancied the ladies; they fancied him back,
For he was good-looking and sure had the
knack.

He'd not been there long before he found out
Which husbands were savvy, and which had
no clout;
Which wives were approachable, and when
and where;
Of what sort of surveillance he should be
aware;
The "ifs" and the "buts," and every detour;
How a confidant's aid one can secure;
How to win over the nurse and the priest,
Even the dog—neglect not the least
Little detail if you want to succeed.
This piece of advice he did certainly heed.
On Nicia Calfucci this guy set his sights,
Vowing to award him all of the rights
Of the Order of Cuckolds, even although
Signora Calfucci did never bestow
Her favors on company whom she received.
Those hoping for more were sadly deceived.
Yet our hero, Callimachus, had better luck,
For as soon as she saw him the lady was struck
By his pleasing demeanor,
Which made him the keener

To lay siege to her camp.
Though she did soon damp-
En his hopes by saying to beat it.
Callimachus, feeling defeated,
Perked up when he saw that Nicia, so stupid,
Was showing the way that the triumph of
    Cupid
Could come about:
There was no doubt
Calfucci would fall for any ploy
That gave him the hope of siring a boy.
Both expert in legal studies,
He and Callimachus soon became buddies.
Nicia was a doctor in canon law,
Which became a tragic flaw:
It led him to place his trust
In a man whose burning lust
For his wife he never suspected.
One day to his friend Calfucci reflected
How much he regretted that he had no heirs.
Whose was the fault for this state of affairs?
He lacked not for vigor;
His wife's shapely figure,
Her good health and youth
Could hardly, in truth,
Be the reason they couldn't conceive.
"In Paris, would you believe,
A master of secret black arts,
Who had come from exotic parts,"
Said his friend, "was just passing through.
There were quite a few secrets he knew.
And he taught them to me.
One just happens to be
The answer, I think, to your plight.
The Grand Mogol has used it each night
On his wife for the past several years.
Princesses, princes, and peers
Have used it with great success.
I've seen the results, no less.
It's a drug the wife should take
From a plant that's called the mandrake.
Its beneficent juice
Has been known to produce
A greater effect when drunk
Than the shadow of a monk
(Which many believe
Makes women conceive).
I'll make you a dad: in ten months if you
    want

We'll be carrying the child to the baptismal
    font."
"Is this for real?" "But I've seen it in action.
The Grand Mogul himself has found satis-
    faction.
He's not a guy you should try to deceive.
I know the magician in fact did receive
When all was said and done,
Quite a tidy sum."
"That's terrific! I'm so excited.
Lucretia will sure be delighted
To learn that we'll be so blest
As to have a babe at her breast.
I'll name you godfather, my friend, if I may.
It's only right. Let's get started today."
"Hold on," said the other. "Not quite so fast.
I have something to tell you that might tend
    to cast
Things in a different light.
Though the problem is rather slight.
But to avoid disappointment
This fly in the ointment
Should be faced before we begin.
Of course, there never has been
Any good without some ill attached.
The juice of the mandrake, whose virtue's
    unmatched,
Has one little defect,
That's its fatal effect
On the first who would dare to embrace
The lady—which in this case,
Would, I'm afraid, be you.
Those who survive it are few."
"Thanks, but no thanks. Count me out.
With your plant I certainly doubt
I'll have anything more to do.
And let's leave her out of it, too.
What good does it do me if I
Become a new father, but die?
Better look for some other guy."
"You certainly go to extremes.
You were hopeful at first, but it seems
You've lost your perspective.
You need a corrective
To your definite lack of persistence.
Allow me to offer assistance.
Listen to what I've to say.
Where there's a will there's a way.
We simply employ,

From the hoi polloi,
To go before you in bed
(Don't worry, he soon will be dead)
Some poor young loser
(Who will not refuse her,
For a beggar's no chooser).
The unfortunate bloke
Will indubitably soak
Up all of the dangerous part.
And then, my friend, you can start,
With no hesitating,
Your procreating.
We should choose a guy who's not too smart,
But nevertheless can look the part.
For we must consider in our dealings
Your beloved Lucretia's feelings.
He shouldn't have too rough a touch
For she likely would not like that much.
No doubt she's used to your delicate hand.
Indeed, she may even refuse your demand,
When push comes to shove,
That she should make love
With this bedtime guest.
We'll just do our best
To make the experience bearable,
Or at least not impossibly terrible.
We must choose a fellow who's young
    enough
To draw off all the poisonous stuff.
Not a drop will remain
Of that venomous bane,
I make you my personal promise."
But Calfucci now played doubting Thomas.
All these intructions to follow
Seemed a bit hard to swallow.
What about his reputation
If arose this situation:
Suspected of complicity
In the death by toxicity
Of a citizen of Florence?
There even could be warrants
For his arrest.
As for the rest,
Lucretia had scorned the attentions
Of dandies with urbane pretensions.
And now to be placed in the arms
Of a bumpkin with rustic charms?
A mere peasant?
Not pleasant.

Not wanting his project aborted,
Callimachus dryly retorted:
"Then we should pick one of high caste
Who will doubtless take care to broadcast
To all he may know
An account, blow-by-blow!
To wish for that would be odd.
The advantage of choosing a clod
Is that folly and fear
Will make him adhere
To silence's code.
Though the money bestowed
Will the same end no doubt have effected.
You should not, let me add, be deflected
From this goal by a mistaken impression
That you would come into possession
Of a cuckold's horns in this matter.
Permit me, my dear friend, to shatter
That illusion. On the one hand,
Your wife, you must understand,
Not choosing of her own volition
To engage in this coition,
Gets no pleasure. In the same way,
The substitute does not betray
Her husband, for his desire
Is simply that he acquire
The contractually promised gold.
So you'll not be a cuckold.
But who's to say he won't die?
All the more reason why
The mandrake's dreaded bane
Must work its will in vain
On the fellow we will use
And whom we must choose
By tomorrow night.
To do this right,
This evening the potion we'll give to your
    spouse.
I have some already stored safe at my house.
My valet will find us a victim.
Keep out of sight once he's picked him.
My servant's discreet, and worthy of trust.
In addition to what we've so far discussed,
I'd forgotten to say that we'll blindfold the
    guy.
That way there's nothing that he can reply
If someone should ask him where he had
    been.
Was he out of town or in?

He wouldn't know.
It's better so."
This was to Nicia's taste.
But the problem that he now faced
Was how to persuade his better half.
She thought he said it for a laugh
But when she saw that he was serious
She became extremely furious.
She swore on her soul she'd rather he slew
    her
Than that word should get out among people
    who knew her.
The sin was too grave to contemplate.
Besides, making love had not been that great
With Nicia Calfucci, and he ought to know
That she had only done it for show.
And now some oaf would put her through
    her paces?
A man devoid of all the social graces?
"Some clod, misshapen and ill-bred,
I should accept into my bed?
No! No one in my husband's stead."
Lucretia being hard to budge, he called on
    the assistance
Of a friar, who preached at her with eloquent
    insistence.
At last she yielded, thinking it a penitential
    act.
She was assured the fellow would not be
    someone who lacked
A good physique, which she could not en-
    dure,
Nor be too redolent of fresh manure.
The magic drug was dutifully taken.
In order to make sure he'd be mistaken
For one who earned his living in a mill,
Our hero spread flour on himself until,
Having added, too, a beard,
To Calfucci he appeared
(Since he did not apprehend
That the stranger was his friend)
To be the man who'd save his life
By kindly sleeping with his wife
The valet brought him in that night,
Blindfolded and all powdered white.
In between the sheets he slipped.
All was silent as a crypt.
Lucretia awaited her fate.
And yet, strange to relate,

She was attractively bedecked:
What did that reflect?
For whom so carefully adorned—
The oaf of whom she'd been forewarned?
The man she awaited in dread
As she cowered in her bed?
The truth about these things
Is whether it's millers or kings
A woman always aims to please.
A double honor's hers if she's
Able to arouse the sluggish
(Even if he be thuggish)
And awaken to love a heart born without it.
Our hero could see, no doubt about it,
It was time to drop the miller's disguise.
She had come to realize
That he was a genuine suitor
Whose gender wasn't neuter.
No time was wasted in sleeping.
"Whose company am I keeping?
This fellow has such nice skin.
I regret the danger he's in.
As each moment our pleasure enhances
His death the closer advances."
Calfucci meanwhile was conflicted
Because of what he'd inflicted
On his wife, who with an air of queenly
    pride
Took all that her bed-mate could dish out in
    stride.
Although for the sake of pure decorum,
And not for any ill will that she bore him,
From returning his kisses she chose to re-
    frain.
Our hero decided it was time to explain
Who he was, that he'd always adored her.
A surrender now was in order:
She should accept his suit
And return his affection, to boot.
He humbly begged her pardon for the deceit.
"Accept my martyrdom, laid at your feet."
(The confession, as you see, was incomplete:
No word of the poison being fake.)
"From love for you this sacrifice I make.
Doesn't matter what you say
I shall perish anyway,
Yet die a very happy man.
Better than a poison can,
The joy of making love to you

"The man who'd save his life / By kindly sleeping with his wife" (Eisen).

Will doubtless slay me through and
    through."
Lucretia did till now resist,
Not from lack of interest,
But only for decorum's sake.
But this was more than she could take:
Torn 'twixt love and shame, she wept
And to the bed's far side she crept.
How could she show herself to this man
    now?
She'd made a bad impression, anyhow.
He must think she was ungrateful
If not in fact downright hateful.
It just was not her fashion
To make a show of passion.
The edge of the bed was the terrain
Where her resistance would prove vain.
Her assailant was soon her possessor,
Though this did not seem to depress her.
Tears, shame, and scruples were soon seen no
    more.
Happy are those who, tricked, are better off
    than before.
Dawn came too soon for him but also her.
So when he said they needed to deter
The venom's power by doing more of this
She agreed, and took it not amiss.
They did this for nights in succession
Assuring Calfucci possession
Of his cuckold's horns. Then her lover
    thought it best,
When the work was finished, to go home
    and get some rest.
He'd hardly hit the sack before the husband
    came to tell
Him all about the miller and how things had
    gone so well.

"At first," he said, "I tiptoed to the bed so I
    could hear
The poor guy on his way, and then I whis-
    pered to my dear
To tell her to be sure to give some kisses to
    this schmuck
Who had no notion he was in for such atro-
    cious luck.
'You have to keep his courage up, so don't be
    too reserved.
It's important that he do it, so my life's pre-
    served.
Your beauty won't be harmed if you show a
    little ardor.
It's only for a night or two; just try a little
    harder.
I'll be keeping tabs on you so don't try to de-
    ceive me.
I'm not a man to be hoodwinked—on that
    you can believe me.
If he be less than eager
And his efforts prove too meager
Send for me right away
And I'll come to save the day.'
But for that there was no need.
Can you imagine this hayseed
Actually seemed to enjoy it?
The way he did employ it
It seemed he'd never quit.
I really must admit
I feel sorry for the guy.
It's too bad he has to die.
Ah well. He'll rot
And be forgot.
Phooey on those who wished me woe.
Soon I'll have a child to show."

3. "An Evening in Reims"

I love no city more than Reims,
The jewel and prestige of France.
Not for its oil for crowning kings,
Nor just its wine, but other things
I like, some of which are quite pretty:
Not the towers of the city
But the women of the place.

One I found to have such grace
She'd tempt the taste buds of a king.
To your attention now I'll bring
One who had a painter wed.
Esteemed by colleagues, it is said,
He made his living in this way.
You couldn't ask for more, I'd say.

Those who knew her thought the wife
Quite contented with her life.
Because he had a another talent,
He was a fine husband, but a better gallant.
Many an amorous lady came
Because of his artistic fame
Who after her portrait had been painted
Remained to get somewhat better ac-
  quainted.
I'm no expert, goodness knows.
But that's how the story goes.
When he'd such a one in hand
His wife it seems would understand;
He'd even laugh with her about it.
Since she never went without, it
Mattered not. No jealousy
Because her husband zealously
Paid the marriage debt he owed
To her, and she in turn bestowed
Sometimes in some other direction
Favors, though with circumspection,
Less inclined than he to share
The news of every love affair.
Among the men that she could get,
Two neighbors fell into her net;
Drawn by her free and happy way
With words, these two were led astray.
She was the most deceitful kind
Of woman one could ever find;
Smart as a tack, but liked to laugh.
She soon told her other half
About these guys' infatuation,
How they lacked all education
In the things controlled by Cupid.
In fact, they were just downright stupid.
They thought that they had read somewhere
That the way to show you care
For your object of affection
Was to wade in deep abjection.
They would weep and sigh and moan
And think that in that way they'd shown
How sincere they truly were.
On everything they would confer,
And conspire in each affair.
If one succeeded, he'd then share
The news of conquest with his friend.
Ladies, look out for this trend:
The only goal that men desire,
The thing that sets their hearts on fire,

Is pleasure; if for love you look
Then you'd better try a book.
For love has died, we are bereft.
Nor hide nor hair of him is left.
Girls, you'll be the prey and toys
Of talkative and wicked boys.
That's why you should pay them back.
Don't be shy; plan your attack.
The first to fall within your clutches,
Pluck his feathers; in as much as
He deserves it—if not now,
Then one day, somewhere, somehow.
To accomplish her design
The wife invited them for wine.
"My husband's gone away and won't
Return until tomorrow. Don't
Worry about him at all.
We are sure to have a ball."
On time for their rendezvous,
The found that things can go askew:
A sudden knocking at the door.
What could fate have now in store?
The house that night was locked up tight.
"From the sound it seems it might
Be my husband. I'll go check."
She through the window stuck her neck
And said, "It's him. You'd better hide
Before I let him come inside.
There may have been an accident,
Or maybe he's picked up the scent
Of what's amiss, and come to spend
The night at home, I apprehend."
The two men now were crazed with fear,
But there was a closet near
And into it they quickly flew.
They had barely passed from view
When he came in, sure enough.
"What is all this lovely stuff?"
He pointed to the handsome fare:
Mutton and pigeon, laid out there;
On the spit a lamb was roasting.
"Quite a spread. Whom are you hosting?"
"I've prepared this lovely fête
For Alice and Simonette.
Thank God you've returned to eat;
The party now will be complete.
There's lots of food and drink for all.
It's time I went next door to call
Them in, for now the roasting's done."

It chanced that of these wives each one
Was married to our lustful gallants.
Though closeted, they praised the talents
Of the painter's wife, so able
To account for the fine table
That for them alone was set.
Then Alice and Simonette
Came in, singing as they did.
Their husbands saw from where they hid
Each of their respective Mrs.
Greeted by the host with kisses.
He praised their beauty and their dresses,
Lavishing on them caresses.
The liberties he was enjoying
Were, the husbands thought, annoying.
All was to their eyes exposed,
Because the door was but half-closed.
With rue the prisoners observed
That minus them dinner was served.
Each wife was led in by the host.
Sitting between, he raised a toast,
Then still more, till in the end
The painter's wife had to descend
(No servant there to do this chore)
To the cellar for some more.
She claimed to fear there was a ghost;
Took Simonette, leaving the host
Alone with Alice—pretty lass,
Though of the provincial class,
Frankly coquettish and proud
That she was so well-endowed.
The painter soon began to hold her,
Gradually he got bolder,
Adding to his warm embraces
Exploration in some places.
In the role of fearless flirt
He placed a hand beneath her shirt
And stole a kiss her husband saw.
He'd not broken any law,
For wise husbands do not mind
When an homage of that kind
Is presented to their spouse.
Yet a kiss can well arouse
Something dormant in the one
Who begins this bit of fun.
He must be on his strict guard:
Once awakened, it's soon hard—
Hard, I should say, to dismiss
From the one who plants the kiss.

Satan has a lot in store:
Simple kisses lead to more.
While one hand her breast inspected,
Elsewhere the other was directed.
Rage grew in her husband's brain.
The other spouse sought to restrain
His friend from leaping out of there
To give to both of them a scare;
To beat his wife, the painter curse,
And then perhaps he would do worse:
Show off the strength within his arm
And the neighborhood alarm.
The other whispered, "Dearest chum.
Please do not do something dumb.
You must admit, in this regard
You're hoisted by your own petard.
For your honor, I suggest,
Silent suffering is best.
The rule is golden and quite true:
Do not to others that which you
Would not want to see them do.
We should the strictest stillness keep
Until our host is fast asleep.
Not till then should we emerge;
Until that time, resist the urge.
That's the way to face our fate.
Don't pick a fight, for it's too late.
There's nothing left you can prevent.
She has signaled her consent;
The rest's a mere formality."
It was a sad reality
Not to the injured husband's taste.
Things transpired with too much haste
Between Alice and her seducer
For her really to produce her
Protests (she'd have made them louder
Had there been more time allowed her)
To a meaningful extent.
When the painter's lust was spent,
Delicately and with care
Alice rearranged her hair.
You'd not have guessed what just took place
But for some redness in her face.
The painter's wife returned meanwhile
With Simonette, and aimed a smile
At Alice. Feasting once again
With grilled meats and fine champagne
(For which that region is renowned),
Their hosts they toasted, then a round

"Adding to his warm embraces / Exploration in some places" (Duplessis-Bertaux).

In honor of which of the three
Ladies present would soon be
The first to be crowned with success
In her quest for happiness
Of the extramarital sort.
They once more had to resort
To getting more wine, with all the toasts.
Because she still had fear of ghosts
The painter's wife required assistance.
Alice, though, put up resistance,
Remembering what she'd just enjoyed;
She'd rather be *that* way employed
But had to go down all the same.
Simonette now played the game.
Feigning the prude, she first appeared
To want to leave, but soon was steered
Otherwise, under duress;
For he'd grabbed onto her dress;
She couldn't let such good clothes tear.

The sight her husband could not bear
And would have leapt right out of there.
"Hold on!" the other said. "I seek
No advantage. Just be meek.
Accept the honor I have earned;
Cuckoldry should not be spurned.
Didn't we say, "an even split"?
We'll just have to wait a bit.
He's had one; along this route
The other soon will follow suit.
She must join the merry dance,
If needed, I will hold his pants.
Like it or not, she'll get her due."
Indeed, the painter followed through.
He gave his all, with no reserve;
Her beauty no less did deserve.
His wife stayed downstairs long enough
For her spouse to do his stuff
And Simonette to have the leisure

To fully enjoy her pleasure.
Although replenished from below
With wine, all chose now to forego
Further feasting; it was late.
The painter had had a full plate,
And licked it clean. Goodnights were said.
After he'd gone off to bed,
She freed the captives from their jail.

Sadly, they'd managed to fail
In the plot so well begun.
Angry at her for what she'd done
They wished somehow that they could do
To her what their wives had gone through
And thus their cuckoldry repay.
My story's done, that's all I'll say.

4. "The Enchanted Cup"

The cruelest of misfortunes is but a bagatelle
Next to a husband's torment when he's
  caught beneath the spell
Of jealousy, which makes him madly wel-
  come every doubt,
No matter what you say when you try to help
  him out.
He can never rest a moment, for his mind is
  tempest-tossed.
When he feels his ears are burning, then O
  heavens! All is lost.
He's a cuckold in his dreams, and so it must
  be true.
Except he hardly ever sleeps; the jealous
  rarely do.
A suspicious husband's wakened by the least
  little sound;
Should there be about his wife some fly
  buzzing round
It's Cuckoldry in person whom he's seen
  with his own eyes.
The impression is indelible, all logic it defies.
To become a fool is the goal for which he's
  straining:
A cuckold in his mind, if not in flesh and
  blood, remaining.
But is cuckoldry indeed to be viewed with
  such alarm?
Does it really have the power to do us that
  much harm?
It amounts to nothing when the husband's
  unaware;
And when he's not, it really isn't all that
  much to bear.
Although you may persist in feeling that to
  be betrayed

Is something at whose prospect you should
  always feel dismayed,
You'd better change your mind or you might
  well wind up
Like the man who drank from the enchanted
  magic cup.
Profit from the story of another's tribulation.
If for your irritation you could find some
  consolation
In the story of the cup, then I soon will tell
  it—though
There's something very pertinent that first
  I'd like to show.
I'd like to state the arguments thanks to
  which I find
That to be a cuckold is entirely in one's
  mind.
Does it make your hat no longer fit?
Not the teeny tiniest little bit.
Does it leave a trace?
Does it show upon your face?
Does it keep you from your pleasure?
In no way that you could measure.
Therefore my conclusion:
It's only an illusion.
Despite the vulgar, common herd
Who so glom onto the word,
Despite the rep that it has had
Cuckoldry is not so bad.
Yes, I'm sure you'll say, but when my honor is
  at stake!
But who said it wasn't? That's no error I
  would make.
Honor, honor, honor: seems it's all I ever hear.
But what honor is in Rome is not the same as
  here.

In Paris a wronged husband who in his grief
    will wallow
Is taken for a fool, not a paradigm to follow.
Yet one who laughs and can be mellow
We take for a decent fellow.
Cheer up, smile, and don't be sad:
Cuckoldry is not so bad.
That it's advantageous is in fact not hard to
    show:
When you're a cuckold, the whole world will
    smile at you, you know.
Your wife's as pliant as a glove,
You'll find some other one to love:
Twenty mistresses you'll keep
And not a soul will make a peep.
When you speak, your words are praised;
In your honor toasts are raised.
At banquets you're the one served first;
Waiters vie to quench your thirst.
Young men on the make, you'll find,
Will to you be very kind.
They'll say they're your biggest fan;
To them you're, as one says, *the man.*
Ipso facto, Q.E.D.
Cuckoldry is good, you see.
Losing at cards? The other guy
Will put his kings and aces by,
Then he will decide to fold,
And you'll win back all your gold.
Creditors breathing down your neck?
Thousands will offer to write you a check.
Besides, your wife will stay in condition,
And bring her charms all to fruition.
In Helen Menelaus found when Paris had
    his way
Perfections that the lady hadn't known she
    could display.
Your wife will be no different, for you'll want
    her to be pleasing.
A prude's no good in bed, because her tem-
    perature is freezing,
And such a one will never learn
How to make her husband yearn.
Ipso facto, Q.E.D.
Cuckoldry is good, you see.
Its subject is the reason this prologue's been
    rather long,
For to treat it cavalierly would, I think, be
    wrong.

And now at last I'm ready for my tale.
There was a man—I'll not go in detail
Concerning name, rank, and address.
The only thing I want to stress
Is he vowed that all his life
He'd take no woman for a wife.
Girlfriends, yes, but never a bride.
I think that I will set aside
The question, was he right or not?
Marriage counting thus for naught
The god of Love could intervene;
He was the only go-between.
This man's needs, as best he might,
Cupid saw to, day and night:
A woman's favors did provide
Who bore a daughter, but then died.
The poor man wept and groaned and sighed,
Not as a bridegroom for a bride,
For often husbands only mourn
Their wives like clothes that they've out-
    worn.
This man's grief was more profound.
In her he'd lost the friend he'd found,
His joy, his heart, his very soul.
The daughter grew, and then the role
Of woman she would soon assume.
From bassinet to nubile bloom
Time passes all too fast.
This father was aghast
At the thought his little lass
Being of her mother's class,
Might in her own conduct falter,
That she'd preempt priest and altar
(Two things that take away the fun
Of giving yourself to someone).
Leaving her to her devices
Might lead to untoward surprises.
A nunnery was just the ticket
To prevent her being wicked.
Instead of games that lovers play
She would learn how to crochet.
No books there for her to read
That in any way could lead
To ideas of the worldly sort.
That the nuns would surely thwart
In one so young.
Love's native tongue
Was one she'd never speak
(It might as well be Greek);

Pious words would there suffice.
Should a nun say she looked nice
"My God," she'd gasp, "don't ever cherish
Features which one day will perish.
They are earthly, fit for worms"—
Et cetera, and in such terms.
None could sew as well as she,
Nor spin nor weave fine tapestry.
In those talents she surpassed
Such famous ladies of the past
As Clotho (she's the Fate who spun),
Or Athena (when outdone
By Arachne, for she spied her
Weaving well, made her a spider).
The girl was beautiful and wise.
Her wealth it was made her a prize,
Attracting from throughout the region
Suitors whose numbers were legion.
Girls in convents stayed a while
Before they trod the marriage aisle.
The dad legitimized his daughter;
All the things the sisters taught her
When she left the nuns behind
Were no longer on her mind.
For to Calista (that's her name)
Troops of handsome suitors came.
Blond and brunet, bourgeois, knight,
Each hoping he'd be Mr. Right.
She chose of her own volition
One of easy disposition—
So it seemed, and handsome, too.
Her father, thinking he would do,
To the marriage then agreed.
A dowry for her every need
He gave. The boy, an only heir,
Like her, brought wealth as well to share.
A very happy girl and boy,
In each they found their greatest joy.
Two years they lived in pleasant ease;
They had but to love and please
Each other. But then jealous doubt,
O hell of hells, began to sprout
In the husband, who when faced
With a rival, felt disgraced.
He behaved like such a dope
He gave the other man some hope.
All the time his rival spent
To solicit her consent,
Had he not been so distraught

Would have simply gone for naught.
What's a husband then to do
When a fellow tries to woo
His wife? Zilch, *nada*, I reply.
Just go to sleep and close your eye.
If she likes what he has to say
Nothing will make her turn away;
For each forestalled, hundreds appear.
But if she doesn't lend an ear,
You could make her change her mind
If you're of the suspicious kind.
This wisdom Damon (that's his name)
Was lacking, but he's not to blame.
He took some bad advice, you see, and so
    could be excused,
Though if he had been wiser that advice he'd
    have refused.
The able sorceress Neria flourished at that
    time,
A mistress of black magic at the acme of her
    prime.
Circe, by comparison, who charmed Ulysses'
    crew,
Was a rank beginner, then just learning what
    to do.
Neria could hold hostage fate, and through
    her many minions
Exerted sovereign jurisdiction over vast do-
    minions.
Hurricanes she could unleash; the west
    winds were her pages;
Her footmen were the northern winds, who
    when winter rages
Are prompt but not polite.
Yet she whose magic might
Could stop the sun from shining
For Damon now was pining.
Up against a power that was greater than her
    own,
In vain did she desire to have a night with
    him alone.
Had it been just kisses that Neria had in
    mind
Those she could have gotten through the
    power to her assigned.
But she wanted more than that, and wouldn't
    compromise.
Damon, though he found that she was easy
    on the eyes,

Would not break his marriage vow and so refused to bend.
He wanted this enchantress to simply be a
friend.
Where are such husbands to be found? Their
race has gone extinct.
Though I'd suggest that maybe we consider
the distinct
Possibility that husbands like that never
were.
A hippogriff or magic lance are things that I
prefer
To think within the realm of scientific plau-
sibility,
While a faithful husband truly strains all
credibility.
But other errors I've let pass so here I will
again.
I guess that one could say that we don't live
as they lived then.
The love-struck enchantress made prodigal
use
Of potions and spells this man to seduce
But when these all failed
It was time she availed
Herself of more properly feminine wiles,
Like come-hither looks and simpering
smiles.
Whatever it took,
Every trick in the book:
All these she tried
But still he defied
Her attempts to arouse
His passion. The vows
He made when he wed
Were the reason, he said.
His resistance left her both astonished and
amazed.
"Your fidelity," she said, "is worthy to be
praised.
But I wonder if Calista feels the selfsame
way.
If you learned she had a lover, I wonder what
you'd say?
If she were two-faced
Would you still be chaste?
I'm obliged to confess
You should have more finesse.
The conclusion I draw:

You're insufferably *bourgeois*.
You're in line for more than mere domestic
satisfaction;
Don't turn down the chance to get some hot
and heavy action.
Have you never set your sights
On love's more intense delights?
Must you take strict measures
To ban illicit pleasures
From your domain?
Let them remain!
Let them be your friends!
They can serve your ends.
Give them a try, and then you'll see:
They'll spice up your marriage, I guarantee.
At least make the effort to learn if it's true
That your dear wife is faithful to you.
I just happen to know there's a guy
Who's often around her, and wonder why."
"Erastus," he said, "is a good friend of mine."
"Call him a friend if you want, that's fine,"
The enchantress said, in shame and spite.
"But Calista has charms, and Erastus is
quite—
Just between me and you—
Appealing too.
And has a talent
For being gallant.
That can bring disaster in a hurry."
Damon now began to worry.
A high-spirited wife,
In the prime of life,
And enjoying that game
I don't need to name;
In expertise at the head of her class,
With an attitude as bold as brass;
Attractive as any one could find:
How could he have been so blind?
Friendship's very well and good
But even a monk beneath his hood
To break his vows would be disposed
When a breast is half-exposed,
And a girl gives a look that seems to say,
"What would you say to a roll in the hay?"
He could already see it taking place.
On such a basis did he trace
Many a chimerical, groundless fear.
Of the way he felt she soon did hear
And from her repertoire drew out

A trick to propose that would turn his doubt
Into such unyielding certitude
That he would at last conclude
His wife was untrue. The trick would consist
Of rubbing a potion on his wrist
That would give him the bearing, the voice
    and the face
Of Erastus, so Damon could take his place.
Working as if by hypnosis
This "water of metamorphosis"
Would cast such a spell
His wife couldn't tell.
"How beautiful you are today,"
Damon disguised came to say.
"You look like springtime come to earth."
Calista knew what that was worth,
Just a silly platitude,
So took a mocking attitude.
Damon had to change his tack,
Tried tears and sighs, "alas" and "alack."
Those tears and sighs were thrown right
    back.
She was a rock, immune to attack.
At last he tried money, an enormous sum.
Now she showed signs she might succumb.
Her anger gone, she listened to reason.
But he was shocked to hear such treason.
She'd have yielded, and money have talked,
Had not the disguised Damon balked.
Gold, that happy metal, is the master of the
    world.
You may be handsome, eloquent, and wear
    your blond hair curled,
Leaving nothing to chance,
But some mogul of finance
Will sweep the woman off her feet from
    right beneath your nose
And make you look absurd. All this time,
    goodness knows,
After a year at your sluggard's pace
You weren't even able to get to first base.
So money could bend her inexorable heart!
Instead of a rock, a lamb played the part.
An accommodating lamb, sweet and tender,
A sacrificial lamb prepared to surrender,
And pledging that with a kiss.
He could take no more of this.
He decided to pause,
Not wanting to cause

His own dishonor and shame.
His original face and his name
He resumed, and said to his wife,
"I've loved you more than my life,
Calista; you've loved me as well.
Is money so precious you'd sell
Yourself at the cost
Of our union, now lost?
I should pay with your blood for this terrible
    shame
But I cannot for I love you the same.
Only my death, for which I now long,
Could possibly blot out this undeserved
    wrong."
Seeing her husband drop his disguise
Was for Calista a shocking surprise.
Stunned into silence, she only could weep.
Damon was plunged into pondering deep,
Wondering was he a cuckold or not?
Though not in deed, she'd sinned in thought.
Neria proposed to straighten him out:
"Here's a way to settle your doubt,"
She said. "Put wine in this magic cup
And then attempt to drink it up.
It was formed by a hand so skilled
That when with liquid it is filled
Someone made a cuckold for real
His true state it will reveal.
When he tries to drink he won't be able;
It will spill on his beard, on his chest and the
    table.
But if he is no cuckold, then he will know
Because there'll be no overflow.
No doubt on his honor can anyone cast
For he can drink every drop right to the
    last."
Damon decided to settle the matter:
He drank from the cup: not a drop did he
    splatter.
"That's a comfort," he said. "And yet I know
Had it not been for me it would have been
    so.
Why do I need a cup?
The jig is already up.
She'd have gone ahead
And jumped into bed
Had I not called a halt.
The whole thing's my fault,
No, there's no getting around it

I'm a cuckold, confound it!"
These words sounded queer
To Calista's ear.
What a disgrace to the whole human race!
If for fear of a little disgrace
Husbands around here get tied up in such
	knots
Let's go live with the Hottentots.
Damon for fear of worse to come
Put Calista under his thumb,
Surrounding her with many spies—
A course of action I'd not advise.
For when gallants are forbidden
The desire for them, though it is hidden,
Will exponentially increase.
Damon then did never cease
To use the magic apparatus
Checking on his cuckold status.
Believing in its wondrous power,
He drank from it every quarter-hour.
After a week, no sign of disgrace.
But then some wine splashed on his face.
O fatal knowledge! Honor destroyed!
Knowledge he'd have done better to avoid.
He tossed out the window this chalice from
	hell,
And was ready to throw himself out as well.
He put his wife in a tower where none could
	approach her;
Morning and night for her sin he'd reproach
	her.
The news of the shame—that he ought to
	have buried
In silence—throughout the province was car-
	ried.
Soon everyone knew what he'd done to his
	wife.
Calista meanwhile led a very sad life.
She could not bribe her jailor, who adhered
	to the rules,
For Damon deprived her of money and jew-
	els.
One day when Damon was feeling randy
She found the opportunity handy—
Since now for once he was paying atten-
	tion—
To plant an idea that would end her deten-
	tion.
"I know it's a terrible thing I've done.

But am I really the only one?
Unhappily, no. Few men are spared
This kind of thing; the burden is shared.
May he whose shame has never been shown
Be the first to cast a stone.
Why is your grief so uncontrolled?
Why refuse to be consoled?"
"I'll accept some consolation,
And will stop your incarceration
When I've been able to assemble
A legion of husbands who resemble
Me in this unhappy way.
When my soldierly array
Has grown to such enormous size
That it would be 'royal' in men's eyes,
Then my labors I will cease
And you from prison will release.
What better way to gather them up
Than to employ the enchanted cup?"
Damon got busy right away.
Whenever a fellow passed his way
He'd invite him in to sup,
And then present the magic cup.
"My wife, alas, has left me for another man.
Want to know if yours is faithful? With this
	cup you can.
Take a drink; here's how it works.
Should nothing spill, no lover lurks
Within the corners of your house.
But if it happens that your spouse
Acts like Venus toward her mate,
The Vulcan who endured the fate
Each husband hates to undergo,
This the cup is bound to show.
If your wife's engaged in sin
It will dribble on your chin."
Each and every guest
Submitted to the test.
In almost every case
It trickled down their face.
Some laughed; some cried.
Some bore with pride
The cuckold's horns they'd been assigned,
Depending on their state of mind.
Soon the army of shakers and movers
Had grown to such size it could go on ma-
	neuvers.
They now could attack a fortified city,
Demanding surrender, showing no pity

"If your wife's engaged in sin / It will dribble on your chin" (Fragonard).

For any commander refusing to yield.
They'd hang him, for they had more men in
    the field.
To achieve "royal" size, they lacked but a
    few;
Two or three months would probably do.
He had no need to recruit with a drum
Because every day new adherents would
    come.
In cuckoldry different ranks and degrees
Signify various expertise.
The rank of infantryman was meted
To the husbands who'd been cheated
By their wives only one time.
While the victims of greater crime
When inducted into the force
Were allowed to ride a horse.
Those who'd suffered even more
Were promoted to the officer corps.
The basis on which these posts were filled
Was how much the liquid spilled.
One fellow splashed it on his lap:
A general's what they made that chap.
There were colonels and majors and captains
    galore,
And superintendents to manage the store.
When they'd more than enough to go on
    campaign
Renaud, the nephew of Charlemagne,
One day by the castle happened to ride.
He like the others was beckoned inside.
Our Damon again proved a genial host.
At dinner he offered the usual toast,
Praising the cup's fantastic ability
To judge the scope of domestic tranquility,
Giving the speech he'd made to the ranks.
Renaud replied, "Thanks, but no thanks.
I believe my wife chaste, and that faith will
    suffice.
What need do I have of this useless device?

If the cup tells me something I already know,
What do I gain, to know it is so?
I sleep well already, thanks be to the gods.
What more do I need? What are the odds
That my right hand might happen to shake?
What consolation from that could I take?
What if I don't hold it perfectly straight?
I can't help if I'm clumsy—a personal trait.
What if the cup from which I were drinking
Should make a mistake, and somehow be
    thinking
That I were another, and not Renaud?
Sir Damon, I think to you I can show
Perfect compliance in all you request
But please do not ask this of your humble
    guest."
Renaud departed, refusing the bait.
Damon was moved at this juncture to state:
"Behold, my dear sirs, a very wise man.
All the same, I think we can
Console ourselves with the comforting
    thought
That of our number there are really a lot."
Soon there were members enough on the roll
For him to reach his exalted goal.
His army at last was "royal."
To his promise he proved loyal,
Freeing Calista from her cell.
Henceforth he'd love her just as well
As ever before, whatever befell.
Renaud shows you how to live.
So to the cup no credence give.
It would have been better for the band
Had Renaud been in command.
Whether Roland or Renaud,
No mortal man can ever know,
Should he the test of the cup attempt,
How from danger to remain exempt.
Charlemagne himself, did he partake,
Would have made a big mistake.

5. "The Falcon"

I recall I said somewhere
The stingy lover ought to share
The fate of sinners sent to hell,
While generous ones should get to dwell,

If the logic of contraries applies,
In that realm up in the skies
We call celestial paradise.
(Syllogisms this precise

Are, I'm told, quite often done
At the world-renowned Sorbonne.)
A man in Florence loved a woman so
There were no lengths to which he wouldn't
   go—
He'd even sell his soul.
To please her was his goal:
When she desired diversion
He'd have no aversion
To spending all he could,
Because he understood
In love just as in war
That's what money's for.
Silver, though precious, should be cast
Like seed, to knock down doors and blast
Through walls; defenses it will breach.
With its help your goals you'll reach.
When enough money you choose to
   spend
Dogs cease to bark; maidservants defend
Your cause with fervor, as if they meant it,
With an eloquence worthy of the Roman
   Senate.
All things considered, money's power
Is such that it will leave no tower
Untoppled. Yet here it failed,
For the lady, though assailed,
Held firm where it mattered.
Frederic's hopes were shattered,
And his bank account, too.
He had owned not a few
Fine titles and estates,
But in his dire straits
He had to sell all he'd acquired
Except a farm, where he retired.
Few friends were left; those that remained
Were in their zeal somewhat restrained.
To buck him up, they'd maybe say,
"Too bad things turned out that way."
But none of them, I think, were prone
To giving anyone a loan
Unless the debtor would agree
To offer as a guarantee
Some collateral of worth.
But Fred had nothing left on earth
Except his little country seat.
All those friends he used to treat
To gifts now showed no gratitude.
They'd clean forgot the attitude

He'd had toward wealth, which was to share
   it—
Forgot, too, his personal merit.
They showed not one ounce of pity
For the man who'd courted Clytie.
(That was her name, and as I said
The name of this poor guy was Fred.)
Back when his cash was flowing,
The parties kept on going.
There were dances and theatricals,
Tournaments and madrigals—
Not only great enjoyment
But also good employment
For merchants and musicians,
Tailors and technicians,
Butchers, bakers,
And monogram-makers.
This hospitality brought such prestige
The women of Florence all laid him siege,
Hoping by some glance or word
That he to passion would be stirred.
But none by him were ever kissed
For every time they aimed they missed.
He'd prefer his Clytie, however coy,
To even a willing Helen of Troy.
Yet despite his willingness to spend
The stubborn lady would not bend.
His costs increasing at a terrible rate,
He sold off from his estate
The lands he'd owned as a marquess.
Then still having no success,
As his expenses still did mount
He sold what he had owned as count.
This was a sad fate to befall:
He missed that title most of all.
To be a count is the fond dream
Of every Italian; it would seem
That with us it's a marquis
That every Frenchman wants to be.
In other lands, a baronet
May be the hope of the smart set.
Which one's best? I sure don't know.
But if one were to market go
To trade the title for some dough
One would come back just the same
As one had been with the name.
I'd say if I had to choose
Between the two, I'd sooner lose
The title and the income keep.

Clytie's husband owned a heap
Of property himself, so she
Was living rather cozily.
She never did accept a gift
From Fred, yet never once did lift
A hand to stop him from bestowing
Those parties on her he kept throwing.
While his suit the lady still did spurn
She thought she owed him nothing in return.
I seem to recall I've already made mention
Of the little farm it was his intention
To inhabit, the last land he still had.
Its condition was pretty bad.
Nothing but a tenant house, which was quite
    poorly built.
There our lover hid himself, because he felt
    some guilt
For having failed to win, despite six years of
    wooing,
The woman he still loved, but who was his
    undoing.
Another reason was in Florence had had felt
    the shame
Of his newfound poverty. So to the farm he
    came.
On his own unworthiness Fred placed all the
    blame;
No complaint from him for her coldness ever
    came.
Our disappointed lover on that farm lived all
    alone
With no servant to assist him, save a tooth-
    less crone;
A cold kitchen rarely used: no guests came to
    his table;
A good, though not pure-blooded, horse
    resided in his stable.
But yet he owned a falcon, with which he
    hunted prey
Around his little farm, passing all the day
In melancholic moping as he would sacrifice
Many a pitiful partridge to the woman made
    of ice.
Thus did our poor Frederic live, after the
    demise
Of his extensive fortune, though it would
    have been more wise
To have lost at the same time his unrequited
    passion,

A passion that yet spurred him on, rather in
    the fashion
Of a rider mounted on his horse behind him
That no matter where he went would always
    find him.
Clytie's husband, as it happened, died.
There was but one child to divide
The estate, and not long for this life.
The boy was sickly, so he'd named his wife
As heir if the son should perish.
This child whom she did greatly cherish
Soon afterward in fact fell ill.
She loved her son as mothers will,
With an ardent zeal that can bring harm,
All the more because of her alarm.
Every moment of the day of him she would
    inquire
How he felt and if there was something he
    might desire,
Some dish that he might want to taste, or
    play with some toy
That she would bring to him in hopes that it
    would please the boy.
But always he opposed
Whatever she proposed.
What he said he wished instead
Was the falcon owned by Fred.
He screamed and carried on to such extent
Even saints would find their patience spent.
A child's imagination must be humored
    without fail
If one does not aspire to have to hear him al-
    ways wail.
You should understand
That Clytie owned some land,
Castle included,
In a secluded
Spot five hundred paces
Distant from, of all places,
Frederic's humble habitation.
Thus the falcon's reputation
Had even reached the ears
Of this child of tender years.
Legends had been told of how the bird was
    skilled:
Never did a partridge escape from being
    killed.
Morn and afternoon the body count was
    handsome;

His master'd never sell him, not for a royal
   ransom.
How could she ever ask, she thought,
Him to give her what she sought,
The only good thing he possessed
After he'd lost all the rest?
Even if she had the nerve
To ask, she did not now deserve
Such favor, with the attitude
That she'd shown, ingratitude
And contempt, by her behavior.
But still he could be the savior
Of her precious son!
Yet she had been the one
Who had caused his ruination.
Could she have a conversation
With this man whom she'd wronged so?
Thus her thoughts went to and fro,
Between her moral shame and wretched grief
And her understandable belief
That with the falcon of her lover
Her dear son might well recover.
For in his pouting mood
He had refused all food.
All day the child would cry;
At this rate he would die
Unless something soon was done.
For the sake of her dear son
The distraught mother one fine day
To Frederic's farmhouse made her way,
With neither retinue nor coach
To assist in her approach.
She seemed an angel to his eyes
Freshly come down from the skies.
Yet he felt shame and beat his breast
Because he'd nothing for his guest
To dine on but a poor repast.
He felt embarrassed and aghast.
He asked of her, "Why is it
That you should deign to visit
The humblest one of those who fell
Beneath your beauty's potent spell?
I'm now a simple peasant.
You must not find it pleasant
To go slumming here.
This honor is, I fear,
Too much for such as I.
Perhaps the reason why
Is you'd some other place in mind,

Nevertheless you were so kind
That you thought that you would break
This other journey for my sake."
"No, no, my lord, the aim I have in view
Is to dine this morning here with you."
"But I've neither cook nor pot.
What can I offer?" "Do you not
At least have bread?"
He quickly sped,
As he was alert and pragmatic,
To grab some bacon from the attic,
Together with eggs from the chicken coop.
He saw his falcon and in one fell swoop,
With no thought his haste to check,
Picked up the bird and wrung its neck,
Plucked its feathers, made a fricassee,
Added spices, like a busy bee
Hurried and scurried here and there
While his maidservant took care,
Rummaging in the linen chest,
To find what cloth would look the best,
Set the table, went outside
For rosemary and thyme, and tried
With half a dozen flowers for a festive look.
The dish was served; Clytie partook,
Pretending that she liked it. When the meal
Was done, she knew that it was time to steel
Herself to the task,
For now she had to ask.
"It's mad of me, my lord, I know,
To trouble a former lover so;
Indeed, to come tear out your heart
Again by asking you to part
With your only source of joy.
But I do it for my boy.
He's dying, but he could be cured
If I could give to him your bird,
Which is his heart's desire.
Reason would require
That I be refused
Since I've so abused
Through indifference and blindness
Your so many acts of kindness.
Your peace, your honor, and your wealth
Have all been spent upon myself.
My unfeeling nonchalance
Was a very poor response
To the tender love that you once bore me.
More than your own life did you adore me.

"You see, he is no more, because on him you've dined" (Duplessis-Bertaux).

And now I dare to ask—but what's the
  use?—
For your falcon. I have no excuse:
Rather should I perish, with my son,
Than from you such a painful boon be won.
Instead of that request the one I'll make
Is that you let a mother, for the sake
Of her only son, the thing most dear
That she has in all the world, appear
Before you so that she might yield
To tears because his fate is sealed,
Confiding in your kindly breast
The grief by which she's so oppressed.
By your pain you've paid the cost;
You know the price: you've loved and lost.
And thus she dares to make entreaty of this
  kind."
"Alas, my dearest Clytie! My falcon you'll
  not find.

You see, he is no more, because on him
  you've dined."
"He is no more!" she cried, perplexed.
"I fear it's so, and I am vexed.
Would God it had been my heart
That had played the fatal part
Allotted to this bird.
What has just occurred
Is fate's way of making sure
That my plight will have no cure.
My sad destiny won't waver:
Ne'er from you will I find favor.
I had no chickens for the feast;
They all were eaten by some beast.
I saw my bird: my path was clear.
Who counts the cost when a queen is here?
For you I'll find another, don't despair.
Good falcons cannot be a thing so rare."
"Dear Frederic, no. I'll ask no more.

You've never shown to me before
A greater mark of love.
Whether Heaven above
Restores my son as I desire
Or the Fates his death require
To you I'll always grateful be.
And hope that you will visit me."
She left, but first held out her hand,
A sign by which we understand
That Love her heart had overpowered.
Fred her hand with kisses showered,
As well as with his tears.
Within two days, the mother's fears
Were shown to be well founded.
The child did die. With unbounded
Grief the stricken mother's tears did flow.
Though there's no pain of heart we undergo
For which we don't seek comfort in the end.
Two doctors soon did have her on the mend:
One was Time, the other sweet Romance.

She married Fred with pomp and circum-
stance,
Not only from a sense of obligation
But also through a heart-felt inclination.
Indeed, through Love. And yet be not mis-
led.
Just from this one case it cannot be said
That hoping for this outcome you should go
And on a woman you desire bestow
All your wordly goods and then expect
That from your rash investment you'll col-
lect.
Gratitude among the female sex
Is not the thing a knowing man expects.
Apart from that I find them charming crea-
tures.
No other creature has such pretty features.
I'm only speaking of the ones who're nice.
As for those whose hearts are made of ice,
They'll have to find another to entice.

6. "The Courtesan Who Fell in Love"

Though Cupid may appear to be a child
The lengthy list the ages have compiled
Of all the wonders he has done makes clear
That in his craft he really has no peer.
He can change a Cato of stern mien
Into a dapper dandy who'll be seen
With girls and likely even will have kissed
'em.
By him are fools turned into fonts of wis-
dom;
He changes raging wolves into tame sheep.
The people whom he alters only keep
Their name: all else is new, like Hercules
Or Polyphemus, both of whom could
squeeze
The life out of a man, they were so strong.
The latter on a rock sat all day long
To sing unto the winds his lovesick woes,
And to charm the pretty nymph he chose
He trimmed his beard and gazed upon his
face
Reflected in the water, seeking grace.
The other changed his club into a spindle
Because a girl his passion's flame did kindle.

I know a hundred tales like these; there's one
Boccaccio tells unlike the common run:
Simon was a very handsome youth,
But in his manners terribly uncouth.
He was about as witty as a bear
But soon became a man most debonair.
Two lovely eyes it was that made him gape;
Love took charge and licked him into shape.
(In the Middle Ages folks believed
That bear cubs were born shapeless and re-
ceived
From their mother's tongue the form re-
quired,
Though I should think that she'd have got-
ten tired!
That's the way the turn of phrase arose—
So at least I'm told the story goes.)
The story, though, that I've in mind to tell
Concerns one of that class of girls who sell
Their charms to carefree youngsters without
shame.
Yet her heart could lodge an honest flame.
Haughty and capricious, hard to please,
It was in Rome she plied her expertise.

To place a miter or a bishop's staff
At her feet would be to make her laugh.
Monsignors and the like weren't worth her
    time;
Her ambition greater heights did climb:
You had at least to be of cardinal rank
Although on that you could not even bank.
The thing you needed to sustain your hope
Was that you were a nephew of the pope.
His Holiness would be a bit hard pressed
Should he himself have wished to be ca-
    ressed
By this creature, for she did not see
How he could be too good for such as she.
Her dresses were in keeping with her pride,
With diamonds glittering on every side;
By trimming and brocade they were be-
    decked.
But Cupid had decided to correct
The high-and-mighty ways of this proud
    heart,
To which a wounding love he did impart.
Its object, whom the god of Love selected,
Was a handsome youth, rich, well-con-
    nected.
Camillo was the fellow's name, while hers
Was Constance (La Fontaine, it seems,
    prefers
To wait until his story's well afloat
Before revealing names [translator's note]).
Although Camillo was an easy guy
To talk to, Constance suddenly turned shy,
Fearful her beloved to apprise
Of her desire in other ways than sighs.
Until now neither modest nor reserved,
She was by her new passion quite unnerved.
It was the first time she had ever faltered—
Which just shows how much she had been
    altered.
Because no one would think that love could
    dwell
In such a heart, Camillo could not tell
What she was going through, although her
    eyes
Were ever fixed on him, as were her sighs.
At parties she was always in a dream.
Her beauty started fading, it did seem;
Her rosy luster turned a lily white.
Camillo had a gathering one night,

The company was mixed, joy at its peak,
For few among the women wished to speak
Of Plato or Aquinas—their bons mots
Was based on baser thoughts. The to and fro
Of witty banter, though, held no appeal
For melancholy Constance. When the meal
Was over and the guests had said goodbye
Our heroine remained there on the sly.
Before they all had left she turned aside
And in a certain bedroom went to hide.
No one noticed, for they all assumed
She'd gone home indisposed, or had resumed
Her duties as a lady of the night.
Because he wished to be alone to write
Camillo told his servants they could go.
A piece of luck for her that it was so,
For now he was alone; the coast was clear,
Though Constance trembled, suffering from
    fear.
She didn't know exactly what to say.
But it was time to act now, come what may.
She stepped forth from the shadows to the
    light:
The astonishment he felt was hardly slight.
"Madame," said he, "do I apprehend
That you are fond of startling a friend?"
He made her sit, and after he recovered:
"How was it you remained here undiscov-
    ered?
Who showed you where to hide beside the
    bed?"
"Love," she said, and then her cheeks turned
    red.
Embarrassment, which caused her face to
    burn,
Is rare among her cohorts, who to turn
Their skin that color use some other potion.
Camillo had already got the notion
That he'd been made an object of desire.
No novice he; in order to acquire
More certain proof, a little fun beside,
And to see this heart so full of pride
Abase itself right to the bitter end,
That he was made of ice he did pretend.
Constance sighed, but now felt so much pain
That she her speech no longer would re-
    strain.
"I don't know," she said, "what you will say
When you see me come here in this way

To declare to you my passion's flame.
I cannot think upon it without shame.
To hide behind the mask of my profession,
Now that I have made you this confession,
Is not a thing a courtesan can do
For when she falls in love she bids adieu
To her vocation and to its defenses.
O that I could make my past offenses
Vanish from your mind! At least excuse
My frankness, though whatever words I use
It seems that I displease you. It's my zeal
That harms me. But I'll tell you what I feel
Despite what harm may come. I do adore you.
Do your worst, but still I come before you
To declare my love. Show your contempt
For me as you may wish. I cannot tempt
You. Beat me, kick me out, do something
    worse
If you think you can, but I am yours."
"I'm not one," he said, "to criticize
But your words do come as a surprise,
As I'm not sure that it is all that wise
For a woman like yourself to say
What might or might not happen in the way
Of love between the two of us some day.
Besides your sex and forms one should ob-
    serve
In what you've said yourself do you ill serve.
What was the point of all this eloquence?
I would have been subdued at less expense
By your charms alone. I don't approve
When a woman dares make the first move."
His words came like a bolt out of the blue.
"I deserve this cruelty from you,
But dare I say what's really on my mind?
To my misdeed you'd doubtless have been
    blind
Had not my loveliness lost all its glow.
It's mere flattery that you bestow
In talking in this way. For I well know
My faded looks hold no more charm for you.
But why have they faded? Think it through:
Was it not the case, in earlier days,
And not that long ago, each man would
    praise
The charms that once were my most prized
    distinction?
Those precious gifts have since met with ex-
    tinction.

The love I bear has brought this harm to me.
No longer beautiful enough, I see,
Am I for you. But were my beauty saved
Then, of course, I'd not have misbehaved."
"Later, on this point more may be said,
But it is late and I must get to bed."
Hearing this, she thought there was a chance
That she might share what in a rapid glance
She saw, the bed that was prepared for him;
But fearing that the likelihood was slim
That he would grant her wish, she made no
    sound.
As if perplexed, Camillo looked around
The room in silence, then he said, "Oh, dear.
What shall I do without a servant here
To help me to undress?" "Then shall I ring,"
She said, "for one?" "You will do no such
    thing.
I don't want them to see you in this place,
Nor that my staff should know in any case
That a courtesan had spent the night."
"To prevent your suffering that plight
I could hide where I had hid before.
But instead of that for you I could do more:
Let no one come; your Constance will today
Serve you as your own private valet.
As reward for carrying out this task
The honor of the post is all I ask."
When Camillo'd given his consent
She approached and to her task she bent.
The buttons she undid with greatest care.
To touch his person Constance did not dare,
But just his clothes. Nor did she refuse
To do the chore of taking off his shoes.
That she could this with her own sweet hand
Is something I find hard to understand.
And yet there's one I love for whom I'd do
Exactly the same action if the shoe
Were on, as one could say, the other foot.
To bed Camillo then himself did put,
Without inviting her there as his guest.
She first had thought this was some kind of
    test,
But now it seemed too much for a mere jest.
Things had gotten worse; to be precise:
"The air," she said, "is turning cold as ice.
Where shall I sleep?" "Just suit yourself," he
    said.
"Then on this chair?" "Oh, no; come into bed."

"Would you please unlace my dress for me?"
"It's too cold; I've nothing on, you see,
And can't get out of bed. Do it yourself."
Nearby she saw a dagger on a shelf.
She took it from its sheath and cut her dress,
Destroying what two months of skilled
 finesse
Had labored to create; fabric bedecked
With gold, fit for a princess, was soon wrecked.
With no sign of regret she caused to perish
What more than life itself most women
 cherish.
Lsdies of France, would you have done as
 much?
I think not, in fact I'm sure, though such
A deed in Italy would find appeal.
To the bed she secretly did steal,
Believing that this time he'd not invent
Some new stratagem that would prevent
Attainment of the ease that she desired.
But then Camillo said, "I am quite tired
Of beating round the bush: I'll not abide
A woman who is forward. At my side
She'll never have a place, though at my feet
You may go, if you should find it meet."
At those words her soul was seized with
 pain.
With that dagger she'd herself have slain,
Had it chanced to still be in her grasp.
But hope had not yet given its last gasp.
Constance knew Camillo well enough
To think that he was made of sweeter stuff
Than his words would lead one to believe.
Surely he'd just said thcm to deceive.
She lay then by his feet; not only this,
She began those very feet to kiss,
But gently so he'd not take it amiss.
Camillo's joy to have her at his feet
Was great, for now his triumph was complete.
He'd brought low this head till now un-
 bowed;
He had overcome this heart so proud;
Of her dazzling beauty I would speak,
But to describe it would take me a week.
Its only fault was just the small detail
Of her complexion, which was rather pale.
Though the reason, once one knows the story,
Gives her loveliness a lustrous glory.
Camillo then stretched out, as if to rest

His weary feet upon her lovely breast,
A breast so white it put ivory to shame.
Then he pretended he'd achieved his aim
Of yielding to the charms of blessèd sleep.
Constance could her sobs no longer keep
From racking her sad frame, and then the
 flow
Of tears of wretched grief did grow and grow.
It seemed the end. But then Camillo called
 her
In a tone of voice that quite enthralled her:
"I'm very happy with your love," he said.
"And now I think that you should come to
 bed."
She slipped in; he spoke into her ear:
"Am I the cruel brute that I appear?
Do you really think me that severe?
If that's what you believe then you don't
 know me.
I did all these things so you could show me
How much to please my heart you were
 inclined.
Now I know you well and what I find
Rejoices me and gives great satisfaction.
Should you wish to make a like exaction
On the man who loves you, go ahead.
I say I'm your lover, but that said,
I also say I wish to see us wed.
There is no other woman on this earth,
Whatever be her rank or social worth,
Whom I'd rather have, in this my life,
To be at once my mistress and my wife.
Of the past we will no longer speak.
Our wedding will be secret. Do not seek
To ask me why. You must already know.
In fact, our marriage would be better so,
As I'd be spouse and secret lover both.
By the way, before we plight our troth,
As we await the coming of the priest,
How about a foretaste of the feast?
You can trust your lover to be true.
I will stand behind his pledge to you.
To all this Constance said not a word.
Camillo, though, her silent answer heard
Because he was no novice in such things.
As for the rest, with all that passion brings,
That should remain a mystery, perhaps
It's best we keep such matters under wraps.
And this is how our Constance did succeed.

"Nor did she refuse / To do the chore of taking off his shoes" (Duplessis-Bertaux).

Nymphs like her should profit if they read
This tale, take it to heart, and do likewise.
Love's training school such females oft sup-
    plies,
If one but take a closer look inside.
In fact, I'd rather take one for a bride
Than many whom men choose to be their
    wife.
A woman who has not spun all her life
Will go through many trials with no
    complaint—
Like Constance, who showed heroic restraint.

The pain her tests imposed was quite acute
But she received abundantly their fruit.
Nuns with whom I have had conversations
Would not flinch at such initiations.
Though it is hard to credit, yet it's true:
What Constance now was tasting seemed
    quite new.
All the pleasures she had had before
Prepared her not for what love had in store.
All those earlier delights did she disdain.
But why is this? Let one who loves explain.

7. "Nicaise"

There was a fellow once
Who was a sort of dunce
In matters of the female heart,
Not knowing how to play his part

Or even how to start.
An apprentice in the draper's trade,
Learning how money from cloth was made,
And things like weft and warp and weave,

His name was Nicaise, suggesting "naive"—
And seemed to fit him, I believe.
What one thought of erotic play
Was different in our fathers' day.
Boys' lessons in love did not begin
Until they had hair upon their chin.
Youth today gain such knowledge
Long before they go to college.
This poor guy, in any case,
Was proving a sluggard in the race,
The reason he was falling behind
Was his slow-wittedness of mind.
Yet he a beauty's heart had caught,
For his master's daughter thought
"He's just the man for me."
As lovable a girl as ever there be,
Nor one to beat around the bush,
She thought he needed a little push,
For she was eager but he was shy.
Some find that forward—but not I.
May a woman make the opening move?
When she's a goddess, I approve.
Of this the girl was well aware.
She had wit and looks and money to spare,
So many young men came seeking her hand.
He would be happiest in the land
Who'd be the one to pluck that flower
That's in the god of Marriage's power
To award to the one she'd wed.
But that's what she'd said
That she would give Nicaise.
Despite what anyone says,
The god of Marriage proposes,
But the god of Love disposes.
She had chosen the apprenticed youth
Because (since I must tell the truth)
The fellow was handsome and young and
    fresh.
No lady despises the joys of the flesh:
Though in the spirit she may dwell
The body will please her just as well.
For each whose soul the door to Love supplies
A thousand are invaded through the eyes.
This one, then, among the most vivacious,
Found a thousand ways to be flirtatious,
Providing the lad renewed incentive
To be somewhat more attentive.
She'd flutter her eyelids and, all the while,
Give him a pinch and then a smile.

Over his eyes her hand she'd put
And then she'd step upon his foot.
To this speech the sole replies
That he could make were heartfelt sighs,
Interpreters of his desire.
Each sighed so much, at last the fire
Consuming them both was overtly declared.
No promises, cuddles, nor kisses were spared.
The apprentice had learned in his work how
    to count
But the number of kisses reached such an
    amount
That he was hard pressed to keep track
Of every smooch and smack.
Their love was with such action packed
There was but one thing that they lacked:
It is a sort of ritual
That has become habitual
When such a love is realized,
But which a girl is well advised,
In my opinion, to forgo.
But she did some interest show.
She said to him, "I wish I might
Be taught the secret of this rite.
It's from you I want to learn it.
Otherwise, I think I'll spurn it
All the rest of my whole life.
But don't think I must be your wife
Right after it is done,
Or else become a nun.
I'd love to marry you, you know,
But wishing will not make it so.
Such is your love you would not aim
To bring upon me any shame.
Several men have asked for me;
My father soon will choose, you see.
But whether he who I am sent
Is Councilor or President,
You may hope, indeed believe,
No matter if it be the eve
Or the day itself I'm wed,
You shall have my maidenhead."
He gave his thanks as best he could.
A suitor came who looked quite good,
Of lofty rank and well-filled purse.
"I think," she said, "we could do worse.
And so with him I say, 'So be it.'
He's not a man, the way I see it,
Who looks at things with much precision."

She told Dad of her decision;
Soon the plans were underway
For the blessed wedding day.
She was betrothed, and things began—
I ask you please to understand
That by "began" I only meant
That she had given her consent
To the marriage, not that she'd
Begun the thing that she'd agreed
To offer to Nicaise before.
In fact, on that particular score
She was cautious: Just in case
Before the marriage could take place
The groom-to-be should chance to change
    his mind,
For she suspected something of that kind,
She told Nicaise he'd have to wait
Until the wedding's actual date
Before she would go through
With what she'd said she'd do.
For it would be bad for her
Should some accident occur.
And yet it was a happy fact
That she was brought to church intact.
She spoke her vows by candle light;
The husband wanted her that night
To go with him to bed.
She, however, said
That she'd prefer a day's delay;
Though it was hard, she got her way.
By now the hour was almost dawn.
Instead of undressing she put clothes on,
It was a dress fit for a queen;
Pearls, gems and diamonds were seen.
It lacked for nothing; for in fact
By the terms of the wedding contract,
She was made a lady; while outside,
Nicaise would make a woman of this bride,
For in the garden they had planned to meet.
To ensure the tryst would be discreet,
A woman friend of hers would serve as sentry,
Keeping watch so no one else gained entry;
She was in on the secret of what they con-
    spired.
Having said to her servants that she had
    desired
To gather some flowers, the bride got there
    first.
When Nicaise arrived, he made this outburst:

"This place is too wet; your dress will be soiled.
The fabric is rare. We can't let it be spoiled.
Just hold on a moment until I have found
A carpet for us to spread on the ground."
"My God, forget about the dress!"
The new bride exclaimed, in sore distress.
"I can always say that I slipped and fell down.
What does it matter? My husband may frown,
But the cost will mean nothing to him.
    Rather,
The time has come for us to gather
Our last-minute rosebuds while we may.
We may not get another day.
I'd sooner see each stitch destroyed
Than our quarter-hour employed
In doing such as you propose.
I would prefer all fancy clothes
Be ruined, and through the mud be drug
Than you should fetch your stupid rug.
While other folk are toiling for the sake
Of my wedding, I should think you'd take
No chance to let such moments slip away.
These words are hardly right for me to say,
But I love you and would like to, if I can,
Make of the naive boy you are, a man."
"You know," he said, "it would be nice
To save a fabric of that price.
On you it looks so spiffy.
I'm off; I'll be back in a jiffy."
He was gone without giving her time to reply.
His foolishness left her wondering why
She'd ever felt tender toward the guy.
What shame she felt! He was such a ninny!
"Go on," she thought. "I won't miss you any.
Any other slob
Could have done a better job.
My guardian angel must have thought
That the talent you have got
Was not sufficiently meritorious
For a gift as blessedly glorious
As the one I almost gave.
From now on I pledge to save
For my husband all affection.
So that from my old connection
No passionate spark bursts into flame,
I'll hurry back from whence I came,
My dear beloved husband's house,
And there I'll offer to my spouse
The gift Nicaise might have received,

"Nicaise, with carpet, was returning" (Duplessis-Bertaux).

If I had not been undeceived."
At these words, she left the spot
Where they'd have sated passion hot,
But now it was her anger burning.
Nicaise, with carpet, was returning.
Lovers, listen as I say:
Not every moment of the day
Does the hour for love chime.
In Love's book I've read that time
Stands still for no man with a maid.
So do not be by caution stayed.
He who hesitates is lost:
For this did Nicaise pay the cost.
Out of breath from having run,
Happy he'd his errand done,
Rejoicing in his draper's skill,
He was ready to fulfill
The purposes he had in mind
(Though each of a quite different kind)
For both his mistress and his rug.
But suddenly he felt less smug

When he saw the spite expressed
On the face of the well-dressed
Woman he had thought to bed,
Returning to the man she'd wed.
As she disappeared from view
Her flame for him was dimming, too.
She to her spouse perhaps was bearing
That which girls are always swearing
That they possess—but was it true?
I think she did, but don't construe
This means that I'd defend that claim
With my finger on the flame.
All I know is this:
I think that when a miss
Is obligated to reply,
It's not a sin to tell a lie.
Thanks to Nicaise, it is a fact,
The newlywed was still intact.
As she was, grumbling, homeward bound
The bride her former boyfriend found.
Nicaise, his mood somewhat deflated,

Asked, "Why could you not have waited?
On this lovely carpet spread
You your girlhood soon could shed.
Now I could my zeal express
With no danger to your dress.
Let's return there right away."
"Perhaps," she said, "some other day.
Your health in fact has got me worried.
You're out of breath because you hurried.
Take it easy, breathe in slow.
There's nowhere else you have to go.
The draper's trade has been till now
Your study, but you should somehow

Acquire some knowledge of romance.
It would your life, I think, enhance.
The process would go faster
If you studied with a master.
But you can't study it with me.
For you a better choice would be
Some humble serving maid.
You're expert in your trade,
In pricing garments and the like.
But as for knowing when to strike,
And how to discern it—
Better go learn it.

8. "The Saddle"

A painter there was, who was jealous, alas.
When he went to the country, he painted an
  ass

On his wife's belly-button, to serve as a seal.
To a colleague of his she had great appeal;
He paid her a visit, and the ass was erased.

"'Take a look,' says his wife. / 'Everything is correct'" (Duplessis-Bertaux).

(Don't ask me how!) This painter replaced
This ass with another, in the same spot.
But a saddle he added, because he forgot.
The husband returns, and decides to inspect.
"Take a look," says his wife. "Everything is
  correct.

The ass will bear witness that I have been
  true.
"The hell," says the husband, irate through
  and through,
"With this witness and whoever saddled it,
  too!"

9. "The Kiss in Exchange"

Guillot with his wife was passing by.
She proved appealing to the roving eye
Of a gentleman of rank, who said:
"Who gave *you* such a pretty wife to wed?
If I were to kiss her, would you mind?
I promise I would pay you back in kind."
"You surely may," the other man replied.
"She is at your service, my sweet bride."
The gentleman then promptly went ahead,

And kissed her with such force that she
  turned red.
One week later he got married, too.
To the vow to Guillot he was true.
He told him, "Here's *my* wife. Now claim
  your kiss."
"Too bad," said Guillot, "I'd not known of this
A week ago for now I wish instead
Of kissing her you'd taken her to bed."

"If I were to kiss her, would you mind?" (Duplessis-Bertaux).

10. "Time to Confess"

Alice was ill, and soon would be dead.
"You must go to confession," somebody said.
"For surely you'd wish for your soul to have
　　ease."
"I certainly do. Would somebody please
Go find Father André quickly for me
For he's the confessor whom I always see."
A fleet-footed messenger took on this chore,
And forcefully rang at the friary door.
"Who is it," they ask, "you've come looking for?"

"The good Father André's the monk whom I
　　seek,
The one to whom Alice will usually speak
When she's impelled to make a confession
Of every sin and moral transgression."
"I see," said a friar. "The confessor of Alice.
I hope you won't think I'm sounding too
　　callous,
But André would be hard to find, it appears—
Confessing in heaven the last ten-odd years."

"Go find Father André quickly for me" (Duplessis-Bertaux).

11. "Portrait of Iris"

I know you paint in a gallant style,
Perfecting your skill on Cythera's isle,
Where all the goddess of Love adore.
Make an effort, we implore:
Paint Iris's portrait. She's not here,
Nor have you met her, but don't fear

(Be grateful that for your repose
You have not, for heaven knows
That charming girl would break your heart)
For this is all you'll need to start:
Lilies and roses, laughing *putti*.
But on second thought, her beauty

"Two more alike were never seen" (Duplessis-Bertaux).

Is such that no one could tell:
Paint Venus, as you do so well—
Two more alike were never seen.

Returning to the Cytheran scene,
Where this Iris you may take,
From her a Venus you could make.

12. "Cupid the Intruder"
(with apologies to Edgar Allan Poe)

Once upon a midnight dreary, in my comfy
   bed I lay,
Plunged in gentle slumber (though I don't
   enjoy that every day)
When I was awakened by a tapping at my
   chamber door.
Noisily a boy was rapping whom I'd never
   seen before.

It was raining hard that night, a cold and
   windy winter storm.
"Let me in," the urchin said, "for I've no
   clothes to keep me warm."
Since I'm such a decent guy and charity have
   always shown
I consented to admit the visitor, chilled to
   the bone.

"What's your name?," I asked the child, but
he provided no reply,
Though he said he'd tell me later, after he
had gotten dry.
To the hearth I went to light a fire, but then
I felt alarm
When I saw him check to see if rain had
caused his bow some harm.
Though I felt dire apprehension, I ap-
proached the child to take
His cold fingers in my hands to warm them,
since for goodness' sake
What was I afraid of? Did I think that I'd be
overpowered
By this kid? He was no Samson. I was acting
like a coward.
Then the imp picked up his quiver, set an
arrow to his bow,

Shook his golden locks, then shot. The shaft
right to my heart did go:
I was conquered since the arrow was by gold
and not lead tipped
(Cupid's quiver is, you see, with arrows of
both sorts equipped;
Leaden ones will quench the fires of romance, while the other sort
Always make you fall in love—that god just
toys with us for sport).
"This is your reward," he said. "Now don't
forget Clymène the fair.
And remember Cupid, too. That's me, in
case you weren't aware."
"I know who you are," I said, "you cruel and
ungrateful boy.
When you show your gratitude are these the
means that you employ?"

"Then the imp picked up his quiver, set an arrow to his bow" (Duplessis-Bertaux).

He made a little joyful leap and wickedly he
said to me,
"Though the storm rained on my bow it's in
fine shape as you can see.

You, however, are not quite so fortunate
upon that score.
"Your heart is sick. Will it recover?" Quoth
the Cupid: "Nevermore."

13. "The Quarrel between a
Beauty's Mouth and Eyes"

Before the Judge of Amathonte, on Venus's
sacred isle,
The suit opposing Mouth and Eyes had now
come up for trial.
Each of these two aspects of a pretty
woman's face
For Eros' highest honors would now seek to
make its case.
Lovely Mouth was first to speak: "To hearts
I make my plea,
And ask them if they think of Eyes the way
they think of me.
When you examine our respective roles, our
charms and features,
You will find we really are quite different
sorts of creatures.
They're many things that I can do, but let it
not be said
That by me at any time have any tears been
shed.
These I gladly leave to my opponent to
supply.
Only to the sense of sight can Eyes appeal,
while I
Have the gift of pleasuring not just one sense
but three,
For smell and hearing also can take blissful
delight in me.
Sweet nothings I can whisper, charming bal-
lads I can sing;
My sighs evoke the fragrance of sweet violets
in spring.
And yet I know a hundred other ways to
please a lover:
Most of them I leave to your discretion to
discover.
If between us two there is a conquest to be
sought,

Eyes will strain and strive and try to give it
their best shot,
But all I have to do is speak, and then the
battle's won.
Besides, there's not much Eyes can do after
the day is done.
When they're closed they've nothing more to
offer, I should think;
While I inside have mother-of-pearl and
outside, coral pink.
My treasures are available at all times for in-
spection
And when opened up, you then will find a
rich collection
Of pearls that number thirty-two—for the
eyes, a feast
More pleasing even than the jewels imported
from the East.
The least of them excels in beauty and in
brightness too
Any pearl that one could find from here to
Katmandu.
Not for a million francs would I exchange,
not thirty-two,
These treasures of my mouth," she said—and
now her speech was through.
For Lovely Eyes a lover spoke, and he took
care to say
That it's through Eyes that Love into each
heart will find a way.
"If we find fault with tears," he said, "then
shouldn't we with sighs?
Lovely Mouth was wrong, for neither one
should we despise.
There are tears of ecstasy, though on the
other hand
There are sighs too meaningless for one to
understand.

Lovely Mouth, it seems to me, does not
   know what she's saying.
The claims she makes for her allures are really quite dismaying.
She should shut up, for heaven's sake, about
   her so-called powers.
What does she have in that regard that can
   compare to ours?
We know a hundred ways to please, by
   sweetness and by looks;
We know the fascinating art of catching
   hearts with hooks.
For that, the Mouth takes us to task, but
   there's where we find glory.
For every conquest she can boast of we can
   tell the story
Of a hundred more than that; and as for
   every song
That celebrates her charms, I hold that one
   would not go wrong
In estimating that there are more than a
   thousand ditties
That sing of us at court, on Mount Parnas-
   sus, and in cities.
Those places resonate with praise for Love
   and Lovely Eyes.
Wherever we appear, each lover yields up all
   his arms,
Surrendering to us because of our seductive
   charms.
Behind a mask our brilliancy has often
   proved deceptive,
When to a mediocrity one finds oneself re-
   ceptive;
A woman whom at other times one wouldn't
   look at twice
Now seems, thanks to the power of Eyes,
   quite able to entice.
Who is this dazzling beauty? is the question
   all will ask.
But that will only happen when she's covered
   by a mask
Through which only her eyes appear—a tribute to our powers.
Lovely Mouth proclaims her love out loud;
   by contrast, ours
In silence is expressed, and for that reason
   pleases more

Than all her pearls and singing and than her
   supposed store
Of oral talents she can call on when she's in
   the mood."
Lovely Eyes' fine lawyer had decided to
   conclude
By calling to the stand a beauty who would
   demonstrate
Directly to the judge which party should win
   this debate.
"My argument up to this point," he said,
   "has shown some whimsy.
But now I have some proof there is no way
   one could call flimsy.
Just take a look at Phyllis here, especially her
   eyes—
And then pass judgment: I am sure that we
   will win the prize."
Although embarrassed, Phyllis turned upon
   the crowd her gaze.
Her look spoke with such eloquence they fell
   into a daze.
The papers they were holding in their hands
   dropped to the floor.
The Eyes now won the audience, if they had
   not before.
But Lovely Mouth, who was aware of what
   had just occurred,
Replied, "To all these arguments I need say
   but one word:
I still can do my work when night has come,
   while Lovely Eyes
Have nothing more that they're good for, I
   hope you realize.
They go to sleep and all their vaunted silent
   eloquence
You'll find at such a time to be of little consequence."
The jury found this argument compelling,
   and awarded
To Lovely Mouth the victory, although it
   was recorded
That Lovely Eyes did win on certain points
   other than this.
The Mouth bestowed upon the Judge a long
   and luscious kiss.

14. "The Wonder Dog"

Treasure chests and hearts share the same
  key—
Or if not hearts then favors, you'll agree.
Most triumphs that the god of Love enjoys
Come from this stratagem that he employs.
When he's used up the arrows in his quiver
He knows that this device will still deliver.
To his philosophy I do subscribe,
For who among us would refuse a bribe?
Kings, princes, judges don't find them too
  shady
To accept, so when I see a lady
Think herself entitled to the same
Consideration, I will not cry "Shame!"
If Themis who, blindfolded, holds aloft
The scales of justice has not always scoffed
At offers litigants have sent her way,
For Venus too I think that it's OK.
Besides, she's not a goddess that I care
To start another quarrel with, I swear.
A Mantuan judge named Anselm chose to
  wed
Young Argie, who was beautiful. That said,
There was a certain difference in age
That caused the fires of jealousy to rage
Within that old gray-bearded judge's heart
But in the eyes of others did impart
An even higher value to his bride.
And so she was besieged on every side
By would-be lovers each of whom was sigh-
  ing—
With no success, though not for lack of try-
  ing.
As Cupid did his best to legislate
In Anselm's house, for some affair of state
The Mantuan court decided they should
  send
An envoy to the Pope, and to extend
To Anselm, whom they valued for his pru-
  dence,
His lofty rank and learnèd jurisprudence,
An invitation to become that envoy.
His first response was not to leap with joy,
Because he rightly feared his stay in Rome
Would be so long that meanwhile back at
  home

God knew what things could happen to his
  spouse.
She might invite in lovers to the house!
He could be gone for six months, maybe
  more.
For envoys there is cuckoldry in store
When they're obliged to stay long at their
  post.
These fears in Anselm's mind were upper-
  most
When to the court's request he gave assent.
But hoping such misfortune to prevent,
He made his wife a long haranguing speech
In which he sought fidelity to teach.
"I have to go away," he said. "I hope,
My dear, that in my absence you can cope
With those temptations that are sure to
  come.
On this, you know where I am coming from:
I am, as you well know, the jealous sort.
So tell me, what's this eager, lovesick cohort
Of suitors doing just outside our door?
Up to this point, you'll say, what they've
  come for
They've not achieved, and I agree, but yet
I think that we should counteract their
  threat.
We own, you know, a country hideaway:
I'd like for you to move there right away.
Flee the city, and those suitors too,
And most of all the gifts they would give
  you.
Of Cupid's machinations, those I find
Far worse than all the other ones combined.
They never fail to win some poor wife's
  heart,
Persuading her from hubby to depart.
On lovers' gifts you must your war declare,
And equally of flattery beware.
As soon as you sense men approaching you
Close tight your eyes and ears, and your
  hands too.
For all your needs I promise to provide,
To you the management hereby confide
Of my estate and wealth. Here, take the keys
To access cash and deeds. Make sure the fees

And rent that we are owed are always paid.
My total confidence on you is laid.
The only thing of you that I demand
Is to know what pleasures you have planned.
None do I withhold, except for one
Which you must save for me when I have
    done."
In this he went too far, I must insist,
Because without that one, they don't exist.
Argie promised to obey this rule:
She'd be deaf and blind, as well as cruel;
Were any gift proposed, she'd just say no.
When he got back, he would be sure to
    know
That she was just the same as she had been
The day he left, and bore no trace of sin.
Anselm went to Rome; meanwhile his wife
Began to taste the joys of rural life.
Soon lovers flocked to see her in that place
She sent them packing: they were in her
    face,
Disgusting and quite boring, truth be told.
To all their tales of passion she was cold.
But one there was to whom she took a liking:
Well-built, and of a beauty that was striking.
To her, his quality was quite apparent.
Atis was his name; his trade, knight-errant.
Yet suffer as he might, he could not steal
Her cruel heart, although he made appeal
With many sighs and prodigal expense.
The sums he lavished on her were immense.
He should have stuck with sighs, which don't
    run out.
But money does, and soon he was without.
A poor man now, what course does he de-
    cide?
He seeks some desert land in which to hide.
Along his path he meets a churlish hick
Who is doing something with a stick,
Poking at a bush to get a snake.
Why was he doing this, for goodness' sake?
That's what Atis asked. The yokel said,
"I'm gonna stomp that thing until it's dead.
Ever time I find a snake around
I beat that sucker right into the ground."
"But friend," said Atis, "Please, I pray, don't
    strike!
Is not a serpent made by God, just like
All other beasts, and precious in his sight?"

I must explain at this point that our knight
Did not have the fear that most folk share
Of serpents and their like, for he was heir
To Cadmus, who the serpent's teeth did sow
In myths that Ovid told so long ago,
And who became a snake himself when old.
On Atis' coat of arms one may behold
In honor of his lineage, a snake.
One sees the difference that that would
    make.
The peasant was compelled to let it be.
To safety slinked the snake; eventually
Our lover found a home within a wood,
A silent and a lonely neighborhood,
Its stillness broken only by some bird
Whose song, with its echo, were all one
    heard.
Joy and woe upon that spot of earth
Looked just alike, and were of equal worth,
Just as they were for wolves in that sad place.
And yet Atis no peace there could embrace.
His unrequited love stayed close behind
Each step he took; indeed he could not find
In solitude the comfort that he sought
For now he had more time to grow dis-
    traught
As he did nothing all day but lament
That Argie from his life now was absent.
"I must return," he said. "Such is my fate.
I'd rather see again that sweet ingrate
Cruel though she is, than be bereft
Of the only pleasure I have left.
Goodbye, sweet streams and lovely wooded
    vales,
Farewell, sad songs of lonely nightingales;
Inhuman though she is, she calls to me,
And far from her, I neither hear nor see."
This fugitive who had from bondage fled
Will put back on the chains that he had
    shed,
For though from their duress he nearly per-
    ished
They are, alas, by him too dearly cherished.
As he approached the walls of his home
    town
(Mantua, which treasured its renown
Of having been erected by the hand
Of a fairy), and approached the strand
Of Mincio, the stream that flowed nearby,

And dawn was glowing in the eastern sky,
A nymph appeared, appareled as a queen,
Majestic, beauteous, of charming mien.
Atis was startled from his meditation
Concerning his fruitless infatuation.
"Your happiness," she said, "I do desire
And my power to grant it is entire.
I am a fairy; Manto is my name.
To be your friend and servant is my aim.
My name is one whose fame you doubtless
    know.
The town of Mantua quite long ago
Derived its name from mine because 'twas I
Who built these walls that soar up to the sky
And which will last for just as long a while
As Memphis' pyramids beside the Nile.
The Parcae cannot cut a fairy's thread:
The one thing we can never be is dead.
But though we can do miracles, we're sad:
For fairies, immortality is bad.
The problem is, despite it we must face
All troubles native to the human race.
Besides that, weekly I become a snake.
Do you recall the effort you did make
Not far from here to save me from that
    peasant
Who would have done to me something
    unpleasant?
Atis, I want to give you this reward:
You will enjoy the one you've long adored.
Go see her now and I will guarantee
Before two days are out that you will see
Argie and all those who guard her honor
Won over by the gifts you'll shower upon her
And on them as well—no holding back.
Gold coins for this endeavor you'll not lack.
For me does Lucifer a treasure keep,
Hidden safe within a cavern deep.
This treasure's yours, because I will it so.
Our magic power your lady soon will know.
To smooth your way and soften her hard heart
I'll go with you disguised, acting the part
Of a little dog that loves to prance
In circles on the lawn, in sprightly dance.
You a humble pilgrim's part will play,
Sounding your bagpipes to lead the way.
Its tunes will draw me on until we've caught
The eye of her whom you so long have
    sought."

No sooner said than done—behold the pair
Transformed within an instant then and
    there.
Atis became a pilgrim who now sang
Like Orpheus, while Manto twirled and
    sprang.
So now to Argie's castle they did go,
And for the servants put on quite a show.
The dog was cute, his capers so entrancing;
The tunes from Atis' bagpipes had them
    dancing.
Argie heard, and told her nurse to run
And find out what it was. "Come join the
    fun!"
A servant told the nurse when she got there.
"This spaniel's so amazing, I declare.
He can understand each word you say,
Can speak and dance in such a charming
    way:
A miracle of nature. I just bet
Madame would love to have him for a pet.
In my opinion, nurse, you really ought
Whether he is willing or is not,
To make his master part with his possession
By gift or sale—leave that to his discretion."
The nurse therefore presented her request.
To name his price Atis soon acquiesced,
Though spoke it low so only she could hear:
"The dog is not for sale, let that be clear.
Nor would I give for free that which can give
Me everything I need with which to live.
All I have to do is to command
And from his paw descend into my hand
Not fleas but francs, doubloons and other
    cash,
Plus rubies, sapphires, pearls all in a splash.
Your mistress, though, has what it takes to
    buy it.
I have a need, and she can satisfy it:
Just let me in her arms for one night sleep,
And then the wonder dog is hers to keep."
The nurse was shocked at his bold proposi-
    tion.
"To think," she thought, "that one of her po-
    sition,
The envoy's wife, would welcome to her bed
A lowly vagabond, unknown, ill-bred!
That from her bed madame would gaze upon
A pilgrim's large and hefty stiff baton!

What if, dear God forbid, the news got out?
Some fleabag hospice sheltered both no
    doubt,
The pilgrim and his dog, why just last night.
And yet my eyes he does in fact delight,
Well-built and fair of face he is indeed.
In love such qualities always succeed.
Perhaps in fact the thing could be arranged."
I need to note that Atis had been changed;
In face and other aspects so disguised
That by no one could he be recognized.
The nurse continued her mature reflection:
"How could one so handsome meet rejec-
    tion?
Besides, he owns a dog of such great worth
There is no Emperor on all the earth,
In China or Tibet, Bangkok or Siam,
Who has the gold that it would take to buy
    him.
A night with her is worth a treasure, too."
As the nurse was thinking all this though,
The pilgrim to his dog appeared to mumble;
Into his hand ten ducats soon did tumble.
He offered them to her; but there was more:
A diamond too fell out onto the floor.
He smiled and picked it up. "This is for her.
To you I'd be obliged, I am quite sure,
If you'd present it with my compliments.
Please also say unto Her Excellence
That I have placed myself at her disposal."
Of the dog and of the man's proposal
The good nurse hurried off the news to tell.
Argie didn't take it very well.
She almost beat her poor nurse black and
    blue.
The nerve of her this topic to pursue!
"That beggar I would welcome to my bed
When I had not let Atis in instead?
My cruelty to him weighs on my mind
He never made proposals of that kind.
If I would not accept it from a king,
However large the gift that he might bring,
Then why would I accede to the request
Of this shiftless pilgrim, so ill-dressed?
I am the envoy's wife, have you forgot?"
"Madame, even a goddess can be bought.
At least I think our man would have a shot.
As for your knight Atis, I should think not."
"But my husband made me take a vow!"

"What makes my mistress think that pledge
    somehow
Is more binding than the one brides say
At the altar on their wedding day?
Besides, who'd ever tell? And who would
    know?
I know wives on whom it doesn't show.
They walk with head held high, but heaven
    knows
They would not if a spot upon their nose
Were there to tell the world what they had
    done.
But are there tell-tale signs? No, there are
    none.
Madame, one would be hard-pressed to
    detect
A change upon a mouth that's been suspect,
Employing its attractions and its leisure
For the sake of an illicit pleasure,
Compared to one in which there is no
    shame.
Give yourself or not, it's all the same.
For whom are you preserving all your
    treasures?
For one, I think, who'll seldom taste their
    pleasures.
When he returns, he'll hardly wear you out."
All that remained to settle was the doubt,
So well the wicked nurse had pled her case,
Concerning if the man was fair of face,
And if the dog could do all that she said.
The pair were ushered in; Argie in bed
Was slow as ever dawn had been to rise.
Our pilgrim boldly crossed to where she lay.
It seems he'd seen some boudoirs in his day.
He bowed with grace that she found quite
    disarming;
She was surprised that he could be so
    charming.
"You don't," she said, "seem like the type of
    fellow
Who's walked the route to Saint-Jacques
    Compostello."
(For those who might not know I'll make it
    plain:
That is a pilgrimage to western Spain.)
Now came the time for Atis' little mutt
To make his entrance and begin to strut
His stuff for Argie and her nurse, although

He'd never for the Judge perform that show.
He did his dance and then began to shake,
And pearls came out, all which the nurse did
take
For chambermaids to gather on a string
To make into a pretty little thing
The pilgrim put around his lady's arm,
Of which he praised the whiteness and the
charm.
So strongly did his looks to her appeal
That for the dog they soon did make a deal.
She gave for her down payment a fine kiss;
When evening came he found it utter bliss
To hold her in his arms, where he became
Himself again, in body and in name.
That added piquancy to her enjoyment
Because it honored our husband's
employment
As papal envoy, and her social status.

Their trysts continued on with no hiatus,
As Argie spent her nights with her sweet
knight.
Because it's hard to keep this out of sight,
The servants knew, for one cannot be blind
To what young lovers do when they've a
mind.
Months passed; meanwhile the Judge who'd
gone to Rome,
His mission done, at last could come back
home.
No doubt as envoy he had known success,
Paid in pardons and papal largesse.
To see if things at home were still well-or-
dered,
As he approached his house he reconnoi-
tered.
He asked his overseer if he thought
That all had done their duty as they ought.

"She was surprised that he could be so charming" (Duplessis-Bertaux).

They had; with this, the neighbors all con-
    curred.
Of what was really up, he heard no word,
Neither from valet nor chambermaid;
By all utmost discretion was displayed.
Although subjected to interrogation,
The nurse and maids still gave no indication
Of what they knew the Judge would like to
    know.
But Satan among women loves to sow
The seeds of trouble, and he did so now.
Argie and her nurse began somehow
To fight so much they almost came to blows.
In vengeance did the latter then disclose
To Anselm the affair he'd overlooked,
Even if it meant her goose was cooked.
His rage, indeed his fury, was so great
That it's beyond my talent to relate.
I will simply point to its effects,
Which show how much this news the Judge
    did vex.
To one of his valets he gave the task
Of taking to his wife a note to ask
That she leave the castle very quickly
For Mantua, where he was feeling sickly.
In the past she'd always had to stay
In the region where the castle lay,
While he had traveled up the road and
    down.
"When you bring her on the way to town,
Be sure," he told his man, "to put some dis-
    tance
Between her and her train, so that resistance
On her part would be completely vain.
What I have in mind I must make plain:
I've been shamed by my unfaithful wife
And I intend for you to take her life.
Stab her with a knife, but take your time.
Then flee; avoid detection of your crime.
Take this gold to cover your expense.
Do my will, and punish the offense,
And then no matter where on earth you live
What assistance you may need I'll give."
Off to locate Argie went the knave.
Her little dog, however, warning gave.
How could a dog a thing like that express?
By barking, growling, pulling at her dress,
By whining so that if one isn't dense
One can grasp the underlying sense.

This dog did more than that, for in her ear
He said exactly what she had to fear.
"But go," he said, "despite his well-laid trap,
For I'll make sure that you avoid mishap."
On their way they passed a wooded glen
That at that time had been a robbers' den.
The cruel agent of her husband's wrath
Sent her entourage on down the path.
Then he announced the order that he bore,
But found he couldn't see her anymore,
For Manto had enshrouded her in mist.
He told Anselm of this surprising twist,
The angry Judge, frustrated in his plot,
Went himself to see the very spot
Where this confounding miracle took place.
A lovely castle occupied the space
That just an hour ago was empty land.
Anslem found this hard to understand,
Yet he admired its beautiful façade,
Built not for a man but for a god,
He thought, in that it seemed that lowly
    mortals
Would not have been allowed to pass its por-
    tals.
Within were gilded rooms, exquisite chairs;
Without, delicious groves and fine parterres.
One would be hard pressed to find today
Such a place as this one on display,
Magnificent and easy on the eyes;
Its existence all logic defies.
Strange to tell, each door was wide ajar,
But no one was around—this seemed bizarre.
Except, that is, a hideous, thick-lipped
    Moor,
Who must have been the doorman, he was
    sure.
Anselm thought he looked both Ethiopian
And like the Grecian fabulist, Aesopian.
"Please tell me, friend," he asked with cour-
    tesy,
"What god owns this, because it's clear to
    me
It's too good for a king, however great."
"It's mine," he said. The Judge fell down
    prostrate
In adoration, and he also prayed
Forgiveness for the rudeness he'd displayed.
"My lord," he said, "I simply didn't know
And surely meant no disrespect to show.

No income to be found in all the earth
Could pay the price this fine château is
　worth."
"I could give it to you as a present,
On one condition you may find unpleasant,"
Said the Moor. "My offer is sincere.
"You'll be the lord of all that you see here,
If you agree to serve me for two days
As my boy of honor, in the ways
That Ganymede once faithfully served Zeus,
Who put him to a very special use.
Do you understand or do I need
To draw a picture? Else we can proceed,
Unless that is you find you're of a mind
To leave this princely residence behind.
Of course you're not as young as Ganymede,
Or nearly as good-looking, I concede."
"My lord, it seems that you are making
　merry
With my age and the judiciary."
"Not at all..." "My lord..." "Say yes or no..."
Anselm at last agreed to have it so.
What will the love of gain not make us do?
Suddenly his costume was all new:
His hat became a cap, and in short pants
He looked just like a page upon first glance,
Except for one detail that it appeared
Had been forgotten, and that was his beard.
Anselm, boy of honor, in that get-up
Had to trail his master without let-up.
Meanwhile Argie, in a corner hidden,
Saw her husband do as he was bidden.
The Moor in fact was Manto in disguise.
By her skill in fooling human eyes
She'd built the castle, and despite his age
Had turned Anselm into a costumed page.
At last his wife her presence did reveal.
"My God, are you Anselm? This is surreal!
It cannot be. My husband is too wise
And virtuous to put on such disguise.
And yet it's really him—for that's his beard—
Our papal envoy, man of law revered,
At your age you've started playing dress up?
So you're a man who likes... Oh, please don't
　fess up!
Don't make me blush to hear of your repen-
　tance.
For my affair you issued a death sentence,
And yet I nearly caught you in this place

In a strange and curious embrace!
I, at least—of this you can be sure—
Have never for a lover had a Moor.
My conduct now should really be excused.
Could a man like Atis be refused,
Who offered such a gift as this to me?
Take a look and then perhaps you'll see
Whether one could reasonably insist
That a girl continue to resist.
O Moor," she said, "become a dog again."
He did. "Now dance." And he began to spin.
Then to the Judge the dog held out his paw.
"Make money," she commanded. Then they
　saw
Doubloons descending in a mighty stream.
"Now do you see," she asked him, "what I
　mean?
His gift to me was this best of all creatures.
And this palace, with its lovely features,
Was constructed by this clever hound.
Can a princess or a queen be found
Who'd refuse an invite to cavort
In exchange for presents of this sort?
And when the donor is so fair of face,
As he is in this particular case,
And loves and should be loved, and much
　caressed,
A woman has to do what she thinks best.
He exchanged the wonder dog for me;
I gave him what you didn't need, you see.
Deficient I'd be in household finance,
You'd think, if I had not seized on the chance
To get a dog like that at such a price.
Do you know that this château so nice
He has built entirely from thin air?
The château for which you'd... Let's not go
　there.
Order that my death sentence be stayed:
I just fell in the trap that Atis laid.
Lucretia (who when raped, took out a knife
And for what she had lost took her own life),
I'd like to see how her story would end
If she had had with these arms to contend.
Let's shake hands, make peace, call off our
　war.
With doggie here, your threats I can ignore.
I fear not steel nor poison, he's so zealous
To defend me from those who are jealous.
So cease to be so, since you know our sex

Will, if you constrain us, then perplex
Your mind with doubts, put horns upon your
    head."
He consented to all that she said.
In return for this, Argie agreed
To tell no one he'd been a Ganymede.
But this meant that she kept in reserve
A useful weapon that one day could serve
To give to Cuckoldry some elbow room
Should she adultery choose to resume.
(For this she was grateful.) Each did yield
And under these conditions, left the field.
What happened to the palace? some will ask.
To go in such detail is not my task.
It vanished in a *poof!* The dog? He stuck
To Atis, did his bidding, brought him luck

In amorous adventures—oh, what fun!
He found with women one can't stop with
    one.
Dog and master strayed but oft returned
To the mistress whose affection was well-
    earned.
Atis no more her lover, but a friend,
And yet much time together they would
    spend.
To the Judge she solemnly did swear
That never again would she have an affair;
Anselm for his part a vow did make
That whatever happened he'd no umbrage
    take,
And said to take a whip and lay it on
If ever again a page's togs he'd don.

15. "Clymene"

*It will seem to the reader that the comedy I'm
adding here is not in its proper place, but if he reads
to the end, he will find a story that is not exactly like
those in my tales but that doesn't completely depart
from them either. There is no division into scenes,
as the thing was not written to be performed.*

Clymene—A Comedy
Characters: Apollo, the Nine Muses, Acanthus
Location: Mount Parnassus

Apollo to the Muses was complaining
The other day, "It's not exactly raining
Decent poems on love, you know.
The market has been pretty slow.
In these sad, depressing times
Love inspires no worthy rhymes.
The reason is, one cannot write
Of something that does not delight.
Nor can one speak of love with art
Who doesn't feel it in the heart.
I do my best to place some zest
For love within the human breast,
But my success with this is less than great
Since the ladies won't cooperate.
Neither love nor poems get respect.
So farewell, beauties; henceforth I expect
To occupy myself performing chores
For Fouquet, Colbert, and Louis Quatorze.

And yet I just saw by the Hippocrene
Acanthus all entranced by some Clymene.
There are some charmers who go by that
    name
Whose attractions have brought them some
    fame;
But this one I don't know, I must confess.
She must come from the provinces, I guess.

ERATO: I know her as a friend—a country
    lass,
    And so a stranger to the ruling class.
URANIA: I know her, as well.
APOLLO: You do? That's swell.
    Polyhymnia and Terpsichore,
    Euterpe too, I think could tell me more.
    Given that their realms are here below,
    Unlike yours, Urania, you know.
POLYHYMNIA: Each of us, O sire, could do
    that task.
APOLLO: If therefore it's not too much to
    ask,
    In front of me let each of you take turns
    Praising her for whom Acanthus burns,
    But be original—because I'm bored:
    Let each in her own way strike some new
    chord.
EUTERPE: Give us the liberty that we require

In this trifle, for you know, O sire,
All nine of us can imitate with ease.
APOLLO: Let's start with Euterpe, if you
please.
EUTERPE: If Terpsichore could join, we'd be
all set
To do this as a pastoral duet.
APOLLO: Assist her, Terpsichore, but please
avoid
The old clichés by which I've been annoyed.
I must have something new;
Nothing else will do.
TERPSICHORE: I'll begin; Euterpe will reply:
The sun had made his trip across the sky.
As he traveled through the universe
A hundred masterpieces, all diverse,
Fell beneath his gaze
But what did amaze
The solar deity and made him boast
To Téthys, the sea, by far the most
Were not those things he'd seen or had
created
But that he'd viewed Clymene and was
elated.
EUTERPE: Get up, Clymene, the Dawn to
greet.
No, stay in bed, sleep is too sweet.
Soon you'll seem yourself another Dawn—
Equally as lovely—so sleep on.
TERPSICHORE: Clymene's as pretty as can
be;
Just needs a little passion, see.
She's friendly, but that's not enough;
She needs some of that potion stuff:
Five or six love drops ought to suffice.
She'd be perfect then, to be precise.
EUTERPE: Love can keep you up at night;
Pain is mixed with its delight.
You know the moan of the turtledove?
Don't blame Clymene for fleeing love.
TERPSICHORE: Venus has long been
dismayed:
Clymene puts her in the shade.
Just yesterday, in fear she'd been outdone
By a mortal, Venus asked her son,
Was the rumor of her beauty true?
"It is. I'd like to show the girl to you."
APOLLO: Watch out. You've left the pastoral
mode somehow.

EUTERPE: Apologies. We'll go back there
right now.
Love divides his empire in four parts.
Half goes to Acanthus; rival hearts
In love with her possess a fourth and
more;
More than three-fourths is therefore
Clymene's score.
For other girls, what's left makes up their
share.
TERPSICHORE: Clymene's heart is one that
doesn't care.
Three-fourths of its indifference is fated
For Acanthus, whom we see elated
To know that of his suffering the rest
Goes to rivals equally oppressed.
EUTERPE: The woods, I think, have turned
a greener hue
Since we began this subject to pursue.
TERPSICHORE: Birds, men, and gods, may
every singer choose
Henceforth the theme of fair Clymene to
use.
EUTERPE: For her the roses dress up lovely
Spring.
TERPSICHORE: For her the Zephyrs perfume
everything.
EUTERPE: For her each bird in harmony
unites.
Reign, Clymene, reign over such sweet
delights.
TERPSICHORE: Love, Clymene, love; give
some man happiness:
Your reign thereby yourself with charms
will bless.
EUTERPE: Of her admirers whom would you
suggest
She love?
TERPSICHORE: Acanthus.
EUTERPE: Why?
TERPSICHORE: He loves her best.
Sire, are you pleased?
APOLLO: Rather. Let Melpomene
In tones that move us introduce Clymene.
And Thalia, you'll act the lover's part
Who won't constrain the torment in his
heart.
MELPOMENE: My sisters, you can see that
I'm Clymene.

THALIA: And I'm Acanthus in this touching
    scene.
APOLLO: Marvelous. We're all anticipation.
    Please fulfill our eager expectation.
CLYMENE: You're wasting your time; you'll
    have no success.
    If you want to be loved, love us a bit less.
    Don't say the word "love": that's my
    advice.
ACANTHUS: Not say that lovely word that
    sounds so nice!
    You mean that I, Acanthus, nevermore
    Will be allowed my Clymene to adore?
    Permit, at least, my keeping what I've
    earned:
    The torment which so long my heart has
    burned.
    Am I so dangerous? Alas, I'm not.
    Although to be beloved is what I sought
    (Fond hope! I don't deserve such happi-
    ness.)
    What I hope for now is so much less:
    To die in loving you's the dream I hold,
    A dream dearer than life a thousand-fold.
    Let me keep my love, in heaven's name.
CLYMENE: There's that word again, always
    the same!
ACANTHUS: The word I find melodious
    To you is only odious?
    So many women if they had their druthers
    Would hear that word and never hear the
    others!
    Both sexes in like measure
    Hear that word with pleasure.
    Only in you does it cause such stress.
    Was there ever a time when it displeased
    you less?
CLYMENE: Love in the past has caused me
    some pain,
    That's the reason for my disdain.
    Having said that, I'll no longer conceal
    That I find in your passion some appeal,
    And admit I take some pleasure
    In being the one whom you so treasure.
    Nor would I say you are devoid
    Of personal merit. So why avoid
    All talk of love? Not out of disrespect
    But because I fear its dire effect.
    I ask you not of love to speak

Because I know that I am weak.
The word is pleasing to my ear;
It's love's misfortunes that I fear.
ACANTHUS: All the misfortunes will fall to
    me;
    Of that you have my guarantee.
CLYMENE: You're worthy of trust, Acanthus,
    I know.
    The problem is with Cupid, though.
    The god is a tyrant, I know too well,
    With a demon's power to cast a spell.
ACANTHUS: It's not toward you he behaves
    that way;
    It's only the men that he makes pay.
    We're the ones who suffer pain
    From women's hearts and their disdain.
    It's the price we men pay for our ardor.
CLYMENE: So instead of making your life
    harder
    Why not relax and just go with the flow?
    Far more pleasant that would be, you know.
    Rather than strive against my will
    It would be better to fulfill
    My own desire and then receive
    Rewards from me. For I believe
    That I could make you happy.
ACANTHUS: So you say
    But you would do so in a certain way:
    The happiness of brother or of friend,
    The same sort of regard that you'd extend
    To simply anyone, any connection.
CLYMENE: No, no, for you I'd have much
    more affection.
    I'd take an interest in all things that touch
    you.
ACANTHUS: But would you take an interest
    in me, too?
CLYMENE: What distinction do you have in
    mind?
ACANTHUS: One important in degree and
    kind.
    For example, in your case,
    I love your person, full of grace.
    But your qualities are not the same
    As you; there's one that merits blame.
CLYMENE: Tell me which quality, and I'll
    correct it.
ACANTHUS: It's that you don't love Love,
    but you reject it.

CLYMENE: I don't hate Love, as I have said
   before,
  But I fear its power. You'd please me more
  If you turned your ardor for Clymene
  To friendship, or something that's in-be-
   tween:
  A bit more than no fire in the grate,
  Yet something less than is your present
   state.
ACANTHUS: So this is what you really want,
   I guess?
  To love you less tomorrow, the next day
   even less,
  While your attractions simply grow and
   grow?
CLYMENE: That's exactly what I said, you
   know.
ACANTHUS: Did you say it in your soul?
CLYMENE: Don't you doubt it.
ACANTHUS: But maybe you should think a
   bit about it.
  Could it be that you might find
  A spite that grows within your mind
  In secret when you hear me say
  I'll love you less each coming day?
  Few women would behave like you.
CLYMENE: Acanthus, I'm a woman too.
  But I know Love, and know it's right
  Against its poison sweet to fight.
  You claim that you love your Clymene
  And yet to me you are so mean.
  Don't speak to me of pleasures sweet.
  With my repose they can't compete;
  It's sweeter still, so I'll abstain
  From what would only bring me pain.
  You can believe I will not fail:
  Against myself I will prevail.
APOLLO: Of pathos that is quite enough.
  Give us now some funnier stuff,
  And on the same topic too.
MELPOMENE: Who's to speak?
APOLLO: Why, the same two.
  Acanthus and Clemene.
MELPOMENE: But sire,
  That would much more skill require.
  Make him funny? I despair.
APOLLO: He's insane: that's halfway there.
MELPOMENE: But he's crazy to excess.
APOLLO: All the better for your success.

We like our lovers just that way:
Exaggeration on display.
To connoisseurs they're a delight.
A wealth of examples I could cite.
MELPOMENE: Therefore we will obey. Do
   you recall,
  My sister muse, the morning when in
   thrall
  To sleep Clymene did in her sweet bed lie
  But with a start was woken by a sigh
  And right away against Acanthus fumed?
  She'd not seen him yet and she assumed
  She'd closed the door but who else could it
   be?
  No one could sigh like him. "Truly," she
   said,
  "They way you say 'Alas!' would wake the
   dead.
  You've quite a talent for that but should
   learn
  To make your sighs more softly when you
   yearn."
  He apologized; it did no good.
  "Your heart more racket makes than a
   forge would.
  Such are its only pleasures, I surmise.
  If I should show my foot, here come the
   sighs.
  You're always in some grief that has no
   name.
  You do this hoping I'll love you the same."
ACANTHUS: I make no claim to that.
CLYMENE: Sit on this bed.
ACANTHUS: Who, me?
CLYMENE: Yes, you.
ACANTHUS: Permit ...
CLYMENE: Enough's been said.
  I want to see you there.
ACANTHUS: But ...
CLYMENE: There, I say.
  See how he finds it so hard to obey
  His mistress when she asks him to sit
   down
  Upon her bed. Just look at that sad frown!
  You know what? I'd like to laugh today.
  No mournful speeches; send them all
   away.
  No "alas, alack"—no, not a peep!
  And banish all those sighs hostile to sleep.

Find a way to show your love that's new.
But what's it now your hand intends to
    do?
ACANTHUS: Simply to obey your wish, and
    to show my zeal.
CLYMENE: That sort of obedience is prema-
    ture, we feel.
    You need not go that far, Acanthus; just
    sit peacefully.
    And tell me, is it still the case your soul's
    on fire for me?
ACANTHUS: It's all on fire.
CLYMENE: It never stops nor gives
    you any peace?
ACANTHUS: No, none.
CLYMENE: Always those tears and
    sighs that only do increase?
ACANTHUS: That's right.
CLYMENE: On you I'll pity take
    And so a promise I will make.
ACANTHUS: And what promise might that
    be?
CLYMENE: My friendship.
ACANTHUS: Why make fun of me?
CLYMENE: There it goes again, that song so
    blue.
    It's true, although you do not want me to
    I want to love you as a friend, but love in
    such a fashion
    That there would be just one step in be-
    tween that love and passion.
ACANTHUS: Is that a step that you would
    ever take?
CLYMENE: Never would I make that dire
    mistake.
ACANTHUS: To your offer then I must say
    no.
CLYMENE: Are you aware what you'd be
    missing, though?
    I kiss my friends, and give them fond ca-
    resses,
    While my suitors have no such successes.
ACANTHUS: I have no yearning for that kind
    of kiss.
    Madame, do I see you laugh at this?
CLYMENE: How can I help it? When Cly-
    mene
    Proposes a kiss, you flee the scene!
ACANTHUS: So is it your firm belief

That for a kiss always too brief,
    And often cold, I would exchange
    My love? I find that passing strange.
CLYMENE: In that case, have twice as many.
ACANTHUS: From others yes; from you, not
    any.
CLYMENE: Try it and maybe you'd find out.
ACANTHUS: What are you upset about?
CLYMENE: Who, me? Why, not a thing.
ACANTHUS: And yet
    I can see that you're upset.
    My having turned your kisses down
    Has made your mind in secret frown.
CLYMENE: It's true, the fact that you refused
    Has left my self-esteem quite bruised.
    That you my kisses could disdain!
    It does the powers of reason strain.
    You're too clever by half, I see:
    Today you were going to vow to be
    My friend, but tomorrow you'd resume
    The role of the lover, I presume.
ACANTHUS: Such joking around you would
    allow?
    Wouldn't a kiss have aroused you somehow?
CLYMENE: What does it matter? Calm
    would have returned.
    A dozen such kisses by now you'd have
    earned.
ACANTHUS: Madame, that's too many.
    What good would they do?
    In their place I'd prefer one true love-kiss
    from you.
CLYMENE: I'd make it too short; you'll lose
    at this game.
ACANTHUS: Madame, let's try it all the
    same.
CLYMENE: It's only from friendship that
    these favors come.
ACANTHUS: Then for the moment a friend
    I'll become.
CLYMENE: I fear that under that friend's
    skin
    There'd be a lover hidden within.
    Don't you have somewhere to go? It's late.
ACANTHUS: If I did, then it could wait.
    Moments like these are much too sweet.
CLYMENE: I must dress. Bye! Now retreat.
APOLLO: Are you about done?
MELPOMENE: Not soon enough

For virgin ears. The kind of stuff
The words that we have said contain
Would not suit those you disdain.
APOLLO: Who, me? Why just the other day
I heard two girls of fifteen say
Things revealing they knew more
Than your lovers on that score.
What I find lacking with your two
Is, one moment, it's all "boo-hoo";
The next, they're laughing to beat the
    band.
The only way to understand
That pair is if you see that each one wears
    a mask.
MELPOMENE: You asked that it be funny:
    how else approach the task?
APOLLO: It's true I wanted something droll,
But consistent with their role.
In character, is what I mean.
THALIA: But sire,
Acanthus' inconsistency is so entire
One moment to the next one wouldn't rec-
    ognize
The man. In love or business he'll
    surprise.
Sometimes he's happy; then he's sad.
One day he thinks his chances bad;
The next he thinks all will be well.
Frankly, with him you just can't tell.
Clymene's quite a kidder; yet
When he's complaining, all upset,
Exuding sighs and discontent,
Her pity is sincerely meant;
The friendship then, it does appear,
On her part is quite sincere.
APOLLO: Bring us some diversion now, Clio.
CLIO: I'm ready, sire.
APOLLO: Something à la Marot.
CLIO: Perhaps a *triolet*?
APOLLO: Let's not get carried away.
Composing in that form is tough;
Would not a couplet be enough?
It's not some antique style you should be
    looking for
Made up of words no one knows any
    more.
Go back to Marot but stop right there.
His style is what we need in this affair.
CLIO: Sire, I understand and will obey.

But still Your Majesty should deign to say
Its choice: an *epigramme, ballade, rondeau*?
Myself, I like *dizains*.
APOLLO: That may be so,
But for so fine a subject my advice
Is to avoid *dizains*—they're too concise.
You'll need a form more ample to give
    voice
To what you have to say: *ballade*'s my
    choice.
CLIO: From a distance once I saw Clymene
And took her for a Grace, one of the
    three.
In fact, a new one—that is what I mean.
The loveliest of all, it seemed to me.
I closer came, and rubbed my eyes to see,
Then suddenly I just had to declare
It was Venus who was standing there.
No, I had mistook: it was not so.
It could not be the goddess, that I swear.
Such is not the Venus whom we know.

Let's think this through: Now Venus is the
    queen
Of pulchritude; on this artists agree.
I counted the attractions to be seen
In this girl as they appeared to me
In order to find out how it might be
That Venus' total with the girl's would
    square,
But found that hers do not even compare
To those the gods on Clymene did bestow.
What is, I wondered, this bewitchment
    rare?
Such is not the Venus whom we know.

Acanthus as I counted now was seen;
This beauty made him sit beside her knee.
I heard it all; no breeze disturbed the
    scene.
He complained to her of cruelty,
Of her intransigence, deaf to Love's plea:
Those things a lover says in his despair.
She took it in with a distracted air.
Love's mention made her to look shame-
    faced, though.
If Olympian chronicles don't err,
Such is not the Venus whom we know.

Don't seek out, Acanthus, other fare.
You'll not find a better anywhere
Than Clymene in this poor world below,
Nor in worlds above who can compare.
Such is not the Venus whom we know.
APOLLO: It's your turn, Calliope. So try
One of two paths traced in times gone by
By two famous writers: one, Malherbe
Who praised his heroes in a style superb;
The other one, Voiture, could write so well
He'd find a way to praise the king of hell
Together with his queen, objects of fear,
In a sunny style full of good cheer.
CALLIOPE: The two you name, sire, are too
    great
For me to hope to imitate.
APOLLO: I didn't mean to say that you
Should imitate one of the two.
You shouldn't seek to imitate
Originals who innovate.
The only time that imitating
Should be done is in translating.
Servile imitators are like sheep
Who in lockstep with their leader keep.
Were he into a river to go down
All the rest would follow and then drown.
I only wish that you might demonstrate
In the style in which Malherbe waxed
    great
Some sample of the beauties of the ode;
Or if that genre's no longer the mode,
And takes a bit too much time to prepare,
While for the other you've a greater flair,
Then lavish fair Clymene with gallant
    praises
In the style of Voiture's graceful phrases.
The incense fine that from his pen arose
Was not around when he was writing
    prose.
CALLIOPE: One stanza I will try, since you
    insist.
But should it not go well, make me desist.
APOLLO: I find it hard to think that you'd
    fall short.
CALLIOPE: Why not? I often have. The
    ode's a sort
Of poem that's very tricky to compose,
The high-toned ones above all, heaven
    knows.

O god of Love who makes even immortal
    gods obey
The passions of mere mortals, will you tol-
    erate today
Clymene's insensibility to blows that come
    from you?
Her behavior should a different character
    acquire.
For the honor of your temples, Love, you
    should require
            That she love just as we do.
URANIA: Muses do not love.
CALLIOPE: And who would think they
    do?
That *we* does not refer to us. Instead you
    should construe
That it means the female sex, of Love the
    devotees.
APOLLO: Calliope is right; let her finish, if
    you please.
CALLIOPE: I'd like to stop while I'm ahead.
I fear she made me lose the thread.
APOLLO: Polyhymnia, now try your hand.
POLYHYMNIA: What kind of tone from me
    do you demand?
APOLLO: I see that our attempt at ode was
    not
The glorious success I might have thought
That it would in the end turn out to be.
It was clever of Calliope:
The interruption served as an excuse.
No point in keeping on; it was no use.
And so a tone less lofty I'd suggest.
The tones Horace adopts would suit you
    best.
I love the authors who use him as guide;
To imitate them would success provide.
POLYHYMNIA: Well said, but still remains
    the task.
Do we Muses have, I ask,
The wit that we once could inspire
In that poet on the dire
Prospect of great Rome's decline?
Nothing's any more as fine
As it once had been in this our sacred vale.
APOLO: Indeed, I've even seen my oracle to
    fail.
There's nothing, men or gods, but does
    decay.

But what to do? Just hide ourselves away
And keep silent, since it's clear there's
  nothing that will last?
I don't concern myself with what I once
  was in the past
But think of what I might become if I am
  still around.
We all get old; we gods as well by such
  constraints are bound
All the more because we are the fruit of
  human fiction.
By my diviner's art I can foresee the dere-
  liction
Into which poets and poems will fall;
For them the universe won't care at all,
When your divinity will end, and mine
  will end as well.
On that prospect though, I do not think
  that we should dwell.
Instead enjoy the time we have; let not sad
  thoughts detain us.
Polyhymnia, it's now your turn to enter-
  tain us.
POLYHYMNIA: In thinking of the means I
  might employ,
Only one would give me any joy.
I hope it survives your critique:
It is to make Acanthus speak.

How happy is a girl who's passing fair!
The moments of her life are always sweet.
A mirror on one side in which to stare,
On the other, lovers at her feet!

Their praise is pleasant, their love still
  more so.
To count the hearts she owns: a joy not
  slight.
One dies, one sighs, another in his woe
Consumes himself in grief for her delight.

Clymene, make good use of what you've got.
One day your charms will all have been
  withdrawn.
Charon will take you over but will not
Take your lovers: by then they'll be gone.

Your charms will not live near as long as you.
Will I be faithful always? I can't tell.

My desire will wither as they do.
A beauty fades; a lover does as well.

Spring's the time to love; that's when it's
  done.
Do not put it off till fall—too late.
Winter will come soon: time stops for
  none.
Hurry, Clymene. No one can make time
  wait.

Sire, for good or ill, that must suffice.
  Though I admit
It has Horace's moral but it doesn't have
  his wit.
APOLLO: Erato, what's the meaning of your
  taciturnity?
You've not been taking part in our poetic
  potpourri,
Though you love to laugh, do you not?
ERATO: I must confess that I was lost in
  thought.
APOLLO: Concerning what?
ERATO: The question that was raised
  not long ago.
APOLLO: To wit, if muses love?
ERATO: That the reply was no
  Was once a source of pride for me, but
    now I must confess
  That if someone asked "Do you love?" my
    answer would be yes.
APOLLO: And why?
ERATO: I don't think it is cool
  To be a *précieuse ridicule.*
APOLLO: If at that attribute you take offense
  With vows of chastity we will dispense.
  All you have to do is take a lover.
ERATO: I'd need a bit of marriage as a cover.
APOLLO: "A bit," you say? That's pretty good.
ERATO: I would not marry; yet I would.
APOLLO: So you'd get married as did Oriane
  With Amadis, is that the plan?
  (She did wed him, it's believed,
  Only after she'd conceived.)
ERATO: Yes, Sire.
APOLLO: The method then is sound.
  But where's a husband to be found?
  On Mount Olympus I see no one who
    would like to wed;

The forest gods are not the sort whom you
    would take to bed.
ERATO: I'd take an author.
APOLLO: A goddess like you?
    Erato would an author pursue?
    An unsuitable choice for you for many rea-
        sons, I would say;
    It's seldom you can find an author who at
        home will stay.
ERATO: That's more an advantage than the
    reverse
APOLLO: Another time we will converse
    About your wedding plans. Meanwhile
    Sing us something in a style
    Neither sweet nor amorous,
    Nothing at all serious:
    The French call it a *bagatelle*.
    In this form once did excel
    Voiture and Clément Marot.
    They did it better, as you know,
    Then the poets of the present day.
ERATO: Sire, my skill at that's in disarray.
    It would take longer than one might
        suppose
    May I a *dizain* in its place propose?
APOLLO: Of course.
ERATO: Bur have we not praised her
    enough?
    Graces, smiles and cupids, all that stuff—
    Once through the list I've worked my way
    What is there that's left to say?
APOLLO: You could list each charm,
        attraction,
    Things that drive men to distraction.
ERATO: And then what things?
APOLLO: There's thousands, really:
    Not to mention *rose* and *lily*:
    Just take those themes, and work them
        round.
ERATO: In *satire* many more are found.
    For each thing praised, hundreds to
        blame.
APOLLO: So blame Clymene in whom no
    flame
    Can kindle any more desire.
ERATO: That topic has been treated, sire,
    By Polyhymnia, my sister muse.
APOLLO: And yet there still remain motifs
    to use.

The subject can be infinite;
Our cabal always finds more in it.
ERATO: It would be a blunder
    To steal my sister's thunder;
    I hope that she'll forgive me if I do,
    And only do this, sire, in hopes of pleasing
        you.
POLYHYMNIA: That's a lot of whoop-de-do
    for just a bagatelle.
ERATO: This one's a special order.
APOLLO: What would be the cost,
    pray tell,
    Of a dizain?
ERATO: Everything costs, but it's time I
    began.

Clymene is wrong. I think that she
Should love our liege tomorrow, today;
She should love him immediately.
Love can suffer no delay.
Each moment is priceless, I attest,
When one has a lover who's stood the test.
They're many lovers on this earth,
Where they too plenteously abound;
A hundred bad, though, are not worth
The good one who's so rarely found.
APOLLO: There's just Urania left, and then
    we're done.
    But all things considered, I for one
    Find that this much praise sometimes can
        pall,
    Especially when one person gets it all.
    Were this panegyric to go on
    I think that you would see me start to
        yawn.
    How is it at a funeral that the mourners
        keep
    When hearing the departed's eulogy from
        falling sound asleep?
    There's no eulogist, it seems,
    Who isn't a Morpheus, bringer of dreams.
    Urania, you'll have to put away
    The sweet words you were about to say.
    Besides, who better to speak of Clymene
    Than Acantus? To the Hippocrene!
    We're sure to find Acanthus there;
    He'll doubtless prove diversion rare.
    How lonely are these forest groves!
    Poets pullulate in droves

Today—too many poems to count.
We'll have to find another Mount
With three peaks and not just two
And bigger than Mount Atlas too.
Yet my court in vain does wait
For worshippers to celebrate
Our mysteries—no devotee,
Or at most just two or three.
Seek the reason in the sky,
Urania.

URANIA: The reason why
Is not so far too seek, O sire.
I'll tell you why our state is dire,
So many authors one has never seen, with-
out a doubt.
And on their anvils each of them their
verses hammer out.
But as for poetry herself, that princess is
dead.
No one seems to care about her. What we
have instead
Is that with little bits of rhyme, of this
make no mistake,
A hundred versifiers in a day for you
they'll make.
That language divine, and those figures of
such charm
That in the past could even the most
hardened souls disarm,
By which the forests and the rocks were
sometimes even moved
And of whose beauties even Mount
Olympus once approved,
All that, I say, is gone; it no longer is in
use.
On you and us and on that language they
just heap abuse.
"What's this?" someone will say. "Some
verses." And that is enough
To bring folks running. So why would one
seek out finer stuff?
A poetaster doesn't need the beauties we
supply;
Without us he already has the crowd's es-
teem, is why.

APOLLO: You have spoken very well. But
what's this I hear?
We're near the Hippocrene; Acanthus
speaks. Let's lend an ear.

ACANTHUS: Gentle breezes, hearken to my
voice,
For now I have a reason to rejoice.
In the past you sent back sad echoes
Of sighs and sobs as I told you my woes,
But today I've found at last success.
Let me tell you of my happiness.
And then the news I'd like for you to share
With Mount Olympus and the gods up
there.
O god of Love, what offering to place
Upon your altar for the signal grace
That you have shown your servant here
today?
And you, who to these banks so often
stray,
O muse-encouraged poets, let me say...

APOLLO: Good grief. He's off his rocker now.
But let's listen anyhow.

ACANTHUS: O poets, now to me your worship bring:
For I'm, if not a god, at least a king.

ERATO: Hey, Acanthus!

CLIO: He can't hear.
He's lost in reverie, I fear.
I doubt that you could draw him out.

ERATO: Even if I have to shout
Until my throat has laryngitis,
Don't permit that man to slight us,
For that would be too appalling.
Acanthus, it's Erato calling!

ACANTHUS: Oh, hi. It's you. What is it?

ERATO: The reason for my visit
You'll soon know; just follow.

ACANTHUS: Ye gods! I see Apollo!
O sire, please pardon me. I fear
I did not know that you were here.

APOLLO: Arise and tell us one and all
Of the favors, great or small,
Granted you by Venus' son.

ACANTHUS: Gladly, sire, I'll tell what he has
done.
Near Mount Parnassus' height late
yesterday
The god of Love I saw making his way
In close pursuit, perhaps, of some young
maid.
Though still far off, he saw me, and
conveyed

His wish that I approach, and I obeyed.
"Your poetry," he said, in sweetest tone,
"Has made my name and power more
    widely known.
In fact, I am your only theme.
As a mark of my esteem,
Here's what I will do for you,
For such recompense is due.
Tomorrow at the break of day
Clymene in her soft bed will stay.
I know that you will find her there,
Sleeping with her breasts quite bare.
Exposed as well you're sure to see
Some other part that recently
I saw as well, and can attest
Its beauty fits in with the rest.
But what it's called, I will not tell,
Although I'll say it pleased me well.
I'll let you be the judge, monsieur;
I know you are a connoisseur.
You'll have the opportunity
Because she'll be asleep, you see,
Of kissing one among the three:
Her mouth, her breast, or should you
    choose,
The other; she cannot refuse.
With Morpheus, the god of sleep,
I'll speak, so he her soul will keep
Engaged in blissful slumber.
Remember that the number
Of things that you may kiss
Is not more than this.
ERATO: Her mouth, her breast ...
    As for the rest—
    I want to know, but nonetheless
    Don't tell me: let me guess.
ACANTHUS: O muse, two guesses I'll allow.
ERATO: Her arm?
ACANTHUS: No. There's one guess left,
    now.
ERATO: Was it her foot, then?
ACANTHUS: You guessed right.
    Cupid said it was so white
    It even ivory surpassed.
    He said that she would be aghast
    And angry when she woke—
    Might even take a poke
    At me, but not to fear
    Because he would be near,

Fending off the blows
She'd aim at my nose.
Instead of going "Wham!"
She'd be a little lamb.
Fate and he would take a hand.
And they did, you understand.
Things turned out just as he said.
This morning she was in her bed—
I found her there, and it would take
All day were I to undertake
To tell you of her splendor.
For did not slumber lend her
The blush of a red rose?
The better to disclose
The whiteness of the rest,
Especially her breast.
Naked was each lovely peak
There is no word that I could speak,
Despite my expertise that way
To tell the beauties on display.
The rise, the fall, each gorgeous thing
That made me feel I was a king—
Just through my eyes, you understand;
For no part here was played by hand.
Then fate permitted me the treat
Of gazing at her lovely feet.
Imagine those of Venus, eyed
By Tritons when the goddess vied
With the Naiads for first prize.
Perhaps you've seen with your own eyes
The ones of which I speak; although
If not, then Mars could let you know.
The foot that I now had in view
Was of an alabaster hue,
Or marble, while the underside
Seemed with deep vermillion dyed.
One of Clymene's lovely feet
Extended from beneath the sheet.
I stared at it, in reverie,
Wondering which of the three
Locations I would want to choose
For the kiss she can't refuse.
Her mouth appealed, with its perfume.
Cupid then entered the room—
I don't know how—I'd locked the door.
Then it was time her breast to explore.
I thought to myself it was such a
    temptation
That if I were king I'd be filled with elation

If only this treasure I could possess,
My crown by itself would be worth so
  much less.
Then by a whim I was drawn to the third
Of the beauties, the one I now preferred.
Perhaps it was this I chose to select
As a way of showing my deepest respect.
Then too, such a striking osculation
Would doubtless prove a rare sensation:
A chance, it was very plain,
That might never come again.
She awoke and saw me, then took fright,
Hid under the covers, out of sight,
Safe for the moment from my pursuit.
Shame had rendered her totally mute.
At last without moving or showing her
  face
She said, "How could you be so base?
I'm very unhappy. Now please get out."
Of her anger the tone in her voice left no
  doubt.
"Cupid," I told her, "had said I could stay.
Look, there he is. Now what do you say?"
"Cupid, schmupid.
Do you think I'm stupid?"
"Gently, gently," Cupid said.
Hearing his voice, she turned her head
And quickly assumed a docile air.
"It appears," she said, "in this affair
I'm not the strongest of the three.
I should have shut the door, I see.
I'm clearly outnumbered—and one's a god,
  too.

For Acanthus to leave, what must I do?
What's it to be? Just don't let him linger."
Cupid was pointing, I saw, with his finger.
His meaning at first was not clear to me.
Then I saw that his gesture led me to see
Her beautiful mouth, and the sense now
  was clear:
If I had the courage, I could kiss her here.
A real lover's kiss, if truth be told,
I'd never enjoyed. "Now kiss her. Be bold,"
He said in a whisper. "I will assist
By holding her hands. She won't resist."
I went ahead, and then what transpired—
The miracle—was by Love's power in-
  spired.
APOLLO: What miracle's this?
ACANTHUS: She met me half way.
POLYHYMNIA: You mortals are mad about
  love, I must say.
  The gods from their ladies get more than
  this
  Yet aren't transported to such realms of
  bliss.
ACANTHUS: The reason for that is easy to
  see.
  Gods have more perks than mortals like
  me.
APOLLO: I was a god, yet Daphne wouldn't
  surrender—
  An episode I'd rather not remember.
  Acanthus, let your joy be unrestrained.
  Farewell. We're pleased, our troupe's been
  entertained.

BOOK FOUR

1. "How Girls Get Smart"

There's a fun-filled game I know
For which desire will always grow.
No brains are needed for this game.
Can you guess what is its name?
You play this game, and so do we.
It amuses equally
The cute, the ugly, day or night.
You can play by candlelight
Or even in the dark, this game.
Can you guess what is its name?
Its finer points no husbands know;
They are known to lovers, though.
No umpires needed for this game.
Can you guess what is its name?
No matter what we call this game
It's very useful, all the same.
For it brings, I would submit,
Increased intelligence and wit.
We see this truth quite readily
In many a little bird and bee.
Before Eliza learned its use
She was as clueless as a goose.
Before then all that she did know
Was how to spin and how to sew.
Tasks like those made no demands
Upon her mind, just on her hands.
Her intellect thus unemployed
Was of thought quite as devoid
As was her dolly's empty head.
Each day Eliza's mother said
About a hundred times, "Go find
Some wit, you ninny, for your mind."
Thinking that the power of thought
Was a thing that might be bought,
Of neighbors, shame-faced, she inquired
From whom this wit might be acquired.
They laughed at her, but in the end

One of them did recommend
She knock on Bonaventure's door—
Of wit the friar had a store.
Eliza right away did go
To see the holy man, although
She feared to make an imposition
On a man of his position.
I doubt, she thought, that he'd be keen
On helping me—I'm just fifteen.
The innocence such thoughts reveal
Gave her even more appeal.
"Reverend father," she began,
"I have come to understand
That wit in this place might be bought.
Of money I don't have a lot
But if on credit I could buy it
Then I think I'd like to try it.
Maybe you'd accept this ring;
Next time something more I'll bring
If the price of wit is higher."
As she said this to the friar
She struggled to remove the ring
From her finger, but the thing
Would not come off; it was too tight.
Seeing poor Eliza's plight,
Bonaventure said, "See here.
There's no need for that, my dear.
What you want, I will supply it;
But you will not have to buy it.
Come on in, just follow me.
No one can hear; no one can see.
The monks are all at prayer today.
The porter does whatever I say;
These walls will keep their secrets well."
She followed him into his cell.
There he threw her on the bed,
And tried a kiss; she turned her head

"Is this the way that one gives wit?" (Duplessis-Bertaux).

And asked, "My goodness, is this it?
Is this the way that one gives wit?"
"Indeed, of that I can attest,"
He said, his hand upon her breast.
"That too?" "Oh yes." "But that also?"
Patiently she let him go
About his work of wit-instilling,
For she in fact was not unwilling.
He pushed his point to such extent
That in the end she was content.
Just as much, of course, was he.
Eliza laughed quite happily.
He felt that he could diagnose
The need to give a second dose.
Nor was that all; there came one more—
The friar had charity galore.
He asked, "How do you like this game?"
"It was not long before wit came,"
She said. "But if it goes away?"

"We'll see to that another day,
I know of other remedies."
"I like this one, if you please."
"Should the need arise, we might
Repeat until we get it right."
This idea sounded good to her.
The rising need soon did recur,
The friar, again to action spurred,
The remedy administered.
At last she curtsied and retired,
Musing on what had transpired
As she made her way back home.
Her thoughts indeed began to roam,
A thing they'd never done before.
What shows the progress even more
That her wit had made somehow
Was her attempt to find just now
A lie so Mother'd not berate
Her wayward girl for being late.

Two days later came a visit
From a friend who asked, "What is it
That you've on your mind, my dear?
Your dreamy look makes you appear
To be beneath some potent spell."
Eliza first refused to tell.
Her friend, however, did insist.
The girl found she could not resist,
And so recounted all of it:
The size of Bonaventure's wit,
How it began and then did end,
The whole shebang she told her friend.
"Now you," Eliza said, "should name
Through whom it was to you wit came."
She said, "The one from whom I got it
Was your brother." "Who'd have thought it?

I'm astonished. He's so dumb,
How could wit from him have come?"
"Silly girl, so unaware!
Learn from me, in this affair
One man's as smart as any other.
Don't believe me? Ask your mother.
She knows how the game is played.
Or if to ask her you're afraid,
Then ask a neighbor—she will say
'Give me a dumb one, any day.'"
Eliza felt this would suffice;
She had no need of more advice.
Her lips henceforth would be sealed tight.
You can see that I was right:
A better game one can't devise
For making those who play it wise.

2. "The Mother Superior"

To follow the example that others have set
Is useful to do sometimes, and yet
Is not always good to do
For sometimes harmful things ensue.
Which of these options should carry the day
Is not really something that I have to say;
I simply have a story to tell.
Some folks will say that the abbess did well
Others will view what she did with alarm
And claim that she caused irreversible harm.
For good or for ill, my story will show
How much like sheep most people go,
Just like the sisters in my tale.
Before the first step, each will quail,
But once the bravest takes the chance
The rest soon enter in the dance.
Should one sheep venture in a stream
No other lamb would ever dream
Of remaining contentedly on the shore;
They'll all tumble in, and drown by the
    score.
Rabelais told of just such a case;
I do not think it will be out of place
To tell it before my narrative starts:
Panurge set sail for foreign parts.
Consulting an oracle was the end
That on this trip did Panurge send.
What bee he had inside his bonnet

Was urgent, depend upon it;
But what it was, I do not know.
Another traveler, Dindenaut,
On his own ship was passing by,
And called him a cuckold. In reply
Panurge said he'd like to buy
One of the sheep that Dindenaut
Was carrying there in his cargo.
Dindenaut started to praise his sheep
To justify a price too steep;
Panurge showed he had the gold,
And in the end the sheep was sold.
He took the sheep and immediately
Tossed the creature in the sea,
Right into the briny drink.
The other sheep followed, quick as a wink.
There perished the flock, the whole wooly
    host;
It was devil take the hind-most.
Hoping to save a ram at least,
Dindenaut grabbed onto the neck of the beast
But both of them drowned, the sheep and its
    master:
That qualifies as a real disaster.
Now back to the tale I have in mind,
About heedless sheep of some other kind.
But not all that different, you understand.
First one, then another, then the whole band,

"They viewed her condition with serious dread" (Duplessis-Bertaux).

Till at last the woman whose job was to keep
Them safe followed suit along with her sheep.
Grosso modo, that's my tale.
But here's what happened in detail:
A Mother Superior was feeling faint,
With the pallor of a Lenten saint.
She called in the doctors and they all said
That they viewed her condition with serious
  dread.
She'd get a fever and then she'd die,
Unless ... unless she'd agree to try
(Though what reason they had for this cure
May appear somewhat obscure)
One remedy that might avail:
To make love with a lusty male.
(Doctors the truth do not disguise.)
"Jesus!" she cried, in pained surprise.
"The very idea! Most certainly not!"
"Madame, the malady you have got

Will most assuredly seal your fate
Unless you choose to conjugate
With a man imbued with all the right stuff;
If not, then one won't be enough—
You'd need two to get it done."
She secretly thought it might be fun,
But what would the rest of the convent say?
Sister Anne saw it this way:
"I know this cure has a taste that's bad,
But other ailments you have had,
And a hundred times imbibed
Each medicine that they prescribed.
Why then should this one bother you?"
"So you say, but if the shoe
Were on the other foot, as it were,
Would you do the same?" "Why, sure.
I'd do whatever they propose.
In fact I'll say—for goodness knows
Your health's important—for your sake

If someone had to undertake
Such a treatment in your stead
I should never want it said
That I was not the very first
To volunteer to face the worst."
The Mother Superior thanked her friend.
The doctors' call came to an end;
Since she their remedy was spurning,
They said they would not be returning.
The mood among the nuns was bleak
But to them Anne began to speak
(She was, you see, sharp as a tack).
"There's just one thing that holds her back:
It is her pious sense of shame.
If somehow she overcame
That misplaced modesty, I'm sure
She would undertake the cure.
The thing for which I truly pray
Is some brave soul would show the way.
That'd be a loving act, indeed."
To this the sisters all agreed.
Throughout the convent went the call;
The rest responded, one and all.
Old and young, big and small.
An invitation was sent out,
And, white or brown, thin or stout,
A motley crew of men replied,

Large enough to well provide
For each and every nun inside.
Nor were they slow to show the way.
As much as any nun would they,
By their intense, sincere devotion,
Get Madame to drink her potion.
Barely had one of the sheep
Over the fence made the first leap
When another followed suit;
Then a third, a fourth recruit.
None would wish to stay behind.
With zeal and fervor unconfined,
Like Dindenaut's flock lost at sea
They jumped in with utter glee.
Their good example took effect:
No longer did Madame reject
The remedy that she had dreaded.
With a man she soon was bedded.
Youth and vigor did the trick.
No more was the Abbess sick;
To her cheeks the bloom returned
Thanks to the cure no longer spurned,
A cure that's sweet to give or take,
A cure for nearly every ache.
Except, I'm sad to say, for pride—
For which one can no cure provide.

3. "The Wife Swappers"

A change of diet's good for you,
Not just for men but women too.
I don't know why the Pope won't say
That trading spouses is OK.
You shouldn't do it all the time
But once a lifetime is no crime.
Perhaps a special dispensation
Could be granted to our nation:
The fickle French delight in trade;
That's the way that we were made.
Near Rouen, a Norman town
Whose citizens enjoy renown
For being very sharp in trade,
The tale that I will tell is laid.
Two villagers at home each had
A sturdy wife whose looks weren't bad
For those whose tastes aren't too refined;

The kind of mistresses assigned
To prelates aren't always required.
Now of his wife each had grown tired.
Both with a lawyer friend were drinking
When one said, "You know, I'm thinking
Maybe we could make a deal.
You'd find it interesting, I feel."
Then to the lawyer he did say,
"I should think, Sire Oudinet,
That among those suits and torts
You've seen contracts of all sorts.
Do you think you could create
One for folks to swap a mate
Just as they might swap a mule?
Did our priest break any rule
In trading parishes? No way.
Yet you know I've heard him say

"Maybe we could make a deal" (Eisen).

'I'm married to my flock.' But see:
He swapped *that* spouse. So why not we?"
His friend came up with this reply:
"That's fine, but you cannot deny
Mine's much the prettier of the two.
I'll tell you what we have to do:
Throw in your mule. Sire Oudinet,
Would that break the law some way?"
"Throw in my mule? Come down to earth!
Every woman has her worth.
Wife for wife should be the trade.
Too much attention can be paid
To beauty and that sort of thing.
Besides, my mule ... why, he's the king
Of mules! Don't ask. It isn't fair.
Wife for wife, and then we're square."
Oudinet then jumped in here
To say, "It's true it does appear
Antoinette has more than Jeanne
Of what can turn a fellow on.
At least that's what the folks here say.
But things a woman hides away
Are the things that I prefer.
Looks are deceiving, that's for sure.
So are women, and so it's best
Not to put them to the test.
Now friends, this proverb I'll invoke:
Don't buy a pig that's in a poke.
I'm sure that neither one of you
Would purchase what was hid from view.
So let's take each one's lovely bride
And set them naked side by side
Just as God did them create."
Neither husband took the bait.
Instead each man preferred to boast
Of qualities he valued most
In his better half. "Now she's
Free from hoof and mouth disease.
No mange on her, my Antoinette."
"My Jeanne's as clean as a bright new cent,
And gives a most delicious scent,
A precious balm." "My Antoinette
Has a taste you won't forget."
"You've no idea what Jeanne can do
In making love, I'm warning you."
"The only time we have a spat
Is about who's best at doing that."
"My Jeanne's expert in all the ways;
You'll be telling me about it in a couple of days."

"Let's drink to that." He took the cup;
They toasted round. "Now let's drink up."
"Here's to Jeanne and Antoinette.
Do we have a deal? Are we all set?"
The bargain was at last concluded:
Wife for wife, the mule included.
Oudinet was most explicit:
Their contract was real and licit.
He made sure that he was paid
For the document he made.
Who then satisfied this debt?
It was Jeanne and Antoinette.
No one of this pact should know;
Both men said they wished it so.
But somehow the priest found out;
The church took its cut too, no doubt.
Although I wasn't there, I'm sure it
Wasn't just the local curate
Who came by and claimed his share;
The vicar too in this affair
Collected handsomely because
In canon law there is a clause
That says nothing must go to waste.
The husbands found themselves ill-placed
To carry out their change of spouses
In a town where both had houses.
For fear of what townsfolk would say
They pulled up stakes and moved away.
Things went well, thanks to God's grace,
At least at first, in their new place.
They made a very fine quartet,
The men and Jeanne and Antoinette.
When the women were alone
They spoke of swapping on their own.
Said one, "I hate the same always:
What do you say we switch valets?"
Whether they did we'll never know.
The other swap worked out well, though.
The first month all four were well pleased,
But after that their passion eased.
Etienne, much to be expected,
Began at length to feel dejected,
Weeping for his Antoinette,
In the throes of deep regret.
In the exchange he felt he'd lost.
Meanwhile Gille could count the cost.
He thought that he had been a fool
To have traded off his mule.
What came next took place this way:

Wandering in the woods one day,
Etienne just happened to see
Antoinette beneath a tree
Sound asleep, beside a stream.
He soon woke her from her dream.
Yet she was only half awake
And therefore made a slight mistake,
For the swap she quite forgot.
He soon saw the iron was hot
And therefore it was time to strike it.
He found that he sure did like it;
Antoinette in some strange way
Seemed tastier than on the day
When they'd first made love. But why?
On this law you may rely:
Food you steal and hide to eat
Will always seem more of a treat
Than cuisine you've baked or bought.
For love and wedded bliss are not,
Despite what pains you care to take,
Dishes you should ever bake
Together in the oven. See
Beneath the spreading chestnut tree
Etienne and Antoinette
Feasting on a banquet set
By Love's artful, practiced hand—
More skill than Marriage can command.
After she went home, he thought:
"Gille some secret drug has got.
For else how could it be my wife
At no time in all her life
Has been as pretty as today?
Let's get her back, the Norman way.
According to our local laws
Every contract has a clause
By which one can undo a deal.
A bailiff will affix his seal
To my writ that will announce
That I this contract do renounce."
Gille fought back as best he could,

Maintained the contract still was good.
It was, decreed the court of law,
Among the things *it* oversaw.
The judges called Sire Oudinet
And asked him what he had to say.
After due consideration,
They gave their interpretation:
Etienne was sad to learn
That his wife could not return.
The reason: he had just enjoyed
His Antoinette, so null and void
Their marriage surely had to be;
Ipso facto, Q.E.D.
There was still the chestnut tree,
Where she would often sing her song.
Thus the wait was never long,
Although if this had not been so
His love for her would surely grow
Because the pleasure would be stronger
If he had to wait the longer.
This doctrine should be widely preached.
Folks of this class it hasn't reached.
Though those of whom this tale I tell
Were really doing rather well
Till one of them deceit did try.
The game they played was rather sly,
One I'd think more worthy of
Persons of class somewhat above
The ones who figure in my story.
But I cannot claim the glory
Of inventing it, alas.
It's so unlike the peasant class
And yet it really happened so.
The suit to Rome's court did not go,
Though Rouen's judges took the case
And deemed the lawyer a disgrace.
God save Maître Oudinet
From falling in the hands one day
Of some judge whose wife is pretty,
For I'm sure he'll show no pity.

4. "A Clear Conscience"

Poets love to lavish appellations
That cast an aura on their fond creations
(Lavishness like that does not cost much).
Shepherdesses, woodland nymphs and such

Are all that in their world do ever dwell,
Though sometimes goddesses show up as
    well.
Horace, noted ancient Roman poet,

Knew such names and he would often show
  it.
His host's maidservant showed up in his
  bed?
She was the nymph Egeria, he said—
Or lent her some such legendary fame.
Adam gave to each species a name;
Apollo, god of poets, did the same;
God told him to do it one fine day.
Even over kings poets have say,
Choosing epithets that best display
The glories of their reign triumphantly.
Humble versifier though I be,
I'm the selfsame privilege allowed.
In this story I could have endowed
My Anne and Thomas with names from
  some myth
Or fairy tale that would have had more pith,

Like Adamas the Druid or Elvire;
No comeuppance would I have to fear.
Although all things considered I prefer
To keep their names exactly as they were.
Anne was quite a clever girl.
Village folk called her a pearl.
As she sat beside a brook
One day she chanced to get a look
At a young man bathing nude.
With spirit was the girl imbued.
Yet she was honest and upright.
The boy was pleasing in her sight.
He had no faults that she could tell.
Even had she known him well,
As long as she had loved him too,
Love would have hid those faults from view.
No tailor ever can disguise
Defects so well as lover's eyes.

"The boy was pleasing in her sight" (Duplessis-Bertaux).

Anne was hid by willow trees,
So she could spy on him with ease.
The willow leaves she peered behind
Were fashioned like a louvered blind.
Lingering around each feature
Of this divinely sculpted creature,
Tall and straight, well-formed and shiny—
Nothing on this guy was tiny.
Four steps back she took in shame;
Eight steps forward then she came.
Drawn on by love, she then recoiled—
All by scruple nearly spoiled.
How could she from sin abstain?
Is there some way one can restrain
Desire when chance puts in one's way
Its object, there as clear as day?
She tried resisting; then she thought
Sin at a hundred feet is not
Perhaps a sin at all. She sat
Upon the grass and thought on that.
And still she stared at what she saw,
Just as artists learn to draw
From looking at a model placed
Before their easels, who is graced
With comeliness, but not with clothes,
Some Eve or Adam in a pose.
Deep within her memory, Ann
Engraved the image of the man.
She'd be there still
Except that Gil
(That's his name)
Just then came
Upon the shore.
Anne then tore
Herself away.
She couldn't stay.
The enemy
Of chastity
Was close now.
She somehow
Defeated Love's intention.
Knowing that prevention
(As I, too, believe)
Is easier to achieve
Than would be a cure.
Love had been so sure
That he'd the victory won,
After he'd begun
In Anne to instill

Those images of Gil.
Although Love was defeated
Because the girl retreated,
Not wanting to display
To Gil *her* charms that day,
She yet did not deny herself the thrill
Of thinking of the finer points of Gil
When she had the leisure
To pursue that pleasure—
The points, that is, that made her feel
    ashamed,
Points that in good conscience can't be
    named.
Easter came, and with it came some stress
Because it was the season to confess
All the sins that one had done till now.
Anne thought she could fool the priest
    somehow,
But Father Thomas didn't let it pass.
As if beneath a magnifying glass
He looked at each detail
And made her tell the tale
More than once to make sure that he knew
What kind of penance she would have to do.
He came down hard upon the girl and fussed
And fumed because her eyes had sinned in
    lust.
"Your soul is in grave danger inasmuch
As it's the same to look at as to touch."
The penance that the father chose
Wasn't bad as penance goes.
On that point I will not dwell
Though I'll say the clientele
Of the curates in those parts
Often found it in their hearts
To pay a tribute to the priest
Who from guilt their souls released
When he heard them make confession
Of each sin and indiscretion.
The tribute's size was greater or was less
Depending on what each had to confess.
This year Anne was worried how to pay
But as it happened Gil came back one day
From the river having caught a pike
So large that he was sure that she would like
To have it, as a mark of his affection.
Quite pleased, she made her way in the di-
    rection
Of Father Thomas to give him the prize,

A tribute that she knew he'd not despise.
The gift was worthy in his view.
"I think, my child, that this will do."
He smiled, his hand upon her shoulder.
"I'm having company," he told her.
"Fellow priests will come to eat.
Once a month we like to meet.
Tonight I am the host.
What would please me most
Would be if you could make a tasty dish
Out of this extraordinary fish
And bring it here the moment of the feast.
That will be your tribute to your priest.
You see, my cook is new and so still learning;
My double gratitude you would be earning."
Back home she ran.
The meeting began;
Guests went to the cellar to sample the wine,
Then back upstairs they gathered to dine.
The dean took his place at the head of the
    table.
He greeted them all; but I am not able
To tell you everything they said
As they waited to be fed.
We don't have that much time at our dis-
    posal.
At least a hundred times came the proposal
That each to each their parish they would
    trade,
But not a single such exchange was made.

Many toasts, with a wink,
To his mistress each did drink,
Although no scandal was observed.
The soup and salad both were served,
Side dishes and the like,
But still no sign of pike.
Time to serve the fruit:
But where was Anne's tribute?
What had happened was, when Gil
Learned that Anne had paid her bill
For confession with his pike
He made known his great dislike
Of the deal she had transacted
And required it be retracted.
Minus fish, the guests departed.
Thomas the host was brokenhearted.
That ungrateful Anne he went to find;
He'd give her a piece of his mind.
He almost had the crudity
To bring up the nudity.
Yet he refrained.
Though he complained,
"Is it now the vogue
To treat me like a rogue?
Are priests and curates mere riffraff
Whom you can trick and then just laugh?"
Anne, who was sly,
Had this reply:
"Do not think that I have been a cheat;
It's just the same to look at as to eat."

5. "The Devil of Popefingerdom"

Pope-omania, says Rabelais,
Is where one is happy all the day.
Restful slumber in its perfect form
Is for Pope-omaniacs the norm.
What we call sleep is just an imitation.
I would love to travel to that nation.
If I live long enough I will go there,
God willing and if Saint John hears my
    prayer.
Folks all day long do nothing there but
    snore;
That's the job that I've been looking for.
Now if there were some sex thrown in for
    free

Then that would be for sure the place for me.
On the other hand,
There's another land
Whose population fares much worse
Because they live beneath God's curse.
You can tell who's from that place
Because they have a sad, thin face.
Long, luxurious sleep is banned
From that most unlucky land.
Therefore, readers, should you ever see
A ruddy face whose smile expresses glee
Belonging to a guy who eats a lot,
A Pope-omaniac is what you've got.
But if your man is thin, depressed, and pale

Then you can call this fellow without fail
Popefingerer, for once upon a time
His forebears committed the grave crime
Of raising to a picture of the Pope
Their middle digit. Now they have no hope
Of prospering in this world or the next;
Everything they try to do is hexed.
The island where they live, says Rabelais,
Was ceded to the Devil, who holds sway.
A host of little devils can be seen
Who to local folk can be quite mean.
Tails they have, and horns and claws;
They enforce their Master's laws.
One day a member of this curious crew
Approached a man who knew a thing or two.
The cleverest of peasants on this isle,
He had a gift for trickery and guile.
The man that day was plowing in his field.
He had to struggle hard to make it yield.
The earth was truly cursed and hard to till,
But he pursued his task by force of will.
The little devil tried to play the part
Of a lord, but wasn't very smart.
He was the sort whom Jesus did assure
That they were blest because they were the
    poor
In spirit—that is, who were short of wit.
This one showed that he was poor in it,
Ignorant and easy to be had.
A gentle sort, because when he got mad
The only evil he had ever wrought
Was some hail upon a cabbage plot.
That's all the damage he knew how to make.
"Peasant," said the devil, "I don't take
The burden on myself of honest work.
Toil like yours is something I can shirk.
The reason is that I'm of noble birth.
You know we devils own all of this earth.
This island was made excommunicate;
That's when it passed into our estate.
You live here under our command.
Legally I could demand
This land's fruit
As my tribute.
But because I'm nice
I think it will suffice
If we agree to share
What this field will bear
With no quibbles over splitting the dough.

What kind of grain do you plan to sow?"
"I've decided on touselle.
It's a grain that grows quite well."
"That's one of which I've not heard tell.
What did you say it was—touselle?
Don't know that—the name sounds odd.
But touselle it will be, by God.
Now get to work, without delay.
Toil like a peasant, every day.
Work like a dog, no help from me.
For I'm too good to work, you see.
I'm a gentleman, as I said.
I can stay all day in bed.
I need neither till nor sow;
There's nothing that I have to know.
Here's how we'll divide the crop:
I take the bottom, you the top.
Yours, what grows above the ground;
My share, all that beneath is found."
Harvest came, and the touselle
Was gathered in, its roots as well,
Because that was the devil's share.
He thought the seeds would be found there,
And that the stalk and golden ear
Were useless grass, dried up and sere.
The plowman tied it for him well;
The devil took it off to sell.
But people scoffed; no one would buy.
The devil looked about to cry.
To his partner he returned.
The peasant hid what he had earned,
Sold it unthreshed, still in the sheaf,
Fostering the false belief
That he'd not prospered in the deal.
"You crook, you sure know how to steal,"
Said the devil. "You're a pro.
While I such subtle tricks don't know.
What grain next year will you sow?"
"Instead of grain, I think I'll go
With carrots, to diversify,
Or turnips. But you can rely
On this: your bags will overflow,
So much that they'll be hard to stow.
Unless it's beets that you'd prefer."
"Turnips, carrots, beets, whatever
You would like to plant is fine.
But all above the ground is mine.
The stuff inside to you will fall:
I'll brook no argument at all.

Please don't try to change my mind
For it's made up, as you will find.
I'm off to tempt some little nuns,
Young and very pretty ones."
Did he succeed? Well, Rabelais
Unfortunately doesn't say.
Harvest-time now came once more.
The peasant gathered quite a store
Of lovely beets; the devil's share
Was only leaves, which he did bear
Upon his shoulders into town.
Folks there jeered at this sad clown.
"Where," they asked, "does that crop grow?
Where is it that you plan to stow
All the cash those weeds will bring?"
The devil found these words to sting.
Without the cash he'd thought he'd earn,
Angry at suffering this ill turn,
He'd tell the peasant what he thought.

He found him at home, laughing a lot,
Enjoying himself with his wife there.
Many an oath did the devil swear:
"By blood, by death, by gosh I say,
I'll find a way to make him pay.
I'll give him a thrashing he'll regret,
But before I do I mustn't forget
There's a lady I know who needs assistance
To vanquish that last little bit of resistance
That's keeping her from giving in.
She wants to, then wants not to sin.
Once my work is done with her
And cuckolds on her spouse confer
Membership and all its rights
On you, Phlipot, I'll set my sights.
I'll beat you till you're black and blue.
Once I get my claws on you
No more will you get your kicks
From playing your confounded tricks.

"Lifting up her dress, she flashed" (Duplessis-Bertaux).

We'll see which one of us will yield
And lose the produce of this field.
I have the right to simply deem,
By my authority supreme,
The field as mine, its crop and seed.
Yet such unfairness I don't need
To practice. But Phlipot no more
Will you triumph as before
By stratagem and clever ruse
For this time I am sure you'll lose.
In a week I will be back.
When I return, I will attack.
Let's shake on it. Look: here's my claw."
The peasant shrank from him in awe,
So scared he couldn't say a word.
But Perrette chuckled when she heard.
She was his wife, wise in the ways
Of love, for ever since the days
When she first tended sheep she'd known
More than tending sheep alone.
She said, "Phlipot, now don't you cry.
I'll make this devil say good-bye.
He's just a novice and still green;
They're many things that he's not seen.
Though he seems to think he's kinky
There's more mischief in my pinky
Than he has in his whole body."
Phlipot fled, which was quite shoddy,
But the fellow wasn't brave.
Instead of cowering in a cave
On the day the devil came
In a church he hid his frame
In a font up to his chin
In the water there within,

With a stole upon his head,
While around him priests did tread,
Chanting, "Satan, get behind me,"
As he prayed, "Oh please don't find me."
I think that we can leave him there
Cold and wet and lost in prayer.
Meanwhile at the house, Perrette
At the door the devil met.
Her hair askew, rage in her eye,
She let forth a blood-chilling cry.
"O, the horror! I've been maimed!
The wicked man should be ashamed
For the harm he's done to me.
In the name of God, sir, flee!
He was in a rage because
You two were to fight with claws.
The fighting, he said, would be hard
Because there would be no holds barred.
Just for practice, here he slashed."
Lifting up her dress, she flashed
The devil, who was seized with fright,
Almost fainting at the sight.
He crossed himself, such was his fear.
A gash that looked like this one here
Was one he'd never seen before.
If Phlipot's claw did that and more
He'd better not pursue this fight.
Quickly, he fled out of sight.
Perrette's neighbors marked the day
In a very holy way,
In the manner they thought best,
Making it a day of rest.
The clergy took their cut as well,
In this triumph over hell.

6. "Ferondo in Purgatory"

The Old Man of the Mountain, it is said,
In Arabia inspired such dread
Not because his empire was so vast,
Nor because his wealth was unsurpassed,
But from what he printed on the mind
Of his men, so they would be the kind
Of fighters who would always persevere
Because they never ever suffered fear.
He selected those who were most brave;
To them a taste of paradise he gave—

Paradise as taught in the Koran.
Its every aspect seemed real to each man;
So persuasive was the trick, they all believed.
But how exactly was this trick achieved?
First, he gave his Turks too much to drink.
Soon they lost the faculty to think.
They fell unconscious; he took them away
To gardens where they would find an array
Of beautiful young virgins on display.
A harvest of such bounty, for the reaping!

It seemed they had awakened from their
    sleeping
In the garden Mohammed awards
To those he deems to merit such rewards.
The young Turks to the maidens made ad-
    vances;
The charming maidens joined with them in
    dances.
All were engrossed in amorous pursuits.
Nightingales accompanied by lutes
And rivulets made music 'neath the trees.
Even other joys there were than these,
All pleasures that our senses can excite
Were present in this garden of delight.
The finest wines in rich variety
Took a toll on their sobriety.
The Turks fell in a stupor, to a man,
And were transported back where they
    began.
What was the upshot of all this carousing?
The certainty that they would all find hous-
    ing
In this splendid heaven when they die,
Provided every peril they defy
Waging war with bravery undaunted,
Doing everything Mohammed wanted.
The Old Man of the Mountain thus could
    boast
Of having an unconquerable host.
No empire could defend against the on-
    slaught
Of those who for this happy paradise fought.
On this subject I've gone on at length
In order that I might show you the strength
Of such a staged illusion so that you
Will see the following story could be true:

Ferondo had money but not much sense.
His job was to care for the wealth and ex-
    pense
Of the lands and estate of a white-robed
    Abbot—
Of the Dominican order, to judge from his
    habit.
There are some monks in that garb I know
Who are fully the equal, as those things go,
In helping out men whose libido's gone slack
By pleasing their wives, as those who wear
    black.

He never thought about tomorrow;
If he hadn't been rich, he'd have had to bor-
    row.
His whole ambition was to find good wine,
The tastiest meats on which to dine,
Complaisant housewives and, lest we forget,
Nuns open to lust. He didn't let
His fellow monks join in the fun,
He never shared with any one.
Ferondo had a pretty bride
Who to the abbot was allied:
The latter's uncle was her dad.
This uncle, now deceased, had had
The post our abbot now enjoyed.
As abbot, he'd his powers employed
To give the daughter he had sired
To Ferondo, who desired
Not only the girl but the honor as well.
It's an acknowledged truth, as I have heard
    tell,
That an illegitimate girl, to be blunt,
True to her parents' blood, will hunt—
For lovers, that is, and she bore this out.
Ferondo, though foolish, yet had no doubt
There was something afoot between her and
    the abbot.
For it had become her continual habit
To go to the abbey—on business, she'd claim.
"To help with the abbot's accounts" she
    came.
Over this work she'd often fret.
Now a purchase, now a debt,
Now an account she had to pay.
There was hardly an hour, hardly a day
When she wasn't by zeal consumed
To share in the duties her spouse had as-
    sumed
As manager of the abbot's estate.
When she came, the abbot would consecrate
His time to her, dismissing his staff.
Despite this precaution, her better half
Still had his suspicions, and when she got
    back
Would erupt into rage and give her a whack.
There was never a husband who raised such a
    fuss.
With rural minds it is often thus.
Folks in the city have more sense;
In such situations they don't take offense.

As far as the abbot was concerned,
For he was accustomed to pleasures un-
     earned,
This interference was hard to take.
Loving pleasure for pleasure's sake,
He hated hard work, which was no surprise,
For he saw the world through Vatican eyes.
That's not my style, I'd say, at all.
In besieging a fort I'd climb up the wall
Rather than simply walk through the gate.
Of tactics in battle I'll not debate.
I speak of love, and not of war.
But now I'd like to tell you more
About Ferondo and the story
Of his time in purgatory.
By means of a powder inducing sleep
He was put in slumber deep
By the abbot. Through this scheme
To the naked eye a corpse he'd seem.

About his body monks gathered round,
Chanting a psalm with an eerie sound.
Ferondo awoke to his surprise:
The attendants looked strange to his won-
     dering eyes.
He found himself within a tomb
But could move about the room,
Which led to a cave beyond the bier.
At first our man was seized with fear.
Was he dreaming? Was he dead?
Or was he beneath some spell instead?
He asked his guardians, "Who are you?
Why are you here, and why am I, too?
It seems I'm imprisoned: What did I do?
Have I incurred divine damnation?"
One of them said, "Take consolation
In the knowledge that in a mere
Thousand years you'll be out of here
And dwelling in one of the higher locations.

"The experience will definitely whiten your soul" (Duplessis-Bertaux).

But in the meantime, we've scheduled priva-
tions
The better to purge you of all your sin.
It's purgatory that you're in.
The experience will definitely whiten your
soul."
The angel who spoke these words to console
Followed them up with eight or ten blows
Of a stout whip, adding that those
And more of the same were due because
Rebellion and jealousy were awful flaws
Displeasing to God, which it would take
Ten hundred years of such scourging to
shake.
Rubbing his shoulder, Ferondo sighed:
"A millennium of this to be purified!"
The angel with the whip in fact
Was a monk putting on an act,
Dressed up like an angel, as were the rest.
Ferondo forgiveness tried to request:
"If I to earth could be returned
I'd show that I have my hard lesson learned.
I'll never be jealous, not the least little bit.
Do you think that maybe you could omit
These thousand years of anguish somehow?"
They held out some hope, though not for
now.
He'd have to spend at least a year
But he'd have what he needed, not to fear,
To sustain his body for the time
It would take to cleanse him of his crime:
A cot to sleep on, bread to eat,
Twenty lashes delivered neat
Each and every day unless
The abbot could somehow make it less
By praying God to let him cut back
The number of times the whip ought to
crack.
The prelate possessed a merciful heart
And was sure to ask if at least some part—
A fourth, or half—could be subtracted
From the sum to be exacted.
"No doubt the abbot for you is pleading;
By prayers to heaven he's interceding.
To have suspected his virtue was very
wrong,"
The Angel said; his sermon was long.
"Would a man of the church have such a
thought?

A white-robed abbot? Certainly not!
Had you accused a monk robed in black
All you'd have got was ten blows on your
back.
Nothing additional would be required.
So get rid of the doubts your error inspired."
He promised he would; what else could he
do?
Yet his wife and the prelate lost precious few
Of the moments they had; in fact, not any.
Their opportunities were many.
Ferondo inquired how his wife was faring
While he this punishment was bearing.
"She's doing fine," the Angel said.
"By our abbot she's been comforted.
And his estate is doing well,
Despite the change in personnel."
"Does she visit the abbey as much as before?"
"She certainly does, in fact even more
Since that poor woman now bears all the
weight
Of overseeing the abbot's estate."
This news was distressing, and took its toll
On poor Ferondo's suffering soul.
A "soul" was all he was, I say,
Since his body was wasting away,
Having been given so little to eat.
A month of fasting now was complete;
The abbot his good works pursued
With vim and vigor yet renewed.
The pains he took weren't without fruit
The ground was fertile; something took root.
Father abbot now could claim
To be a father in more than name.
This was not news to be revealed,
But the birth couldn't be concealed.
Therefore he prayed so ardently
That Ferondo was set free.
His soul emerged lighter than air
Because they'd nearly starved him there,
In that phony purgatory.
This redounded to the glory
Of the abbot, who folks thought
Must be a saint, for he had wrought
This miracle (one but few
Had first believed was really true).
Having now returned to life,
Ferondo went back to his wife.
His own he took the child to be

Though if he did the math he'd see
Such could hardly be the case.
Two miracles had taken place:
The posthumous child and his father's re-
    turn;
God all the more Te Deums did earn.
That year there'd been sterility

Despite the assiduity
With which the monks performed their vow.
They did their best, but still somehow....
Let's leave the steward and his bride,
Renounce all jealousy and pride,
And hope we can of this be sure:
We'll never need *that* kind of cure.

7. "The Psalter"

This time, dear nuns, I promise is the last
That in a tale of mine you will be cast.
Your escapades are those folks like to tell.
They have a grace that's without parallel.
Just one more, this one that will make three.
Oh no, it will make four! How dumb of me.
There was Mazet, and then the sick abbess
Who underwent her cure under duress.
That one was pretty racy, I'll admit.
Nor should we Sister Joan and child omit.
That's it so far. And so we will have four.
You nuns no doubt will say that you deplore
My having given you such pride of place.
It's not because I wish for your disgrace.
Yet really it is not my fault at all
But rather yours, for you so often fall
From grace and would do better just to pray
Than from the straight and narrow path to
    stray.
So let's get started with the tale at hand.
There was a nunnery, you understand;
A young man lived nearby who often went
To gaze upon the nuns to his content.
There were those who found him to their
    taste,
Who'd look at him with thoughts that were
    not chaste
And smile at him and do all that they could
To please the youth, but yet it did no good.
Inside the convent walls there wasn't one,
Young or old, no not a single nun,
Whom he did not impel to dream and sigh.
He soon saw what was going on and why.
It didn't cramp his style, which stayed the
    same.
One sister—Isabella was her name—
Was able to acquire him for her use,

For reasons we can easily deduce:
A gentle disposition, well-endowed,
(If such an explanation be allowed)
In places where it matters, and quite new
To the nun's vocation, it is true.
On top of all of that, so lovely too.
The sisters had two reasons to be jealous:
Her lover and her charms; so they were
    zealous
To spy upon her, should some fault appear—
Each good with ill does come; each pleasure,
    fear.
They kept such careful watch that one dark
    night,
The kind whose shadows should conceal de-
    light,
They heard some words emerging from her
    cell
That didn't come from prayer books, they
    could tell;
Nor did the topic nor the tone of voice.
"We've got him now," they said, and did
    rejoice.
In triumph, someone ran to bring the word
To the abbess, and those who hadn't heard,
While others stood as sentries at the door.
They trembled, knowing something was in
    store.
Upon the abbess' door a sister pounded.
"Wake up!" she said, "For you will be as-
    tounded
To find that Isabella has a man
Inside her cell. Please hurry, if you can."
The abbess had not been engaged in prayer
Now was she sleeping, but she had in there
Father Jean, the local village priest.
Not wanting to arouse doubts in the least

She rose and hastily began to dress.
Distractedly she grabbed what by her guess
Would be the veil the sisters call a psalter,
But in the dark it seems her hand did falter
For it was not the veil she donned; instead
She wore the padre's pants upon her head.
Thus attired, she opened up and heard
A full account of what had just occurred.
The erring Isabella she berated:
"Our convent I won't let be desecrated
By that daughter of the devil, God forbid.
I pray that God, despite the thing she did,
Can restore good discipline somehow.
We must call a meeting here and now."
The nuns were brought together and they
    met.
With tears was Isabella's face all wet
As she recalled with sad pangs of regret

The way her lover had made gentler use
Of the face now suffering abuse.
"A man," exclaimed the abbess, "in this
    place!
That God's house should suffer such dis-
    grace!
Have you not already died of shame?
A creature such as you I dare not name.
Who made us welcome you? Who is to
    blame?
'Sister' is a title that you've lost
Now that it's too late you'll count the cost.
So simply 'Isabella' I will call you.
Do you know the fate that will befall you
By our rules not later than tomorrow?
Before then you will learn it, to your sorrow.
What have you to say in your defense?"
The trembling nun regretted her offense.

"She wore the padre's pants upon her head" (Duplessis-Bertaux).

From her embarrassment she was too weak
To move a muscle or indeed to speak.
But as luck would have it, she could spy,
When she raised her head, something awry.
It was the strange headdress that took the
    place
Of the psalter-veil above the face
Of the abbess, which no one else had seen,
For their excitement had just been too keen.
The girl screwed up her courage and she
    said,
"What's that thing that's hanging from your
    head?
You should readjust it." What she'd seen
Were drawstrings for the codpiece. What I
    mean
Is, tailors at that time would oft equip
Men's pants with laces where today we zip.
It seemed to Isabella that the veil
Looked a lot like pants; she didn't fail
To notice, having seen both in the flesh;
And her recollection was quite fresh.
Not that Father Jean had quite the fashion
Sense of the young man, or showed his
    passion.
But close was quite sufficient, in this case.
"And yet she dares to laugh right in my face!
Such insolence must signify perdition.
Her sin ought to have led her to submission.
Does she really think her shameful taint
Will lead the church to make of her a saint?
Leave my veil alone, you imp of hell.
It's on your *soul's* adjustment you should dwell."
The Mother Abbess did not end her song

Until her sermon grew to be quite long.
"Fix your veil," the nun then said again.
This time, the sisters did at last begin
To look—the young to laugh, the old to
    grumble.
The abbess couldn't find a word to mumble,
Though in her sermon she had been verbose.
Irate and shamed for having made so gross
An error, there was nothing she could say.
The hive was all abuzz, and in this way
The sisters' diverse thoughts were on display.
Recovering at last, the abbess said:
"It's much too late to vote now. Go to bed.
Our meeting till tomorrow we'll adjourn."
But on the morrow she did not return
To the matter, nor did she the next.
The wisest in the convent weren't perplexed:
They drew the conclusion that it meant
One should speak no more of the event.
Too much scandal would, they knew, be bad.
The reason that the nuns had once been mad
At Isabella was because she had
What they wanted but could not attain.
When they saw their efforts would be vain
To make her share, they came to the decision
That each for her own needs would make
    provision.
Gentlemen, old friends, were now invited.
Sister Isabella was delighted
To get her lover back; while the abbess
Could once more the village priest possess.
So far the union of the sisters went
That men to those without were sometimes
    lent.

8. "King Candaules and the Professor of Law"

Many have been the instrument of their own
    demise.
King Candaules bears witness to this truth.
    He was unwise.
In the annals of stupidity he plays a major
    part
For an act of imprudence that wasn't very
    smart.

To his vassal Gyges one day he spoke of the
    queen:
"You know her lovely face, but the parts you
    haven't seen
Far surpass in loveliness the ones that you
    have viewed.
You haven't seen a thing until you've seen her
    in the nude.

I'd like to let you stare
At her beauty bare
And I know a way
That I can display
Her unencumbered beauty to your viewing
Without her knowing what it is I'm doing.
But if this boon I gave,
Gyges, you must behave:
I'm sure you realize
Desire must not arise.
I would not be pleased, and that's for sure,
To hear that you made vows of love to her.
Tell yourself that what you will be shown
Is but a lovely statue made of stone.
When you've seen her I want you to say
Not art nor thought nor wish in any way
Could go as far in beauty as she's gone.
She's in her bath and so has nothing on.

A connoisseur like you can now attest
That my felicity is of the best."
They go. Gyges admires
But more than that, desires.
He tries to fight the impulse, but it's violent.
If he could he'd rather remain silent,
But fearing that the king would sense his
    state
He finds it better to exaggerate.
Abandoning all shyness and reserve
He praises each detail he can observe.
"Ye gods!" says Gyges. "How can I begin?
Such a body, such a satin skin!
All the pretty parts revealed to me!
What a happy husband you must be."
Fortunate it was that she'd not heard
Of Gyges' hymn of praise a single word.
For the queen would surely have exploded.

"What a happy husband you must be" (Duplessis-Bertaux).

In that era, though it seems out-moded,
The fairer sex were shy and timid creatures.
If today you chance to praise their features
Their ears won't burn, nor will they mind a
    bit.
In Gyges' eyes the queen was exquisite.
He sighed and felt the love within him grow.
The king led him away, but seemed to know.
Gyges was on fire,
Burning with desire.
It does no good to flee;
Love wins eventually.
Though with the king he showed careful
    discretion
The queen became aware of his obsession,
Then discovered how it came about:
The king told her the prank he'd carried out.
What did her most provoke
Was that he took it as a joke.
It was dumb of him to think that she
Would not mind to hear such raillery.
Even had she laughed within her heart
She'd have felt obliged to play the part
Of an avenging Fury, for her honor.
But the rage that now had come upon her
Was real, and she did dream
Of a vengeance most extreme.
To get back at him for her disgrace.
Put yourself, dear reader, in her place—
That's the only way that you could know
Just how far her vengeful thoughts did go.
"That a mortal, a mere mortal, can now say
He's seen my hidden beauties on display!
The only eyes allowed to view those things
Are those of deathless gods—I mean of kings.
Either sort, I guess, would suit as well.
Which is best, I guess I cannot tell."
Such thoughts running through her mind
To vengeance made the queen inclined.
Shame, spite, and ire: all these her heart
Found uses for, and in the plot
The god of Love played his role too;
There is nothing he can't do.
Gyges was handsome, therefore without
    blame.
Her husband, though, who'd brought on her
    such shame,
On him fell all her hate, which was immense.
For to be a husband's an offense

Itself, and any sin he may commit
Can bring the penalty of death with it.
The queen's in love with Gyges now; the
    king she does detest,
A cuckold in the catalogue along with all the
    rest.
A distinction few strive to acquire, but which
    he sure does merit
Because of his stupidity. He'll have to grin
    and bear it
And be best buddies with the husband of
    adulterous Venus—
It's Vulcan I'm alluding to, the model of the
    genus.
That was bad enough but now the Fate who
    cuts the thread
Has her scissors out for him, and soon he
    will be dead.
The lovers a dire plot have hatched:
To Hades is the king dispatched;
It was poison sent him there.
Henceforth is Gyges free to stare
To his content on beauty bare,
And satisfy his fond desire.
Whether by her love or ire
He's now installed, in Candaules's stead,
Upon the throne and in her bed.
Of this tale I have no more to say.
It is well known, yet in a striking way
It fits in well with my design,
The moral back in my first line:
"Many have been the instrument of their
    own destruction."
The story coming up will offer us the same
    instruction.
Although the first I do admit
Perhaps could do as well as it.
This scene's the town of Rome we know,
Not the Rome of long ago—
That sad, severe, and cheerless place
From which were exiled love and grace—
But the city of today
A lovely, charming place to stay,
Where life is lived in modern fashion:
All one thinks about is passion.
If you're twenty-five or so
That's the place where you should go.
Recently in Rome there lived a master in
    that art

That on "mine" and "yours" finds its founda-
    tion in large part,
By which I mean the law, of which posses-
    sion is nine-tenths:
A man who loved to mock and always put in
    his two cents
And often found diversion at another one's
    expense.
Professing jurisprudence,
He had among his students
One from France who was, he saw,
More apt to study love than law.
One day the lad looked out of sorts.
"Reading Bartolo on torts,"
The prof said, "when school's not in session
Is not with you a big obsession,
Though I'm surprised a guy like you
Doesn't have a girl or two.
After all, you come from France
Don't you just live to seek romance?
Rome's not short on girls, nor you on skill.
Here, the Lord be praised, you'll have your
    fill."
"Rome," the student said, "is new to me.
But it seems, as far as I can see,
Apart from those who charge
The choice just isn't large.
Fellows looking for some action
Don't seem here to get much traction.
How can a guy have any fun
When each girl's penned up like a nun?
Double locks on every door.
Frowning matrons mind the store;
Guards and husbands, eagle-eyed,
Keep close watch on those inside.
Success for me will not come soon;
I might as well wish for the moon."
"The honor that you do our city
Is unmerited. I pity
Boys from out of town like you
Who've no idea what they should do.
It's not as hard as you presume.
Cease to dwell in gloom and doom.
Know that we have wives galore
Who'll trick their husbands, and what's more
Will do it right beneath the eyes
Of their husbands' loyal spies.
You have but to hang the sign
And then, my friend, you'll do just fine.

Go to church and by the holy water take
    your place.
When a lovely lady comes you offer some
    with grace
On your fingertips, by which gesture she will
    know
That you seek adventure. If she plans then to
    bestow
Her favors on your person, she'll be sure to
    send you word.
She'll find out your address although it's one
    she's never heard.
An old decrepit dame who is well versed in
    the lore
Of lovers and their secrets will come knock-
    ing at your door.
She'll take charge of setting up a private ren-
    dezvous.
So you see, it's in the bag; that's all you have
    to do.
Except there's something else that I really
    have to mention:
The women here in Rome demand you give
    your full attention
To the task at hand.
By that, please understand
Although in France I'm told that women
    love flirtatious chatter
The women here get to the point; the rest
    just doesn't matter.
Signoras' appetite is such
They'll work you half again as much
As you're used to back at home."
"I'm sure I'll like it here in Rome.
I would not be bragging if I said
I am pretty good in bed."
He may not have really been—
Boasting's such a widespread sin.
The counsel the professor gave was good:
To the church in which the young man stood
The prettiest signoras of all Rome came
    every day:
Graces, Aphrodites, female angels on dis-
    play.
Beneath their veils were dazzling eyes that
    gave off sparks of fire.
The place he chose was fortunate, so much
    there to admire.
To every lady passing by

The student sweetly gave the eye.
With reverence he bowed, and with devotion
He offered water in a sweeping motion.
One angel took the water with a grace especially fine.
The student said within his heart, "I know she will be mine."
He went home; the go-between arranged the rendezvous.
How it turned out in each detail I needn't go all through.
Suffice to say he did his duty
Many times to this fair beauty.
With everything that transpired his professor he regaled.
I fear discretion is a virtue that the French have failed
To see the virtue of, and consequently see no flaw

In telling of their triumphs—modesty is so *bourgeois*.
The teacher felt that some congratulation
Was due to him because the education
He gave the youth had yielded such good fruit.
Besides, he thought dumb husbands were a hoot!
"Shepherds have a hundred lambs to guard,"
He said, "but husbands seem to find it hard
To guard just one! It's difficult, I know,
But not impossible, as such things go.
Although I do not have a hundred eyes
And though she might some subtlety devise
I'd defy my wife to get away
With a trick like that one any day."
You'll not find it easy to believe,
Dear reader, that the wife you saw deceive
Her husband in the way that I've just shown

"The sight of him brought mirth to all the class" (Duplessis-Bertaux).

With the youth was the professor's own.
The worst was that the more that he found
   out
About her, then the less that he could doubt,
As his pupil told him of the hidden charms
Of the woman he had held within his arms
And the things the two of them had done in
   bed,
That the wife in question was the one he'd
   wed.
Though there was one detail that held him
   back,
It was that he assumed that she must lack
A certain talent that came in for praise
When the student told of all the ways
That she amused the lad in bed.
To himself the jurist said:
"She's never done that one for me
So I think that I am free
To think that it cannot be her,
Which is of course what I'd prefer.
The other points, though, coincide.
The question is hard to decide.
At home my wife will only dream,
While this one talks on in a stream
Of vivacious words and wit.
It really does not seem to fit.
Yet the figure, the face, and the hair are the
   same."
So back to the other position he came.
After swinging to and fro
He concluded, alas, that it was so.
That he was enraged you can understand.
"Is there a second meeting planned?"
"The first one went so well we thought we'd
   have another go."
The prof approved. What was her name?
   The student didn't know.
"But what's it matter? She makes me so glad.
Her husband, let me tell you, has been had.
If there's anything that we've left out
We will get to it next time, no doubt.
Tomorrow we're to meet.
It will be so sweet.
At a time and place I will be led
To a room where she awaits in bed,
A field of battle where it's meet and right
For lovers to pursue their kind of fight.
Not in some attic filled with gloom

But in a clean and gilded room.
Last time I was taken down a hall
Where no light of day came in at all.
The crone then led me to a place
Replete with love's delights and grace.
Take my word—I swear it's true."
Imagine what was going through
That professor's worried head.
But to go himself instead
Was the plan he now devised.
He wanted her to be surprised,
So surprised that for years to come
People would speak of what he had done.
Yet silence would have been a better plan.
It's better just to take it like a man
And then await the place and time
When best to avenge the crime.
Once a wife has brought a husband to the
   cuckold's state
There's nothing he can do, because by then it
   is too late.
He did not agree.
He was in error, as we'll see.
This legal eagle yet believed
Something still could be achieved,
Something saved from this disaster
If the student now his master
(Having sponsored his admission
In accordance with tradition
To the ranks of cuckolds grim)
Were replaced in bed by him:
The cuckoldry might be reversed.
But who's to say he'd been the first?
Was she as pure as driven snow?
He went, hoping no one would know
That he went in the other's place,
In silence and with hidden face.
Alas, things did not come out right.
The old crone had with her a light.
Though he was learnèd in the law
She knew who it was she saw,
Cleverer than he by far;
That's the way those old crones are.
Unfazed, she said to him, "Wait there.
I'll let her know, for I don't dare
To let you in her room unless
She's warned. Meantime, you must undress.
That's the right attire
For what will soon transpire."

After this he was propelled
Into a room where he beheld
Nightgown, bathrobe, laid out neat;
Nightcap, slippers for the feet,
Colognes and perfumes of the best—
As if for an honored guest.
He took his clothes off, now was stark
Naked, stumbling in the dark.
By her hand the crone assisted
Him along a path that twisted
Till at last they found the door.
She pushed him in. He stood before
His students in the school of law.
They all started to guffaw
When they saw him enter nearly nude.
Had their law professor come unglued?

Had he just come from some lusty lass?
The sight of him brought mirth to all the
    class.
The news ran throughout Rome
Meanwhile, back at home
The scandal caused his wife to file a suit
Claiming that her spouse was dissolute.
Her relatives joined in, said he was mad;
It was his fault that things turned out so bad.
The marriage was dissolved; she left to enter
An institution known to be a center
For rituals of a very private sort,
Where prelates sometimes show up to
    cavort.
She became a kind of nun
Where she could really have some fun.

9. "Putting the Devil in Hell"

A fellow afraid of love, I'd say,
When he sees a girl should run away.
I'm not a very daring guy;
I've been burnt, so I'm twice shy.
Girls have power in their eyes:
A fellow languishes, and dies.
We're helpless while they have their fun:
Courtship's too great a risk to run.
As proof, I'll tell you of a beauty
Who made a monk forget his duty.
This one's joy was genuine
Except for this: it was a sin.
I must say I was annoyed
By the woman who enjoyed
A cooling drink, and then could say,
"What delight this could convey
If it were a sin as well!"
Against that thought I do rebel
For sin should not be part of pleasure
Added in for extra measure.
One should always fear its taint,
Even if one is a saint.
Truer words were never spoken.
This monk his vows would not have broken
Had he had a healthy fear
And not permitted to come near
That girl so simple and so nice
For whom he fell within a trice.

Alibech, as I believe,
Was her name. She was naive.
One thing she read, and took to heart:
That saints had lived their lives apart,
Far from the world and its distractions;
Solitude had its attractions.
They lived like angels in the wild,
Which seemed romantic to the child.
"I sure would like," she said one day,
"To live my life in just that way."
So fixed was she upon this goal,
She left and did not tell a soul.
Nor mom nor sister nor friends knew,
For this girl did not bid adieu.
She journeyed at a steady pace,
Never stopping in one place,
Until she came upon a wood
Where an old man's cabin stood.
He may once have had some vigor;
Now he cut a sadder figure,
Just skin and bones and looking tired.
"Sir," she said, "I've been inspired
To be a saint and have my day
When folks would think of me and pray.
O what pleasure it would be
If each year they'd offer me
Flowers and presents as I'd stand
With a palm branch in my hand

And a halo on my head.
Tell me of the life you've led:
Is it hard to be a saint?
I can fast till I feel faint;
That's one talent I have got."
"Girl, give up that foolish thought,"
Said he. "I tell you as a friend,
Saintliness does not depend
On something anyone can do.
God save the girls, and women too,
Who fast and yet no virtue gain.
If you would saintliness obtain
They're other things that you must do,
Plus virtues that I never knew,
But which a hermit in this wood
Will teach you better than I could.
Go see him now, for it's not right
For you to be within my sight."
Saying this, he left her there,
Shut and locked his door with care.
This was wise to do, no doubt,
Trusting neither age nor gout,
Hairshirt nor fasting to prevent
Thoughts her presence would have lent.
Not far from there our saint did find
The hermit he had had in mind.
This one his soul in God invested,
Though of faith as yet untested;
Rustick was the young saint's name.
Alibech to his door came.
Briefly did the girl acquaint
Him with her urge to be a saint,
An urge so pressing in her case
One day her child might bear the trace.
(She didn't seem to know, he thought,
Exactly how a child was got.)
Smiling at her innocence,
He said, "Though my experience
And knowledge of this trade is small,
You are welcome to it all.
The little that I have I'll share,
As you for sainthood I'll prepare."
He in judgment sure was lacking
Not to send this pupil packing.
Look what came of his mistake.
He had tried his soul to make
Perfect as a soul could be.
He prayed with assiduity,
Made vigils, fasted, and—this hurt—

Often wore a rough hair shirt.
"But," thought he, "that's not enough.
Saints are made of sterner stuff.
Now to hold fast to my duty
When alone with some young beauty
And my innocence preserve
Would great recompense deserve.
Such triumph only angels know;
It's unheard of here below.
I'll let her stay, for if I might
Resist her charms I'd reach the height
Of purity that I so crave."
He let her stay—which was quite brave,
For he'd do battle with two foes:
The Devil and the flesh. What woes
Those two enemies can cause!
Such a prospect should give pause.
From rushes Rustick made a bed,
A better place to lay her head,
In her novice situation,
Unaccustomed to privation,
Than the hard, unyielding floor.
For supper, all he had in store
Was some fruit and bread so old
It was showing signs of mold.
To drink, just water, with no wine.
Yet her appetite was fine.
He didn't eat; when she had fed
She thought it time to go to bed.
Alibech on her cot slept
While he tormented vigil kept.
Though he tried his very best
The Devil gave his mind no rest.
A serpentine demonic beast
Demanded entrance to the feast.
He let him in only to find
That Alibech obsessed his mind.
The lovely lines of her young face
Her innocence, her girlish grace,
The charming manners he'd observed,
Her figure, and the way it curved,
And especially a breast
Which it seemed did never rest,
Moving here and moving there,
It pushed against her underwear
Despite her efforts to restrain it,
Within her corset to contain it.
It had a mind all of its own
And spoke in an enticing tone

In its own peculiar fashion.
Our poor Rustick, moved by passion,
Meditated on this text.
The hairshirt he abandoned; next,
His whip, and then all piety.
Banned from the society
Of saints, he headed for her bed.
"Wake up," he said, "you sleepyhead.
To go to sleep so soon's not good.
I think before you do we should
Do what pleases God so well:
Emprison Satan in his hell.
It was for that he was created.
Let's proceed." His purpose stated,
Rustick slipped into her bed.
Puzzled by what he'd just said,
Knowing nothing of this rite,
She did not put up a fight.
Halfway forced and halfway willing,

She her own desire fulfilling,
In the end, she was content,
Feeling like a penitent.
Quite humbly now she thanked the friar
For letting her this way acquire
The lesson she now knew so well:
What was the devil and his hell.
Henceforth, if sainthood she would know
Martyrdom was the way to go.
She'd left virginity behind.
Martyrs, not virgins, were the kind
Of saints that Rustick here would make.
She'd not again make that mistake.
She'd still not quite her lesson learned,
Because she said, "The Devil's earned
The name he has for raising hell:
He's broken things inside his cell.
Just look! Not that I would complain.
In fact, he should come back again."

"He headed for her bed" (Duplessis-Bertaux).

"So be it," Rustick then replied.
And such loving care supplied
That in the end hell came to yearn
For Satan often to return,
If that was all right with the friar.
"But yet I fear that one will tire
—At least," she said, "so I've heard tell—
Of even the softest prison cell."
Soon she'd reason to complain:
The cell its inmate called in vain.
The devil could no longer hear.
Hell was now devoid of cheer.
As was she, who now did seem
No longer of sainthood to dream.
Rustick no longer, for his part,
Wanted sainthood to impart.
Soon she left all on her own,
Furtively, and quite alone,
Returning home the shortest way.
I'd love to know what she did say
To her parents, to explain.
No doubt she said she'd hoped to gain
A saintly crown, but now she knew
It's something that one cannot do.
Her parents took her at her word—
Or seemed, for it may have occurred
To them that that which she called hell
Had suffered damage. Yet the cell

Is dark; its jailors often fail
To know the truth about their jail.
Alibech was wined and dined.
From simplicity of mind
She her closest friends did tell
The mystery of Satan's hell.
"You didn't need," they said, "to roam
All that far away from home.
That secret lesson can be taught
Not ten paces from this spot."
"My brother," one said, "I'd have lent."
"Or my cousin I'd have sent,"
Said another. "And what's more,
There's Néherbal who lives next door.
He is very qualified.
Besides, he wants you for his bride.
Accept his hand in marriage now
Before he learns of this somehow."
And so his wife she did become.
The dowry was a tidy sum;
The groom was also pleased because
She was pretty, while the flaws
Of her hell remained unknown.
With such grace as was here shown,
The gifts of Marriage let's employ.
God grant to all such wedded joy,
Just as in that desert cell:
He his devil, she her hell.

10. "The Farmer and His Mare"

Father Jean was a priest
Who seldom preached save at a feast.
When he was inspired by wine
Then he sermonized just fine;
Then his triumph was divine,
An angel's voice in paradise.
He had another favorite vice,
Which I'll forbear to mention here,
But whose sense no doubt is clear
To the readers of today.
For this, to Father Jean's dismay,
The opportunities were rare.
Father Jean would often share
His knowledge and sagacity.
Indeed, in this capacity
Wives and husbands came to see

Father Jean for his advice.
He also found it very nice
To direct the spiritual life
Of each young and eager wife.
He found this easier and quicker
Than to trust it to the vicar.
A good shepherd knows his sheep,
And faithfully his rounds will keep.
Those on whom he liked to call
Included Farmer Pierre. Though all
This good man had in rents and lands
Were his strong back and his two hands,
Plus a hoe, with which he tried
For his household to provide.
He had a wife who wasn't bad,
Young and pretty; though she had

"Next, to hills somewhat more grand" (Eisen).

A weathered face, what remained
Was still firm, and well maintained.
That rustic sort is not my type,
But country curates do not gripe
Nor turn their noses up at dishes
Such as these. Indeed their wishes
Find their consummation here.
Father Jean when she was near
Would always give a sidelong glance,
As a dog awaits the chance
To grab a juicy-looking bone
And chew on it when he's alone.
He devoured her with his eyes;
His passion he did not disguise.
Yet she was quite innocent
And didn't know what it all meant:
Neither his attentive look,
Nor the pains he often took
To bring her gifts, bouquets of flowers.
These were beyond her modest powers
Of comprehension—might as well
Have used a foreign tongue to tell
The things these gestures couldn't say.
But Father Jean thought of a way.
Pierre was, frankly speaking, dumb,
About as stupid as they come.
"Pierre," he said, "one can't refute
The fact that you are destitute.
But if for you I did a thing
That made you happier than a king,
What would you give me in return?
What gratitude would this gift earn?"
"If you could do what you propose,"
The farmer said, "you could dispose
As you wish of all I have.
My wife's milk cow is soon to calve;
Our pig has now grown very fat:
I'd gladly give you all of that."
"I'd want no pay for this good deed,
Just to help a friend in need.
Here's what I propose to do.
Magdeleine I'll turn into
A mare by day, by magic spell,
Then the wife you know so well
She'll become again at night.
Your profit will be far from slight:
The ass on which you now depend
Is slow, the market's at its end
By the time that he arrives.

You cannot sell your beans or chives,
Your cabbage, garlic, or your peas.
But with a mare you could with ease.
And the mare your wife would make
Would be sure-footed, no mistake.
When she returned at end of day,
No bread or soup, but just some hay
Is all you'd need to feed the beast."
"You sure are a learnèd priest.
That's what it means to go to college.
I wish that I could buy such knowledge."
"I'll teach you what you have to do,
The formula, the gestures too.
All the magic incantation
That brings about the transformation.
She'll be a good, strong breeding mare.
There's just one thing you must beware:
Your silence must be absolute,
Else the charm will not take root.
And later, never say a word
About whatever has occurred.
Your lips are sealed, though you will see,
And afterwards do just like me."
The farmer promised he'd keep mum.
"Magdeleine," the priest said, "come.
You must remove all of your clothes.
Do not your will to ours oppose.
Take off your sleeves and now your skirt;
Remove your petticoat and shirt."
She began to blush with shame.
She said she'd rather stay the same
And the change to mare forego
If it meant she had to show
Her nakedness, so she said "No!"
Pierre inquired, "What's the big deal?
You've merely yourself to reveal,
Then we'll know how you appear
As God made you. What's to fear?"
Then he said, "Don't make a fuss.
You know, my wife, it's only us."
But still she seemed quite ill at ease.
"But when, my dear, you look for fleas
What do you do? Why, you discard
Each stitch you have. Is it so hard
To do the same for this good cause?
Is it the priest who gives you pause?
But Father Jean's a family friend.
He won't bite. Let's put an end
To all this haggling, anyhow.

He could have finished up by now."
He then took off his wife's clothes
And put his glasses on his nose
To watch the progress of the plan.
By the belly Jean began.
"May a mare's chest here come forth!"
He said, while moving farther north.
Then his hands moved east and west,
As each embraced a generous breast.
Next, to hills somewhat more grand
Located in a distant land
He now turned his close attention.
It's a place we will not mention
By its name, for we revere
All within that hemisphere.
At each spot the priest would pause
And he would intone the clause
About how every feature there
Should become part of a mare—
The back, the breasts, the flanks, the thighs.
All this passed before Pierre's eyes,
Who thought it seemed to take too long.
Was there something going wrong?
He made a prayer to God to hurry
Up the change; it made him worry.
But for the magic not to fail
One step remained: to place the tail.
Just an ornament, no doubt,
But one should never leave it out.
Father Jean therefore proceeded
To attach the tail where needed.
Farmer Pierre screamed his dismay.
You could have heard him miles away:
"Don't put the tail on! Oh God, no!
You're attaching it too low!"
But Pierre was not fast enough;

Already Jean had done his stuff—
Or would by then have done, at least,
Except that Pierre tugged at the priest,
Who said to him, "You bloody fool.
Don't you see you broke the rule?
You must stay quiet, I had said.
But you intervened instead.
You've brought the magic to a halt.
The spell is broken—it's your fault."
Pierre now groaned in desolation.
Magdeleine showed irritation.
She in fact was quite irate.
She said, "You'll never leave the state
Of poverty you're in today.
And then you have the nerve to bray
At me, your poor long-suffering wife,
About the misery in your life.
From the goodness of his heart
He's offering us a fresh new start,
Our gracious pastor Father Jean,
A way to make our woes be gone.
And this he would do for free.
But you, my husband, just don't see.
You don't deserve, you loser, you,
All the good that this would do.
Father Jean, pay him no mind.
Tomorrow morning you will find
Me most willing to be turned
Into the mare that he has spurned.
While my husband's occupied
In getting all his onions tied
Come on by and cast your spell,
That voodoo you do so well.
Pierre said, "No more mare, alas.
I'll be contented with my ass."

11. "Eel Pâté"

Change is a prerequisite,
For beauty, even exquisite,
Will, lacking variety,
Lead to stale satiety.
I need more than one kind of bread:
White, whole wheat—or rye instead.
Sometimes I am really fickle
And yearn for some pumpernickel.

Variety's the spice, you see.
Try it. It sure works for me.
That girl with a dark complexion
Stirs in me a strong affection.
Now why is that? Because she's new.
While that one, of a lighter hue,
Whom I conquered long ago:
Her heart says yes, but mine says no.

"Must I eat it every day?" (Fragonard).

Why is this? It's clear to me:
Variety's the spice, you see.
I've said it in another place,
But I still like a change of pace.
So too did a certain guy
Whose wife was nice, but by and by
His flame flickered and went out
Because of boredom, I don't doubt,
Caused by marriage and possession.
There was nothing there to freshen
Passion, so he soon was cured
Of the love he'd once averred.
His valet's wife was rather cute.
The master, sly and dissolute,
Soon added her to his collection;
The valet plunged into dejection.
He had caught them in the act
And felt his rights had been attacked.
"She belongs to me," he said.
So too did the marriage bed.
His wife and he began a feud;
The names he called her were quite rude.
He was wrong to make a stink
Over that, is what I think—
God preserve us from much worse.
He preached a sermon, chapter and verse,
To his master: "To each his own.
You should leave my wife alone.
God and Reason are agreed;
You should make this rule your creed.
Do you think you have no spouse?
The lovely wife inside your house
Is worth a hundred wives like mine.
The honor you bestow's too fine.
A gentleman as grand as you
She doesn't need. What we should do
Is draw our water from the well
We each have been assigned. I tell
You, if I'd a wife like yours—
And I'm sure that connoisseurs
Will back me up in what I say—
If God had sent your wife my way,
I wouldn't change her for a queen.
But since I cannot contravene
What has already taken place
I simply wish you'd have the grace
To be content with what you own
And leave my darling wife alone."
His master did not let him know

Whether he agreed or no,
But told his staff it was his wish
That the valet's favorite dish
Be served to him at meals each day.
It was a dish called eel pâté.
The first and second times he ate
He thought it tasted really great.
But when the third time came as well
He found he couldn't stand the smell.
For something else he reached his hand
But was prevented. By command
Of his master, the valet
Could have no dish but eel pâté.
"Just stick with that one, I'd suggest.
Why complain? You like it best."
"I've had my fill," said the valet.
"Must I eat it every day?
For me it has no more appeal.
Could I at least have *roasted* eel?
Or some other dish instead?
If not, I'd rather just have bread—
Some of yours, if you don't mind.
By hell or heaven I must find
Bread or something else to eat.
I fear that when my life's complete
And I am lying in my tomb
I will still have to consume
Yet again some eel pâté."
His master then came by to say,
"My friend, I frankly am surprised
That a dish you highly prized,
That is so good and tasty too,
Should seem distasteful now to you.
Did you not say the other day
Your favorite dish was eel pâté?
It seems to me a little soon
For one like you to change his tune.
But in my case you'd lots to say
When you viewed with such dismay
My giving up what you thought tasty.
You, it seems, have been more hasty
Than I was. But learn from me
That it's not stupidity
For those who have the appetite
To substitute brown bread for white.
Variety's the spice, you see."
After this soliloquy,
The valet felt somewhat consoled,
And yet at the same time was bold

Enough to put in his word, too:
"Should the only aim in view
Be one's private search for pleasure?
Change is good, but spend some treasure
To persuade the ones concerned."
This suggestion was not spurned,
For the master tried it out.
Using golden words, no doubt,
They say he like an angel spoke.
When I golden speech evoke,
My sense to everyone is clear;
Each will know just what I mean:
When gold appears upon the scene,
As I've often said before,
It can open every door.
It persuades the demoiselle,
Her maid, her little dog as well—
Everyone within the house.
Sometimes that even means the spouse.
In the present instance, he
Needed winning over, see?
And he was the only one.
Soon some gold the trick had done,
For the valet was not blind
To seduction of that kind.

One's often left without defense
Against that kind of eloquence.
Cato and Demosthenes
Had no golden words like these.
Having started out defiant,
Our jealous husband turned compliant.
They even say that he became
One never happy with the same
Object of lustful devotion,
Converted to his master's notion
That it did behoove a man
To have a short attention span.
From then, all one ever heard
Was of adventures that occurred
In the valet's new career.
He was now quite cavalier,
Ever longing to pursue
Objects that were always new.
Whether amateurs or pros,
The girls and women whom he chose,
In every one he took delight
As he fed his appetite,
Reveling in diversity.
Variety's the spice, you see.

12. "The Eyeglasses"

I'd give up nuns, I'd said before,
Because there is an ample store
Already in the tales you've read.
They're other things you'd like instead
Of nuns to hear of in a tale.
No doubt such sameness can grow stale.
But, you see, I can't refuse
What is given by my muse.
I'm afraid it's just this simple:
All she's given me is wimple.
(Wimple, should you care to know,
Is the cloth designed to go
Like a veil beside the face;
Nuns wear it with becoming grace.)
Wimple here, wimple there,
Wimple, wimple everywhere.
My muse provides more than enough.
What can I do with all this stuff
Except to tell yet one more tale

Of what goes on behind the veil?
But if I must tell tales like these
I want nuns with expertise
In the finer points of lust.
Someone now may say, "But must
The subject be exhausted thus?"
To which I say: preposterous!
Of nuns there is so much to say
I'd write forever and a day,
Except of course I really think
That first I would run out of ink.
If I attempted to refrain
Some case might send me back again,
Some case of convent love, perhaps,
Would cause me to once more relapse.
I'll speak no more of any nun
Once the present story's done.

A fellow once of fifteen years

Passed for a girl, so it appears,
Thanks to his so far beardless chin,
And thus was able to get in
A convent, taken for a nun.
Among the nuns he soon found one
Who shared his taste for having fun.
She profited as well as he
From their liaison, but she
Found the profit in her case
Became a thing more like disgrace.
She found that she'd enlarged her girth;
Subsequently she gave birth
To a child who was the spitting
Image (as of course was fitting)
Of the nun who was its dad.
The consequence was very bad.
The convent's nuns were all atwitter:
Whence had come this little critter?

This darling little *champignon*
Did not get here all on its own.
Amid ensuing wild turmoil,
"Who has dared our name to soil?"
Demanded the prioress, irate.
Jail became the mother's fate,
But still the prioress had to know
Who was the man who'd done her so.
How did he come? How did he go?
Twice-locked the gate, and high the wall,
The gatekeeper ancient, the opening small.
Could it be a boy in a girl's disguise?
A wolf who would our sheep surprise?
Wanting to get to the bottom of this,
And to test out her hypothesis,
The prioress issued to all the command
To remove their clothes and nakedly stand.
This posed a problem for one of the sheep,

"Our young man, amid such splendor" (Duplessis-Bertaux).

Who did not see how he could keep
His gender a secret if he were nude.
As his options he reviewed,
He thought perhaps that if he tied it
With some luck he might could hide it.
What "it" was, I fear to say.
Let's see if I can find a way:
In ancient times the human race
Had in the trunk an open space,
A window through which one could read
What was within, which served a need
For doctors practicing their art.
But a window on the heart
Was not so good, the women thought.
It spoiled the privacy they sought.
Mother Nature, always wise,
A good solution did devise.
Two drawstrings did she provide,
To close it up, should one decide.
Both men and women had this right
But women laced theirs very tight.
A bit too much, but still they thought
Things weren't as hidden as they ought.
Men laced theirs the other way:
Loosely, leaving in some play.
This difference between one sex
And the other did perplex
Mother Nature: it seemed wrong
That men's excess should be so long
While that of women was so short.
It's easy now to guess the sort
Of thing he tied to not be seen,
The excess part of the machine.
With some thread he tied up that
In such a way it seemed as flat
As any nun's. But bear in mind
That thread or silk or any kind
Of bridle never could contain
That which he tried to restrain.
I fear that it will escape
And assume a different shape.
Bring me angels, bring me saints:
Theirs would break from their restraints
Unless they were unusual creatures
When they saw the lovely features
Of the twenty nuns assembled,
Who the Graces so resembled:
Charms the sun has never spied
Save upon the other side

Of the ocean, where they say
Naked tribes are on display.
To peer at them without their clothes,
The prioress put on her nose
Her glasses, for a better view.
Think of the torture he went through,
Our young man, amid such splendor
Served up by the female gender.
He could not help but observe
Each secret charm, each flowing curve,
Fine proportion, swelling breast,
Luscious skin, and all the rest.
Those secret beauties, suddenly seen,
Set in action the machine.
It escapes, breaks the thread;
Like a stallion, shakes its head.
Then it rears and up it goes,
Strikes the prioress on the nose,
Sending those eyeglasses flying
To the ceiling. No denying
The prioress, who almost fell
Herself was now as mad as ... Well,
Let's just say she was provoked.
The convent's chapter was convoked,
The event discussed by all the nuns.
It was ruled the older ones
Would at the faker have first crack.
Tied to a tree, they bared his back
And all of his anatomy.
They savored this with godless glee.
One ran in to fetch a broom;
Another found whips to the arsenal room;
A third put under lock and key
Young nuns who might show sympathy.
Thus on the victim fate did smile,
Postponing punishment a while.
While they were gone along came by
A miller on a mule, a jolly guy
Who delighted in women's company.
"Oho!" he said. "What's this I see?
It's rather funny and very quaint,
A peculiar way to martyr a saint.
Young man, who put you in this fix?
Have those nuns been up to tricks?
Or have you undone a nun?
Was she pretty? Was it fun?
For you seem to be the sort
Who with sisters loves to sport."
"Just the opposite," he said.

"It's me they want to get in bed.
God give me patience to get through
This trial, for that I'd never do.
My scruples forbid such a thing,
I would not, even for the king.
To their appeals I will prove cold,
Were it worth my weight in gold."
The miller laughed, untied the rope,
And then said, "You utter dope!
You have scruples? You're a serf!
Things like that are more *our* turf!
Our curate wouldn't be that dumb.
I'll take your place and get me some.
You're not suited to such work.
I'll ask no quarter, no task shirk.
Bring on the nuns; I'll do 'em all.
It looks like we will have a ball."
Hearing it once was good enough;
He tied him to the tree and said, "I'm off!"
The big-shouldered fellow, now stripped
   bare,
Awaited joys that he'd find there.
The squadron arrived, in solemn procession
With whips and rods in their possession.
As they passed, each struck a blow
Preventing him from letting them know
He wasn't the man they took him for,
Toward whom those nuns such malice bore.
"Mesdames," he said, "just wait a sec.
Your conduct here is not correct.
Take a closer look at me.
I am not that enemy
Of the fair sex, that nincompoop
So full of scruples he won't stoop

To satisfy female desire.
Try me out. I never tire.
Cut my ears off if I lie.
For you-know-what you may rely
On me. But take those whips away.
That's a game I will not play."
"Whatever is he talking about?"
One of the toothless crones cried out.
"You mean you're not our baby-maker?
Too bad. You'll still pay for that faker.
We've not gathered here today,
With weapons, just to stop halfway.
We'll play the game we've come to play."
The whips and rods now came back out.
The nuns bore down; he tried to shout
In terms that would be understood,
Just as plainly as he could,
"If that's what you want to do
Then I'm your man: I can scru ...
ple you with the best.
Just put me to the test."
The more he spoke along that vein,
The more they strove to cause him pain;
The memory would long remain.
While the miller was getting whipped
The mule in the meadow happily skipped.
What became of either I know not;
I've not given it much thought.
It's enough to have saved the youngster's skin
From the wages of his sin.
None of my readers would want to trade
Places with him in this escapade,
Even if they were in the mood
To see those sisters in the nude.

13. "Convincing Kate"

Fresh-baked biscuits, soft and warm
Are great, but they don't have the charm
Of my Kate's white and satiny breast,
Which one fine morning I caressed.
I'm fonder of them than any food
But she wasn't in the mood.
"Let your rooster roost elsewhere,"
She said to me, "for I don't care."
She hoped that she might hold out long,
But my desire was getting strong.

I was in a narrow strait,
Hoping for a better fate.
So asked again, but nothing got.
The more I tried, the more she fought.
Struggling, I tried to say
In a rather plaintive way,
"Alas, poor me! in such a fix!
The boatman of the River Styx
Is calling me and I must go.
Yet still you want to treat me so!

Don't be mean and cruel to me.
I'm your humble captive, see?
My body's yours, liver and spleen."
"Thanks," she said, "but I'm not keen
On what you offer. When it comes to
    wooing
I want one who knows what he's doing."
"I swear," I said, "and certify
That I hope one day, by and by,
I'll see your defenses fail;
Then I your fortress walls will scale.
The god of Love has up his sleeve
Many tricks, so don't believe
Your heart is safe from every harm.
He's flexing even now his arm
And you, I fear, will feel its force.
Contempt is not the wisest course."
"You've misconstrued," she said, "my
    thought.
I don't doubt I will be caught
In Love's subtle traps and snares,
But I'll be taken unawares.
Not for a fortune—no, I wouldn't
Do a thing I know I shouldn't.
So if you would, please go away
And put an end to our affray.
"To use," I said, "a vain excuse
When one could make better use
Of an opportunity
Is to err most terribly.

When one won't participate,
Second thoughts will come too late.
But the man who is rejected
Never will stay long dejected.
He will be a real go-getter
And find something even better,
Somewhere else—hence this thought:
Strike the iron while it is hot.
Vain clamors are not attributes
Of my amorous pursuits.
Flowers and roses are my style;
Such nice things often beguile.
Soon enough come tears and pain
For lost time one can't regain.
In pleasant pastimes therefore spend
Your lovely days before they end."
Thus did I preach to pretty Kate
With the aim to motivate
Her to ler her heart grow fonder
And to let my fingers wander.
It was by lover's right I took
That liberty; a sexy look
In her eyes now seemed to say:
"Lover, you may seize the day."
I clearly heard it, for no man
Can pay attention like I can
To the voice within those eyes.
As for the rest, I will apprise
The reader of this humble rhyme
In more detail some other time.

14. "The Tub"

Be a lover, if you would be clever:
Trick or ruse or stratagem you'll never
Lack; the novice wet behind the ears
Once he loves is wise beyond his years.
The desire to court
Won't come up short
Should on invention its success depend.
Love always gets its way in the end.
There's a tale of a tub I know
That shows just how this is so.
In some little country town
Whose name has earned such weak renown
There's no point in giving it now
Lived a cooper who got by somehow

And his wife—Anne was her name.
The god of Love to their house came
With Cuckoldry, his special friend.
Rich or poor the house, they'll condescend
To make themselves at home, and bivouac
Whether it's a mansion or a shack.
Thus it happened at the cooper's house
That a man caressed the cooper's spouse.
They had reached a point in their caressing
When interruption would be most distress-
    ing.
Because, you see, they'd gotten pretty far.
Just then, the husband came home from a
    bar

All breathless with excitement, bearing news.
The precious moments that he made her lose
Did not the cooper to his wife endear.
She had to hide her lover, that was clear.
She led him quickly to the yard outside,
Found a tub and placed the man inside.
"Good news!" the cooper said. "I've found a
  buyer
For our tub." "How much, might I inquire?"
"Fifteen francs." "Such a paltry sum?"
She asked her husband. "That was dumb.
You can thank my skill in trade
For I've come to your aid
And sold that tub already for eighteen.
The buyer at this moment may be seen
Inside his purchase, I expect,
Making sure that all's correct,
Making a piece-by-piece inspection,
Searching for any imperfection,

Running his hand from stem to stern
To see what flaws he might discern.
You'd get nowhere without me.
While you were off drinking, see,
I was hard at work right here.
I've enjoyed till now no cheer,
But rest assured that now I will;
Henceforth I plan to get my fill.
Your liver must be pretty good,
With all the drinking it's withstood.
It's really hard for me to see
How you deserve a wife like me."
"Please, my dear, don't make a stir,"
Said the cooper. "Pardon, sir.
Why don't you come out of there
And I will scrape it with great care
On all sides, and then I'll get
This tub of yours completely wet:
That will prove it's water-tight.

"While he was checking for a crack" (Duplessis-Bertaux).

You will see I've made it right."
The man emerged at his demand;
With a candle in his hand
The cooper scraped the inside clean
While an interesting scene
On the other side occurred,
Which he neither saw nor heard.
While he was checking for a crack,
Love and Cuckoldry came back.
It may be supposed
The task they imposed
On the lovers was a different kind
Than the labor that had been assigned
To the husband in the tub,
Who had to scratch and scrape and rub.
So the lovers now took heart

And each of them resumed the part
He or she had played
Before the cooper'd made
His unannounced return.
You don't need to learn
Exactly what transpired.
All I was required
To do was prove my thesis;
No need for exegesis.
Thanks to the wit that they deployed
Greater pleasure they enjoyed.
Another thing I can report:
Neither was novice at this sport.
I've substantiated my contention:
Love is the mother of invention.

15. "Mission Impossible"

A demon not as bad as he was black
For performing wonders had the knack.
Using what he knew of magic art,
He conquered for a guy a cruel heart.
The contract that the two of them had
    signed
Was somewhat unusual in kind:
He did not become the demon's slave,
But it would be he who orders gave.
The difficulty was, no sooner done
Than he would have to give another one.
The demon would perform that promptly,
    too.
He'd have to think of orders ever new.
This would never stop and never slow;
It would always be exactly so.
If he couldn't think of a command,
His soul and body Satan would demand,
To do with as he wished. The man consented
To this condition, thinking it presented
No special problem, for he thought it easy
To command; the thing that made him
    queasy
Was obeying. Off he went to see
The lady he desired so ardently.
There he tasted pleasures never known,
Except he found that he was not alone;
In this place of amorous enjoyment

The demon was awaiting new employment.
And so the lover to the demon said
Whatever thing would come into his head.
He sent him off to build castles in Spain,
To raise a storm upon the bounding main,
To make his wallet overflow with ducats,
To come from Rome with pardons stuffed in
    buckets.
None of these feats took more than a second;
Meanwhile his inamorata beckoned.
To think of new commands and then still
    more
Was using up his wits; his brain felt sore.
To his mistress he at last complained.
He told her everything, the pact explained.
"So this is why," she asked, "you look for-
    lorn?
Don't worry, I will soon remove that thorn.
When the devil comes, you will display
What I'm holding here, and you will say
Uncurl this for me; take out the kink."
Then she gave him something which I think
Comes from that region known as Venus'
    garden.
I hope that my allusiveness you'll pardon,
But what it was is difficult to name
Without incurring from someone some
    blame.

It's called the fairies' labyrinth as well.
A duke in honor of a demoiselle
Thought up the Order of the Golden Fleece,
Based on a myth that comes from ancient
  Greece,
But also based upon the golden hair
The duke in secret saw his mistress wear.
The lover told the demon, "Take this thread;
It's curved; now make it straight instead.
Get to work and leave us now, I say."
The devil disappeared, and right away
He put the thread beneath a heavy press.
But this effort did not bring success.
He tried with hammer blows to smash it flat,
Then tried soaking; nothing came of that.
Nor of other techniques he applied.
Despite the charms and magic spells he
  tried,
The demon only met with failure still:

He could not make the thread bend to his
  will.
It fought back against the wind and rain;
Snow and fog could not its force restrain.
The more the devil toiled,
The less the thing uncoiled.
"I've had enough.
What is this stuff?"
The demon said at last.
"I really am aghast.
Never in my whole career
Have I seen a thing so queer.
It's something without parallel
To resist the powers of hell.
Any devil would be foiled
By this thread so tightly coiled."
He went back to his master and he said,
"Here it is, your precious little thread.
I give up the task.

"Take this thread" (Duplessis-Bertaux).

The only thing I ask
Is that you tell me what the hell
It is that can resist so well."
"That you quit so soon I do regret,"

The lover said. "They're more come with the
    set.
Because they're just as frizzy
They'd sure have kept you busy.

16. "The Magnificent One"

A dash of mother wit, besides a lot
Of handsomeness of face, and then you've
    got—
When you add a willingness to spend—
Three qualities in gallantry that blend
To form an overwhelming triple threat
That's scaled the heights of many a parapet.
Lofty though they be, they can be taken
And the proud defender's will be shaken.
The victory, I say, goes to the gallant
Who's generous, good-looking, and has tal-
    ent.
Such a man as he will win the prize,
Though sometimes it's won by other guys.
Nevertheless, I'd say that as a rule
It's better not to be an utter fool:
Some intelligence will be required.
The avaricious never are desired;
The ugly on the power of words depend;
But best is he who's not afraid to spend.
All three of these qualities were seen
In Magnifico, a Florentine.
On the battlefield he'd earned the fame
That gave him every right to have that
    name.
As did the way he lived, his courtesy,
The lavish gifts with which he was so free.
He was clean-cut, good-looking, and up-
    right,
Well-dressed, flirtatious, and always polite.
A certain lady caught this fellow's eye.
The social status she enjoyed was high
And she was beautiful, which only doubled
The strong desire by which this man was
    troubled.
As a prize, Madame did nothing lack:
There'd pleasure be, and glory, back to back.
To get around her husband would be hard,
For Aldobrandin kept a careful guard.
If that spouse had had ten thousand eyes,

He'd have used them all as jealous spies.
Yet Arguses like him are often tricked.
This foolish husband thought he could pre-
    dict
That tricked he'd never be, and showed
    defiance.
But Love knows how to counter such reliance.
Apart from this, he was acquisitive,
And thought it better to receive than give.
Till now Magnifico had said no word
That the wife could possibly have heard.
There was, it seemed, no way she could have
    learned
The fire with which his martyred passion
    burned
(The old same song again—it's never new).
And even if she knew, what could he do?
The reader doesn't need for me to say.
To get back to our lover's sad dismay
At his utter inability
To tell the doctor of his malady
(The physician being in this case
The one who made him sick in the first
    place):
His frustration makes him feel tormented;
He paces aimlessly like one demented.
There is no window, not a jalousie
That would allow Magnifico to see
Her beauty, nor her lovely voice to hear;
There'd never been restrictions this severe.
Yet there was a way, and don't you doubt it.
So I'll tell you how he went about it.
I'd said before the husband found it pleasant
To receive (not give!) sometimes a present.
Our gallant had a horse that was endowed
With a gait of which he was quite proud.
He showed it off; the husband was en-
    tranced,
And praised the stallion for the way it pranced.
Our lover cleverly made the suggestion

That he trade for it. "Out of the question,"
Aldobrandin said. "I must refuse
For in such deals I know I always lose.
Although it's true I really like your horse."
Magnifico knew what this meant, of course.
"Since at bartering," he said, "you balk,
The horse is yours if I can have a talk
With your wife; you can be present, too.
It's just a little thing I'd like to do.
Besides, your bosom friends should have
    some kind
Of notion what thoughts dwell within her
    mind.
A quarter-hour is all that I request."
The husband interrupted, feeling stressed.
"And just like that, I'd let you have my wife?"
Aldobrandin cried. "Not on your life!
I don't want your horse at such a price."
"But you'd be present. Wouldn't that suffice?"
"I'd be present?" "That would be the deal.
Nothing bad could happen, don't you feel?
While someone with as sharp an eye as you
Is keeping watch on all we say and do."
The husband now began to meditate;
The thoughts he had soon made him
    vacillate:
"What he says is right, because as long
As I am there, then nothing can go wrong.
I'm sure to gain; the fool is sure to lose.
But just to be more certain I'll refuse
To let my wife say one word in reply,
Although he will not know I've been so sly
As to insert this hidden complication."
He consented. Now a stipulation
Came from the other side in this affair:
"You must place yourself so far from there
That the words we say you cannot hear."
No problem, since it seemed to him quite
    clear,
Thanks to the clause he'd secretly provided,
Their conversation would be quite one-sided.
He went to get his wife; when she arrived
Magnifico's enchantment was revived.
When they'd been introduced, the two
    retired
To a corner of the room, as he'd required.
In chairs they sat; he left out the preamble,
Went straight to the point—no time to
    ramble.

"It's not the hour or place I'd have preferred,
Yet I can say it all in just one word:
Your loveliness has got beneath my skin.
Would responding to that be a sin?
You've too much sense to think it would, I'm
    sure.
If I'd the leisure, doubtless I'd refer
In long detail to my consuming flame,
And of all I've suffered do the same.
But in what would take six months to say
In fifteen minutes now I must convey.
And more than that, because that is not all:
A lover's passion would be rather small
And cold, if he did not go all the way.
But what's this? Have you no word to say?
Is this how you reject a man like me?
God made you divine but I don't see
Why it is you cannot answer prayer.
Oh, I see—your husband over there
Has played a trick on me and will deny
The possibility of a reply.
He will say it wasn't in the deal.
But two can play that game, is what I feel.
I know a way around it. What I'll do
Is supply the answers here for you.
The look from out the corner of your eye
Communicates—to translate I will try.
It says: 'Do not believe I'm made of stone.
All the attentions that to me you've shown,
The serenades, the emblems on your shield,
The tournaments, the jousting in the field,
Are all so many signs of love, I know.
I'm not offended by the love you show.
Far from it, for the arrow that struck you
From Cupid's bow has pierced me through
    and through.
But what can we do?'—What can we do?
Since we are agreed, this very night
Let's taste the fruit that comes from our
    shared plight.
And thus we will repay the jealous zeal
Aldobrandin displays, the imbecile.
We'll laugh at him and take our pleasure hot.
For this, your garden is the perfect spot.
Go there tonight. Don't doubt we will suc-
    ceed.
For I am sure your spouse will feel the need
To try out his new horse at his estate.
While he's in the country and it's late,

And your duennas are all fast asleep,
Come down there our rendezvous to keep.
Get up from your bed and hurry down;
Take nothing with you but a fur-lined gown.
Because there's too much traffic in the street
It will be wiser and much more discreet
For me to come across the neighbor's wall.
I know that he will not object at all,
I've bribed him to come over to our side.
A ladder by the wall I will provide.
So you see, there's nothing you should fear.
'Magnifico, how much I love you, dear!
How gratefully I ratify your plan!
I will come as quickly as I can.'
These are your words. God grant that from
　my seat
I could arise and dare embrace your feet!
'Magnifico, you soon will have that chance

Without the fear of someone's jealous
　glance.'"
He rose and left, pretending to be mad,
And grumbled to her husband, "I've been
　had.
It's not what I had reason to expect:
The words I spoke to her had no effect;
I might as well had been there all alone
Than with that silent woman made of stone.
If you can find more horses at that price,
Then you should buy them—that is my
　advice.
At least the horse I had will whinny at you
Which is not the case with that cold statue.
I've been outmaneuvered by the best.
If someone thinks that he would like the rest
Of the time I've bought, I'll sell it cheap."
The husband laughed so hard he had to weep.

"Their conversation would be quite one-sided" (Duplessis-Bertaux).

"These young whipper-snappers," he then
    said,
"Always have some scheme inside their head.
You gave up too soon, which is too bad.
For with persistence you could well have had
That which you desire. Yet all the same
I'll keep a sharp eye on you in this game.
The horse is mine that had been yours be-
    fore;
You won't need to feed it any more.
Now that our transaction's been completed,
It's on his back that you will find me seated,
Trotting at a comfortable pace
On the road up to my country place."
By nightfall his prediction had come true;
Our lovers likewise made their rendezvous.
To say exactly what that night took place
Would, I think, here take up too much
    space.
She was young and frisky as a kitten,
Beautiful as well, and both were smitten.
Three times they met, each other to possess;
Such a lovely one deserved no less.

They ran no danger, were not interrupted.
Magnifico her guardians corrupted,
Gold and silver keeping them asleep;
A sentinel he hired, close watch to keep.
A cottage in the garden was assigned
By them a use of quite a different kind
Than what Aldobrandin had intended—
Though the new use was, I think, more
    splendid.
He was made a cuckold through and
    through;
With his new horse he found so much to do
That just one day, he thought, would not
    suffice;
He stayed away for three, to be precise.
Unperturbed by any doubt or worry,
He did not see why he should have to hurry.
In this he'd better luck than some, of course,
Who have a wife but do not have a horse.
What's worse is when it happens that one
    knows
What is taking place beneath one's nose.

17. "The Painting"

I've been asked to tell in a decorous way
The tale of one of those paintings we never
    display
But keep behind curtains because they're
    risqué.
Delicate lines must spring from my head
That say certain things yet leave them un-
    said,
And all the same be understood
By innocent girls who've always been good—
Though that's not hard when you bear in
    mind
That such a girl you'll never find.
Catullus said, in ancient Roman days,
That any matron would just love to gaze
Upon the gift Priapus got from Juno,
Which was a very long and large ... well, *you*
    know.
If a lady finds that thing offending,
Then I think that lady is pretending.
Since we allow our sight

Pleasure and delight,
Why then do we fear
To offend the ear?
But since we do, I'll have to try my best
Not to reveal, but only to suggest.
Each and every fine detail
I will cover with a veil.
But nothing will be lost, because
That veil will be of see-through gauze.
Subtle thoughts expressed with grace
May anything at all embrace.
Instances of this abound;
In writing poetry I've found
When a word is well selected
Ladies pardon, not reject it.
An object delicately named
Makes no one to feel ashamed.
No one hushes;
No one blushes.
Yet the meaning is quite clear.
That subtle art's what I'll need here.

"But why," I'm sure someone will ask,
"Such precaution for this task?
Women are not prone to fainting
When they gaze upon a painting."
Ears are chaste, is my reply,
But bold and saucy is the eye.

I come now to the work at hand:
It's a painting, understand.
I must explain to ladies fair
The reason for this broken chair,
And that lout upon the floor.
Muses, help me with this chore.
On second thought, ignore that call.
I forgot, you're virgins all.
Of the game of love, you know
Absolutely nothing. Though
I'd be grateful if you'd ask
Apollo's help with this tough task.
My choice of words requires his aid;
Otherwise I'd be afraid
I'd say what could bring on some chuckles
But get rapped across my knuckles.
This painting tells an episode
That took place at the abode
Of Venus: isle where loves abound.
Near Cythera there once was found,
At the edge of town, a monastery
That the goddess made a seminary.
Nuns in that place did dwell,
But lovers came as well.
From the city and the court
They came in search of amorous sport,
Many a doctor, many a priest.
Among the visitors, not least
For whom the convent was a draw:
Those who studied canon law.
One especially was seen,
Well-spoken, always shaved and clean,
Sheeny hat and spotless collar;
No shame attached to this fine scholar.
The best thing that he had going
Was, two nuns were each bestowing
Charms on him, a welcome guest.
One of them had just progressed
Beyond the novice level, while
The other'd not yet passed that trial.
The first, seventeen years of age,
Had consequently reached the stage

When she a thesis could defend—
One about love, I contend.
Point by point they had been taught
By their guest, who knew a lot.
"Learn by doing," he would say.
It was really best that way.
These two sisters made a date
For him to come—they couldn't wait.
To make the fête especially fine
They'd prepared some food and wine.
Where you Bacchus and Ceres find
Venus won't be far behind.
The crystal goblets were so clean
One's own reflection could be seen.
The table set with style and grace,
All was in its proper place.
Crystal, china, wine on ice,
Flowers to make the room look nice,
In arrangements so designed
They formed letters intertwined,
Initials of each sister's name,
With their lover's, to proclaim
The passion that he could engender.
Cloistered nuns enjoy such splendor.
Their beauty whets the appetites
Of lovers knowing the delights
Their habits hide from most men's eyes.
These two were nearly the same size.
They had fair skin and lovely features;
Well-proportioned, charming creatures,
They were lithe and firm of breast.
Love found a thousand sites to nest
In, here and there, where never sun
Can shine its light upon a nun
Except when lovers lift the veil
So they can view in more detail.
To each sister Venus' son
A thousand times each day would run
With open arms because he thought
She was his mother, whom he sought.
But he had not yet come, their guest;
In fact was late, and this distressed
The two, who started to berate
The absent one for being late.
They had planned to entertain him:
Did some other loves detain him?
Was he too sick to come and sup
Or did some business hold him up?
Said one, "If he should now return

He would have to wait his turn."
While this mystery they pondered
Near their door a servant wandered.
I once told of a Mazet
Who to a convent came to stay,
A man quite up to any task
Who did all the nuns would ask.
I'll call this servant by that name
Because his duties were the same.
This Mazet today was headed
To a nun he'd often bedded;
An older one, who was entrusted
With the convent's keys, and lusted
After what he could provide.
Errands that he ran would hide
The reason he came to her door.
Although he'd come this way before
The door that he by error found
And on which his hands did pound

Was not the one he'd been assigned
(He did not have the keenest mind).
Instead, it opened to the cell
Where our pair of nuns did dwell.
They opened eagerly the door.
They were surprised; they cursed and swore.
Then they saw he was a treasure.
They laughed. One said: "Let's take our
    pleasure
With this doofus. He would be
Just as good, it seems to me.
Did we make all this preparation
Just to hear a fine oration?
Eloquence is over-rated
And is not what we've awaited.
For the aim we have in mind
This rustic bumpkin's worth, I find,
The scholar and his teacher, too."
The judgment that she made was true.

"At the peak / Of her discourse" (Duplessis-Bertaux).

His easy-going ways, his girth,
His witlessness showed them his worth.
He didn't even seem to think;
All he did was eat and drink.
Soon the nuns had made him tame,
Ready for whatever game
They intended that he play,
Their very own private Mazet.
I've filled in the missing parts;
It's at this point the action starts.
Apollo, please don't leave me now.
I'll still need your help somehow.
Tell me why this clod, there seated,
To such blandishments is treated
And lets all the work be done
By one and the other nun.
Would it not have been more fitting
For the sisters to be sitting?
It might have been more debonair
To have let them have the chair.
Ah, but now it seems I see
Lord Apollo telling me:
"Hold on there. It doesn't suit
To make inspection too minute."
I understand. Cupid, that child,
Sometimes gets a little wild.
I was wrong, too late I see,
To let that wicked boy emcee.
Once he's let into a room
Rules and laws will just go "BOOM!"
He runs things by his own whim.
Stuff gets broke? OK by him.
Violence he has in store.
Soon the rustic's on the floor.
The painting does not indicate
If the chair cracked from his weight
Or because it was too weak
Or if it was that at the peak
Of her discourse, fraught with emotion,
Sister Teresa was in motion.
Whatever happened, we do know
The chair did break and he did go
Right to the floor, a rough conclusion
To this stage of the confusion.
Censors, here please keep away.
To those of good will, though, I say:
Sister Claudia, you see,
Turns this sad catastrophe
To her advantage and her profit.

Teresa having fallen off it,
Claudia the tiller took.
Teresa, with demonic look,
Tried to take it back and seat
Herself again, but it seemed sweet
To Claudia to own that throne
To which she'd now accustomed grown,
And to fend her off, resisted.
But watch out! Here's a two-fisted
Nun who is prepared to rumble.
"Bring it on! I will not tumble
From my seat, and will defy
All comers." That's a good reply.
One will when being that lascivious
To all else be quite oblivious.
I'm not surprised she should disdain
For greater good a little pain.
Despite the anger on the face
Of the one who'd lost her place.
Claudia, though, just kept on,
As did the man she sat upon.
Meanwhile, the other nun bemoaned
Her loss; in her distress, she groaned.
Venus' pleasures are delights,
But they often lead to fights.
For example, think of Troy,
Which Greek armies would destroy
In bloody combats that dismay us
All because poor Menelaus
Couldn't hold on to his wife.
That a clod could cause such strife
Between two nuns is no surprise.
You'll see hostilities arise
If you disturb one in her joy,
Just like the battle fought in Troy.
In the battle for this charmer
Neither nun did wear much armor.
Venus was likewise attired
When her bouts with Mars transpired.
Ladies, such deshabillé
Always makes a fine display.
The uniform that Venus wore
Brought many splendors to the fore.
The armor that the Cyclops made
By hers were all put in the shade.
This painting, with these sisters' charms,
Would have made Achilles' arms,
Especially the wondrous shield
He carried on the battlefield,

Had Vulcan put it in, I'm sure,
Shine with even more allure.
Thus for better or for worse
I have told in rhyming verse
The story of this battle royal.
Although I have tried to be loyal
To the truth and not distort
Doubtless I have fallen short
For I could never quite portray
In words what to the eyes convey
Fine paintings, just as art cannot
Depict on canvas action hot
In all its movement and its force.
Words and colors aren't, of course,
The same; neither are ears and eyes.
Too long I've left, I realize,
Dethroned Teresa in the lurch,

Waiting to regain her perch.
She had her turn at last; Mazet
Did such diligence display
Each was content. The tale ends here,
Although it seems to me quite clear
They must have paused to drink and eat,
To make their pleasure more complete.
But what about the guest they thought
Would show up—did he come, or not?
If he never made it to the feast
The sisters could console themselves at least
With the one who did share their repast.
If the invited guest arrived at last,
They'd have hid both Mazet and the chair.
And then have made their guest feel wel-
      come there.

THE UNCOLLECTED TALES

1. "The Ephesian Matron"

If ever there was a twice-told tale
That runs of the risk of growing stale,
It would be the one that I
Would at present like to try
To fit into my rhyming verse.
"Your choice could hardly be much worse,"
Someone surely will complain.
"What do you think you have to gain?
It would be erroneous
To think that old Petronius
Could be by you improved upon.
You'll only make your readers yawn."
Answering critics I can't do,
Except to make the story new.
In Ephesus, in Asia Minor,
Of all the matrons none was finer,
None more wise and virtuous—
The vote, it was unanimous—
Than the one of whom I'll speak.
Folks came from far and wide to seek
The matron out and they would stare,
Because they knew she was so rare.
Her notoriety was based
Upon the fact she was so chaste:
A model of domesticity
And conjugal felicity.
Mothers-in-law would speak with awe
Of her to their daughters-in-law.
Husbands to their wives would say
Hers were virtues they should display.
The ancient and most venerable house
Of prudes descend all from this spouse.
Her husband loved her madly, but
He died; I need not say of what.
His entire estate he left
To his widow, too bereft
To be in any way consoled

By his silver and his gold.
Many widows tear their hair
In grief, and yet they take due care
Of their property's upkeep;
They'll count the money as they weep.
But this one's sorrow was astounding.
Throughout the town there went resounding
Lamentations quite heart-rending
That threatened to become unending,
Though in such cases we do know
Complaints are greater than the woe.
Though desperate the soul appears,
Exaggeration's in the tears.
This advice her friends did stress:
"Moderation, not excess,
Even in grief, we do implore."
This only made her grieve the more.
She did not wish to gaze upon
The light of day, now he was gone,
But went into her husband's tomb,
Resolved to die within its gloom,
In the place his corpse was laid,
And then accompany his shade
As it descended into hell.
As proof a friend can love too well—
An impulse that can lead to madness—
A female slave, moved by her sadness,
Chose to keep her company,
Prepared to die too, if need be.
Although it was quite brave to do
She hadn't really thought it through.
The slave, the wiser of the two,
Gave to her mistress' grief its due,
Allowing it at first free rein
Before attempting to restrain
The widow and make her conform
To something closer to the norm.

200

But her efforts bore no fruit:
The widow kept at her pursuit
Of every means that she could try
To join her spouse—that is, to die.
The quickest way and thus the best
Would be a dagger to the breast.
But she wanted still to feast
Her eyes upon the man who'd ceased
To be, but whose dear body lay
Where she saw it on display,
This sight the only thing she fed
On in that chamber for the dead.
Starvation thus would be the gate
Through which she'd go to join her mate.
One day, and then two days did pass
In which she sighed and said, "Alas!"
But no nourishment did take.
Imprecation she did make
Against the gods, nature, and fate.
All three did she excoriate.
For one who had such grief to tell
She expressed herself quite well.
Close by the tomb, there came to stay
Another corpse, though in a way
That was different, for he
Was hanging from a gallows tree.
He this scaffold was adorning
So that he might serve as warning
To those contemplating theft:
They too would be dangling left.
A soldier was well paid to stand
Nearby, subject to the command
The hanging body to defend
From any relative or friend
Who'd try to spirit it away.
Should he fail, he'd have to pay
By undergoing the disgrace
Of taking the condemned man's place.
This penalty was inhumane
But thus the state did crime restrain.
From the tomb he saw at night
Through its fissures, glowing light.
Curious, he went to peer,
Then the widow's cries could hear.
He entered, was surprised and said:
"Can you not be comforted?
Why those tears upon your face
In this melancholy place?"
Her grief was so extravagant,

The attention she paid him was scant.
But then he saw the corpse and guessed
The reason she was so distressed.
The slave explained that, by grief torn,
To die of hunger they had sworn.
Though he'd no gift for oratory,
Life, he said, while transitory,
Was a gift not to refuse.
She paid attention to his views
And as she listened to him speak
Her grief began to grow more weak.
Time was having its effect.
"If your vow makes you reject
All food," he said, "then don't decline
To gaze upon me while I dine.
It won't prevent your own demise."
The women liked this compromise.
Thus he ate his soldier's ration.
The slave now felt the strong temptation
To renounce the vow she gave
To join her mistress in the grave.
"Madame," she said, "I've had a thought.
Would your husband care a lot
Whether you should live or die?
If you'd died first, would he deny
Himself the rest of his life span?
We should live longer, and we can.
Why go to our grave at twenty?
Of time to spend there we'll have plenty.
Death comes too soon—no need to race.
I'd rather die with a wrinkled face.
Why bring to Hades charms so fair?
What good would they do you there?
Sometimes when I see the grace
With which the gods adorned your face
I feel that I'm not all that keen
On burying treasure sight unseen."
When this flattery she heard
From her stupor she was stirred.
To her senses now she came.
The god of Love took careful aim
With the arrow in his bow.
Toward the soldier it did go,
Striking him right to the quick;
Immediately he was lovesick.
A second arrow now took flight;
It grazed her with a wound more slight.
The beauty by which she was graced
Was such that men of finest taste

"Why those tears upon your face?" (Fragonard).

"Let's make a little substitution" (Duplessis-Bertaux).

Would have loved her all their life
Even if she'd been their wife.
The guard was moved not just to pity
But to love, she was so pretty,
Though the tears that she did show
Made her seem all the more so.
She listened as he sang her praise,
Poison that is love's first phase.
She found its taste to be so sweet
That he persuaded her to eat.
A corpse, however well-preserved
And handsome, doubtless less deserved
Her love than this fine living fellow.
She began at last to mellow.
Little by little came the change;
I do not find this to be strange.
A lover spoke into her ear
Who soon became a husband dear.
This took place, you may suppose,

Right beneath the dead man's nose.
While these two were getting married
The hanged man was getting carried
Off by a thief. The soldier did run
When he heard the noise, but the deed was
   done.
He returned to tell his tale of woe.
He'd have to hide: where could he go?
The female slave took things in hand:
"They've stolen your corpse, I understand?
And you'll be subject to execution?
If Madame consents, I have a solution.
Let's make a little substitution.
Her husband on the noose will go.
No passerby would ever know."
Seeing her lover in this pickle,
The widow consented. Oh how fickle
Women are! Some are pretty;
Some are not, and more's the pity.

But if some were made of faithful stuff,
They'd be beautiful enough.

Prudes, to boast would not be wise.
You may resist what we devise,
But our will's as strong as yours.
You'd be surprised by what occurs.
Not to be sanctimonious,
And pardon me, Petronius,
But what the Matron did was not
So fantastic that it ought

To be recalled in tale and song.
The only thing that she did wrong
Was to have so loudly cried
And to plan her suicide.
As for the matter of the switch
And the alacrity with which
She placed her husband on the rope,
It was the other's only hope.
All things considered, women have found
The humblest soldier still around
Beats a Caesar in the ground.

2. "Belphegor"

to Mademoiselle de Champmeslé
With your name I decorate
My latest book of tales to date.
May they all succeed so well
Some future age our praise will tell.
I win fame upon the page;
You, by acting on the stage.
Our names, here linked in what I write,
Together will traverse the night
Of shadows that the ages cast
On all that's happened in the past.
As now in hearts and minds you reign
In memory you'll long remain.
The roles you've played are known to all.
As Phèdre you held us in thrall,
As Berenice, Chimène so sad,
And as Camille when she was mad.
Who's not enchanted when he hears
This voice that moves us all to tears?
None else but you can play these parts
And speak like you right to our hearts.
To praise all that's divine in you
Is something that I cannot do:
Since you're with every grace replete
The task would never be complete.
Of all the loves that I have had
You'd have been the first—too bad!
And you'd have had my soul entire
If I'd have shown somewhat more fire
In telling you how I did burn.
To be beloved in return
Is what those who love desire.
I felt that I could not aspire

To please you, so I merely said
I was your friend, though in my head
And heart I knew that I was more.
How I wish upon that score
I had had a better fate.
That said, it's time now to relate
A story that I'd like to tell.
One day Satan, King of Hell,
Passed his subjects in review.
They were sure a motley crew:
Many kinds all in a mass,
Princes with the lower class.
Many wept within the crowd;
Satan found the noise too loud.
He asked each, "Now who's to blame?
Who cast you in the pitiless flame?"
In each case the answer was
A wife or husband was the cause.
Satan called his minions in
And said, "If this is why they sin,
We can with ease increase our glory
If we can verify their story.
In order to achieve this end
A crafty demon we should send;
One who's very prudent, too.
Marriages he'll closely view.
To learn about it at first hand
He'll become someone's husband."
They consented with one voice.
Belphegor soon was their choice.
His ear acute, and keen of eye,
He was one who loved to pry.
The truth of any situation

Yielded to his penetration.
For the mission to succeed
He was given what he'd need:
Letters of credit; as for cash,
Here and there he'd find a stash.
He was granted, in addition,
Power to alter the human condition:
Good and bad, pleasure and pain—
These were things he could ordain.
He could escape predicaments
By his tricks and diligence.
On earth he'd be obliged to roam,
Nor could he die, nor come back home
To Hell until ten years had passed.
Through space he traveled very fast,
Establishing his residence
Where luxury and much expense
Were the order of the day,
Florence. There he could display
His boundless wealth. He took the name
Of Signor Roderic, became
A figure in society,
Gaining notoriety
For his house and retinue,
And for being well-to-do.
All pleasures were his to command.
The dinners that he gave were grand.
One of the pleasures he loved most,
Besides the one of playing host,
Was that of flattering a guest.
Poets seemed to like it best;
In return they'd sing his praises
In artistic paraphrases.
Many honors he received—
More, it is widely believed,
That any citizen of Hades.
And he had from all the ladies
Declarations of affection.
He encountered no rejection,
For money when it is bestowed
Smoothes out the bumps in any road.
Those who have enough will win.
I've said it before, and will again:
No other motive have I found;
Money makes the world go round.
All this time he kept an eye
On marriages, to certify
If spouses were content or not.
Of those who weren't, there were a lot.

In the other category
It was quite another story.
There were so few that he felt pained.
For Belphegor all that remained
Was himself to make a trial
Of the married state. Meanwhile,
Florence had a lovely lass,
Beautiful, of noble class.
Not much money, but much pride,
For she had virtue on her side.
Roderic asked for her hand
(By proxy, you must understand).
Honnesta—that was her name—
Had many suitors, was the claim
Her father made, but of them all
To Roderic the choice might fall;
Dad needed leisure to reflect.
The suitor strove now to affect
An alteration in her heart,
With feasts and serenades did start
To lavish her, spared no expense
To gain from her the preference.
The funds he'd brought were much reduced
But thereby he indeed seduced
Miss Honnesta, for she said yes.
Her lawyer came, which did distress
This devil quite a lot because
He saw how love was spoiled by laws.
Does one acquire a wife, he thought,
The same way a château is bought?
He had reason to complain.
Litigiousness you see's the bane
Of human existence. Must
We abandon simple trust?
Contracts, legalese, and clauses
Are of civil strife the causes.
Solemn vows and laws cannot
Stop the battles that are fought
Between Love and Marriage, for
Only hearts can peace restore.
The married state is not the same
As other states that I could name:
All's forgiven between *friends*;
The delights that Eros sends
Make *lovers* think that all is well.
But for *spouses*, life is hell.
They're bored, they're tired—and why is
  this?
It's Duty's fault things are amiss.

It's just the way we're made, I guess.
Then is conjugal happiness
Impossible on earth to find?
I've pondered this within my mind.
A perfect marriage can exist:
Of pardoning it must consist.
When each forgives the other's folly
Then the marriage will be jolly.
When Belphegor brought home his bride
He found that he was misallied.
For Honnesta was more demonic
Than he was—which was ironic.
Constant arguments and fights
Kept the neighbors up of nights.
They'd come running when they heard,
Wondering what had occurred.
"To treat that way someone like me,
Born with the finest pedigree,
Someone made of fine alloy!
You should have stuck with the hoi polloi.
I'm too good," she'd shout, "for you!
I'm a woman of virtue."
Prudes who claim they're without fault
Should be taken with some salt.
Squabbles were most vehement
Over money that she spent
On gambling, clothes, and furnishings—
All the myriad of things
Invented just, it seems, to spoil
The modest fruits of honest toil.
This poor devil began to miss
The tranquillity of Hell's abyss.
The worst of the mess he now was in
Was having to put up with her kin.
There was her father and her mother,
Her big sister and kid brother.
He had to purchase sis a suitor
And cover the expense of the brother's tutor.
But the principal reason for his downfall
Was his steward, who took it all.
Such is the nature of the beast:
He profits most when profits least
His master, who's obliged to spend
On fees and taxes that won't end,
While the steward's free to save by stealth
And little by little build up his wealth.
So he bides his time till his boss must sell,
Then buys the estate and does quite well.
But when the steward an owner becomes

He too must lay out massive sums
And see his savings whittled away.
Now should it happen that one day
The other's made steward of his former estate,
His wealth he could gradually recreate
And they could resume the roles they'd
    played.
But Belphegor was too dismayed.
He chose to invest in trade,
Which he thought would fill his purse,
But it turned out to make things worse:
Agents unworthy of his trust,
A ship that sank; the venture went bust.
He borrowed to cover; when the loan came
    due,
His creditor came; he had to skidoo.
He ran to the country to escape his pursuer,
Hid out on a farm that reeked of manure.
He said to Matheo, who was his host,
There were two things that he feared most:
His creditors, and a wife who was worse,
That the only way out of this double curse
Was to find a body in which to hide
And there for a time he could reside.
No one, he thought, would find him there.
Should Honnesta repent, what would he
    care?
Maybe she regretted being so pure,
But he'd heard enough, that's for sure.
To thank Matheo for his aid
Belphegor this promise made:
From the bodies where he'd hidden
Three times he'd come out if bidden.
He entered a body that very day;
What happened to his, I cannot say.
An only daughter was the victim;
Matheo was hired to evict him.
Then the devil went to Rome,
Found a new one for his home.
Matheo said the magic word
After this, there was a third.
All were female. Don't forget
Three like this were all he'd get.
Belphegor became a squatter
Inside the King of Naples' daughter.
She had been much in demand;
Princes came to seek her hand.
On her the family's hopes were pinned;

"The devil skedaddled, and off he flew" (Duplessis-Bertaux).

Therefore they were much chagrined
When her soul became possessed.
Exorcists had done their best
But fearing his wife was still about
Belphegor would not come out.
Throughout the countryside and town
Matheo's skill had gained renown.
They offered him a princely sum
But Matheo would not come.
Though he'd love to make a killing,
Belphegor would be unwilling,
For his three times had all been used;
So he reluctantly refused.
Just an ordinary guy,
He said, who knew no reason why
He'd been able a time or two
To make some devil bid adieu
To a body he possessed.

"It must have just been luck," he guessed.
"That devil had been pretty weak,
Unlike the one of which you speak."
But his objections were in vain;
They dragged him off, and under pain
Of death by hanging, said that he
Had to perform his specialty.
He had until the sunset hour
To display his magic power.
The king stood by to keep an eye
Upon the battle where would vie
The devil and the exorcist.
A spectacle not to be missed,
There was no mother's son at court
Who didn't run to see such sport.
Rope and scaffold on one side,
In case he failed at what he tried;
On the other, should he succeed,

More money than he'd ever need.
He eyed the coins there on display.
Belphegor smiled and said, "No way.
Three times you've had—that's all you get."
Matheo now began to sweat.
He begged, he pleaded, wept great tears.
But all this fell upon deaf ears.
The devil only laughed. Poor Matt
Announced he'd failed. And that was that.
They grabbed him then, for he would hang.
About to make his last harangue
(A quaint tradition of the time:
One convicted of a crime
Could speak to those who'd come to see
His rendezvous with destiny),
To him a good idea did come:
He told the drummer to bang his drum.
The sudden noise to the devil gave
A terrible shock. He exclaimed, "You knave,
What's this deafening sound I hear?"
"It's Honnesta; she'll soon be here,
Roaming the earth in search of you."
The devil skedaddled, and off he flew
To deepest Hell. In Satan's court
Of his success he made report.
"Sire," he said, "the marriage knot
Is with seeds of damnation fraught.

Down to Hell they fall like rain,
The souls that we through Marriage gain.
I myself have tried it out.
The thing is good itself, no doubt,
But surely has seen better days,
For everything at last decays.
Marriage is hellishly cruel:
Your crown has no finer jewel."
Satan believed him, and he earned
His recompense, though he'd returned
Before the stated ten years' time.
But how could that have been a crime?
What else in fact could he have done?
A devil at your ear's no fun,
The same sound always in your head.
It's no wonder that he fled.
At least Hell has some variety—
Less cruel than her society.
I wonder how long a saint would last?
Job would have lost his patience fast.

What conclusions from this tale?
Don't turn your house into a jail.
And if you really have to wed
Don't take an Honnesta to bed.
Though here's some news I'd like to share:
Wives like her are actually rare.

3. "The Little Bell"

Man is such a weak and feeble creature!
Inconstancy's his most consistent feature.
Previously I did announce
That naughty tales I would renounce.
Alas, it was two days ago I swore
Of such frivolities I'd write no more.
It just goes to show you cannot trust
A poet, who'll do what a poet must.
Wisdom's not for those who haunt the
    Muses.
On the other hand, their art amuses.
That their words are sweet you can't
    refute,
But steadfastness is not their strongest suit.
And yet I'd like to find a compromise.
Perhaps I could propose it in this guise:
Let's suppose my matter is defective;

Could my form not give it some corrective?
Let's see what I can do upon this theme.

In a meadow close beside a stream
In the area not far from Tours,
A fellow liked to go make overtures
To the lovely girls who came by there.
Their teeth were white, their pretty feet were
    bare.
Each cow they took to pasture wore a bell.
For one of these young cowherds this guy
    fell.
The trouble was, she wasn't yet of age,
Because thirteen is too young to engage
In the game this gallant had in mind.
Although it's true the laws in fact do find
That at this age a girl can be a bride,

That's in the city, not the countryside,
Even if in fields love seems to flower.
The young man tried all that was in his
  power,
But it was in vain. Maybe it was

Her inexperience that was the cause,
Or her timidity—or her distaste.
Perhaps it was all three, but she stayed
  chaste,
And made it clear that her reply was no.

"He ... took / The bell and made it tinkle" (Janet-Lange).

All was fair in love, he thought, and so
As twilight fell he led a cow away
From those she was entrusted with that day.
Being young, the girl did not keep track
Of how many followed the path back.
But the lack did not escape her mother,
Who sent her daughter back to get the
    other,
With some angry words that made her cry.
So she returned and called—but no reply
Except her echoes in that lonely dell.
He had found a way to mute the bell
That hung about the heifer's neck, then took

The bell and made it tinkle so she'd look
Deep in the woods, where he led her astray.
Imagine then, my reader, her dismay
When she discovered him and not her cow.
"My torment's so great as to allow
A tactic that might not seem to be fair."
When he spoke these words she knew de-
    spair.
She filled with screams that ill-frequented
    spot.
But no one came. Now girls, there is a lot
That you can learn from such a tragic case:
Avoid the woods, that dark and silent place.

4. "The River Scamander"

For naughty tales I'm more than ready now.
Love demands it; he laughs at my vow.
Cupid holds both men and gods in thrall.
All of them must answer to his call.
When I sing henceforth in my rhymed tales
Of the power of Love, I must use veils
To soften and disguise whereof I speak
So that I will not abuse the weak.
I'd rather that my lines would have no wit
Than they for tender ears should be unfit!
If in my poems I should introduce
A charmer and the girl he would seduce
My purpose is to warn the fairer sex
Of such deceivers and the ill effects
That ensue from falling in their traps.
You can't be too careful with some chaps.
Ignorance has made a thousand stumble
For every one who at my verse msy grumble.
An orator, I've read, who was esteemed
In ancient Greece, the land that once was
    deemed
To be the sovereign mistress of the arts,
Was obliged to leave for foreign parts.
Banished from his homeland, now he sought
To visit where the Trojan War was fought.
He took his friend Cymon, who would
    enjoy
The chance to see the ancient site of Troy.
From its debris a new town was constructed
Whose inhabitants seemed uninstructed
In their noble past; Hector and Priam

Were nothing more than names, consumed
    by Time.
Ilium, your name for me is magical,
Inspiring poets often to wax tragical.
It's too bad I'll never see that town,
Whose walls the gods first built and then
    tore down,
Nor the fields of furious campaigns.
Of those fabled times no trace remains.
Though on ancient times I love to ponder,
I'll get to the point and cease to wander:
By the river known as the Scamander,
Which near Troy flows through a lovely dale,
Walked Cymon, the hero of our tale.
An innocent young girl soon was there seen,
Drawn to the river's banks, so cool and
    green.
Her veil was floating gently on the breeze.
She had a naive beauty that did please.
Simply dressed, she seemed a shepherdess.
Cymon was taken by her loveliness,
Which made him think that on those banks
    that day
Venus conspired to grant him a display
Of rarest treasures. Nearby was a cave
Into which she went, for she did crave
Its coolness as a respite from the heat;
Its solitude to her seemed also sweet.
The fault as well must lie with wicked Cupid
For this decision, which was rather stupid:
Not just following this lonely path,

She decided too to take a bath
Where the river flowed into the cave.
Our man's vantage point there to him gave
An unobstructed view of beauty bare;
On a hundred charms did Cymon stare.
People in that far-off time believed
The earth was full of gods, so he conceived
The clever plan of posing as one too.
He crowned his head with wet reeds to
　imbue
Himself with all the splendor of the god
Of the river, hoping she'd be awed.
To Mercury and Cupid did he pray.
An innocent against such an array
Of tricksters really didn't have a prayer.
She revealed a foot whose whiteness rare
Would drive a Galatea to despair
(A famous milk-white beauty bore that
　name).

She plunged it in the water, then with shame
Saw her lilied nakedness reflected.
Her attention in this way deflected,
He approached her. In a state of shock,
She took cover deep within the rock.
"I am," he said, "the god of this domain.
Be my goddess and with me you'll reign.
Few rivers have the qualities I own;
I want to share my life with you alone.
My heart is purer than my crystal wave.
Come marry me, and dwell within my cave.
For you the riverbank with flowers I'll spread.
If you consent to join me in my bed
And your image in my depths admire,
Your friends shall all be nymphs, should you
　desire,
Divinities of river, mountain, wood,
For throughout the world my powers are
　good."

"'I am,' he said, 'the god of this domain'" (Duplessis-Bertaux).

His eloquence, her fear that she'd displease,
Allowed him to achieve his goal with ease,
Despite her modesty and sense of shame,
Which to some degree did spoil the game.
Religious superstition has its flaws:
Of many accidents it is the cause.
Cupid also helped her doubts to quell.
Flushed with success, Cymon bid her
    farewell.
"Come back," he said, "and here again we'll
    meet.
But be sure that you remain discreet.
We'll conceal the secret troth we've plighted
Until I've spoken to the gods united
On Olympus and the news imparted."
The new goddess at these words departed.
Was she content? The god of Love would
    know.
For two months each to the cave would go,
Unnoticed by a soul within the town.
Eventually, his passion did slow down.
His visits to the cave became more rare.
Is happiness so burdensome to bear
That once possessed, it must be thrown
    away?
There was a wedding in the town one day.
A crowd of onlookers stood in the square.

The goddess saw her lover standing there.
"Behold," she cried, "Scamander! He's a
    god."
People gathered round and thought this odd.
"We are wife and husband, he and I.
We'll celebrate our marriage in the sky."
At this they laughed, because it was absurd.
Some threw stones at him, their anger
    stirred.
He fled as best he could to save his skin.
The chastisement that he'd get for his sin
Were he living now would be more dire.
Such crimes back then did not, it seems, re-
    quire
The retribution they'd incur today.
Times have changed, is all that I can say.
Scamander's wife was teased, but nothing
    more.
A lover found her prettier than before.
To each his own. He offered her his hand.
The gods cannot spoil things, you under-
    stand.
Should they bring a girl loss of esteem,
Money has the power to redeem.
Just a larger dowry endow
And she'll doubtless find a spouse somehow.

5. "The Unwitting Go-Between"

Love's the greatest talker that I know.
His arguments are gestures he can show,
Like gentle looks and smiles and tender
    tears.
In war as well his mastery appears.
Sometimes he goes to battle pennants flying;
Sometimes it's on finesse that he's relying.
When the case for subtle tactics calls
By stealth he'll take those well-defended
    walls.
He gets my vote. Imagine two châteaux:
One to Mars, the war god, we'll expose;
The other we'll propose as Cupid's prey.
Let the former gather his array
Of soldiers and attack with all his might.
I predict the damage will be slight.
But Love unarmed and naked will win his;

At tricks and stratagems he is a whiz.
Some I've read of, some seen with my eyes;
But this one I'll now tell of takes the prize.

Young Amantha to Geronte was wed;
She deserved a better man instead.
He was boorish, difficult, and old,
A jealous type whose heart was rather cold.
She was young, had never loved, and apt
To be by the first man she saw enrapt.
Cleon, young, well built, handsome and wise,
Was the one on whom she cast her eyes.
Responding to this tribute, he succeeded
Too well perhaps, more so than was needed.
She tried to follow Duty and resist
But when the moment comes Love will
    insist.

When that happens, Duty bids adieu.
All that she at first wanted to do
Was talk to him, and find some consolation
In telling him of her deep desolation.
I'm sure that's why she thought they would
    be meeting,
But appetite will always come through eat-
    ing;
The best is not to sit down at the table.
Amantha thought with Cleon she'd be able
To keep things on the up and up—just chat,
Show him her esteem, no more than that.
Friendship and a little more is fine,
But nothing else that would be out of line.
Rather death than to commit a sin!
The difficulty was how to begin.
Letters can spell trouble if they're seen.
What she needed was a go-between.
How to find one? Geronte inspired fear.

I've said before that Love will persevere
And one way or another find a way.
This will be the proof of what I say.
Cleon had an aged relative,
An upright prude who to herself did give
The power to rule him like a governess.
Amantha came to her in feigned distress
To say, "Madame Alis, I don't know why
He should think it worth his while to try,
But Cleon has been making eyes at me.
I've never cared for him, it's plain to see;
I never have; I'm sure I never will.
But he seems to get some kind of thrill
From passing by my window without fail
Every day; he's always on my trail.
He sends me notes that make me blush for
    shame,
Delivered by a friend I will not name,
Although you know her. Please do me a favor

"And here's my portrait" (Duplessis-Bertaux).

And make him stop this terrible behavior.
Something bad will come of it no doubt.
My husband would explode if he found out.
Cleon's attempts will only failure find.
Tell him that for me, if you don't mind."
Alis praised her attitude and swore
She'd make sure he bothered her no more.
Cleon on Aunt Alis soon came calling.
She told him his conduct was appalling.
Poor Cleon denied it, and averred
That the very notion was absurd.
She said she had no faith in his denial,
He was a child of Hell and full of guile.
He should have to face the consequence
Of lying and denying his offense.
Whether what he claimed was true or not
Amantha is a woman whom one ought
To never think of in that sort of way.
To her honor one should homage pay.
She is a faithful wife, so don't pursue her.
Cleon agreed, but now began to view her
In quite a different light than he'd before.
What mysteries, he wondered, were in store?
Three days had not quite passed when she
 returned
To tell Alis that Cleon's passion burned
Brighter still. Had she not had occasion
To exercise her powers of persuasion
On her nephew and make him refrain?
Alis her anger hardly could contain.
Once Amantha left she sent for him.
What she had to say was pretty grim.
I don't think I have the strength to tell
You all she said. It had to do with Hell;
She called him Satan, Lucifer, and worse.
She said that he deserved to bear God's
 curse.
Her elaborate admonishment
Threw Cleon into dazed astonishment.
He didn't really know what he should do.
To say that he'd done wrong would be untrue.
He went home to ruminate and muse.
At last he thought: "Perhaps it is a ruse.
What she complains of is what I should do.
She says I woo her: therefore I should woo.
I love Amantha with all of my heart,
For she's not just beautiful—she's also smart.
I could not at first make all this out,
But now I understand. Without a doubt,

Amantha sees a passion to be shared.
I'd go and see her right now, if I dared;
Full of confidence, I'd let her know
The violence of my desire. And so
Perhaps I should go over to her house.
But what if I were caught there by her
 spouse?
That's a fate I really do not need.
Wiser would it be to let her lead."
Three days later, she was back again
At his aunt's house, as if to complain,
But really to continue his instruction.
"I believe that he wants my destruction.
He thinks that with some presents I'll be
 bought,
That I'm that kind of woman. Well, I'm not!
Look at these jewels he has given me.
And here's my portrait. Look—and do you
 see?
It must have been from recollection done
Because my husband has the only one.
With these gifts this morning to me came
The woman whom I mentioned but won't
 name.
These presents should be thrown back at his
 head.
If at this moment he were here I dread....
I'm so mad I don't know what to do.
But hear the rest: he let me know he knew
That my husband has been called away
On some business to our farm today,
And that is where tonight Geronte will sleep.
Once the servants are in slumber deep
Cleon will make his way up to my room.
What does he hope to get? I must assume
A rendezvous or something of that kind.
I think the guy must be out of his mind.
Were not that it would implicate my spouse
I'd put a band of watchmen round the house,
So that if he came he would be caught,
Or forced to flee in shame, as well he ought."
At this, Amantha left. Cleon returned;
The first thing Alis did, because she burned
With anger for the shame and the disgrace
Was throw the gems and portrait at his face.
She would have wrung his neck too, if she
 could.
"Do you think you've acted as you should?
But that's nothing, for the rest is worse."

By chapter she recited and by verse
Every little thing Amantha said—
A message that Cleon correctly read.
"It's true," he said, "that I once loved this
   beauty.
But now I see in which way lies my duty.
Since it's clear that now all hope is gone
I've concluded it's best to move on."
"That's the proper path to take," she said.
But to Amantha's house that path now led.
At midnight sped our hero, all elated,
To the place she'd clearly indicated.
All alone she waited at the door;
The servants were asleep, and what is more,
The clouds hid moon and stars with their
   thick veil.

All had been arranged in fine detail:
When he entered, she led him above,
Without a word, up to the room of love.
Once there, he felt impelled to declare
He found her beauty far beyond compare;
Her magnanimity he praised as well.
"Now be so kind," he asked her, "as to tell
Me how you came up with this stratagem.
For really, it's the *crème de la crème*.
The god of Love knows of none that are wit-
   tier."
She blushed, which made her then look all
   the prettier.
He extolled her body and her soul—
I only hope he didn't just extol!

6. *"The Remedy"*

If the image of the truth can please,
Ought we not the truth itself to seize?
Often in the tales that I relate
I try it, and its force is always great.
The truth draws to itself every mind.
Although one must in writings of this kind
Conceive false names, the rest can all be told
Precisely as the story did unfold.
But on the names we ought to cast a veil.
That's what I do in the following tale.
Near Le Mans, a place where folks are wise,
And subtleties they like to analyze,
A girl from there had not so long ago
A delicate, fresh-faced, and handsome beau.
He was so young a one that on his chin
His adolescent beard had not come in.
She had charms and wealth, so many tried
To court her, and to win her for their bride.
But in vain, because the girl, in truth,
Had such an inclination for the youth.
The parents, though, had someone else in
   mind.
Their way of thinking was the Norman kind;
The art of marriage was to them the science
Of family to family alliance.
But she wheedled and cajoled with such
   success
That her parents granted him access.

Their indulgence, or the lad's ability,
Perhaps also his blood and his nobility,
Had made them change their mind—which,
   I don't know.
But with lucky folks it's always so.
Unlucky ones just never get a break.
The parents liked the lad for his own sake;
To his merit and his zeal they paid due heed.
Besides those things what else does one
   need?
Lots of cash. The values of the past,
The golden age, are but a shadow cast,
For only money talks today, I fear.
O golden age, you'll not again appear.
Not in Le Mans, in any shape or fashion.
Your innocence, though, would have helped
   his passion
To achieve its goal with less delay.
The parents' slowness so got in the way
The girl, who in her heart already viewed
The two as wed, decided to conclude
The rest of what the mystery contained
According to the usages maintained
In the realm of Love on Venus' isle.
Our old novels, in their pleasant style,
Often told of such *faits accomplis*.
People still do that, it seems to me,
Supping ere a priest can say the grace.

The god of Love performed in that priest's
   place;
For the parents he stood in as well,
The notary, and all his personnel.
Cupid got this done with no delay,
Far from the Norman dilatory way.
Behold our lover glad and satisfied,
Passing nighttime hours with his "bride."
To tell you how would not be hard at all:
Duplicates of keys, holes in the wall,
Little presents given to the maid—
That's the way, you see, the game is played.
The "husband" in this fashion could now
   savor
In calm, and yet in secret, his "bride's" favor.
One evening, though, the girl, feeling un-
   well,
Her ailment to her governess did tell.
The governess was not one in the know

Concerning secret goings to and fro.
The girl should have an enema, she said,
To be given in the morning while in bed.
At midnight the young "husband" showed
   up there;
Of these arrangements he was unaware.
With a vigor normal for his age
He had come his passion to assuage.
The sleep that follows when this course is
   run
Had for the fellow only just begun
And in the east the rosy-fingered glow
Of dawn had just begun to show
When at the door the woman did appear,
Remedy in hand, full of good cheer.
Fortunate it was that there were two—
Doors, I mean, which hid them from her
   view
The time it took for her to make her way

"He ... placed himself instead / In the place where she was supposed to be" (Duplessis-Bertaux).

To the inner door. In that delay
All the girl would have to do was hide
Him in the covers, and show her backside.
But she wasn't sly enough, and fear
Made her panic and to disappear
Beneath the sheets herself; to him she said
In two words the nature of her dread.
He was wise, and placed himself instead
In the place where she was supposed to be.
The governess, who so that she could see
Had put her glasses on, then tried her skill
Upon the person who she thought was ill.
She bid adieu, and then did disappear.
Godspeed to her and all who interfere
With lovers and their secrets. There are
    those
Who, hearing what I've told, will now suppose

That I've made an error, for they'll find
That the girl was not the clever kind
That they thought she'd be. "She's lacking
    wit.
Therefore we think your prologue doesn't fit.
Your claim to tell the truth does not con-
    vince."
Snide remarks like that just make me wince.
I could show a hundred ways they're wrong.
But if I did, then it would take too long.
The argument in fact would never end.
Though on this you really may depend:
There's nothing that I've said that wasn't
    true;
It's based on faithful witnesses who knew.
It's on these guarantors that I rely.
No one can say as much on this as I.

7. *"Indiscreet Confessions"*

Paris, that lovely city without peer,
Within its walls has had no girl so dear,
So ravishingly easy on the eyes,
As the young Amantha. Quite a prize
She was to win. Her father didn't lack
For money; still her mother held her back
Beneath her wing until the day arrived
When handsome Damon fell for her, and
    strived
To win her heart. Winningly he gave
The impression that he was her slave.
This strategy allowed him all the faster
To become her legal lord and master—
Not in a way that was the least bit phony,
But in the lawful bonds of matrimony.
When they'd had a year of wedded bliss
They still got along, nothing amiss.
In fact, they loved each other more and
    more.
But one day Damon said, "What I deplore,
Though you're the sweetest girl I've ever
    known,
Is that I cannot say that you alone
Have reigned within my heart, for I confess
That I have felt another one's caress.
Indeed there have been several I could name.
I take upon myself the guilt and blame.

I remember that the nymph was sweet;
It was in the woods that we did meet.
The god of Love was there to give his aid;
He did so well that we a daughter made."
"I too have a past that I must own,"
Said Amantha. "I was home alone
When in came a well-placed family's son:
Good-looking, and when all was said and
    done
I felt for him because I am goodhearted
And it wasn't long before we started
To do those things that lovers oft enjoy.
From this adventure I now have a boy."
She was barely done when he erupted;
His soul by jealous madness was corrupted.
Soon he fell into a wild despair.
He ran out of the room and down the stair,
Found a saddle and he put it on,
Cried "I'm a cuckold now!" His mind was
    gone.
Hearing this, all came to get a view,
The parents, servants, and the neighbors too.
He told them why it was he was upset.
I don't want the reader to forget
That till then her parents, good bourgeois,
No family disturbance ever saw.
For all her needs her father did provide,

Even after she became a bride.
The expense of servants and of spouse
Were covered by the master of the house.
Until then they all had dwelled in peace,
But now that fine tranquillity would cease.
The mother now her daughter went to find;
The father followed, for he had in mind
To listen secretly to what they'd say.
He heard the mother cry in great dismay,
"You have made a terrible mistake.
I've seen fools, but you just take the cake.
It really was a stupid indiscretion
To have made that unprovoked confession.
You're not the first girl to sin with a guy;
Men are evil and Satan is sly.
Not that it's excusable, of course.
We'd have to lock up all our girls by force
In a convent till the day they marry.

I myself have a past I carry,
The same fate that you suffer I have had,
And in my heart I really do feel sad.
I had three children before I was wed.
But to your dad have I this secret said?
And is our marriage worse for all of that?"
They'd barely reached this moment in their
   chat
When her husband, listening at the door,
Ran off, like his son-in-law before.
From the saddle he now took the girth,
Providing for the neighbors lots of mirth.
Although they laughed they all did also
   know
That they themselves could put on the same
   show.
Both husbands on the same street made dis-
   play

"I had three children before I was wed" (Duplessis-Bertaux).

Of their madness, each in his own way.
One was belted, and the other saddled;
Both were cuckolds, and their brains were
    addled.
This story has a useful moral too,
And I'd like to tell it now to you.
Lucky Damon turned into a wretch:
His disclosure did disaster fetch.
But his wife's simplicity of mind
Was, it seems to me, one of a kind.
To one's very husband to confess!
What madness, not to mention witlessness!
To say it is imprudent doesn't come

Close at all; let's just say it's dumb.
On these two points I'd like you to reflect:
The marriage knot is worthy of respect,
And faith and honesty, I do believe.
If by mischance it could some harm receive
That could make it topple to one side,
That secret harm you must to none confide.
Don't let your scruples leave you high and
    dry.
Sometimes it's not a sin to tell a lie.
It's doubtless good advice I'm giving here.
But have I followed it? I've not, I fear.

8. "Mixed Up in the Dark"

Dame Fortune likes to get her kicks
From playing on us her mean tricks.
Instead of what our heart is set on,
She gives what we didn't bet on.
There's one she on me did play;
It seems it was but yesterday.
I loved Cloris; she loved me.
After a year she said maybe
She'd yield a little to my passion
In a weak and feeble fashion.
That's all that she had in mind,
Though favors of a finer kind
May be had by him who seizes
Chances to do what he pleases.
One evening I went to her house
In the absence of her spouse.
Alas, he came back at nightfall,
And Cloris wasn't there at all.
As chance would have it, in her place
I found a maid I could embrace.
What her mistress owed, she paid.
Then the mistress played the maid.
Authors often do arrange
Instances of like exchange,
Though such reciprocity
Calls for virtuosity.
When a surprise is desired
Skillful hands are required.
If your reader you'd astound
Your plot must be on solid ground.
For things to happen in due course

Never exert any force.
Cupid, though his eyes are blind,
Pulls surprises of this kind.
Boccaccio's skill in this was ample.
Take "The Cradle," for example.
Though in the version that I told
My hand may have been too bold
And in a thousand places spoiled
The beauties over which he toiled.
It's time to end this preface now
And to find a way somehow
To demonstrate by some new ploy
The powers Fortune and Love enjoy.
The best way to accomplish this
Is to tell what went amiss
To a fellow in Marseille,
And it happened just the way
I tell it. Every bit is true.
His real name I'll conceal from you.
Clidament was a lucky man.
He'd married as well as anyone can.
His wife was honest, virtuous, sweet;
His joy should have been complete.
She was very pretty too.
Still he looked for someone new.
It's a trap the devil sets:
One's never pleased with what one gets.
His lady had a serving-maid
Who nearly the same charms displayed:
The same size and same demeanor,
Lovely figure. If you'd seen her

"Suspicion, scruple, and surprise / Could be read in all their eyes" (Eisen).

You'd say she was just the one
For those looking for some fun.
Her mistress had a few more graces,
But if one could mask their faces
They could easily confuse
And you'd not know which to choose.
A hot-blooded Provençal,
He had not the wherewithal
To delay his mad pursuit.
Besides, Alix was very cute.
Although Alix could be a flirt
Her first response was rather curt.
Then he promised he would pay
A hundred crowns to have his way.
That sum so that she'd be nice
Was, I think, a decent price.
Would his wife have cost as much?
Maybe less, for chance is such
That in these things you never know.
But I err in talking so,
Because she never was inclined
To pay attention to the kind
Of promises that lovers make.
With her it would be a mistake
To offer one's deathless devotion;
It would just be wasted motion.
Nor could gifts with her succeed.
Alas! Why one should ever need
To purchase love? One thing's for sure,
Things are no longer what they were.
Love now has all things for sale,
Nymphs and shepherds at retail.
It is sad and very odd:
Though he used to be a god,
All Love does now is oversee
The proper charging of a fee
For objects we should call divine.
Times, mores, customs: all decline!
Alix at first told him: "No deal!"
And said how mad it made her feel,
Then calmed down and changed her tone
And said that they could be alone
In the cellar the next day
When she thought she could get away.
On these terms they were agreed.
But right away did she proceed
To tell her mistress of the plan.
Maid and mistress then began
To plot a little switcheroo.

The husband wouldn't have a clue,
They were so closely parallel.
It couldn't help but turn out well.
Catching him right in the act
Should have quite a nice impact.
By chance it happened the next day
He met a friend along the way.
He could not contain his joy,
So he told him of his ploy.
Although he also did confess
He wished he could have bought for less.
A hundred crowns was quite a lot.
At this, the friend then said, "Why not
Share the pleasure and the cost?"
Thinking of the crowns he'd lost
The husband thought it might be nifty
To split all this fifty-fifty.
And yet the thing might turn out wrong:
What if she would not go along?
She might fear that they would boast
Of how to both she had played host.
His friend, though, put his mind at ease:
In darkness like that, no one sees.
Alix is a little thick,
Therefore not that hard to trick.
In silence they should alternate,
Entrusting all the rest to fate
Or to Love, who for this tryst
Would doubtless be there to assist.
"That she from us no word would hear
She would attribute to your fear,
And your prudence would convey
That the walls have ears, they say.
To tell a secret to a wall
Is not a good idea at all."
Having settled on these measures,
Both were ready for Love's pleasures.
To the husband's house they sped.
Clidament's wife was yet abed.
Next to her the maid still slept.
By the way her hair was kept—
No elaborate cornette—
He could see that the soubrette
Was for their bout of love all set.
The hour arrived; but now arose
A quarrel over who first goes.
Although the husband was the host
He didn't want to be hindmost.
The preference due to a guest

At such a time did not seem best.
His behavior wasn't nice.
They had to settle it by dice:
To be first the friend was fated.
In the cellar now they waited
For Alix, who didn't show.
In her place the wife did go.
She gently knocked upon the door.
It was opened, and before
She had the time to recognize
The change that made things otherwise
Than she'd expected them to be,
The friend, whose face she could not see,
Did what he had come to do.
Since her face he could not view
He did not feel all the delight
To which his prey gave him the right.
For she was prettier than the lass
And of a higher social class.
This scene had hardly been played out
When Clidament began his bout.
Her consternation was extreme
For the wife would never dream
That her husband could return
So soon, nor with such passion burn.
"He must, in this masquerade,
Be thinking that I am the maid,"
She thought, and vowed that she'd see to it,
Making sure that he would rue it.
When their energies were spent
Each out of the cellar went.
The friend who had gone equal shares
Was the first to mount the stairs.
But when the husband saw his wife
He had the surprise of his life.
Likewise when she saw the friend
At first she did not comprehend.
Suspicion, scruple, and surprise
Could be read in all their eyes.
None had had the time to hide

The turmoil going on inside.
The husband saw he must keep mum;
The wife in her delirium
Was about to tell him all—
Surprising me, for I recall
That women know well how to lie;
On this science they rely,
Even those not blessed with wit.
Alix, some say, by conscience bit,
Feeling bad because she'd not
Earned the money that she got,
For the husband's aggravation
Offered him some compensation,
Putting it upon *her* tab.
Actually, I'll have to blab
And say that here I've told a lie:
It makes a better tale, is why.
I see that folks two questions pose:
The first, is he now one of those
Husbands whom we cuckolds call?
I'd say that he is not at all.
For neither Madame nor his friend
Did this quality intend.
The other bears upon the onus
Of what's called *lex talionis:*
Eye for eye and tooth for tooth.
Is it not in fact the truth
That the wife still has the right
With the friend to take delight
Because when she was with the friend
The first time, she did not intend
To do so, while her husband did?
I think she does, but God forbid
That any harm in such a case
Should come to those who have the grace,
Like her to never be consoled.
Some wives there are who'd be so bold
As to take this all in jest.
Concerning them, silence is best.

9. "A Rearward Glance"

Back in ancient Greece, there were a pair
Of sisters. Each claimed that her derrière
Was as beautiful as any ass
Belonging to a woman of her class.

Because dispute remained which of the two
Could offer up the better rearward view,
An expert came the pair to analyze;
The older one he judged to win the prize.

He married her, for she had won his soul;
His brother did the younger one extol,
And, likewise, took that one to be his bride.
Things went so far the wives came to decide
That they would build a monument to last:
A temple named for Venus-the-Fair-Assed.

I'm not certain what they had in mind
But of the Grecian temples I might find,
In all their rich and multiform variety,
That's the one where I'd have shown most
  piety.

Notes on the Tales

1.1 *"Jocondo" ("Joconde")*

Source: Ariosto, *Orlando Furioso*,
canto 28, octaves 1–74

The story is much older than *Orlando Furioso* (1516). In fact, it is nearly identical to the frame-story of the *Thousand and One Nights* (see Aldo D. Scaglione, "Shahrar, Giocondo, Kote'rviky: Three Versions of the Motif of the Faithless Woman," *Oriens* 11.1/2 [Dec. 11, 1958]: 151–161). As Astolfo calls for Jocondo to come join his court, King Shahryar calls for his brother Shahzaman. As Jocondo, on his way to court, returns home to retrieve a forgotten bracelet and discovers his wife in bed with a valet, Shahzaman, on his way to court, returns home to get a jewel he has forgotten and discovers his wife in bed with a slave. Jocondo is pallid at court, sick with grief; so too is Shahzaman. Jocondo finds consolation in discovering the queen making love to a dwarf; Shahzaman is consoled by beholding the king's wife making love to a slave. Jocondo tells King Astolfo of the queen's infidelity; Shahzaman tells King Shahryar. Astolfo decides to leave the palace and travel with Jocondo; Shahryar decides to leave the palace and travel with Shahzaman. Astolfo and Jocondo share the favors of the same girl in the inn; Shahryar and Shahzaman share the favors of a girl held prisoner by a Jinni. Astolfo and Jocondo return home to find contentment with their wives; but at this point the stories diverge, for when Shahryar and Shahzaman return home the former kills his wife (the latter already had) and begins to sleep with a different virgin every night and slay her in the morning. Sheherazade puts an end to this by telling Shahryar a new tale every night, interrupting it each time to prolong her life. From this frame emerge the 1001 tales.

It is highly unlikely that La Fontaine would have known of the existence of the *Thousand and One Nights*, much less that this was the frame story. But the coincidence that it is the first story in both collections is remarkable.

1.2 *"Richard Minutolo"*

Source: Boccaccio, *Decameron*,
Third Day, Sixth Story

In both "Jocondo" and "Richard Minutolo" *A* (Jocondo, Richard) tells *B* (Astolfo, Catella) that *B*'s spouse is unfaithful and arranges for *B* to go to a secret room where *A* will display that infidelity. While in one tale *A* (Jocondo) is telling the truth, in the other *A* (Richard) is lying. There are actually two rooms in "Jocondo" that parallel, each in its own way, the shuttered room in the bathhouse in "Richard Minutolo": (1) the secret room off the gallery in Alfonso's palace and (2) the room in the inn where the dénouement unfolds. In both (1) and the room in the bathhouse an illicit encounter takes place; in both (2) and the bathhouse a mistake is made in the dark: Jocondo thinks the innkeeper's daughter's lover is Astolfo, as Astolfo takes him to be Jocondo; in the darkened room in the bathhouse, Catella mistakes Richard for her husband (and thinks that her husband is mistaking her for Simone).

Significant Alterations

(1) Richard Minutolo makes sure there are no holes in the wall of the secret room, so no light will come in; he does not do so in Boccaccio's version. This detail parallels the "fentes que le bois laissait" [cracks in the woodwork] (1.1, line 180) through which Jocondo was able to see the queen.

(2) Richard is intent on staying silent to keep up the masquerade, but at a certain point cannot help laughing, which provokes Catella's ire: "*Tu ris*, dit-elle, ô dieux! quelle insolence!" ["*You laugh*," she said. "O gods! Such insolence!"] (1.2, line 155). Neither the laughter nor her reaction appear in Boccaccio. Jocondo's wife makes a similar complaint: "*tu ris* de mon amour" [*you laugh* at my love] (1.1, line 66), which does not appear in Ariosto.

Words Unique to This Tale and the One Before

"Tu ris."

1.3 "The Cuckold, Cudgeled but Content" ("Le Cocu, battu et content")

Source: Boccaccio, *Decameron*,
Seventh Day, Seventh Story

In both this tale and "Richard Minutolo," *A* (Richard, Bon's wife) tells *B* (Catella, Bon) that *C* (Catella's husband, the falconer) is guilty of infidelity towards *B*, and that *B* can catch *C* engaging in infidelity by going to a rendezvous in the dark (the room in the bath house, the garden) disguised as and in the place of the person *C* is expecting to meet (Simone, Bon's wife) and in whom *C* has an adulterous interest. *A*, however, is lying to *B* about who *C* will think *B* is, for *C* will know that *B* is in fact *B*. *A* does all this to facilitate the satisfaction of a sexual desire on *A*'s part.

Significant Alterations

(1) Bon's wife claims (falsely) that when the falconer tried to seduce her the idea came to her "de lui manger *la vue*" [of tearing out his eyes] (1.3, line 61). This passage does not appear in the *Decameron*, but it does parallel what Catella tells Richard: "Je ... te saute à la vue" [I ... will tear out your eyes] (1.2, line 129).

(2) The stories conclude with consolations: Richard tells Catella "Le mieux sera que vous vous *consoliez*" [The best will be for you to *console* yourself] (1.2, line 198); Bon "des coups se *consola*" [*consoled* himself for the blows] (1.3, line 141). "Jocondo" ended the same way "*Consolons*-nous, bien d'autres le sont qu'elles" [Let's *console* ourselves: many others are as unfaithful as they] (1.1, line 494). There is no mention of consolation in the sources for any of the three stories, except that at an earlier moment in Boccaccio's version, Catella tells Richard (still thinking he is her husband) that she will not be consoled (*Decameron* 3.9.39; McWilliam, p. 234).

Words Unique to This Tale and the One Before

In no other tale will anyone's "vue" be threatened.

1.4 "The Husband Who Heard Confession" ("Le Mari confesseur")

Source: *Les Cent Nouvelles Nouvelles*, story 78

In both this tale and the preceding one a husband disguises himself in someone else's clothing to hear what he thinks will be evidence that he is a victim of infidelity (of his servant's infidelity in 1.3, of his wife's in 1.4). But what he hears turns out to be a pleasant surprise for which he praises God because it fools him into believing that the person he had thought was unfaithful actually was not. The husband in 1.3 exclaims, "Loué *soit Dieu*" [Praised *be God*] (line 132); the husband in 1.4, "Béni *soit Dieu*" [Blessed *be God*] (line 144).

1.5 "The Cobbler and His Wife" ("Conte d'une chose arrivée à Château-Thierry")

Source: Unknown, though perhaps based on an event in La Fontaine's hometown.

In "The Husband Who Heard Confession" a husband is in voluntary concealment (disguised as a priest) while his wife engages in risky behavior (telling the truth about her adultery), which she brings to a halt just in time, at the moment her husband makes his presence known. Similarly, in "The Cobbler and His Wife" a husband is in voluntary concealment (hiding in a corner) while his wife engages in risky behavior (giving the merchant the impression that she will trade him sex for the cancellation of the debt), which she brings to a halt just in time, at the moment her husband makes his presence known.

Words Unique to This Tale and the Two Before

In "The Husband Who Heard Confession" the wife tells her husband that it is strange that an "homme *si sage*" [a man *so wise*] (1.4, line 39) as he cannot solve her riddle. In "The Cuckold..." the husband consoles himself for the blows received in the garden by seeing that his falconer was "*si sage* et si fidèle" [*so wise* and so faithful] (1.3, line 140). The expression "si sage" will recur in "The Cobbler and His Wife," but in no other tale. The cobbler's wife says of the rich man's wife, "chacun n'est pas *si sage* qu'elle" [not all are *as wise* as she] (1.5, line 41). The expression "si sage" appears only in this tale and the preceding two. The adjective, however, changes its meaning as it moves from one tale to the next. The cuckolded husband in 1.3 might have meant that the young man was "sage" in the sense of having "du jugement" [good judgment], that he was "avisé, sensé dans sa conduite" [circumspect, sensible in his conduct] (*Le Petit Robert*). Or he might have meant, to cite another definition, dating from the seventeenth century, "honnête et réservé dans la conduite sexuelle" [upright and reserved in sexual conduct] (*Le Petit Robert*). In the context given the adjective in "The Cobbler and His Wife," it has precisely the opposite sense, as the cobbler's wife suggests that the rich man's wife is capable of commiting an act of adultery without being caught because she is "si sage." Whichever of the two definitions we adopt for the young man in "The Cuckold, Cudgeled but Content," he was praised for being "sage" because he was *not* engaged in adultery, while the shoemaker's wife was ironically praising the other wife for being "sage" because she *was* capable of engaging in adultery—and getting away with it. In addition to this opposition, in "The Husband Who Heard Confession" the context the word is given is just the opposite from its context in "The Cobbler and His Wife": in the former, "sage" is a qualification of the husband duped by his wife; in the latter, it is applied to the duping wife.

1.6 "Bosom Buddies" ("Conte tiré d'Athénée")

Source: Athenaeus, *The Deipnosophists*, Book 12, Chapter 9

In "The Cobbler and His Wife" two persons (the cobbler and his wife) enter into an agreement (with the merchant) in which the two will both enjoy the same object of desire (the grain); when the opportunity arises to get something for nothing (by getting the debt cancelled through allowing the merchant to think he can have sex with the wife), they take it. Similarly, in "Bosom Buddies" two persons (Axiochus and Alcibiades) enter into an agreement (with each other) in which they will enjoy the same object of desire (the woman); when the opportunity arises to get something (the daughter as mistress) for nothing (by denying paternity), they take it.

What the two friends get for nothing (the daughter) is not the same thing that they first entered into an agreement to obtain (the mother), while in "The Cobbler and His Wife" the agreed-upon object (the grain) remains the same. However, there is an equivalent in "The Cobbler and His Wife" to the second object of desire in "Bosom Buddies," and it comes with a parallel opportunity of getting it for free: in the scenario the rich man proposes, that the next time such a situation arises she cough after instead of before, the wife could enjoy the illicit sex without having to pay for it because her husband would never know.

The passage of time during which the debt for the grain matures is paralleled by the passage of time during which the daughter matures, and is marked in the telling by a similar turn of phrase and in the event by an emergence of sexual desire in both instances: "*Le terme échu*" [the term come due] (1.5, line 7), "*Le temps venu* que cet objet charmant / Put pratiquer les leçons de sa mère" [When the time arrived for the grown-up daughter / To practice the lessons her mother had taught her] (1.6, lines 9–10).

Significant Alteration

La Fontaine departs from his source when he has each man claim to be the father of such a beautiful daughter. In Athenaeus, they do not make such a claim: "Later a daughter was born to them, of whom they declared they could not tell whose child she was" (Athenaeus, *The Deipnosophists*, p. 417). In La Fontaine's version, however, they boast of it: "il en naquit une fille si belle, / Qu'ils *s'en vantaient* tous deux également" [there was born a daughter so beautiful that both *boasted* about it equally] (1.6, lines 7–8). This sets up a parallel with the cobbler, who boasted of the trick they played on the merchant: "le mari puis après *se vanta*" [the husband afterward *boasted*] (1.5, line 28).

1.7 "The Glutton" ("Autre conte tiré d'Athénée")

Source: Athenaeus, *The Deipnosophists*, Book 8, Chapter 5

Too much of a good thing turns dangerous when the glutton eats so much of a sturgeon that he will die, then decides to eat the rest of the fish, reasoning that he could afford that pleasure, having nothing more to lose. So, too, is "Bosom Buddies," in which one friend decides to add to the pleasure of sleeping with the mother that of doing the same with the daughter, which is dangerous for she may be *his* daughter. "Je prends sur moi le hasard du péché" [I take upon myself the hazard of the sin] (1.6, line 16). This reverses the order: for the glutton the first pleasure is the dangerous one; for the friend, the second. But both take the attitude that they have nothing to lose from the additional indulgence.

Significant Alteration

In Athenaeus neither of the friends steps forward to say he will take upon himself the risk of the sin; instead, they both sleep with the daughter: "whenever Alcibiades enjoyed possession of her, he would say she was the daughter of Axiochus; but when Axiochus did so, he would say she was the daughter of Alciabiades" (*The Deipnosophists*, p. 417). Thus the element of risk linking "Bosom Buddies" to "The Glutton" was added by La Fontaine.

1.8 "A Model Nun" ("Conte de ****")

Source: Unknown

The glutton eats too much; Sister Jeanne fasts. He persists in his misbehavior; she abandons hers. Both the glutton and the other nuns are told to prepare to leave this world—though in different senses—and both refuse to stop behaving as if they were still in it.

1.9 "Provincial Justice" ("Conte du juge de Mesle")

Source: Unknown

The other nuns imply that their conduct, though imperfect, is far from as bad as Jeanne's; the provincial judge argues that his conduct, though imperfect, is less so than that of judges who don't even bother to draw straws.

1.10 "The Peasant Who Angered His Lord" ("Conte d'un paysan qui avait offensé son seigneur")

Source: Distantly related to *Il Candelaio*, a play by Giordano Bruno

The story of a provincial judge is followed by the story of a judging lord. Both make unjust judgments, though with opposite results: the defendant wins his case in 1.9 but loses in 1.10. Both the unjust decisions are said to be "nothing new," but these words are said with opposite intent. The narrator complains of the lord's behavior toward the peasant "ce n'est chose nouvelle" [is nothing *new*] (1.10, line 4) in the sense that it has been ever thus, alas, between the powerful and the weak. But when the judge says "De *nouveauté* dans mon fait il n'est maille" [There is nothing *new* in my way of judging] (1.9, line 11) he is justifying the action, not condemning it.

The judge also parallels the peasant, for both are faced by a difficult choice. The judge is made "perplexe" [perplexed] (1.9, line 2) by the case before him; the peasant was perplexed by the impossible choice of punishments. In the end, both make a choice that is no choice, but for different reasons. The judge lets chance decide; the peasant involuntarily chooses all three, one after the other.

1.11 "In the Court of Love" ("Imitation d'un livre intitulé «Les Arrêts d'amours»")

Source: Loosely based on Martial d'Auvergne, *Les Arrêts d'Amour*, ca. 1460–66

Although in his Preface to Book One La Fontaine says he added this tale and the next simply to fill out the volume, "In the Court of Love" fits well with its immediate predecessor. It is the third tale in a row to be placed in a judicial setting, and all three the judges rule unjustly. The judges of the Court of Love are unduly influenced both by the

self-interest of the god of Love, their sovereign—who, it is claimed, would suffer if the woman's repose were troubled by a lover's advances—and by the gifts she gave them. They thus parallel the unjustly judging lord, who parallels the provincial judge who does not decide cases by the rule of law but by drawing straws.

In 1.11 are reunited two strands of the sequence that had begun to diverge, law and love. Though remaining within the judicial domain established by the two preceding tales, this one brings the discussion back to matters of the heart.

1.12 "Vulcan's Revenge" ("Les Amours de Mars et de Vénus")

Source: Tapestries at Nicolas Fouquet's Château de Vaux-le-Vicomte

Vulcan "se plaint" [complains] (1.12, line 92) to Jupiter in "Vulcan's Revenge," as the ill-treated lover "se plaint" [complains] (1.11, line 4) before the Court of Love. Both are unsuccessful because their judges are biased by self-interest. The Court of Love ruled against the litigant because the ungrateful beauty persuaded them that if she lost her "repos" [repose] (1.11, line 22) her attractiveness would suffer, with the result that Cupid's arrows would be shot in vain. Vulcan's plea to Jupiter about his wife's adultery will likewise fall on deaf ears because Jupiter is himself an adulterer, and therefore reluctant to punish the same misbehavior in another.

In the Court of Love the beauty's legal defense is predicated on her need for "repos" and Cupid's interest in seeing that she preserved it. In "Vulcan's Revenge" it is in "repos" that Venus is her most unfaithful: "Sur un lit de *repos* voyez Mars et sa dame" [On a bed of *repose* see Mars and his lady] (1.12, line 79). Venus is punished by being given too much repose, paralyzed by Vulcan's net in that state and made the laughing stock of the gods, becoming the "spectacle nouveau / De deux amants qui *reposent* ensemble" [new spectacle of two lovers who *repose* together] (1.11, line 109).

1.13 "The Ballad of the Books" ("Ballade")

Source: Probably original with La Fontaine

The narrator recounts a conversation he says he had with Cloris and Alizon about novels. Prudish Alizon claims to prefer reading the lives of the saints and to want to see books about love consigned to the flames. But after she leaves, Cloris and the narrator discover in her "péchés écrits" [written sins] (1.13, line 27)—a list of one's sins drawn up in preparation for confession—that she secretly delights in

Ariosto's *Orlando Furioso*, especially a scene in which the sleeping Angelica is about to suffer an attempted rape. The allusion is to canto 8, octaves 48–50, where the hermit casts a sleeping potion on Angelica's eyes, and tries to rape her while she slumbers but is unable to sustain an erection.

As also happened to Venus in "Vulcan's Revenge," Alizon's secret sin is laid bare to laughing onlookers—Cloris and the narrator. But La Fontaine's net is more tightly woven than that, for Venus was *asleep* with Mars on the "lit de repos" and Alizon's sin is to fantasize about being "Angélique *endormie*" [Angelica *asleep*] (1.13, line 33). Venus's slumber was itself connected with the ungrateful beauty's desire in "The Court of Love" to be left alone in her "repos" (1.11, line 22) and that the beauty "*Dormit* à son plaisir" [*slept* at her pleasure] (1.11, line 29).

2.1 "Making Ears and Mending Molds" ("Le Faiseur d'oreilles et le Raccommodeur de moules")

Source: *Les Cent Nouvelles Nouvelles*, story 3; Bonaventure Des Periers, *Nouvelles recréations et joyeux devis*, story 9; Boccaccio, *Decameron*, Eighth Day, Eighth Story

There are three sources for this tale, two of which La Fontaine alludes to in the subtitle. The unacknowledged third, Bonaventure Des Périers's "De celui qui acheva l'oreille de l'enfant à la femme de son voisin" [The man who finished the ear of his neighbor's wife's child], is actually the only source in which the specifics of pregnancy and ear-making are present; in all three, however, one man finds a way to sleep with another's wife. But in none of them does the wronged husband take his revenge in quite the way he does in La Fontaine's version (in Des Périers he takes no revenge at all), by fixing the mold for the nose in André's wife. The nose is La Fontaine's invention, and is the perfect counterpart to the ear. "Souvenez-vous de les *rendre pareilles*" [Remember to *make* them the *same*]" (2.1, line 39), Alice told André, alluding to the ears of her unborn child. Guillaume is just as interested in making two things similar, wanting his revenge to match the crime, telling André's wife—and André as well, who hears this from his hiding place: "Je lui *rendrai* si je puis la *pareille*" [I will *do* the *same* for him if I can] (2.1, line 169). By introducing the nose into the story, La Fontaine does more than improve upon Des Périers, where ears were part of the plot but not noses, and more than "les rendre pareilles" in two senses (ear to ear and noses to ears). He also works toward making "pareils" this tale and "The Ballad of the Books," the last in Book One but also the one just before 2.1 in the overall sequence, for a nose was stuck in there too: "Quiconque y met le *nez* devient noir comme un four" [Whoever puts his *nose* in there becomes as black as an oven] (1.13, line 46), in an allusion to *Amadis de Gaule*, a dangerous book to read.

Other connections link the passage in "Ballade" about *Amadis de Gaule* with the scene of Guillaume's vengeance in 2.1. A "four" [oven] is associated with guilt in the line just quoted, where the nose one sticks in the book comes out blackened as if it had been stuck in an oven; four lines earlier in the same passage, sexual guilt had already been linked with the etymologically related word "fournée": "cette bonne hypocrite, / Un pain sur la *fournée* emprunta" [that good hypocrite, / Borrowed some bread in advance from the batch] (1.13, lines 41–42), alluding to Oriane's having conceived a child before marriage. The "pain" [bread] that was taken without benefit of clergy reappears as the "pain" [bread] that is the "pareille" [equivalent] Guillaume gives back to André in making love to his wife: "rendant à son époux / ... *pain* blanc pour fouace" [repaying her husband ... white bread for brown] (2.1, lines 188, 189).

Orlando Furioso, another dangerous book in "The Ballad of the Books," also forms part of the connections linking the tales. Alizon was fascinated by the scene in which the sleeping Angelica is at the mercy of a sexual predator. This recalls Venus asleep "Sur un lit de repos" [on a bed of repose] (1.12, line 79) and imprisoned by Vulcan's avenging net in "Vulcan's Revenge," which itself parallels the "repos" [repose] and untroubled sleep the ungrateful beauty sought in the Court of Love (1.11, line 11).

The dénouement of "Making Ears and Mending Molds" echoes that of "Vulcan's Revenge." Guillaume tells his wife to lend him her aid so that "j'attrape le galant" [I might *trap the gallant*] (2.1.106). In the concluding lines of "Vulcan's Revenge" the narrator asks, referring to the way the lovers were caught in Vulcan's net, "Demandez-moi qui fut bien *attrapé*, / Ce fut, je crois, *le galant* et la belle" [Ask me who was well *trapped*. It was, I believe, *the gallant* and the beauty] (1.12, lines 118–19). Venus and Mars are trapped on a bed; André is trapped between a bed and a wall. Neither André nor Venus and Mars can leave the scene of the crime. While Guillaume made love to André's wife, "André vit tout, et n'osa murmurer" [André saw everything, and dared make no murmur] (2.1, line 195), forced to watch (and, though he did not know it, to be object of Guillaume's attention)—as Venus and Mars were forced to be the objects of others' gaze. A similar paralysis afflicted the sleeping Angelica alluded to in "The Ballad of the Books."

Words Unique to This Tale and the One Before

If André's punishment echoes that of Mars and Venus, it is poetic justice, for his crime included behaving like Vulcan, who caught his prey with "Un *rets*" [a net] (1.12, line 102): André, who preyed upon women, "ne tendait guère en vain ses filets; ... / Sage eût été l'oiseau qui de ses *rets* / Se fût sauvé" [did not lay his nets in vain.... Wise would have been the bird who could save itself from his *nets*] (2.1, lines 8, 10–11). The word "rets" appears in no other tale.

2.2 "The Catalonian Friars" ("Les Frères de Catalogne")

Source: *Les Cent Nouvelles Nouvelles*, story 32

In both "The Catalonian Friars" and "Making Ears and Mending Molds"

(1) A man named André persuades another man's wife (or other men's wives) to engage with him in extramarital sex for the sake of a worthy end (improving the unborn child in 2.1, the wive's salvation in 2.2).

(2) André's success is due to the wives' ignorance: Alice "*ignorait* les malices d'amour" [was *ignorant* of love's wicked wiles] (2.1, line 15); the Catalonian Friars had their way at a time when the feminine sex "vivait / Dans *l'ignorance*" [lived in *ignorance*] (2.2, lines 15–16).

(3) The Andrés tell the wives they are asking only for an excess their husbands do not need. Alice informs her husband that "André me dit quand il parfit l'enfant, / Qu'en trouveriez *plus que* pour *votre usage*" [André told me when he perfected the child that you would find *more than* you needed for *your use*] (2.1, lines 96–97); Brother André tells the assembled wives that what the monks want from them is something for which their husbands "n'ont *plus que* faire" [have *no more* need] (2.2, line 37), a "superflu" [superfluity] (2.2, line 40). He then anticipates the objection that "*notre usage*" [*our practice*] (2.2, line 41) might seem counter to the laws of marriage, but that his ultimate concern is the salvation of their souls. In these parallel passages the two "plus que" have different meanings yet point toward this same conclusion. In 2.1, Guillaume will find more than ("*plus que*") he needs; in 2.2, the husbands are in possession of something they have no use for ("Un bien dont ils n'ont *plus que* faire"). Similarly, "usage" has two different senses in the two passages: in 2.1, "votre usage" means "your needs"; in 2.2, "notre usage" means "our practice" (of requiring such tithes). Nevertheless the two echoing expressions ("plus que" and "votre / notre usage") are intriguingly there, and they serve parallel arguments.

(4) The wives have scruples—but in exactly opposite ways. Alice was worried that what André proposed might be wrong: "Alix dans la pensée / Sur cette affaire un *scrupule* se mit" [Alice in her mind had a *scruple* about this affair] (2.1, lines 64–65). But the Catalonian wives were scrupu-

lous in not holding back their favors from the monks: after a few months, the monks were getting fatigued and would have willingly extended credit but "les donzelles *scrupuleuses*, / De s'acquitter étaient soigneuses, / Croyant faillir en retenant / Un bien à l'ordre appartenant" [the *scrupulous* women were careful to pay their tithe, thinking it wrong to retain what belonged to the order] (2.2, lines 129–32).

(5) Sex is work. In 2.1, what André and Alice are doing is to complete "l'*ouvrage*" [the *work*] (2.2, line 50, 61) of perfecting the unborn child. In 2.2, the wife explains to her husband that the monks are taking a tithe on "les *oeuvres* de mariage" [the *works* of marriage] (2.2, line 178), echoing Brother André's words (2.2, line 66) in his sermon to the wives. That sex is work is also clear from the following passage in 2.1, which is echoed in two separate passages in 2.2: "Philosopher ne faut pour *cette affaire*. / André *vaquait* de grande affection / À son *travail*" [No philosophizing needed for *this affair*. André *attended to* his *work* with great affection] (2.1, lines 45–47). The verb *travailler* returns when the monks "dans la vigne du Seigneur / *Travaillent*" [*work* in the Lord's vineyard] (2.2, lines 12–13); "cette affaire" and "vaquer" return in "le couvent ... / Après avoir à cette affaire / *Vaqué* cinq ou six mois" (2.2.124, 126–27). The combination of "vaquer à" + "cette affaire" is unique to these tales.

(6) The angry husband takes "*vengeance*" (2.1, line 183; 2.2, line 230) on the man who slept with his wife.

(7) The vengeful husband keeps the malefactor "*enfermé*" [locked up] (2.1, line 162; 2.2, lines 218, 249).

Significant Alterations

(1) There was no Friar André in the source for 2.2.

(2) Both Andrés make the argument that they are only taking an excess that the husband doesn't need. Friar André's argument to this effect does not appear in the source.

(3) The husbands' vengeance in "The Catalonian Friars," which is so extreme as to be out of character for the *Tales*, was not in La Fontaine's source, as Collinet notes (Pléiade edition, 1379n). A measure of the importance of these sequential parallels for La Fontaine may lie in the fact that he forged the parallel to 2.1 even if it meant going out of character.

Words Unique to This Tale and the One Before

(1) "cette affaire ... vaquait à" (2.1, lines 45–56); "à cette affaire / Vaqué" (2.2, lines 126–27)

(2) "enfermé" (in the singular)

2.3 "The Cradle" ("Le Berceau")

Source: Boccaccio, *Decameron*, Ninth Day, Sixth Story; a variant appears in "The Reeve's Tale" in Chaucer's *Canterbury Tales*.

The wife in "The Catalonian Friars" complains to her husband, "Vous êtes cause qu'en *demeure* / Je me trouve présentement" [You're the reason I'm past due now] (2.2, lines 182–83) when he won't let her see the monk at midnight. When midnight chimes in "The Cradle," Pinuccio, "Son temps venu ne fait longue *demeure*" [his time come, did not remain long] (2.3, line 77) in bed, but hops up to join Colette in hers. Pinuccio, in other words, does not "fait longue demeure" because he makes his midnight assignation; the wife is "en demeure" because she does not.

The wife had planned to make her payment to the monk "en *chemin faisant*" [*along the way*] (2.2, line 147); that is, as she was passing by the monastery. La Fontaine plants the identical expression in the other tale at the moment when the innkeeper's wife, having been misled by the displaced cradle into entering the wrong bed, decides to profit from the unusual ardor displayed in her husband (whom she takes Pinuccio's friend to be): "*Chemin faisant*, c'était fortune honnête [*Along the way*, it was a piece of luck honestly come by] (2.3, line 125). Here the expression "Chemin faisant" appears to come from the friend's thought that it a piece of honest luck to have found her in his bed, though alternately it could have come from her thought that it was a piece of good fortune that her husband should be in such an amorous mood.

Frère André preached in his sermon to the wives, "Qu'entre *la chair et la chemise* / Il faut cacher le bien qu'on fait: / Tout ceci doit être secret" [That between *the flesh and the shirt* we must hide the good we do. All this should be secret] (2.2, lines 78–80). On her return from having gone to investigate the noise that awoke her, the innkeeper's wife mistakenly believes the cradle has kept her from climbing into the wrong bed: "Près de ces gens, je me suis, peu s'en faut, / Remise au lit *en chemise ainsi nue*" [I very nearly got into bed with these men *naked under my nightshirt*] (2.3, lines 103–4). In this turn of phrase "chemise" and naked flesh are combined, as they were in a different way in "The Catalonian Friars." In the end, the innkeeper's wife does hide what she did beneath her chemise, though it was some time after the act before even she realized what she had done.

Frère André's recommendation that "*Tout* ceci doit être *secret*" [*All* this should be *secret*] (2.2, line 80) is not entirely followed, as one wife eventually tells her husband why she has a midnight appointment, and he subsequently discovers the dimensions of the scandal. But André's advice *is* followed in the concluding lines of "The Cradle," in a combination of "tout" with "secret" that appears in no other tale: "*Tout* fut *secret*; et quiconque eut du bon / Par-devers soi le garda sans rien dire" [*All* was kept *secret*, and whoever profited kept it himself] (2.3, lines 199–200).

Significant Alteration

In "The Cradle" Pinuccio and Colette plan their rendezvous for midnight, which is the same time that the wife in "The Catalonian Friars" tries to go visit her monk. In the source for the latter, that time had been the hour of the angelus, which would have hours earlier. In the *Decameron*, Pinuccio simply goes from his bed to the girl's when he thought everyone else was asleep; the hour is not indicated.

Words Unique to This Tale and the One Before

"tout ... secret."

In the first (1666) edition of Book Two of the *Tales*, "Making Ears and Mending Molds" was immediately followed by "The Cradle"; three years later, La Fontaine published a second edition, adding three more tales that he had published separately in 1667 and 1668 (in the *Recueil contenant plusieurs discours libres et moraux* in 1667, published allegedly in Cologne, but possibly clandestinely in France [Collinet, Pléiade edition, p. 1330], in the *Recueil des Contes du Sieur de La Fontaine, les Satyres de Boileau, et autres pièces curieuses* in 1668). He inserted one of them, "The Catalonian Friars," between these two; he placed the others ("The Hermit Monk" and "Mazet of Lamporechio") at the end of the book. Why did he not place "The Catalonian Friars" at the end of the book with the other two? Georges Couton asks the same question in his notes to the Garnier edition of the *Contes*, and suggests it might have been "to attenuate the scandalous nature of the tales that attack monks and priests" (p. 392n), but it is not clear how the import of this tale of monkish misbehavior could be attenuated by its appearing in one place rather than another. It is more likely La Fontaine placed the tale where he did because of opportunities it offered for forging ties with those on either side, which we have seen to be extensive. His placing it there and not with the others suggests that for him the order in which the tales appear was important. More than that, what he did to this tale between its separate publication and its reappearance in Book Two proves that the parallels to be found between neighboring tales were intentional, for the change he made actually creates one. Line 82 was originally "Voici un beau mot de *l'Apôtre*" [Here is a good word of the *Apostle*] (Collinet, Pléiade edition, 1378n). When the tale appeared in Book Two, the line was changed to "Voici trois mots d'un *bon apôtre*" [Here are three words of a *good apostle*], thereby forging yet another parallel between this André and the André in "Making Ears and Mending Molds," who is there called the "*bon apôtre*" [*good apostle*] (2.1, line 66).

But before "The Catalonian Friars" came on the scene, there were quite a number of parallels between the two tales who until then were neighbors, "Making Ears and Mending Molds" and "The Cradle."

(1) In both, a man makes love to another man's wife in that man's presence.

(2) In both, someone eagerly and naively recounts to the very person who should not hear it the adultery that character has committed. Alice tells Guillaume as soon as he returns home that she has been sleeping with André, blithely assuming her husband would approve of her efforts to improve the unborn child; Pinuccio, thinking he is talking to his friend, regales the innkeeper with intimate details of what he had just done with his daughter.

(3) The father's reaction parallels the husband's. Speaking "d'un ton plein *de colère*" [in a tone full *of anger*] (2.3, line 156), he berates the lovers, telling Colette "il faut que je te *tue*" [I have to *kill* you] (2.3, line 166). Similarly, Guillaume, "outré *de colère....* Voulut *tuer*" [moved *by anger....* Wanted *to kill*] (2.1, lines 86, 88) his wife. The expression "de colère" appears in no other tale in Books 1–4 (which is to say, in any of the tales published by La Fontaine in an organized collection—the tales gathered here in Book 5 never appeared all together in one place in the poet's lifetime).

(4) Noise, and making less of it than one might, is a motif in both tales. Guillaume's first thought is to cut off an ear, or some more pertinent part of André's body, but then decides to avenge the wrong "avecque moins de *bruit*" [with less *noise*] (2.1, line 140). When Pinuccio's friend leaves the room in the dark he reasons that to try to get around the cradle "aurait fait trop de *bruit*" [would have made too much *noise*] (2.3, line 91), so he moves the cradle instead, with what results we know. In other words, the dénouement of 2.1 finds its origin in the desire to make "moins de bruit," while the dénouement of 2.3 likewise finds its origin in the desire not to make "trop de bruit." And it is another noise that sets the catastrophe in motion, the "bruit" (2.3, line 97) that awoke the innkeeper's wife. Similarly, the "bruit" (2.1, line 120) Guillaume intentionally makes as he climbs the stairs sends André into his hiding place between the bed and the wall.

(5) In both tales the verb *irriter* has a sexual nuance. When Guillaume begins to make love to André's wife he is so "*irrité*" (2.1, line 186) that he spares her nothing. La Fontaine here gives a double sense to "irrité": both "angry" and "sexually excited." The second sense is apparent when the word reappears in "The Cradle": prior to the night of their rendezvous, Pinuccio and Colette were frustrated in their desire to be alone together, but "Cela ne fit qu'*irriter*" [it only *inflamed*] (2.3, line 37) their passion.

(6) When Pinuccio approached Colette's bed "*Pas ne trouva la pucelle endormie*" [he did *not* find the girl asleep] (2.3, line 79), because she was waiting for him, ready to join in consummating their passion. Likewise, in the only other appearance of "pas [...] endormi[e]" in the *Tales*, "Le lendemain, pareille heure venue, / André ne fut *pas endormi*. / Il s'en alla chez la pauvre innocente" [The next morning at the same hour, André was *not asleep*. He went to the poor innocent's house] (2.1, lines 55–57). In both passages saying that a person is not asleep is a way of saying that that person is ready and eager for sex.

(7) La Fontaine seems to hint at the parallel between Alice sleeping with André and the innkeeper's wife sleeping with Pinuccio's companion by inserting a word in both tales that appears in no other. In 2.1, it denotes the husband's absence that gives André his opportunity: "Son mari donc se trouvant en *emplette*, / Elle au logis, en sa chambre seulette, / André survient" [Her husband *off buying provisions*, she at home in her room alone, André showed up] (2.1, lines 18–20). In 2.3, it denotes the attractiveness Pinuccio's finds in the innkeeper's wife, despite her age: he "recommence la fête. / La dame était de bonne *emplette* encor" [begins his enjoyment again. The lady was *well-endowed* still] (2.3, lines 122–23).

(8) When the innkeeper's wife got in bed with him, Pinuccio's friend "La mit en *oeuvre*" [went *to work* on her] (2.3, line 111); what André and Alice did was likewise "work": "Demain, dit-il, nous polirons l'*ouvrage*" [tomorrow, he said, we will perfect *the work*] (2.1, line 50); "Et moi, dit-elle, allais par un message / Vous avertir de hâter cet *ouvrage*" [and I, she said, was going to send you a message to hurry up this *work*] (2.1, lines 60–61); "Tant fut *ouvré*" [so much *work* was done] (2.1, line 64). The connection between work and marriage would also play a role in the tale that in the second edition comes, like the cradle, between the two: Friar André exhorts the wives to give the monks a tithe on "les *oeuvres* de mariage" [the *works* of marriage] (2.2, line 66).

Words Unique to This Tale and the One Before

(1) "de colère"
(2) "pas [...] endormie"
(3) "emplette"

2.4 "The Muleteer" ("Le Muletier")

Source: Boccaccio, *Decameron*,
Third Day, Second Story

In both "The Muleteer" and "The Cradle" a woman makes love in the dark to a man she mistakes for her husband. Both are surprised by their "husband"'s unwonted vigor, which they attribute to exactly opposite causes: the innkeeper's wife to joy, wondering "quelle joie / Le fait agir en homme de vingt ans?" [what joy makes him act like a twenty-year-old?] (2.3, lines 117–18); the queen to anger, believing that "la colère / Rendait le prince outre son ordinaire / Plein de transport" [anger was making the king more than usually passionate] (2.4, lines 79–81). The innkeeper's wife sees this as a gift from God: "puisque Dieu nous l'envoie" [since God is giving it to us] (2.3, line 119). The narrator speaks of the muleteer's potency in parallel terms: "En ses présents le Ciel est toujours juste" [In its gifts, Heaven is always just] (2.4, line 82).

In both tales a man pretends to be asleep: the muleteer when the king passes among his stable hands looking for his wife's lover; Punuccio when he pretends to be sleepwalking, at his friend's suggestion.

In describing the ritual the king observed on nights he wished to sleep with his wife, the narrator notes that he would arrive "Presque *en chemise*" [wearing almost nothing but *a nightshirt*] (2.4, line 48). This connection between near-nudity and a "chemise" parallels the innkeeper's wife's concern that she was almost "en chemise ainsi nue" [naked in her nightshirt] (2.3, line 104), and continues a thread begun in Friar André's remarks in "The Catalonian Friars" about keeping the secret between flesh and the "chemise" (2.2, line 78).

Significant Alterations

(1) In Boccaccio's version of "The Cradle," the innkeeper's wife does not wonder why her husband has suddenly turned so passionate.

(2) Nor does she speak of it as a gift from God.

(3) Both tales end in silence in La Fontaine; not so in Boccaccio. In "The Muleteer" the king tells the stable hands that whoever did the deed should remain silent about it: "qui la fait si se taise" (2.4, line 140). "The Cradle" also ends with silence, with all the participants having good reason to keep their secrets "sans rien dire" [without saying anything] (2.3, line 200). But in Boccaccio the participants continue to chatter on about the evening's events.

2.5 *"The Saint Julian Prayer"* *("L'Oraison de saint Julien")*

Source: Boccaccio, *Decameron*,
Second Day, Second Story

In both "The Saint Julian Prayer" and "The Muleteer," a man appears "en chemise" (Renaud, because the robbers have taken his clothes [2.5, line 98]; the Muleteer, because he is disguised as the king [2.4, lines 48 and 59]) at the door of a desirable widow (the queen in 2.4, though remarried, is widow of the late king), is admitted by her maidservant, is bathed and perfumed, exchanges his rags for his husband's clothes (the widow lends them to Renaud; the Muleteer had already attired himself in clothes resembling the king's before appearing at the door), gives the woman the impression that he is her husband (her current husband in "The Muleteer"; her late husband in "The Saint Julian Prayer"), gains entry to her bed, and the two make love.

The muleteer is "en chemise" of his own volition, but Renaud against his will. The muleteer's attire (which included being "en chemise" like the king but also wearing his mantle) was above his station, Renaud's beneath. The muleteer was dressing that way in order to look like the woman's husband; conversely, Renaud's being dressed that way led to his putting on the husband's clothes.

Renaud "*tremble*, et frissonne" [*trembles* and shivers] (2.5, line 146) in the cold before he gains admittance; the muleteer "*tremble*" [*trembles*] (2.4, line 119) in the stable as he awaits the king's return. It is because Renaud is trembling (from the cold) that he is admitted into the widow's house and subsequently makes love to her; in a precisely situation, the muleteer trembles because he has made love to the widow (the queen).

Significant Alterations

(1) In Boccaccio's version, the king was not wearing a nightshirt when he appeared at the door of the queen, and thus neither was the muleteer. Renaud was, however, clad only in his shirt after the robbers took his clothes. La Fontaine evidently took that detail and planted it in "The Muleteer" as well.

(2) His heart beats wildly, but the muleteer does not tremble in Boccaccio's version, though Renaud does: again, a detail taken from one source and planted in the other to produce a further parallel.

(e) Although both the muleteer and Renaud take a bath in Boccaccio's version of these tales, neither is perfumed.

Words Unique to This Tale and the One Before

(1) "tremble" (in a conjugated form)

(2) The muleteer, in preparation for meeting the queen, is "*parfumé*" [*perfumed*] (2.4, line 69); Renaud likewise: "On le *parfume* avant que l'habiller" [He is *perfumed* before being dressed] (2.5, line 215). These are the only times anyone is perfumed in the *Tales*.

2.6 *"The Servant Girl Found Guiltless" ("La Servante justifiée")*

Source: Marguerite de Navarre,
Heptaméron, story 45

While in "The Saint Julian Prayer" a man comes to resemble the owner of the clothes he puts on, in "The Servant Girl Found Guiltless" a woman comes to resemble the presumed owner of the clothing she takes off.

The husband begins his dalliance with the maid by praising her: "il commence à *louer* / L'assortiment" [he began by *praising* her flower arrangement] (2.6, lines 27–28). Renaud began his courtship of the widow with praise as well, "*louant* par le menu / Tout ce qu'il voit, tout ce qu'il n'a point vu" [*praising* in detail all that he saw and all that he hadn't seen] (2.5, lines 279–80). Both women go through the motions only of fending off the man's advances. The widow "résista tout autant qu'il fallait, / Ni plus ni moins" [resisted as much as required, neither more no less] (2.6, lines 294–95). When the husband began to slip his hand onto her breast, she "Se défendit: mais de quelle manière? / Sans rien gâter" [defended herself. But how? Without spoiling anything] (2.6, lines 31–32). In a parallel turn of phrase, between Renaud and the widow there were "*baisers* donnés et pris ... ce *qu'on appelle* ... les préludes d'amour" [*kisses* given and taken ... *what one calls* ... foreplay] (2.5, lines 299–301); the neighbor informs the wife that her husband and the girl began to pick certain flowers "*que baisers on appelle*" [*that one calls kisses*] (2.6, line 84).

After acknowledging that he found his source for "La Servante justifiée" in the *Heptaméron* of Marguerite de Navarre, La Fontaine writes, "quiconque en soit l'auteur ... / J'y mets du mien selon les occurrences: / C'est ma coutume; et, sans telles licences, / Je quitterais la charge de conteur" [whoever the author is ... I put some of my own in according to opportunity. It's my custom, and without such freedom I would give up telling stories] (2.6, lines 13, 14–16). What he puts of his own in this and other tales falls into three categories:

(1) the additions he makes to the narrative, of which all the details of seduction in the preceding paragraph are instances;

(2) the verbal echoes he inserts such as "baisers ... qu'on appelle" / "que baisers on appelle";

(3) and his occasional subtle allusions to the sequential structure and its concomitant repetitions. "The Saint Julian Prayer" and "The Servant Girl Found Guiltless" not only repeat each other but are about the act of repeating. In the garden everything happens twice, so that the second version erases the first. Similarly, Renaud not only repeats the look and the clothing of the widow's late husband (2.5, lines 266–67), as the muleteer had done in the story before, but in a later scene the widow sets out to erase what had happened to Renaud before he arrived at her doorstep by a series of sexual favors: "Voilà ... / Pour le chemin, voici pour les brigands, / Puis pour la peur, puis pour le mauvais temps: / Tant que le tout pièce à pièce s'efface" [That is ... for the road, this for the thieves, then for the fear, then for the bad weather; so that everything piece by piece was erased] (2.5, lines 306–09). The widow's enumeration, point by point, of the different details she makes disappear anticipates the point by point enumeration that will take place in "The Servant Girl Found Guiltless" when every detail the neighbor recounts is answered, and erased, by the wife's "c'était moi" [that was me] (the phrase that La Fontaine singles out for special phrase in the tale's opening lines).

Significant Alteration

In Boccaccio, the widow does not enumerate Renaud's misfortunes and then kiss them away.

Words Unique to This Tale and the One Before

"baisers ... on appelle"

2.7 "The Three Wives' Wager" ("La Gageure des trois commères")

Source: Boccaccio, *Decameron*, Seventh Day, Eighth and Ninth Stories; the second of La Fontaine's three tales parallels "The Merchant's Tale" in Chaucer's *Canterbury Tales*.

In both the first of the three stories told in "The Three Wives' Wager" and "The Servant Girl Found Guiltless" a husband has designs on a chambermaid whose identity is in question; in both, her clothes are part of her disguise, particularly when she removes them. In 2.6, it is the wife who is fooled about the chambermaid's identity; in 2.7, it is the husband. In both, the unfaithful spouse makes love to a "chambrière" [chambermaid] (a real one in one story, a pretend one in the other) without the other spouse finding out.

In both the second story and "The Servant Girl Found Guiltless" a spouse makes illicit love in a garden in full view of a witness and gets away with it. In both, a "dance" of sorts takes place "on the grass." When the husband climbs the tree the second time, he "voit la *danse* / Sans se fâcher" [sees the *dance* without getting angry] (2.7, lines 200–01), a dance paralleling the one the husband performed with his wife in imitation of what he had done with the maid: "tétons d'entrer en *danse*" [breasts entered into the *dance*] (2.6, line 57). Guillot, the lover, pretends to have seen the husband kissing his wife "*sur l'herbette*" [*on the grass*] (2.7, line 161), paralleling the neighbor's complaint that the chambermaid fell and made love "*sur l'herbe*" [*on the grass*] (2.6, line 91). In both stories, a spouse is led to believe that eyewitness testimony is mistaken: the wife puts no credence in what the neighbor saw; the husband does not believe his own eyes. In both, the eyewitness evidence is discounted because of the way a second, parallel event is cleverly invented by the adulterous spouse: what the husband does in the garden with the wife neutralizes the effect of the eyewitness evidence of what he did with the maid; what Guillot claims to have seen the husband do with the wife neutralizes the effect of the first-hand evidence the husband has of what Guillot actually did do with his wife.

The theme of repetition continues into the third story told in "The Three Wives' Wager." Thus, while in "The Servant Girl Found Guiltless" a wife is fooled by her husband into re-enacting a sequence of events in which a chambermaid had taken part with her lover (who was that wife's husband), in "The Three Wives' Wager" a wife fools her husband by claiming to have re-enacted a sequence of events in which a chambermaid had taken part with her lover: tying a thread to her toe, running the thread out the front door to the street, and waiting for the tug at the other end.

Significant Alteration

In Boccaccio, the source for the third tale in 2.7, the wife does not claim to be re-enacting what the chambermaid did.

2.8 "How Old Men Count the Days" ("Le Calendrier des vieillards")

Source: Boccaccio, *Decameron*,
Second Day, Tenth Story

Thanks to the "gageure" [wager] the three wives made with each other, they were all able to enjoy a lover they valued more than their husband. Thanks to a "gageure" (2.8, line 100) she makes—about who can catch the most fish—the heroine of "How Old Men Count the Days" ultimately finds a lover she enjoys more than she ever did her husband. There was no wager in the *Decameron*'s version.

In addition to the wager that frames them, each of the three wives' tales in 2.7 finds something to match it in 2.8:

Richard de Quinzica is exceedingly "scrupulous": He never encountered a day in the calendar where he could not allege some "scruple" (2.8, lines 44 and 76) that would rule out making loving to his wife. The first husband in "The Three Wives' Wager" was scrupulous too, or pretended to be, finding the new chambermaid very fetching but feeling constrained to "feindre du *scrupule*" [feign *scruples*] (2.7, line 63) in her presence. When his wife catches him with her she says that had she known his tastes "J'aurais chez moi toujours eu des *tendrons*" [I would

always have *young girls* on hand] (2.7, line 83); the narrator of 2.8 calls the heroine a "tendron" too, citing her as an example of how parents "Jeunes *tendrons* à vieillards apparient" [match *young girls* with old men] (2.8, line 7). When Bartholomea is kidnapped by the pirate, she "fit son devoir de pleurer / Un demi-jour" [made it her duty to weep for half a day] (2.8, lines 122–23), as the fake chambermaid "Fait la honteuse, et jette une ou deux larmes" [pretends to be ashamed, and weeps one or two tears] (2.7, line 107) when his mistress says that she [i.e., he] is going to have to sleep with her from now on.

In the second wager story, Guillot pretends to complain that the husband and wife are engaging in a display of affection right beneath his eyes, exclaiming "*Devant les gens* prendre ainsi vos ébats!" [To cavort *in front of people*!] (2.7, line 144). Quinzica explains away his wife's absence of affection for him with the same turn of phrase: "la pauvrette est honteuse / *Devant les gens*" [the poor thing is ashamed *in front of people*] (2.8, lines 183–84). The phrase, which appears in no other tale, connects two parallel yet opposite moments, for what Guillot falsely accuses the husband of doing is what Richard falsely claims his wife cannot do, engage in a public display of affection.

The third wager story concludes, as does 2.8, with the happy marriage of a couple who knew each other sufficiently well because they had already made love several times. The pirate and Bartholomea avoided the mistake she had made with Quinzica, "S'étant choisis l'un et l'autre à l'épreuve" [having chosen each other by trial] (2.8, line 252). Similarly, the valet and the chambermaid went to the altar "Se connaissant tous deux de plus d'un jour" [having known each other for more than one day] (2.7, line 322); they had been sleeping with each other for some time. Neither the wedding nor even the couple appears in the source for that tale.

The advice La Fontaine offers in the prologue to 2.8, that like matched pairs of beasts of burden, married couples should be "de force pareille" [of equal strength] (2.8, line 11), is itself matched by his practice of offering us his *Tales* themselves in well-matched pairs, each married to the other—though in a sequence that requires something like serial adultery in that each is wedded to two partners!

Significant Alterations

(1) There is no wager in 2.8's source.

(2) In the source for 2.7's third tale, there is no marriage of a couple (the valet and the chambermaid) who (unlike Bartholomea and Quinzica, but like Bartholomea and the pirate) tested their sexual compatibility before marriage.

Words Unique to This Tale and the One Before

"Devant les gens."

2.9 "A Money-Minded Woman Meets Her Match" ("À femme avare galant escroc")

Source: Boccaccio, *Decameron*, Eighth Day, First Story; a variant appears as "The Shipman's Tale" in Chaucer's *Canterbury Tales*.

Guillot in the pear tree, in the second of the stories in "The Three Wives' Wager," tells the husband below how shocked he is to see he and his wife engaging in love-play "*Devant les gens*" [*in front of people*] (2.7, line 144), while Richard de Quinzica maintains to the pirate who kidnapped his wife that the reason she didn't throw her arms around him and shower him with kisses is that she was too shy "*Devant les gens*" [*in front of people*] (2.8, line 184) to show her affection. Now it is precisely because Gulphar gives Gasparin's wife the money "en présence de gens" [in the presence of people] (2.9, line 45) that she is constrained to hand it over to her husband, and that Gulphar achieves his goal of tricking her into giving him sex for nothing. La Fontaine had to make a change in the story to achieve his end of having this scene echo the two others. In the *Decameron* it is in the presence of only one witness that Gulphar gives her the money. All three scenes—"Devant les gens" in 2.7 and 2.8 and "en présence de gens" in 2.9—offer variations on the theme of making a sexual display in public, except that it is just the opposite here because Gasparin's wife at first thought Gulphar was trying to *conceal* from the "gens" the sexual nature of their transaction by pretending to repay the loan. Only later does she realize he really was paying it back.

The narrator of "A Money-Minded Woman Meets Her Match" complains that in the present age only money talks in matters of love, and indeed Gulphar has to buy the woman's favors. Richard de Quinzica in "How Old Men Count the Days" essentially bought his wife from her parents when he married her, and tries to buy her again from Pagamin. "Mettez un prix ... Je le paierai *comptant....* / *Voilà* ma bourse, il ne faut que *compter*" [Set your price ... I'll pay it *in cash.... There is* my purse, just *count*] (2.8, lines 164–65, 167). His words anticipate those Gulphar will say to Gasparin's wife: "*Voilà*, dit-il, deux cents écus *comptants*" [*There are*, he said, two hundred crowns *in cash*] (2.9, line 46). "Voilà" and the verb "compter" appear together in no other single line in the *Tales*. Pagamin, who refuses to sell her back but would give her back if she wanted to

go, doesn't want to sell what Gulphar doesn't want to buy (but will obtain by pretending to buy).

The narrator of "A Money-Minded Woman Mets her Match" complains that "Le *jeu*, la *jupe*, et l'amour des plaisirs" [*Gambling*, the *skirt*, and the love of pleasures] (2.9, line 30) are resources at Cupid's disposal ("la jupe" standing here for women's clothing in general). Bartholomea's husband links gambling and clothing in recalling his attempts to purchase her affection. "Have I ever refused you anything," he asks, "Soit pour ton *jeu*, soit pour tes *vêtements*?" [either for your gambling or for your clothes?] (line 198). These are the only two lines where "jeu" and clothing appear together in the *Tales*. We will see this connection return in the next tale.

Significant Alterations

Instead of several witnesses ("en présence de gens") to the return of the money, there is only one.

Words Unique to This Tale and the One Before

(1) the verb "compter" +"Voilà"
(2) "jeu" + clothing

2.10 "You Can't Think of Everything ("On ne s'avise jamais de tout")

Source: *Les Cent Nouvelles Nouvelles*, story 37

The wife is constrained to good behavior as long as her guardian is present, as the wife in the preceding tale was constrained to return the money to her husband because Gulphar gave it to her in front of other people.

The narrator's assertion in "A Money-Minded Woman Meets her Match" that "la jupe" [the skirt] counts among Cupid's resources (since a man can buy a woman's love by buying her clothes) becomes true for a different reason here, for it was by getting her "jupe" soiled and sending her guardian away to get another one that the wife was able to see her lover. In the source, it was not another skirt the guardian was sent to find but a dress and a head scarf. La Fontaine evidently made this change to make the connection.

The woman in the soiled skirt "gâte" [spoils]: "on n'avait jeté / Cette immondice, et la dame *gâté*, / Qu'afin qu'elle eût quelque valable excuse / Pour éloigner son dragon quelque temps" [this garbage was thrown, and the lady *spoiled* (her dress), so that she'd have a good exuse for sending away her dragon for a while] (2.10, lines 29–32). The money-minded woman has something spoiled, too: "Elle était jeune, et belle ... fors un point qui *gâtait* / Toute l'affaire ...

elle était avare" [She was young and beautiful ... except for a detail that *spoiled* everything ... she was greedy] (2.9, lines 22–25). Yet the avarice that spoiled her became the means through which Gulphar fulfilled his desire. So not only does the wife "gâter" something in both tales (*dame* is the subject, not the direct object of *[avait] gâté* in "et la dame gâté"), but in both it is thanks to her doing this that the lover achieves his end.

The husband's immediate response when the duenna tells him that his wife has spoiled her skirt and sent her to fetch another is that trick "isn't in my *book* [*livre*]" (2.10, line 27), his compendium of wifely wiles. Not only does he have a book, but the important thing is that something is not listed in it that should be. The husband in the other tale had one too, the account book from whch Gulphar asks him to erase his debt: "Déchargez-en votre *livre* de grâce" [please delete it from your *book*] (2.9. 60). The debt will be *deleted* from the book of accounts, thus providing the perfect complement to the trick that would have to be *added* to the other husband's book.

Significant Alteration

The "robe" and "couvrechef" are changed to a "jupe."

2.11 "The Bumpkin in Search of His Calf" ("Le Villageois qui cherche son veau")

Source: *Les Cent Nouvelles Nouvelles*, story 12

The tale in which a duenna loses sight of the woman she was supposed to be guarding is followed by the story of a man who loses track of the calf in his charge. In both, a surprise comes down from above: the garbage falling from a window and the unexpected voice from the tree that interrupts the lover and his lady, "les arrêtant tout coi" [stopping them speechless] (2.11, line 11). The interruptions have opposite effects, interrupting lovemaking in one instance, making it possible for it to begin in the other. Each "dame" is undressed in the presence of her "galant"—the terms are used in both tales.

2.12 "Hans Carvel's Ring" ("L'Anneau d'Hans Carvel")

Source: Rabelais, *Tiers Livre*, chapter 28; *Les Cent Nouvelles Nouvelles*, story 11

This tale and its predecessor suggest hidden parts of the female anatomy without actually naming them. Hans Carvel puts his finger "où vous savez" [where you know] (2.12, line 48); the narrator of the other tale reports that the gallant exclaims over

what he can and cannot see "Sans dire quoi" [Without saying what] (2.11, line 10). Both Carvel and the man in the tree put a stop to someone else's sexual activity inadvertently—at least initially in Carvel's case, since he at first thought he was putting a ring on his finger; only later does the Devil explain that doing so will prevent his wife from having lovers.

Significant Alteration

The humor of 2.11 arises from the bumpkin's not realizing what the pair below were up to, focusing as he was on what he heard the gallant say about his visual powers. From his high perch where he had gone "Pour mieux entendre, et pour voir dans la plaine" [The better to hear, and to see into the plain] (2.11, line 4) in his attempt to locate his calf, the tree's branches and leaves evidently blocked his view of what was directly below. Here La Fontaine departs from his source, where the tree-sitter did see the naked woman below and misread what he saw, taking her pubic hair to be the tail of his calf.

2.13 "The Boasting Braggart Punished" ("Le Gascon puni")

Source: *La Précaution inutile*, a Spanish play adapted by Scarron in 1655

Both the man looking for his calf and Hans Carvel stumble into a sexual situation without realizing it. That motif continues in "The Boasting Braggart Punished," with a number of parallels between the bragging Gascon and Hans Carvel:

(1) Both men spend the night in bed with the woman they love (Carvel with his wife, the Gascon with Philis although he doesn't realize it),

(2) snoring (Carvel actually doing so, the Gascon making snoring noises—at least Philis advises him to "snore away"),

(3) and are surprised by what they discover in the morning.

(4) What they are surprised by is the realization that what they had thought was non-sexual—Carvel having his finger in a ring, Dorilas in bed with Cloris's husband—turns out to have been sexual.

(5) To soften Philis's heart, the Gascon "eût couché, dit-il, avec le *diable*" [would have slept, he said, with the *Devil*] (2.13, line 65). Carvel meets the Devil in his sleep.

2.14 "The Runaway Bride" ("La Fiancée du roi de Garbe")

Source: Boccaccio, *Decameron*, Second Day, Seventh Story

Alaciel, daughter of the sultan of Alexandria, is betrothed to the King of Garbe. But she undergoes a series of sexual adventures on her way to meet her intended, with the result that she sleeps with eight men before gets there (to each of whom I will assign a number in parentheses in the order of their appearance). She is escorted on the voyage to her future husband by Hispal (1), with whom she had already formed a sentimental attachment. Attacked by pirates along the way, the young couple manage to escape, swimming from rock to rock until they reach land, Alaciel dragging along a little case full of precious stones. With the treasure, Hispal purchases a château; in the surrounding park and woods they pass idyllic moments, consummating their love. When satiety sets in, Alaciel sends him back to Alexandria to reassure her father and to request a more powerful escort for her return. The second escort arrives, and its captain (2) falls in love with Alaciel, who yields to his desire after he threatens to starve himself to death if she won't. Another pirate (3) attacks, wiping out the escort, compelling Alaciel to make love to him under the threat of her own starvation. A neighboring nobleman (4) then lays siege to the château, killing the pirate and his crew, and takes her into his château. Having plied her with drink, he enters her bed when she is sleeping; though surprised and frightened to awake in his arms, she is persuaded to let him continue the affair. One night he allows a friend (5) to take his place in her bed; given the darkness and his silence, she is at first not aware of the substitution. Though initially angry, she soon consents to become a continual object of exchange between the two. Later, she comes to the rescue of a young woman in her retinue, but at the cost of having to yield to the desire of the man (6) who was intent on forcing himself upon the girl. One day she awakes from a nap in the forest to find herself in the presence of a knight-errant (7) who was about to kiss her but refrains at the last moment. He offers to take her back to her father; in return, she will grant him sexual favors en route. He is slain by a band of brigands near Joppa, but bequeaths her and the rest of the favors to his nephew (8), who escorts her the rest of the way back home. The young man's tutor spins a tale for her father's benefit in which he says that Alaciel has spent her time away from home in innocent religious devotion.

La Fontaine's version of Alaciel's adventures is almost entirely different from Boccaccio's, as he says it will be in his opening lines. He writes that he has followed his source in two points only: that she passed through eight men before finding the right one and that this did not bother her fiancé. He might have added that he retained the shipwreck at the beginning of her adventures and the face-saving fiction at the end. Apart from these elements, La Fontaine gave himself free rein to invent each of the adventures his heroine would undergo. As we will see, he took full advantage of this opportunity to devise episodes that would connect this tale in multiple ways with its immediate predecessor and successor in the sequence.

Alaciel in both versions is brought at last to her fiancé, the king of Garbe, passing her wedding night so successfully that, as La Fontaine puts it, "*Veuve* de huit galants, il la prit pour *pucelle*" [The *widow* of eight gallants, he took her to be a *maiden*] (2.14, line 31). Boccaccio does not call her a widow, only a maiden (a *pucelle* in the French translation of the *Decameron* La Fontaine read). By calling her a widow as well, La Fontaine creates a parallel with Philis of "The Boasting Braggart Punished," for she was a widow (a *veuve* in line 38) with something of a *pucelle* about her: "Je ne sais quel air de *pucelle*" (2.13, line 32). In no other of La Fontaine's tales is a woman both. Actually, Alaciel was not exactly an eight-time widow, despite what La Fontaine says in line 31, for not all of her lovers died. Only two or three of them did: the second pirate (3) and the knight-errant (7); the captain of the second escort (2) may have been slain by the second pirate's men, though the tale is not explicit on that point. La Fontaine thus overstates her widowhood, the better to make the two tales match. Not only are Philis and Alaciel widows, but widows without tears: Philis's rich old husband was one of those "que l'on perd sans pleurer" [whom one loses without weeping] (2.13, line 27). When the lord of the neighboring château (4) hanged the second pirate (3), the little love she bore the latter and the civil treatment she received from her liberator "Ne lui permirent pas de répandre des larmes" [Did not permit her to shed tears] (2.14, line 460). (She does weep for the knight-errant, however, in line 718.)

The crime the Gascon committed and his punishment return here. He was not only a braggart but, more seriously, a "*médisant*" [one who *speaks ill* of someone else] (2.13, line 6). The sixth man to make love to Alaciel, from whom she rescued a girl at the cost of having to have sex with him in the girl's place, had a "*médisante* humeur, grand obstacle aux faveurs" [a tendency *to speak ill*, a great obstacle to receiving women's favors] (2.14, line 564). In his edition of the *Contes*, Jean-Pierre Collinet took note of this connection between two characters (p. 1404n). La Fontaine's practice of highlighting a connection between neighboring tales with a word that makes its only appearances in them is evident here, for such is the case with *médisant(e)*. After he has his way with Alaciel, the man shows that his reputation is well-deserved. He had sworn to say nothing of their encounter, but does so just as soon as he can find a listener (2.14, lines 605–11). In neither of the two sources for "The Basting Braggart Punished" is the model for Dorilas guilty of boasting of sexual success, earned or unearned.

Waking up to the shocking discovery of whom one is in bed with, the Gascon's punishment for his "médisance," is three times inflicted on Alaciel, with lovers 4, 5, and 7. A verbal echo connects the first of these to the Gascon. In preparation for it, in the Gascon's case, "on le *met au* grand *lit*" [he was *put in* the big *bed*] (2.13, line 66); similarly, Alaciel is "*mise au lit* par ses femmes" [*put in bed* by the women] (2.14, line 484) before waking up with lover number 4. When she discovered herself in his arms the next morning, "La *frayeur* lui *glaça* la voix" [*Fright froze* her voice] (2.14, line 496). Similarly, when the Gascon thinks that Cloris's husband (who is really Philis) is getting into bed with him "la *peur* se saisit; / Il devient aussi froid que *glace*" [*fear* took hold of him; he became as cold as *ice*] (2.13, lines 68–69).

"The Runaway Bride," at 801 lines the longest of La Fontaine's *Tales*, is in its structure emblematic of the collection, for the eight gallants succeed each other as the tales in sequence succeed each other, each replicating something of his immediate predecessor:

Both Hispal (1) and the captain of the second escort (2) do battle with pirates (the second pirate being the lieutenant of the first), but with opposite outcomes. The captain was conquered by the pirates who invade the château, but Hispal defeated his pirate, cutting in him in two as he stands with one foot on his ship and the other on Hispal's, a situation that is itself a metaphor for the way the successive gallants and the successive tales are related to each other. When reading them in pairs, we typically find ourselves in the peculiar posture of Grifonia the pirate, with one foot in one and one in the other, able to inhabit both at the same time, and to consider each through the other's perspective. Contemplating two neighboring tales at once, we can find ourselves cut in two by "un revers" [a reverse movement of the blade] (2.14, line 97), our attention equally divided between two situations that are the same, yet by a reversal (to play upon the "revers" by which Hispal divided the pirate) are exactly opposite. That happens in two ways in the microcosm of the *Tales*' sequence that the sequence of Alaciel's first two gallants provides. The first way I have already noted, the fact that both engage in a battle with pirates yet with precisely reverse outcomes. The second way comes from the fact that Hispal triumphs over his pirate by cutting him in half, but the captain of the second escort loses to his pirate because he cut his own troops in half: "il partage / Sa troupe *en deux*" [he divides his troops *in two*] (2.14, lines 322–23) as Hispal "coupe *en deux*" [cuts *in two*] (2.14, line 97) his opponent, leaving one half on the shore, and going with the other to the château. A fatal error, for the troops on the shore are slain by pirates. Had his forces been united, he could have repelled their invasion.

Gallants number 2 and 3, the captain and the pirate who defeated him, are related beyond their combat by the parallel—and yet precisely opposite—methods they use to persuade Alaciel to sleep with them. The captain threatens to die of starvation if she doesn't give in; the pirate threatens to make *her* starve.

Gallant number 4, the lord of the neighboring château, lays siege to Alaciel's château as the pirate had, and just as successfully. They differ, though, in their approach to Alaciel: the pirate, by withholding food; the neighbor, by offering it (the wine was particularly efficacious).

Gallant number 5 is the friend of number 4 whom the latter sends to Alaciel's bed while he goes in search of other conquests. Both enter her bed without her knowing it, but with the difference that when gallant number 4 did so Alaciel was surprised to find a man there at all but number 5 did, she was surprised to discover he was not the man she was expecting. In her subsequent lovemaking with number 5 "l'on *n'omit rien*" [*nothing* was *omitted*] (2.14, line 528), echoing what was said of the feast number 4 had prepared: "Ce *n'était* pas pour *rien omettre*" [*nothing* was *omitted*] (2.14, line 472). The two men differ in their approach to conquest (I am combining the military with the amatory sort here): in attacking the pirate's men as they slept the neighboring lord had been able to effect a complete surprise by taking the precaution of arriving in silence; by contrast, though he had instructed his friend to arrive in silence at Alaciel's bed, the friend could not contain his joy without speaking and as a result could not prevent her from discovering the ruse.

Gallants 4 and 5 are interchangeable, not only when the latter first takes the former's place in the princess's bed but even more so later, after she accepts her new lover and forgives the other one for foisting him upon her. These two interchangeable men are followed by two interchangeable women in the episode of man number 6, Alaciel and the girl the man was originally attacking, and for whom she substitutes. At first, Alaciel insists that he simply take her, but he insists on deciding by chance. In the end, chance decides it will be Alaciel, but his unwillingness to accept her initial offer (she fearing the lot might fall on the girl) is significant, for it underscores the interchangeability of the two women. A further connection between gallants 5 and 6 is that both have trouble holding their tongues, 5 because he could not keep from speaking *before* sex (overcome with joy to be in bed with Alaciel), 6 because he could not keep from speaking *after*.

The theme of interchangeable objects of desire comes right back with gallant number 7, who had trouble choosing between kissing Alaciel's mouth or her breast. In his admirable self-restraint, he is just the opposite of number 6, who was "violent dans ses désirs" [violent in his desires] (2.14, line 553). Yet the verb "passer" marks for both the will to achieve one's desire: "Il faut que l'une ou l'autre *passe*" [One or the other will have to do] (2.14, line 591) gallant number 6 had said about Alaciel and the girl; while it was "sur le point d'en *passer* son envie" [on the point of assuaging his desire] (2.14, line 629) that number 7 stopped short.

After his the death of gallant number 7, his nephew, gallant number 8, continues to claim the sexual favors Alaciel agreed to in return for being safely escorted home. But while the favors the uncle received were extensible, on the occasion of the becalming, the nephew had no such luck, as the last of those agreed upon expired when they arrived at the border of her father's domain, at which point the nephew bows out of the picture. Gallants 7 and 8 are also opposed in that the former was loved, as the tears Alaciel sheds upon his death reveal, while the latter was not, the favors he received being purely a way of satisfying what she owed to his predecessor.

The original (1666) version of Book Two concluded with this tale, and appropriately so. A bravura display of the storyteller's art, it also replicates in its structure the structure of the whole, the eight gallants succeeding each other with echoing connections and oppositions like the tales themselves.

Significant Alteration

The prototype for Dorilas in the source for 2.13 does not boast of sexual success; that Dorilas does so boast creates a parallel with Alaciel's sixth sexual partner.

Words Unique to This Tale and the One Before

(1) a woman who is both "*veuve*" [widow] and "*pucelle*" [maiden]

(2) "médisant[e]"

2.15 "The Hermit Monk" ("L'Ermite")

Source: *Les Cent Nouvelles Nouvelles*, story 14

Alaciel, like Philis, was both "veuve" [widow] and "pucelle" [maiden]. The two terms return in "The Hermit Monk," but applied to two different persons, the mother and her daughter: "Toi femme *veuve*, et toi fille *pucelle*" [You, *widow* woman, and you, *maiden* girl] (2.15, line 58). This is the only line in the *Tales* where both terms appear—except for this line in "The Runaway Bride": "*Veuve* de huit galants, il la prit pour *pucelle*" [The widow of eight galants, he took her to be a maiden] (2.14, line 31).

These two tales interlock with "The Boasting Braggart Punished" in the following way: in and only in "The Boasting Braggart Punished" and "The Runaway Bride" is the same person both "veuve" and "pucelle"; in and only in "The Runaway Bride" and "The Hermit Monk" do both "veuve" and "pucelle" appear in the same line. This is a departure from the source for "The Hermit Monk," for in the *Cent Nouvelles Nouvelles* the hermit spoke only to the mother at this moment; in La Fontaine's version, he speaks to both, with the result that the two terms appear in the same line.

Both the girl in "The Hermit Monk" and Alaciel are daughters placed in a sexual relationship by their parent: the marriage (and, thanks to the voyage to her fiancé, eight other love affairs) her father arranged for Alaciel; concubinage with the monk for the daughter, with the mother's consent (though, unlike Alaciel, also the daughter's). A verbal echo marks the parallel: Alaciel had to "*partir de ces lieux*" [*leave this place*] (2.14, line 60), that is to leave her home for the kingdom of Garbe; the hermit's voice tells the girl "Allez trouver mon serviteur fidele / L'ermite Luce, et *partez de ce lieu*" [go find my servant the hermit Luce, and *leave this place*] (2.15, lines 59–60).

Significant Alterations

(1) La Fontaine here made a change in the story that makes the parallel possible. In the *Cent Nouvelles Nouvelles*, she does not move in with the hermit, so never really leaves home. Though he does undress her in his cell and make love to her there the first time, their subsequent trysts take place at her mother's house. By contrast, in La Fontaine's version she dwells with the hermit for eight months—"seven whole months" (2.15, line 177) after she realizes she's pregnant (which would have taken the greater part of a month to discover). Thanks to this change in the story, Alaciel and the widow's daughter more closely parallel each other, both leaving home for a long period of time during which they acquire their first sexual experience, Alaciel with eight different lovers, the daughter with the same lover for at least eight months.

(2) One of the additions La Fontaine brought to Boccaccio's story of Alaciel was the "cassette aux bijoux" [jewel box] (2.14, line 84) she saved from the pirates by dragging it along by "des cordons" [cords] (2.14, line 118) as Hispal swam from rock to rock with her on his back until they reached the shore. The box and its "cordons" find echoes what the hermit and the daughter wear. He "d'une *corde* était ceint ... mais sous sa houppelande / Logeait le coeur d'un dangereux paillard. / Un chapelet *pendait* à sa ceinture / Long d'une brasse, et gros outre mesure" [was girded with a *rope* ... but beneath his cassock lodged the heart of a dangerous rake. A rosary *hung*

from his belt six feet long and of extraordinary size] (2.15, lines 13–17). The rosary (whose dimensions may parallel those of the family jewels inside the robe) "*pendait* à sa ceinture" [hung from his belt] (2.15, line 16), which was "une *corde*" [a rope] (2.15, line 13). The treasure box that held Alaciel's jewels "à des *cordons* étant *pendue*" [was *hanging* on *ropes*] (2.14, line 118). When the widow's daughter prepares to visit the hermit she puts on "Son demi-*ceint*, ses *pendants* de velours" [her *belt*, her velvet *pendants*] (2.15, line 117). This part of her costume—appropriately, given the sexual symbolism attached to the equivalent part of the monk's outfit—will become the unmistakable sign of her pregnancy, though her new taste for sexual pleasure will cause her to want to conceal it: "une certaine enflure / La contraignit d'allonger sa *ceinture*; / Mais en cachette" [a certain swelling obliged her to lengthen her *belt*, but secretly] (2.15, lines 169–70).

Word Unique to This Tale and the Two Before

A verbal link continues a thread begun in "The Boasting Braggart Punished," where Dorilas suffered "la *frayeur* extrême" [extreme *fright*] (2.13, line 108). It continued when Alaciel woke up to discover that she was in the arms of the lord of the neighboring château, "La *frayeur* luy glaça la voix" [Fright froze her voice] (2.14, line 496). It returns in "The Hermit Monk" when the morning after they first hear the voice, the mother tells her daughter that perhaps "la *frayeur* t'avait fait mal entendre" [*fright* had made you not hear correctly] (2.15, line 97). These three passages are exceptional in that they are the only ones in the *Tales* in which *frayeur* appears. But they are linked in other ways, too. Alaciel was frightened upon awakening; mother and daughter were frightened awake; Alaciel is so frightened that her voice is paralyzed; the mother and the daughter are frightened *by* a voice.

2.16 "Mazet of Lamporechio" ("Mazet de Lamporechio")

Source: Boccaccio, *Decameron*, Third Day, First Story

Like the widow's daughter in "The Hermit Monk," who goes to live at the monk's hermitage with the intention of having sex with him (in hopes of giving birth to a pope), Mazet goes to live in the convent in order to have sex with the nuns.

In the prologue to "Mazet," La Fontaine faults parents for sending their daughters to convents thinking it would keep them pure; the widow does the same for the opposite reason, sending her daughter to live with the monk so that she *would*

have sex! In "Mazet," we are told that "le malin" [the evil one] (2.16, line 10) will profit if one sends one's daughter to a nunnery; in "The Hermit Monk," the devil is also called by this term: "Je crains, dit-il, les ruses du *malin*" [I fear, he said, the ruses of the *evil one*] (2.15, line 140).

In "Mazet," La Fontaine argues that nuns, being more constrained, are not less but more likely than other women to have erotic thoughts: "le désir, *enfant* de la *contrainte*" [desire, the *child* of *constraint*] (2.16, line 24). In other words, *constraint* produces a *child*—an instance of his penchant for planting precise reversals in neighboring tales, for the two terms appear in an opposite order of causality in "The Hermit Monk." There, a *child* produces *constraint*: "une certain enflure / La contraignit d'allonger sa ceinture" [a certain swelling *constrained* her to lengthen her belt] (2.15, lines 169–70).

Mazet breaks his silence when he complains to the Mother Superior that he had always heard that a good rooster only has to service seven hens, but he has been burdened with nine, (counting her). Although she takes his sudden ability to speak to be a miracle, it does put an end to his disguise. Just the opposite happens in the other tale when the hermit *begins* his charade with a sudden miraculous voice.

Significant Alteration

Instead of seven hens, in Boccaccio the upper limit was ten. Why did La Fontaine revise this figure downward, and why in particular to seven? So that it would match the only other instance of that number in the *Tales*, the number of months of sex the widow's daughter enjoyed before she had to stop because her pregnancy was too obvious to conceal.

3.1 "Brother Philip's Geese" ("Les Oies de frère Philippe")

Source: Boccaccio, *Decameron*, Prologue to the Fourth Day

Like the parents criticized in the prologue to "Mazet of Lamporechio" for thinking they could protect their daughters from men by enclosing them in a convent, Brother Philip tries to protect his son from women by enclosing him in his forest hermitage. He will turn out to have been just as mistaken. Taken together, the last two tales in Book Two and the first in Book Three feature a hermitage (2.15), a convent (2.16), and a hermitage (3.1). Both Mazet and Philip's son take up an older man's profession when he retires (the convent gardener and Philip); both of the older men take their successors to their place of employment to smooth the transition, and both young men are twenty years old when this occurs.

Significant Alterations

(1) Philippe's son was eighteen in Boccaccio's version, but twenty here to match Mazet.

(2) Nor in the *Decameron* does the son ask to hear the bird sing. By adding that detail, La Fontaine sets up a parallel to Mazet's situation in the convent. Mazet is to the nuns as the birds are to the boy, for Mazet cannot express himself in spoken language as long as he pretends to be mute, and the boy when he was living in the woods could not understand the birds: "Encor ne pouvait-il entendre leur langage" [Yet he could not understand their language] (3.1, line 61). (That detail is missing from Boccaccio as well.) The tale concludes with his request to the bird to make its voice heard: "Oie, hélas chante un peu, que j'entende ta voix" [Goose, alas, sing a little, so I may hear your voice] (3.1, line 159); Mazet's story heads to its climax when he suddenly makes his voice heard to the nuns. Appropriately, in those first spoken words he refers to women as birds (by referring to himself as an overworked rooster). The nuns' response is to take better care of him, making sure he is "bien nourri" [well fed] (2.16, line 190); similarly, the son wants to take care of the goose, to make sure it is well nourished: "J'aurai soin de la faire paître" [I would take care to feed it] (3.1, line 163).

3.2 "The Mandrake" ("La Mandragore")

Source: Machiavelli, *Mandragola* (a play)

In concealing from his son the existence of women, even his late mother's, Philip creates the illusion of a paternity without sex. The exact opposite—sex without paternity—happens in "The Mandrake," in which Nicia Calfucci, though he makes love to his wife, cannot father a child. Calfucci and Philip ask contrasting yet parallel questions related to their own demise and their surviving sons. When Callimachus tells Calfucci that the mandrake that can make him a father can also be fatal, Calfucci asks, "Que servira *moi mort* si je suis père?" [what good will it do *me dead* if I am a father?] (3.2, line 111). This oddly echoes Philip's worry about what will happen to his son after he's dead: "*lui mort* après tout / Que ferait ce cher fils?" [with *him dead*, after all, what would the dear son do?] (3.1, lines 115–16). Philip's question is focused on his son's interests; Calfucci's, comically, on his own.

Other verbal links set up a parallel between Lucretia in her relation to her first adulterous lover and Philip's son in his relation to the first women he meets. When Calfucci first hears of the potion's potential for making him a father, he exclaims that it "doit être à Lucrèce *agréable*!" [should be *agreeable* to Lucretia!] (3.2, line 93). It proved agreeable to her in ways he didn't anticipate. The same adjective with an exclamation mark (the only times this happens in the *Tales*) comes from the son: "Ô l'*agréable* oiseau!" [O what an *agreeable* bird!] (3.1, line 158) the boy exclaimed. When Lucretia first touched Callimachus's fine skin, she asked "Qu'est ceci donc?" [*What's this* now?]" (3.2, line 239), echoing what the son asked when he first saw the opposite sex: "Qu'est-ce là?" [*What's that?*] (3.1, line 153). The son is being introduced to the delights of sex, Lucrèce to those of adultery.

Word Unique to This Tale and the One Before

"*agréable*" accompanied by an exclamation mark

3.3 "An Evening in Reims" ("Les Rémois")

Source: Unknown

In this tale, as in "The Mandrake," a spouse encourages his or her mate to engage in sexual activity with someone else. The juice of the mandrake makes this possible in one tale, the juice of the grape in the other. It was only when the wine gives out, twice, that the painter has the opportunity to embrace first Alis, then Simonette. Both the wine and the poison in the juice must be "drawn": the painter's wife and the wife who accompanies her to the wine cellar are called "des *tireuses* de vin" [*drawers* of wine] (3.3, line 166); the poison in the mandrake juice must be "drawn out," as what is needed is some poor victim, Callimachus tells Calfucci, who "*attire* et prenne en somme / Tout le venin" [*draws* and takes, in sum, all the venom] (3.2, lines 127–28).

Both tales begin with a report of what "each" of her acquaintances thought of the wife: "*Chacun* l'aimait, *chacun* la jugeait digne / D'un autre époux" [*Each* loved her; *each* thought she deserved another husband] (3.2, lines 7–8); "*Chacun* trouvait sa femme fort heureuse" [*Each* found his wife to very happy] (3.3, line 13).

When the victim arrives to sleep with his wife, "*Gardez-vous bien* ... / D'aller paraître en aucune façon" [*Keep yourself from* being seen in any way] (3.2, lines 173–74), Callimachus tells Calfucci. "*Gardez-vous bien de* faire une sottise" [*Keep yourself from* doing something foolish] (3.3, line 141), one husband tells the other when he threatens to burst out of the closet and raise a ruckus. In both tales, the identical expression is uttered to prevent a husband from making himself visible when another man makes love to his wife.

3.4 "The Enchanted Cup" ("La Coupe enchantée")

Source: Ariosto, *Orlando Furioso*, cantos 42–43; for the prologue: Rabelais, *Tiers Livre*, chapter 28

In both "The Enchanted Cup" and "An Evening in Reims" it is when wine cannot be drunk—either because there is, for the moment, no more left, or because the enchanted cup will not allow any to be consumed—that cuckoldry becomes apparent.

When Damon, disguised, tries to seduce his wife, his attempts linguistically replicate those of the two neighbors in "An Evening in Reims." They had tried to win the painter's wife with "leurs *fleurettes*, / *Pleurs et soupirs*" [their *flirtations*; *tears and sighs*] (3.3, lines 38–39). Damon, in disguise, begins the same way, with "la *fleurette*" [flirtation] (3.4, line 292), then "changea de batterie: / *Pleurs et soupirs* furent tentés, / Et *pleurs et soupirs* rebutés" [changed tactics: *tears and sighs* were attempted, and *tears and sighs* were rebuffed] (3.4, lines 298–300). The expression "pleurs et soupirs" appears nowhere else in the *Tales*.

In both tales, hospitality and cuckoldry are intimately connected. The guests either become cuckolds or come to realize that they already are. In both, the host wants to make the company of those invited "complete": Damon eventually reaches his goal, "Le nombre de soldats étant presque *complet*" [The number of soldiers being almost *complete*] (3.4, line 453); the hostess in Reims is delighted to see her husband arrrive, for now "La compagnie en sera plus *complète*" [The company will be more *complete*] (3.3, line 87).

Words Unique to This Tale and the One Before

the expression "pleurs et soupirs"

3.5 "The Falcon" ("Le Faucon")

Source: Boccaccio, *Decameron*, Fifth Day, Ninth Story

"The Falcon" and "The Magic Cup" present two contrasting sorts of hospitality, though in both, guests leave sadder than when they arrived. Damon's hospitality comes from a selfish desire to increase the ranks of fellow-sufferers, while Fred's is unselfishly offered at considerable personal cost.

Clitie's son is a "fils *unique*" [*only* son] (3.5, line 216); Damon and Calista are each an only child: "La fille était *unique*, et le garçon aussi" [the girl was an *only* child, and the son was as well] (3.4, line 150). Their "unique"-ness thus made their marriage possible, since it helped persuade the Calista's father to consent to her choice; "unique"-ness brought about the marriage of Fred and Clitie, too, through their common misery in his losing "l'*unique* et seule chose / Qui lui restait" [the *unique* and only thing that he had left] (3.5, lines 142–43), the falcon, and her losing her "fils *unique*, une unique espérance" [*only* son, her only hope] (3.5, line 216). In other words, in both tales, two marry who either are "unique" or lose the only "unique" thing they own. In *Orlando Furioso* Damon was not an only child.

Earlier in the "The Falcon," the narrative of Fred's trying without success to persuade Clitie to yield to his desire contains embedded references to Damon's attempt, when disguised as Éraste, to seduce Calista. Both Calista and Clitie were immovable rocks: "Caliste était un *roc*; rien n'émouvait la belle" [Calista was a *rock*; nothing moved her] (3.4, line 301), while Clitie "tint bon; Fédéric échoua / Près de ce *roc*, et le nez s'y cassa" [held firm; Fred shipwrecked near this *rock*, and his nose got broken] (3.5, lines 22–23). Nowhere else in the *Tales* is a woman described as a "roc."

Significant Alteration

In *Orlando Furioso* Damon was not an only child.

Words Unique to This Tale and the One Before

a woman as a "roc."

3.6 "The Courtesan Who Fell in Love" ("La Courtisane amoureuse")

Source: Unknown

Jean-Pierre Collinet links "The Courtesan Who Fell in Love" with "The Falcon," noting that "The wealthy prostitute offers a feminine rejoinder to the melancholy and impoverished hero of 'The Falcon,' in counterpoint to him. From one story to the next the same fervent apprenticeship in love is pursued, and the sweetness one can find in forgetting one's self for the loved one" (Pléiade edition, 1429n). As Frederic unselfishly sacrificed his last remaining possession to receive Clitie in what style he could manage, Constance selflessly abases herself out of love for Camille, suffering the indignities he imposes to test her love. The parallel between Constance and Clitie is all the more piquant for the contrast: the virtuous married woman, totally unresponsive to all the expense Frederic had showered upon her, versus the Roman courtisan who never slept with a man except for money.

The women are linked as well in that both "dare" to request something from a man, despite realizing that they do not "merit" its being granted. Entering into the mind of Clitie as she hesitates before resolving to ask for the falcon, the narrator wonders: "et supposé qu'elle *ose* / Lui demander ce qu'il a pour tout bien, / Auprès de lui *méritait-elle* rien?" [and supposing that she *dare* ask him to surrender his only possession, next to him *did she deserve* anything?] (3.5, lines 143–44). Constance says to Camille: "*J'ai mérité* ce mauvais traitement: / Mais *ose-t-on* vous dire sa pensée?" [I *deserved* this ill treatment. But *dare* one tell what you one is thinking?] (3.6, lines 134–35).

Both men must play host to an uninvited woman. Before the woman arrives, both had dismissed their servants; Camille for the night, Frederic for good. Obliged to be hospitable, both are either "confus" [embarrassed] or pretend to be: Frederic is ashamed to have nothing to offer but a miserable dinner, which "Le rend *confus*" [makes him *embarrassed*] (3.5, line 165); having dismissed his servants, Camille, "feignant d'être *confus* / Se tut longtemps" [pretending to be *embarrassed*, kept a long silence] (3.6, lines 155–56). Both men reject the "advances" women make. While Frederic had eyes only for Clitie, when he was still a wealthy man, there was not a woman in Florence who did not try to win his heart, one by an insinuating word, a look of the eye, or "quelque autre *avance*" [some other *advance*] (3.5, line 52); Camille wounds Constance's feelings by announcing, "Je n'aime point qu'on me fasse d'*avance*" [I don't like it when one makes *advances* on me] (3.6, line 131). With the significant exception of the very next tale, as we will soon see, in no other will a woman make an "advance" to a man.

3.7 "Nicaise"

Source: Girolamo Brusoni,
Curiosissime Novelle amorose

"Nicaise," like "The Courtesan Who Fell in Love," is the story of a young woman who sets out to seduce a young man. She tries to signal her interest in various ways: "Sur les yeux lui mettait la main, / Sur le *pied* lui marchait enfin" [She put her hand over his eyes, resorted to stepping on his *foot*] (3.7, lines 57–58). This is the only time in the *Tales* when a woman courts a man through his feet—except for when Constance, as Camillo commanded, placed herself "Aux *pieds* du sire; et d'abord les lui baise" [At his *feet*, and began by kissing them] (3.6, line 222). Implicitly recalling Camille's declaration that he didn't like women who made "advances," and the "advances" to which women subjected Frederic, the narrator says of such behavior here that it was proper, for a goddess "fait ces *avances*-là" [makes those *advances*] (3.7, line 32). Constance's willingness to sacrifice her expensive dress by cutting it with a dagger when Camillo refuses to help her unlace it is paralleled by the girl's willingness to let her

dress by soiled by the muddy earth rather than lose precious moments by allowing Nicaise to fetch a carpet. She exclaims, "*périssent* / Tous les vêtements du pays" [let all fine garments *perish*] (3.7, lines 162–63), echoing the narrator's observation that when Constance cut her dress, two months' work by skilled seamstresses "*périt* en un moment" [*perished* in a moment] (3.6, line 164). Constance's finery displayed "Ajustements ... *de reine*" [ornaments ... *of a queen*] (3.6, line 193), while of the girl's outfit the narrator of "Nicaise" exclaims, "On eût dit *une reine*" [she looked like a *queen*] (3.7, line 135).

Words Unique to This Tale and the Two Before

"avances" made by a woman to a man.

3.8 "The Saddle" ("Le Bât")

Sources: Various, including
Béroalde de Verville, *Le Moyen de parvenir*

We recall that Nicaise worried about what would happen to the costly apparel the merchant's daughter was wearing if they made love on the wet ground. The damage that the friction and prolonged contact inherent in coition can do to what a wife has on is also the subject of "The Saddle"—except that what is damaged is not clothing but something resembling a temporary tattoo. The wife declares that the painted donkey is "*témoin* de ma fidélité" [*witness* to my fidelity] (3.8, line 12), as Nicaise bragged that the rug he had returned with would "*témoigner* quel est mon zèle" [bear *witness* to my zeal] (3.7, line 240). He was hoping it would testify to his ardor, while the painted donkey in its new version does in fact bear witness to the other painter's ardor, as the husband immediately realizes.

Because he is a painter by profession, the husband can see the minute differences between his own work and another's; likewise, it is through the eyes of a professional that the cloth merchant's apprentice recognizes the value of the dress his lover is wearing. The husband's professional eye was helped into awareness by the mistake his rival made of adding a needless decoration to what the woman was wearing. This parallels the dress the merchant's daughter was wearing in the garden, over which she and Nicaise had their dispute, for it too bore more decoration than the dresses she had hitherto worn; it had pearls, diamonds, and other jewels, as well as being made of expensive fabric, like the courtisan's dress in the tale before. In the eyes of both women, their costly outfits were of no more value than the plainest dress when compared to the prospect of making love. Yet there is a difference between the two, for Constance saw her prospect realized, while the merchant's daughter did not. The blame for things not turning out the way she intended should be laid not only on Nicaise, whose professional eye saw the value of her dress and whose professional conscience could not countenance its destruction, but on the merchant's daughter herself. This was not the dress she was married in, but one she specially put on for her garden tryst. Wanting to show off her queenly raiments, the symbol of her new-gained noble status, thanks to her marriage, she came to the rendezvous with her lover wearing the clothes her husband gave her, and in this way resembles the artist's wife who presented herself to her husband wearing the painted donkey his rival gave her instead of the one he had made. The first donkey is to the second donkey as the first dress is to the second dress; both second versions are more elaborate than the first—having a packsaddle in one instance, having jewels in the other—and both betray their origins, having come from the rival of the man to whom they are displayed.

By accident or not, the two donkeys betray the hidden structure of the work in which they appear. If we read the *Tales* in their sequence with close attention to detail, we will keep remembering what we have just read. The second donkey as an imperfect reminiscence of the first is like the second of two sequential tales, resembling its predecessor like an imperfect recollection. Things are somehow the same, yet not.

3.9 *"The Kiss in Exchange"* (*"Le Baiser rendu"*)

Source: Unknown

In both this tale and "The Saddle," a woman is shared by two men, one of whom is her husband; in one case with his consent, in the other without it. In both there are two things that closely resemble and are meant to replace each other, the two kisses and the two painted donkeys. In one, pressure leaves a mark (a redness); in the other, pressure erases one. There is fidelity in both, but of different sorts: the marital fidelity that the wife claimed the donkey would show ("L'âne est témoin de ma *fidélité*" [The ass bears witness to my *fidelity*] [3.8, line 12]), and the gentleman's fidelity to his promise ("monsieur, dit-il, est si *fidèle*" [monsieur, he said, is so *faithful*] [3.9, line 12]). Fidelity of the second sort is potentially at odds with that of the first, as the gentleman, Guillot imagines, might have been so faithful to his word that he would have allowed his new bride to be unfaithful. Both tales conclude with a husband's anger, but for exactly opposite reasons, the painter because his wife has slept with another man, Guillot because his had not.

3.10 *"Time to Confess"* (*"Épigramme"*)

Source: Unknown

It is too late in both tales: ten years too late for Father André to hear Alice's confession, a week too late for Guillot to have offered to let the other man make love to his wife.

3.11 *"Portrait of Iris"* (*"Imitation d'Anacréon"*)

Source: Anacreon, *Odes*

Like Iris, Father André is absent. How can Alice confess to him when he is no longer on earth, and how can the painter do Iris's portrait when she is unobtainable to him, either by sight or memory? The painter is asked to practice his art here, and will return to Paphos and Cythera to practice it there, while the priest used to do confessions here, but now does them in heaven.

Significant Alteration

Alice sends for André for the "*repos*" [repose] (3.10, line 3) of her soul; the painter is informed that it is better for "*repos*" [repose] (3.11, line 5) that he has not met Iris. The absent André would have brought repose, but the absent Iris would have destroyed it. This detail was not in the source for 3.11.

3.12 *"Cupid the Intruder"* (*"Autre imitation d'Anacréon"*)

Source: Anacreon, *Odes*

Iris is interchangeable with Venus; each is the other's double. Doubleness is thematic in "Cupid the Intruder" in an opposite way. In 3.11, two are one; in 3.12, one is two, as Cupid appears first as victim, then as victimizer.

3.13 *"The Quarrel between a Beauty's Mouth and Eyes"* (*"Le Différend de Beaux Yeux et de Belle Bouche"*)

Source: Charles Sorel, "Dialogue des Yeux et de la Bouche"

A single personage presented in two opposing versions (Cupid as victim and Cupid as victimizer), one replacing the other as the story unfolds, is followed in 3.13 by two opposing attributes (Eyes and

Mouth) of the same personage simultaneously struggling for dominance. The most telling difference between the Eyes and the Mouth is presented in the latter's closing argument: the Eyes have to be seen, the Mouth does not have to be seen to exert its power; it can do so just by being heard. This distinction between the visual and the aural coincides with the two manifestations of love's divinity in the two preceding tales, Venus (3.11) and Cupid (3.12). Venus's interchangeability with Iris is entirely visual, while it is what the narrator hears—Cupid's tale of woe—that tricks him into letting Cupid in. The Mouth's advocate convincingly makes the case that it is at night that she can best exercise her powers, when the Eyes cannot; it is at night that Cupid wreaks his havoc on the narrator.

3.14 "The Wonder Dog" ("Le Petit Chien qui secoue de l'argent et des pierreries")

Source: Ariosto, *Orlando Furioso*, canto 43

The Mouth kisses the judge for ruling in her favor; in "The Wonder Dog," a beautiful woman marries a judge.

When Argie's nurse urges her to take Atis for a lover, she symbolically reduces her to a mouth: "il faut être / Bien habile pour reconnaître / *Bouche* ayant employé son temps et ses appas / D'avec *bouche* qui s'est tenue à ne rien faire" [one would have to be pretty good to distinguish a *mouth* that had put its time and charms to use from a *mouth* that had not] (3.14, lines 279–82). This parallels the reduction in 3.13 of a woman to mouth and eyes. In both tales, the mouths are part of a comparision—in 3.13 with eyes, in 3.14 with another mouth.

Atis's dog has pearls to offer ("Aussitôt *perles* de tomber" [Immediately *pearls* began to fall]" (3.14, line 308); so too does Lovely Mouth: "Trente-deux *perles* se font voir" [Thirty-two *pearls* make their appearance] (3.13, line 30). The latter are teeth; while the former are made possible by the teeth Cadmus sowed: Atis saved the serpent from being killed by the peasant, because he, unlike other men, was not afraid of snakes, tracing his descent from Cadmus who became a serpent in old age (3.14, lines 120–22).

Significant Alteration

In the source, Ariosto has Adonio, Atis's prototype, trace his origins to the serpent's teeth Cadmus sowed, while La Fontaine has him descending from Cadmus himself and not the teeth. He adds the detail, not in Ariosto though indeed in Ovid (*Metamorphoses*, book 4, lines 563–89; p. 109), that Cadmus became a serpent in old age. In the context of

"The Wonder Dog," where Atis's rescue of the fairy-as-serpent brings Manto to show her gratitude by enabling him to seduce Argie with the pearls and other treasures the dog can provide, it makes more sense for Atis to be descended from the man who sowed the teeth than from the teeth themselves. Atis handsomely reaps what he sows as far as those pearls are concerned. Indeed, he has the dog scatter the pearls on the floor as Cadmus scattered the serpent's teeth (*Metamorphoses*, book 3, lines 101–05; p. 76).

3.15 "Clymene"

Source: Original with La Fontaine

As La Fontaine writes, "Clymene" will appear to readers to be somewhat out of place in a collection of tales, but if they persevere to the end they will find a tale like the others. He appears to be alluding to the episode in which Acanthus recounts his small measure of success in obtaining a lover's kiss, as opposed to a friendly one, from Clymene. "Clymene" presents itself as a "comedy" rather than a tale, though one meant to be read, not performed. It is at the same time a tour de force of 16th- and 17th-century poetic genres and styles, as Apollo's muses try to imitate some of La Fontaine's favorite poets—Clément Marot (1496?–1544), François de Malherbe (1555–1628), and Vincent Voiture (1597–1648)—and improvise in specific poetic forms (the *églogue*, the *ballade*, the *ode*, and the *dizain*). There is one part of that literary excursion that is of special interest, for it presents in microcosm the structure of the *Tales in Verse* as a unified work of art. As we are seeing, each of La Fontaine's tales repeats elements from the one that precedes it. This is precisely what Euterpe and Terpsichore do beginning at line 32, when they promise to amuse Apollo with an improvised "églogue" [eclogue], which I have translated as a "pastoral duet." Virgil's *Eclogues* and Theocritus's *Idylls* are the classic models for this genre, though it probably appears in many folk cultures as well. In the article "Pastoral," *The New Princeton Encylopedia of Poetry and Poetics* describes this poetry as "amoebaean verses ('responsive verses') whereby verses, couplets, or stanzas are spoken alternately by two speakers. The second speaker is expected not only to match the theme introduced by the first but also to improve upon it in some way." In Virgil and Theocritus the two speakers are shepherds, which is why it is called "pastoral." The imitative nature of the response becomes really evident in the following exchange: "EUTERPE: Pour elle le Printemps s'est habillé de roses. / TERPSICHORE: Pour elle les Zéphirs en parfument les airs. / EUTERPE: Et les oiseaux pour elle y joignent leurs concerts. Régnez belle, régnez sur tant d'aimables choses. / TERPSICHORE: Aimez, Clymène, aimez;

rendez quelqu'un heureux : / Votre règne en aura plus d'appas pour vous-même" [EUTERPE: For her the roses dress up lovely Spring. / TERPSI-CHORE: For her the Zephyrs perfume everything. / EUTERPE: For her each bird in harmony unites. / Reign, Clymene, reign over such sweet delights. / TERPSICHORE: Love, Clymene, love; give some man happiness: / Your reign thereby yourself with charms will bless]. In each of her replies, Terpsi-chore recycles elements from what Euterpe just said, with both repeated words ("Pour elle ... Pour elle") and parallel constructions ("Régnez, belle, régnez ... "Aimez, Clymène, aimez").

La Fontaine's *Tales in Verse*, as we are finding, are one long pastoral duet, in which each tale repeats words from and constructs parallels to the immedi-ately preceding tale.

In "The Wonder Dog" when Atis in his pilgrim's disguise was at last given permission to present him-self before Argie, she was still in bed; "L'univers n'eût jamais d'*aurore* / Plus paresseuse à se lever" [The universe never had a *dawn* more lazy to rise] (3.14, lines 293–94). Clymène is likewise slow to rise, and, like Argie, is compared to the dawn: "L'Aurore vous veut voir; Clymène montrez-vous: / Non, ne bougez du lit; le repos est trop doux: / Tan-tôt vous paraîtrez vous-même *une autre Aurore*; / Mais ne vous pressez point, dormez dormez encore" [Get up, Clymene, the Dawn to greet. / No, stay in bed, sleep is too sweet. / Soon you'll seem *another Dawn—*/ Just as lovely—so sleep on] (3.15, lines 41–44).

Words Unique to This Tale and the One Before

(1) Both Acanthus and Atis receive supernatural help in their amorous quests. When Cupid rewards Acanthus for his poetry, he says "*je veux pour récom-pense*" [I want as a recompense] (3.15, line 561) that he can kiss Clymène. Manto had spoken the very same words in rewarding Atis for saving her life: "*je veux pour récompense*" [I want as a recompense] (3.14, line 173) that he find success with Argie. The expression appears in no other tale.

(2) Both Argie and Clymène are called "inhu-maine" [inhuman] (3.14, 144; 3.15, 649), the only times that adjective appears in the *Tales*.

4.1 "How Girls Get Smart" ("Comment l'esprit vient aux filles")

Source: Unknown

La Fontaine begins by speaking of "un jeu diver-tissant sur tous, / Jeu dont l'*ardeur* souvent se re-nouvelle" [a game diverting for all, a game whose

ardor often renews itself] (4.1, lines 1–2). "Clymene" opens, similarly, with a remark about "ardeur"—and "esprits." Apollo is complaining to his Muses that he doesn't see any more good love poetry being pro-duced because the present generation of mortals is not sufficiently interested in the subject: "J'ai beau communiquer de l'*ardeur* aux *esprits*" [In vain do I communicate ardor to minds] (3.15, line 6), for his efforts go unappreciated. Acanthus proves to be the exception. Full of ardor for Clymène, he is having a hard time persuading her to respond in kind. "Un peu de passion est ce qu'on lui souhaite" [A little passion is what one wishes for her] (3.15, line 46), remarks the muse Terpsichore. "Cinq ou six grains d'amour, et Clymène est parfaite" [Five or six grains of love, and Clymène would be perfect] (3.15, line 48). Eliza is in need of a dose of something, too: wit—"esprit"—which her mother tells her a hun-dred times a day she needs to go in search of. And when she finds it, it takes the form of precisely what Clymene lacks: the renewable "ardeur" of the di-verting game of which La Fontaine speaks in the opening lines of her story.

Words Unique to This Tale and the One Before

Only in "Clymene" and "How Girls Get Smart" is "ardeur" connected with "esprit" or "esprits."

4.2 "The Mother Superior" ("L'Abbesse")

Source: *Les Cent Nouvelles Nouvelles*, story 21; Rabelais, *Quart Livre*, chapters 7–8 (for the prologue)

This tale is a mirror reversal of "How Girls Get Smart." In that tale, a young girl goes to a "couvent" [monastery, in that instance] (4.1, line 99) to have sex with a monk in order to solve her problem (lack of wit); in this one, a young man goes to a "couvent" [here, a nunnery] (4.2, line 99) to have sex with a nun in order to solve *her* problem (poor health). When she was still lacking wit, Eliza was "affligée et *honteuse*" [sad and *ashamed*] (4.1, line 32) to have to ask the neighbors where she could buy it; it was because of their desire that the Mother Superior not feel "*honteuse*" [ashamed] (4.2, line 118) that the other nuns decide to undergo the operation first, by way of encouragement. What the Mother Superior does with the young man is avowedly medicinal; what Eliza does with the monk is cast in medicinal terms when he "Donne d'esprit une seconde *dose*" [Gives a second *dose* of wit] (4.1, line 81), continu-ing the medication motif that began in "Clymene" when Terpsichore said all Acanthus's unresponsive beloved needed was a few grains of love. When

Eliza asks him what is to be done if the "esprit" makes itself scarce, he explains that "D'autres *secrets* se mettent en usage" [Other *secrets* are called into use] (4.1, line 88), meaning secret techniques to induce arousal, and anticipating what sister Agnes will say to the Mother Superior: "Vous faites cent *secrets*, / Faut-il qu'un seul vous choque et vous déplaise?" [You take a hundred *remedies*; why must one shock you?] (4.2, lines 85–86). Here "secrets" means remedies, as Alain-Marie Bassy points out (Folio edition, 521n). Clearly it has that sense in the other tale too, particularly when the monk gives her yet another dose: "Le *secret* même encore se répéta / Par le *pater*" [The *remedy* was repeated, by the father] (4.1, line 95).

The Mother Superior was "*Sage rendue*" [made *wise*] (4.2, line 132) by the nuns' example, and took her medicine. At the conclusion of her story, Eliza was made wise too, as the narrator points out: "Vous voyez donc que je disais fort bien / Quand je disais que ce jeu-là *rend sage*" [You see I was right when I said that this game *makes* one *wise*] (4.1.132–33). Eliza had been made "sage" because she realized that she should keep mum on what she had done with the monk. The Mother Superior is thus "sage" in two opposite ways from Eliza:

(1) She becomes "sage" before making love; Eliza after.

(2) For the Mother Superior becoming "sage" consists in no longer caring that others in her community know about her sexual activity; the others removed that difficulty by engaging in it first. For Eliza, however, becoming "sage" consists in taking care that others in her community *not* find out about what she does in bed.

4.3 "The Wife Swappers" ("Les Troqueurs")

Source: Unknown; perhaps based on a legal case

In both this tale and "The Mother Superior," sex that would under normal circumstances be considered illicit is made licit by a higher authority. The medical establishment ordered the Mother Superior to take a lover; Étienne and Gille's exchange has the full force of law, and Étienne's attempt to revoke it is delayed by both the legal systems of both church and state, who are concerned only by the legal, not the moral, issues of the case.

La Fontaine begins "The Mother Superior" by saying that people are like sheep, "Tant sur les gens est l'exemple puissant" [So powerful on people is the force of example] (4.2, line 10), and by recounting how Panurge played a trick on Dindenaut in buying one of his sheep and then tossing it overboard so that the rest of Dindenaut's flock would follow it into the sea. The nuns in the convent be-

have like the sheep. When the monks arrive to engage in sex with them in the interest of removing the shame that was holding the Mother Superior back from following the doctors' orders, "De ses brebis à peine la première / A fait le saut, qu'il suit une autre soeur" [Of her ewes the first had no sooner made the leap than another sister followed] (4.2, lines 120–21), then another, and soon the whole flock.

Significant Alteration

The motif of imitation is absent from the source for "The Mother Superior"; so too is any mention of sheep. By adding them, La Fontaine laid the groundwork for several connections linking the two tales:

(1) Women are equated with "brebis" [ewes] in both: the nuns, in the passage just cited, and in the following lines, spoken by one of the wife swappers who remembers what their curate used to say: "Mes brebis sont ma femme" [My ewes are my wife] (4.3, line 31), meaning that he felt married to his parish.

(2) When Étienne and Antoinette made love again, illicitly in that they have now been assigned to other spouses, the narrator tells us that "ils *firent le saut*" [they *made the leap*] (4.3, line 119), echoing the sexual leap the nuns also made: "à peine la première / *A fait le saut*, qu'il suit une autre soeur" [the first had no sooner *made the leap* than another sister followed] (4.2, lines 120–21).

(3) In the beginning of "The Mother Superior" La Fontaine asserted that most persons behave like sheep, "Tant sur les *gens* est l'*exemple* puissant" [So powerful on *people* is the force of *example*] (line 10). He finds a way to place "l'exemple" and "gens" again in the same line at the conclusion of the other tale by remarking that the idea these two peasants had of exchanging wives "était pièce assez fine / Pour en devoir l'*exemple* à d'autres *gens*" [was so clever that it should have owed its *example* to other *people* (in the sense that finer folk than these peasants should have been the ones to have set such a clever example)] (4.3.166–67). La Fontaine's insistence on the power of the example in these two tales suggests a subtle self-reference: one tale follows the example of its predecessor.

4.4 "A Clear Conscience" ("Le Cas de conscience")

Source: Unknown; perhaps original with La Fontaine

Like "The Wife Swappers," "A Clear Conscience" is about taking back one's word. Étienne breaks his wife-swapping contract with Gille; Guillot makes Anne back out of her obligation to give the priest the fish.

The two husbands in "The Wife Swappers" were drinking when they came up with the idea of exchanging wives. When the priests are drinking in "A Clear Conscience," they propose exchanging parishes: "On *permuta* cent fois sans *permuter* pas une" [They *swapped* a hundred times without *swapping* once] (4.4, line 135)—that is, they proposed it but didn't actually do it. The two husbands actually compared changing wives to priests' changing parishes, noting that their priest had called his parish his wife. The term used in the priests' projected exchanges—*permuter*—is transformed into a noun to apply to the husbands: "*permuteurs*" (4.3, line 92). Collinet remarks that La Fontaine appears to have invented the noun (Pléiade edition, 1461n). The words appear nowhere else in the *Tales*.

Words Unique to This Tale and the One Before

"permuter" and "permuteurs."

4.5 "The Devil of Popefingerdom" ("Le Diable de Papefiguière")

Source: Rabelais, *Quart Livre*, chapters 45–57

This tale is yet another story of a broken contract, though not one freely entered into by one of the parties. But then neither had Anne freely entered into her obligation to the priest. She offered the fish in fulfillment of the "*tribut*" [*tribute*] (4.4, line 109) all the parishioners in that region owed their confessor. The Devil of Papefiguière also exacts a tribute: "je puis avec justice / M'*attribuer* tout le fruit de ce champ" [I could legally claim for myself as *tribute* all the produce of this field] (4.5, lines 55–56). The devil demands of Phlipot that they split the proceeds from this year's crop. He will take what is underground, Phlipot what is above. "Ne t'attends *pas* que je t'aide *un* seul *brin*" [*Don't* expect me to help you *a* single *bit* (literally, a single "blade")] (4.5, line 71). By an interesting and in fact meaningful symmetry, this responds precisely to the non-appearance of the tribute of the fish at the priest's banquet: "tout le dîner s'achève / Sans brochet *pas un brin*" [the banquet drew to an end with *not a bit* of pike] (4.4, lines 139–40). The expression "pas [...] un [...] brin" makes no other appearance in the *Tales*. Clearly La Fontaine intends for one tribute to parallel the other. He underscores that parallel with another verbal one: at the end of the feast, the guests in "A Clear Conscience" are "*Légère de* brochet" [*Lacking* the pike] (4.4, line 142); at the end of two years of making no money on Phlipot's crops, the devil is "*Léger d'*argent" [*Lacking* money] (4.5, line 118). This expression, too, is unique to these two tales.

Although both tales speak of broken contracts, they only seem to be so from the perspective of the devil and the priest. By their own lights, both Anne and Phlipot live up to their side of the bargain. The farmer gave the devil each time as promised whatever half he wanted, and Anne simply applied the priest's understanding of the relation between seeing and having to the fish. This pair of tales begins (with "A Clear Conscience") and ends (with "The Devil of Popefingerdom") with someone gazing at someone else naked. They both end with a defiant woman making clear to her opponent what seeing really means.

Words Unique to This Tale and the One Before

(1) "pas [...] un [...] brin"
(2) "léger[e] de"

4.6 "Ferondo in Purgatory" ("Féronde ou le Purgatoire")

Source: Boccaccio, *Decameron*, Third Day, Eighth Story

The "long sommeil" [long sleep] (4.6, line 112) into which Ferondo is plunged recalls the "long dormir" [long sleep] (4.5, line 14) that the inhabitants of Pope-omania are said in 4.5 to enjoy. As the abbot "*plonge*" [*plunges*] (4.6, line 112) Ferondo into a deep sleep, Phlipot is "*plongé*" [*plunged*] (4.5, line 161) into the holy water when he hides from the devil. Priests "*chante autour*" [*sing around*] him (4.5, 163), and monks "*chante[nt]*" [*sing*] (4.6, line 113) at Ferondo's burial and then stand "*autour*" [*around*] (4.6. 115) when he wakes up.

The abbot who frequented Ferondo's wife "Pas ne *semait* en une *terre ingrate*" [didn't *sow* in *infertile earth*] (4.6, line 187), since he fathered a child. The verb "semer" makes its only other appearance in the *Tales* when the devil asks Phlipot, "Quel grain veux-tu *semer* pour l'an prochain?" [What seed do you want to *sow* for next year?] (4.5, line 98). The "terre" [land] that was not "ingrate" [infertile] for the abbot contrasts with the "terre ... maudite" [cursed land] (4.5, line 38) Phlipot had to work with. When Ferondo returned from purgatory to a pregnant wife, he took for his own the "*fruit* posthume" [posthumous *produce*] (4.6, line 198), reaping where he did not sow. The devil tried to do the same, telling Phlipot that he could legally take "tout le *fruit*" [all the *produce*] (4.5, line 56) of his field, though he settles for half. After being cheated twice of that half, he appears at Phlipot's door to challenge him to a duel to determine who "jouira du *fruit* de ces sillons" [will enjoy the *produce* of these furrows] (4.5, line 135). The analogy between the produce of the fields and the produce of the womb seems already just beneath the surface at this point, for "ces sillons" are about to be followed by the analogous groove

Perrette will show the devil. Ferondo's premature burial—"on l'enterre" [he is buried] (4.6, line 113)—is analogous to Phlipot's planting because, like a seed, he will one day come out of the earth.

Word Unique to This Tale and the One Before

"semer"

4.7 "The Psalter" ("Le Psautier")

Source: Boccaccio, *Decameron*, Ninth Day, Second Story

Both Isabella and Ferondo are confronted by tormentors wearing false clothing, but they react in opposite ways. The monks' angel costumes fooled Ferondo into thinking he was in purgatory, but Isabella was the first to notice that the Abbess was improperly attired. In an additional mirror reversal, the monks intended to wear their costume but the abbess did not (that is, not her lover's pants on her head), and the monks wanted to be seen so garbed but the abbess did not. La Fontaine even finds a way for the Abbess's headgear to parallel Phlipot's: "d'étoles, dit-on, / Il *s'affubla* le *chef*" [with stoles he *bedecked* his *head*] (4.6, lines 159–60); the Abbess was "de grègues *affublée* ... ce nouveau couvre-*chef*" [with pants *bedecked* ... this new *head-covering*] (4.7, lines 68–69).

Isabella and Fernondo are both accused of *péchés* [sins] (4.7, line 113; 4.6, line 128), and threatened with having their "*âme*" [soul] (4.7, line 118; 4.6, line 130) improved through punishment. Both have to listen to sermonizing: "Pas ne finit mère abbesse sa gamme / Sans *sermonner*" [The Abbess did not come to a stop without *sermonizing*] (4.7, lines 119–120); the monk guarding Férondo "lui fait un long *sermon*" [makes him a long *sermon*] (4.6, line 160). Both are released from their ordeal because of their tormentor's fear of "*éclat*": in the convent, "trop d' *éclat* eût put nuire au troupeau" [too much *commotion* could harm the flock] (4.7, line 138); when the abbot discovers he is going to be a father, "Comme il n'est bon que telle chose *éclate*" [As it would not be good that such a thing *be known*] (4.6, line 190), he lets Férondo go back to his wife so that he will claim the child as his own.

4.8 "King Candaules and the Professor of Law" ("Le Roi Candaule et le Maître en droit")

Sources: Herodotus, *The History* (for King Candaules); Giovanni Fiorentino, *Il Pecorone* (for the Professor of Law)

The two stories told within "King Candaules and the Professor of Law" are related to each other as each tale in the sequence is to its neighbor (the same thing happens in "The Runaway Bride"): a motif in one resurfaces in the other. Each story features a husband who unwittingly makes himself a cuckold, and in each a spouse's nakedness is exposed without his or her consent. A wife is naked in one story, and it is her husband's doing; a husband is naked in the other story, and it is his wife's doing. Nakedness sets off the chain of events in one story, but is their culmination in the other.

But 4.8 repeats elements from "The Psalter" as well. When the Abbess's error is revealed to her nuns, her embarrassment matches that of the professor when he is led, naked, before his students. She has been stripped as naked, figuratively, as he. Wearing a pair of men's pants on her head, she displays the evidence of her own sexual indiscretion, as does he. As the Abbess is embarrassed to appear before all the nuns in her charge adorned with evidence of illicit sex, the law professor is embarrassed to appear with the same sort of evidence before his students. Both, naturally, feel ashamed: the Abbess, "honteuse" (4.7, line 126); the professor, "honteux" (4.8, line 333).

4.9 "Putting the Devil in Hell" ("Le Diable en enfer")

Source: Boccaccio, *Decameron*, Third Day, Tenth Tale

Gyges in 4.8 and a hermit monk in 4.9 both try to combat their desire, the former as he sees the queen bathing naked, the latter as he tries to sleep in the same hut with the enticing Alibech. La Fontaine underlines the parallel between the queen and Alibech with an echo: when Gyges saw the queen in her bath, "Ce *doux objet* joua son jeu" [This *sweet object* played its game] (4.8, line 30)—that is, she had such an effect on him that his desire was aroused. In the opening lines to "Putting the Devil in Hell," the narrator introduces the story by speaking of the kind of "*objets doux*" [sweet objects] (4.9, line 3) that were too much for the monk. (The expression appears only in these two tales.)

Both tales are about a "Maître" [master] and the "écolier" or "écolière" [scholar] who seeks his tutelage. The professor is called "Maître" in the title ("le Maître en droit") and twice in the tale (4.8, lines 133, 317); the student, instructed by him first in law and then in the art of seduction, is twice called an "écolier" (4.8, lines 261, 280). The terms crop up again in "Putting the Devil in Hell": "*Maître* Rustic eût dû donner congé / Tout dès l'abord à semblable *écolière*" [*Master* Rustic should have sent away at the beginning such a *scholar*] (4.9, lines 78–79).

There are the only tales where an "écolier" or "écolière" appear, and neither "master" not "scholar" appears in the source for "Putting the Devil in His Place."

Significant Alteration

No "master" or "scholar" in the source for 4.9.

Words Unique to This Tale and the One Before

(1) "doux objet," "objets doux"
(2) "écolier," "écolière"

4.10 *"The Farmer and His Mare" ("La Jument du compère Pierre")*

Source: Boccaccio, *Decameron*,
Ninth Day, Tenth Story

In both this tale and "Putting the Devil in His Place" a man in holy orders manages to have sex with a naive woman by making her think they are taking part in a worthwhile ritual.

The women are alike in their innocence. "Rustic sourit d'une telle *innocence*" [Rustic smiled at such *innocence*] (4.9, line 78); "La villageoise était fort *innocente*" [The woman was very *innocent*] (4.10, line 48). They are alike in what they wear: Rustic was tempted by a "sein qui pousse et repousse / Certain *corset* en dépit d'Alibech" [breast that pushed and pushed again against a certain *corset* in spite of Alibech] (4.9, lines 121–22); Father Jean issues the command "ôtez ce *corset*" [take off that *corset*] (4.10 line 111), along with the rest of her clothing.

The two holy men parallel each other not only in proposing a phony ritual in order to have sex but also in that both rituals are "plaisant": in Rustic's case, "un fort *plaisant* trafic" [a very *pleasant* arrangement] (4.9, line 13); Father Jean, similarly, "s'avisa d'un *plaisant* stratagème" [thought up a *pleasant* stratagem] (4.10, line 55).

Significant Alterations

(1) In the source for 4.10, it was the wife who asked the curate to perform the miracle; in La Fontaine's version, it is the curate's idea, which creates a parallel to the 4.9, where it is the allegedly holy man—Rustic—who proposes to Alibech that they perform the ritual. Both Alibech and Magdeleine later express the wish to repeat the experiment.
(2) No mention of angels or triumphs in the source for 4.9; no eloquence attributed to the curate in the source for 4.10. These motifs unite the tales, as explained below.

Words Unique to This Tale and the One Before

(1) In contemplating the test of his saintliness that Alibech's presence in his hut would provide, Rustic hopes for a triumph rivaling those of angels: "*Triomphes* grands chez les *anges* en sont" [Such *triumphs* only *angels* know] (4.9, line 92). When Father Jean preached at grape harvests his triumph was angelic: "Il *triomphait*; vous eussiez dit un *ange*" [He *triumphed*; you would have said he was an *angel*] (4.10, line 4). In the source for "Putting the Devil in Hell," there is no mention of angels or triumphs; in the source for "The Farmer and His Mare," the curate is not known to have been especially eloquent.
(2) Alibech wanted to become a saint so that she could receive "des *fleurs* et des *présents*" [*flowers* and *presents*] (4.9, line 48). Magdeleine achieves that goal, to the extent of receiving bouquets and presents, without becoming a saint, as Father Jean showered her with them in vain before devising his stratagem: "Ni ses *présents* ne touchaient Magdeleine: / Bouquets ... / Tombaient à terre" [Neither did his *presents* touch Magdeleine's heart; *bouquets* ... fell to the ground] (4.10, lines 51–53).
(3) When Alibech told the first hermit that she already knew how to fast, a step to sainthood, he replied that "Il faut encore *pratiquer* d'autres *choses*" [There are other *things* that must be *carried out*] (4.9, line 57). Father Jean tells the husband that he is going to show him how to turn his wife into a mare so that he can work the spell later himself (apparently it needed to be done daily): "Toi-même après *pratiqueras* la *chose*" ["Afterwards you yourself will *carry out* the *thing*] (4.10, line 106). By practicing other things the hermit undoubtedly meant other saintly acts and virtues, but the chief act she will practice under the other hermit's tutelage is essentially the same thing that Jean will practice on Magdeleine.
(4) Rustic's own name resonates (and uniquely so, as neither the proper nor the common noun appears anywhere else) the way the narrator describe's Magdeleine's rustic charm: "ce *rustiq* ne m'eût plu" [I would not have found this *rusticity* appealing] (4.10, line 32). The two rustics complement each other: one the sexual predator, the other the prey; one the man, the other the woman.

4.11 *"Eel Pâté" ("Pâté d'anguille")*

Source: *Les Cent Nouvelles Nouvelles*, story 10

In "The Farmer and His Mare" a husband unhappy with his lot is persuaded by a man with designs on his wife to make a change, but later repents; in "Eel Pâté" a husband happy with his wife is persuaded by a man with designs on his wife to make a change and later does not repent. The curate tells the farmer he can share with him "le moyen d'être un jour plus *content* / Qu'un petit *roi*" [the way to be *happier* than a little *king*] (4.10, lines 63–64); the valet tells his master that if he were married to as a fine a woman as his master was, "d'une *reine* ne voudrais" [I would not want a *queen*] (4.11, line 53) and that the master should be "*content*" [happy] (4.11, line 57) with what he has. In other words, the master should count himself happy as a king already.

Significant Alterations

(1) In the source, his dispute with his master was not over the master's wanting the valet's wife, for he had none, but over his disgust with having to procure for his employer a constant supply of new women. By giving the valet a wife whom the master desires, La Fontaine generates a parallel with the preceding tale, where Father Jean desires the farmer's wife.

(2) We saw how Father Jean's angel-like eloquence when he preached at grape harvests echoed Rustic's hope of achieving angelic triumphs; improving upon his source, La Fontaine sets up a second echo to the curate's eloquence, saying of the master that when he seduced women with money, as his valet had advised, "il parlait comme un *ange*" [he spoke like an *angel*] (4.11, line 115).

Words Unique to This Tale and the One Before

The comparison, so central to "Eel Pâté," of a woman to a certain "pâté" was anticipated by Magdeleine's being compared to "pâte": she was not to everyone's taste, but "Pour des curés la *pâte* en était bonne" [her *pastry* was good enough for curates] (4.10, line 33).

4.12 "The Eyeglasses" ("Les Lunettes")

Source: Bonaventure Des Périers, *Nouvelles récréations et joyeux devis*, story 62

The way La Fontaine complains in "The Eyeglasses" about how his muse sets before him "guimpe; et puis guimpe ... *toujours guimpe*" [wimple, and more wimple ... *always wimple*] (4.12, line 5) parallels the valet's complaints about eel pie: "*toujours pâtés* ... / Pâtés tous les jours de ma vie" [*always pâtés* ... pâtés every day of my life] (4.11, lines 75, 77). Eel pâté stood for women in that tale, wimple for nuns in this. The problem encountered by the young man in the convent is the opposite of the valet's. Faced with an abundance of eel pâté, the valet had too little desire; faced with an abundance of nuns, the young man has too much.

The valet is persuaded by his master to accept a change in the object of his desire. The nuns, want-

ing to wreak their vengeance on the intruder, have no problem with a change in the object of their desire for vengeance when the miller substitutes for the actual offender. In the context the two tales together form, the miller performs a substitutionary atonement not only for the young man whose place he willingly takes but also for the master who mistreated his valet. At least that's what several verbal parallels between the miller and the master and between the young man and the valet could be taken to mean:

(1) When the miller arrives on the scene he is described as a "*Bon compagnon*" [a *lusty fellow*] (4.12, line 135). The phrase makes only one other appearance in the *Tales*, when it is applied to the valet's master in the context of what he did to the valet's wife: "Le maître, étant *bon compagnon*, / Eut bientôt empaumé la dame" [The master, being a *lusty fellow*, soon snapped up the wife] (4.11, lines 26–27).

(2) The miller says to the young man that he looks to him like "un vrai *croqueur* de nonne" [a true nun-*devourer*] (4.12, line 143). The valet, after his conversion, became precisely that: "Par où le drôle en put *croquer*, / Il en *croqua*, femmes et filles" [where the fellow could *devour*, he *devoured* them, women and girls] (4.11, lines 142–43).

(3) Although he is indeed a "croqueur de nonne," the young man denies it, protesting, "de commettre une si grande offense, / J'en fais scrupule, et fût-ce pour le *roi*" [I would scruple to commit such a great offense, even for the *king*] (4.12, lines 147–48). Even for the king he would not commit adultery with a nun, as even for a queen the valet would not be unfaithful with a wife as fine as his master's: "je m'y tiendrais, / Et d'une *reine* ne voudrais" [I would stay with my wife, and for even a *queen* I would not] (4.11, lines 52–53).

Given these parallels, what the miller suffers in the young man's place he also suffers as a substitute for the master—as if La Fontaine were granting the valet's wish for vengeance against the master who had twice wronged him, taking his wife and making him eat nothing but eel pâté. The proof of the pudding, or in this case the pâté, is a delicious pun: "on donne au *maître* l'*anguillade*" [the *master* was given the *eel-whip*] (4.12, line 193)—a whip, as Collinet points out (Pléiade edition, 1484n), made of eel-skins. It is not by chance that neither "anguille" nor "anguillade" appears in any other tale—nor that the miller is at this very moment called the "maître" [master]. Poetic justice indeed: the "maître" who gave his valet nothing but eel pâté to eat is followed by a "maître" who must suffer eels in another, more painful form.

Words Unique to This Tale and the One Before

(1) "bon compagnon"
(2) "anguille," "anguillade"

4.13 "Convincing Kate" ("Janot et Catin")

Source: Original with La Fontaine

The moment when the young man's libido breaks through its restraint in "The Eyeglasses" is paralleled by the moment in "Convincing Kate" when the narrator is so aroused that her rejection of his advances can do nothing to calm his ardor. It is already too late: "De ma fressure / Dame luxure / Ja s'emparoit" [Of my innards Dame Lust had already taken hold] (4.13, lines 16–18). His hand caressing Kate's breast, "En tel détroit / Mon *cas* estoit, / Que je quis [chercha] meilleure aventure" [My "case" was in such straits that I looked for a better opportunity] (4.13, lines 19–21), he goes on to say, as La Fontaine plays on "cas" = "case" and "cas" = "genital organs," as Collinet notes (Pléiade edition, 1484n). He was making the same pun in "The Eyeglasses" (1) when he said in the prologue that whenever he would try to avoid telling yet another tale about nuns "quelque *cas* m'y ferait retourner" [some "case" would make me return] (4.12, line 15), (2) when the prioress declares "Sus qu'on se déshabille: / Je veux savoir la vérité du *cas*" [Everyone immediately undress. I want to know the truth of the *case*] (4.12, lines 48–49), and (3) yet again when she put her spectacles on "Pour ne juger du *cas* légérement" [So as not to judge the *case* superficially] (4.12, line 100). One of those "cas" will knock those spectacles off her nose.

4.14 "The Tub" ("Le Cuvier")

Source: Boccaccio, *Decameron,* Seventh Day, Second Story

"The Tub" begins with echoes of the two tales that precede it: "Soyez amant, vous serez inventif: / Tour *ni détour, ruse* ni stratagème / Ne vous faudront" [Be a lover, you will be inventive. Neither trick *nor detour, ruse* nor stratagem will you lack] (4.14, lines 1–3). In "Convincing Kate," the narrator recommends just the opposite: *not* to look for a "détour" or a "ruse": "en amours faut / Batre le fer quand il est chaud, / Sans chercher *ny détour ny ruse*" [in love you must strike the iron while it is hot, seeking *neither detour nor ruse*] (4.13, lines 70–72). La Fontaine was himself looking for a "détour" (4.12, line 59) to express decently what it was the young man tied. These three tales are tied together by the thread of the "détour." The threads of a "ruse" and a repeated "ni" are added to tie "Convincing Kate" ("ny détour ny ruse") all the more tightly with "The Tub" ("ni détour, ruse ni"), a combination unique to those two tales, while an opposition between "chercher" and "trouver" further connects "The Eyeglasses" ("Comment *trouver* un *détour*") with "Convincing Kate" ("Sans *chercher ... détour*").

The three are linked as well by their common focus on the unstoppable machinery of sexual arousal. We saw it in "The Eyeglasses" when the visual delights of the naked nuns were depicted as "ressorts" [springs] that "Eurent bientôt fait jouer la machine" [soon made the machine spring into action] (4.12, lines 108, 109), causing the thread to break, and in "Convincing Kate" when Janot reports in what state Dame Lust has put him and the resulting dire straits in which his "cas" was placed. In "The Tub," when the lover is fondling the wife "Ils en étaient sur un point, sur un point ... / C'est dire assez de ne le dire point" [They were at a point, at a point.... To say nothing is to say enough] (4.14, lines 23–24; ellipsis in the text).

Words Unique to This Tale and the One Before

"ny détour ny ruse" / "ni détour, ruse ni"

4.15 "Mission Impossible" ("La Chose impossible")

Source: Unknown

In both this tale and "The Tub,"

(1) A pair of lovers are interrupted in their lovemaking by an intruder: the husband when the adulterous couple "étaient sur un point, sur point..." [at a point, at a point...] (4.14, line 23), the demon when the lover "Goûte des voluptés" (4.15, line 26).

(2) The woman is quick to come up with a solution.

(3) Her solution is to give the intruder a task to perform that will give the lovers the opportunity to continue their lovemaking.

(4) The task is to work on an object to change its state: to clean out the cask, to straighten the hair.

(5) The object is circular, if in different ways: the cask is round, the hair is a "ligne circulaire / Et courbe" [circular line, and curved] (4.15, lines 57–58)

(6) Force is applied to the object.

(7) Water is applied as well.

(8) The task is repetitive: the husband "repasse / Sur chaque endroit" [passed again over each place] (4.14, lines 60–61), and "regratta" [rescraped] (4.15, line 65); the demon not only gives the hair repeated hammer blows, but tries as many different techniques as he can think of.

The tales are precisely opposed in that the task imposed in "The Tub" is time-consuming but doable, while the one imposed in "Mission Impossible" is, as the title asserts, impossible.

The demon is given "de *l'ouvrage*" [some *work*] (4.15, line 85) to do; the task imposed on the husband is called the same thing, Love and Cuckoldry "imposant un *ouvrage* / À nos amants bien différent du *sien*" [imposing a *work* on our lovers quite different from *his*] (4.14, lines 63–64). When the lover in "Mission Impossible" is with his mistress he "*Goûte* des voluptés qui n'ont point de pareilles" [*Tastes* pleasures that have no equal] (4.15, line 36) but in fact this tasting does find its equal in the joy the wife in "The Tub" tells her husband she has never tasted but that in fact she had been been savoring just before his arrival and that she has already found a way to enjoy again: "Je n'ai *goûté* jusqu'ici nulle joie: / J'en *goûterai* désormais, attends-t'y" [I have until now *tasted* no joy; I *will taste* some from now on, you can count on it] (4.14, lines 46–47).

The hair is named as "le *fil*" [the thread] (4.15, line 62), appropriately echoing the word's appearance in "The Tub," where it denotes the very thing the "*fil*" in "Mission Impossible" enables the lovers to resume: "notre couple ... / Reprit aussi *le fil*" [4.14, our couple ... took up again the *thread*] (lines 66–67).

4.16 *"The Magnificent One"* *("Le Magnifique")*

Source: Boccaccio, *Decameron*,
Third Day, Fifth Story

La Fontaine has planted a number of verbal ties connecting this tale to "Mission Impossible":

(1) The horse with which Magnifico distracted the husband was "bien *taillé*" [well built] (4.16, line 63). The task with which the lover distracted the demon was *taillé*, too, in the only other appearance of that word in the *Tales*: "plus d'un compagnon / Vous aurait *taillé* de l'ouvrage" [more than one companion would have *cut* you out some work] (4.15, lines. 84–85), he tells the demon when he returns, unable to fulfill the order. You would have had, in other words, your work cut out for you with the others, too—which means that he had his work cut out for him with the first one. The horse and the hair are each "taillé," in different senses, but appropriately so as they both serve the purpose of distracting the obstacle to the lovers' getting together.

(2) When Magnifico proposes to give his horse in exchange for a few minutes' conversation with the wife, Aldobrandin "commence *d'y rêver*" [begins *to dream* about it] (4.16, line 85). In the only other appearance of "de + rêver" in the *Tales*, "L'amant, à force *de rêver* / Sur les ordres nouveaux" [The lover, by force of *dreaming up* new commands] (4.15, lines 39–40), soon runs out of ideas.

(3) Both lovers call their beloved "divinité," in the only times in the *Tales* that word appears in the singular. "Le Ciel vous fit ... *Divinité*" [Heaven made you a ... *Divinity*] (4.16, lines 121–22), Magnifico tells Aldobrandin's wife. The lover in "Misson Im-

possible," unable to think of further tasks to give the demon, "s'en plaignit à sa *divinité*" [complained to his *divinity*] (4.15, line 42).

(4) The theme of tasting sexual delights, that began in "The Tub" when the wife said "Je n'ai *goûté* jusqu'ici nulle joie" [I have until now *tasted* no joy] but "J'en *goûterai* désormais" [I *will taste* some from now on] (4.14, lines 46–47), and continues in "Mission Impossible" when the lover "*Goûte* des voluptés qui n'ont point de pareille" [*Tastes* pleasures that have no equal] (4.15, line 36), continues when Magnifico tells the wife how they can "*Goûter* le fruit de ce commun martyre; / De votre époux nous venger et nous rire" [*Taste* the fruit of this common martyrdom: take vengeance on your husband and laugh in each other's company] (4.16, lines 143–44).

(5) When Magnifico pretends to admit defeat, the husband laughs, and makes fun of him for giving up so soon: "vous lâchez *trop tôt* prise" [you give up *too soon*] (4.16, line 181). The lover had made the same taunt to the demon: "vous perdez un peu *trop tôt* courage" [you're losing courage a little *too soon*] (4.15, line 83). (6) Magnifico resembles the demon in another way: both have to contend with an unresponsive femininity. Confronted by this surprising resistance, both are led to wonder, What is this? "*Qu'est ceci*" [*What is this*] (4.15, line 74), the demon asks; "*Qu'est-ce là?*" [*What is that?*] (4.16, line 119), asks Magnifico.

Words Unique to This Tale and the One Before

(1) "taillé"
(2) "de" + "rêver"
(3) "divinité" in the singular applied to a beloved

Significant Alterations

(1) La Fontaine departs from his source in having Magnifico impose a time limit of fifteen minutes to his conversation with the wife. Interestingly, he actually finishes before the allotted time. This is what provokes Aldobrandin's laughter and his remark about giving up too soon, creating a verbal parallel ("trop tôt") with 4.15.

(2) His speediness, which is also demonstrated by his ability to compress six months of courtship into less than a quarter hour, which has no basis in the source either, parallels the demon's speediness in accomplishing all tasks but the last.

4.17 *"The Painting" ("Le Tableau")*

Source: Pietro Aretino, *Ragionamenti*

The difference between what ears and eyes perceive, important in this tale because "The Painting" presents itself as a transformation of something made for the eyes into something made for the ears, is also important in "The Magnificent One," where the title character is obliged to translate what he sees on his beloved's face into the words she would have said had her husband not forbade her to speak. Confronted with a silent picture and asked to make it speak, La Fontaine's situation in "The Painting" parallels the one in which the protagonist of the other tale finds himself. He "reads" her face; La Fontaine reads the picture. Indeed, the picture may be puzzling enough to need some deciphering. All we know of it for sure are two elements—a broken chair and a fallen rustic—which La Fontaine is obliged to explain: "Je veux, quoi qu'il en soit, expliquer à des belles / Cette chaise rompue, et ce rustre tombé" [I want, whatever else, to explain to the ladies this broken chair and this fallen rustic] (4.17, lines 35–36). Everything else in the narration flows from his effort to explain those two elements.

The two constituent parts of the first of these elements were already present in "The Magnificent One":

(1) "cette chaise...": The heart of the action in "The Painting," certainly as far as the picture is concerned, takes place on and around a chair. The scene between the Magnificent One and Aldobrandin's wife also takes place on chairs, his and hers. The nuns, in turn, try using the rustic as a seat of sorts.

(2) "...rompue": The nuns do not need nor indeed want the visitor to say a word. Comparing him to the seminarian they had been expecting, one had said to the other: "Il vaut bien l'autre, que t'en semble? ... / Qu'attendions-nous ici? Qu'il nous fût débité / De beaux discours? Non non, ni rien qui leur ressemble" [He's as good as the other, don't you think? ... What are we waiting for? To hear fine speeches? No, no, nothing of the sort] (4.17, lines 132, 134–35). Like the painting where he sits center stage, the rustic will engage in no discourse, fine or otherwise, while the two nuns improvise their own—the "discours véhément, et plein d'émotion" [violent discourse, full of emotion] (4.17, line 176) of which Thérèse showed herself capable—around him, as Magnifico improvised his—not violent, though likewise emotional and amorous—around the mute object of his affection. Remaining mute, the nuns' guest resembles Aldobrandin's taciturn wife. The nuns' silent guest, La Fontaine remarks, "C'était l'homme d'Ésope" [He was Aesop's man] (4.17, line 142), alluding to an episode in La Fontaine's "Vie d'Ésope le Phrygien" [Life of Aesop the Phrygian]: Aesop was enslaved to Xanthus, who told him to go find a man who took no pains for any reason whatsoever. Aesop searched in the streets, "et voyant un paysan qui regardait toutes choses avec la froideur et l'indifférence d'une statue" [and seeing a peasant who looked upon all things with the coldness and indifference of a statue] (Pléiade edition, p. 17), he brought him to Xanthus. Aldobrandin's wife gives the appearance of

a statue too, which is why the first thing Magnifico reads in her silent countenance is the declaration that she isn't one: "Ne croyez pas, monsieur, / Que la nature ait composé mon coeur / De marbre dur" [Do not think, sir, that nature made my heart of hard marble] (4.16, lines 132–35).

Magnifico says the reason he knows she wants to tell him this is that something in her look breaks through: "ce coin d'oeil, par son langage doux, / *Rompt* à mon sens quelque peu le silence" [this corner of your eye, by its gentle language, *breaks*, I think, the silence a little] (4.16. 130–31). That rupture, in the intertext formed by La Fontaine's careful sequencing of his tales, is connected to that suffered by "Cette chaise *rompue*" (4.17, line 36); the repeated verb's importance is underlined by the fact that it reappears in the scene of the demise of the chair: "l'Amour est en étrange garçon.... / Le voilà qui *rompt* tout.... / Ses jeux sont violents. À terre on vit bientôt / Le galant cathédral" [Love is a strange boy.... Here he *breaks* everything.... His games are violent. On the ground one soon sees the galant chair-sitter] (4.17. 164, 170–72). Love made the chair break; love, one could reasonably conclude, also broke the silence, through the sweet discourse of "ce coin d'oeil."

Thus part of the little La Fontaine had to go on (or the little he reveals to us of the picture), the "rompue" of "Cette chaise rompue, et ce rustre tombé" is part and parcel of the little Magnifico had to go on, the break in the silence.

The Uncollected Tales

As we have seen, La Fontaine arranged his tales in the four definitive volumes (dating from 1665, 1669, 1671, and 1674) in a meaningful order, their sequential connnections even extending in each case from the last tale in one volume to the first in the next. Although he did not live long enough to gather the eight other tales he would eventually publish into a single collection, it is possible to detect the sequence he probably had in mind for them if we take into account the chronology of their publication and, when more than one appeared together, the order of their arrangement there. For the sake of convenience I will refer to them as 5.1, 5.2, etc. "The Ephesian Matron" (5.1) and "Belphegor" (5.2) were published in the *Poème du Quinquina et autres ouvrages en vers de M. de La Fontaine* in 1682; "The Little Bell" (5.3), "The River Scamander" (5.4), "The Unwitting Go-Between" (5.5), "The Remedy" (5.6), and "Indiscreet Confessions" (5.7) appeared in *Ouvrages de prose et de poésie des sieurs de Maucroix et de La Fontaine* in 1685; "Mixed Up in the Dark" (5.8) appeared in the *Oeuvres posthumes* in 1696, the year after La Fontaine's death, probably with his blessing (Alain-Marie Bassy,

Folio edition, p. 549). In addition, "The Ephesian Matron" (5.1) and "Belphegor" (5.2) appeared together (again, in that order) in 1694 in the twelfth book of the *Fables*. There, as I argue in *In La Fontaine's Labyrinth* (pp. 179–86), they show numerous connections with the fables on either side ("Philémon et Baucis" and "Les Filles de Minée") and with each other. There is no evidence that La Fontaine ever intended to publish "A Rearward Glance," which did not appear in print until 1714 (and when it did it was attributed to another poet, Jean-Baptiste Rousseau), so I do not think he intended it ever to appear in a sequence with the other eight or any other tales.

5.1 "The Ephesian Matron" ("La Matrone d'Éphèse")

Source: Petronius, *The Satiricon*

In both "The Painting" (4.17) and "The Ephesian Matron" a man comes to the door behind which two women live and they ultimately accept him as a substitute for another man as a sexual partner for one or both. In neither case did the man seek out the women; rather, the servant in the convent (in 4.17) had merely come to the wrong door, and the soldier (in 5.1) was simply intrigued by the light and the weeping coming from the tomb. The nuns could see that the man who knocked on their door was "un trésor" [a treasure] (4.17, line 127), which is how the Ephesian Matron considered her husband: "la Dame voulait paître encore ses yeux / Du *trésor* qu'enfermait la bière" [the woman wanted to feed her eyes for a while yet on the *treasure* the casket enclosed] (5.1, lines 67–68)—the husband for whom she would find a substitute in the man who came to her door. These are the only occasions in the *Tales* in which a woman calls a man a "trésor."

There are other matrons in the *Tales*, but with one notable exception they are, unlike the Ephesian Matron, given no sexuality. In "The Mandrake," Calfucci, wanting a child, consulted matrons along with charlatans and magicians (3.2, line 18). In "King Candaules and the Professor of Law" a "matron austère" (4.8, line 158) guards a wife's door against lovers. But a remarkably sexual matron appears in "The Painting": "Toute *matrone* sage, à ce que dit Catulle, / Regarde volontiers le gigantesque don" [Every wise *matron*, according to Catullus, willingly looks at the gigantic gift] that Juno gave Priapus (4.17, lines 11–12). Not only do these two tales have the only matrons with any interest in sex; they have the only wise ones: the "matrone *sage*" in the passage just quoted, and the Ephesian Matron, who was "Une dame en *sagesse* et vertus sans égale" [A lady unequalled in *wisdom* and virtues] (5.1, line 12).

In the prologue to both, La Fontaine is "engaged" to tell a problematic tale. "The Painting" may be too scabrous to relate: "On m'*engage* à conter d'une manière honnête / Le sujet d'un de ces tableaux / Sur lesquels on met des rideaux" [I have been *engaged* to tell in a decent manner the subject of one of those paintings one hides behind curtains] (4.17, lines 1–3). "The Ephesian Matron" may be too well-worn: "un conte usé, commun, et rabattu.... Qui t'*engage* à cette entreprise?" [a worn-out, commun, and already-told.... Who *engaged* you to perform such a task?] (5.1, lines 1, 4).

Words Unique to This Tale and the One Before

(1) The narrator is "engaged" ("On m'engage," "Qui t'*engage*") to tell a story.
(2) A woman regards a man as a "trésor."

5.2 "Belphegor" ("Belphégor")

Source: Machiavelli, *The Marriage of Belphegor*

The Ephesian Matron wanted to follow her husband to hell: "Elle entre dans sa tombe, en ferme volonté / D'accompagner cette ombre aux enfers descendue" [She enters his tomb, firmly resolved to accompany this shade which had descended into hell] (5.1, lines 45–46). The tragic figure of the grieving Matron finds a comic counterpart in Madame Honnesta, who chases her husband "par tout le monde" [throughout the world] (5.2, line 260)—everywhere *except* hell, where he goes to escape her at last: "le Diable décampa, / S'enfuit au fond des Enfers" [the devil decamped, and fled to the depths of hell] (5.2, 262–63).

Both women are "prudes." Summing up her conquest by the soldier, La Fontaine comments, "*Prudes* vous vous devez défier de vos forces ... témoin cette Matrone" [*Prudes*, you shouldn't trust your powers to resist.... Consider this matron] (5.1, lines 182, 186). Recounting Honnesta's claims to virtue, he adds, "Il n'est pas sûr qu'Honnesta ne fît rien: / Ces *prudes*-là nous en font bien accroire" [That Honnesta did not sin is not a sure thing. Such *prudes* deceive us] (5.2, lines 140–41). (These are the only passages in the *Tales* where "prudes" appears in the plural.)

Both women make noise at night and attract the curiosity of someone nearby who comes to investigate. The soldier guarding the hanged man sees light through the cracks of the tomb. "Curieux, il y *court*, entend de loin la Dame / Remplissant l'air de ses clameurs" [Curious, he *runs* there, hears from afar the lady filling the air with her clamors] (5.1, lines 97–98) of grief. First he runs, then he hears the noise she's making; in the case of Honnesta and the neighbors, it's the reverse: "Le bruit fut tel que madame Honnesta / Plus d'une fois les voisins éveilla: / Plus d'une fois on *courut* à la noise" [The noise was such that Madame Honnesta more than once woke up the neighbors. More than once they *ran* to the disturbance] (5.2, lines 131–33). The Matron's noise is her cries of grief for her lost husband; Honnesta's, her expressions of anger at hers.

In the dedication to Mlle de Champmeslé that was part of "Belphegor" in its first appearance (as a tale) but was deleted when it was published (as a fable) in the twelfth book of the *Fables*, La Fontaine writes, "Nos noms unis perceront *l'ombre* noire" [Our united names will pierce the black *shadow*] (line 7 [Pléiade edition, p. 897]). I think this is a subtle nod in the direction of the Matron's intention "D'accompagner cette *ombre* aux enfers descendue" [to accompany this shade which had descended into hell] (5.1, line 46). Though the word "ombre" appears several times in other tales, only in these two is it connected to death. In this passage from "The Ephesian Matron" it denotes the "shade" of the Matron's late husband; in the prologue to "Belphegor" it denotes "la nuit des temps" [the night of time] (line 5), time after the death of La Fontaine and Mlle de Champmeslé that their fame can pierce. Later in "Belphegor," a similar expression, "l'éternelle nuit" [eternal night], denotes hell itself: Belphegor "traverse ... / Ce que le Ciel voulut mettre d'espace / Entre ce monde et l'éternelle nuit" [traverses ... the space God put between this world and eternal night] (5.2, lines 42–44). In other words, in his prologue to "Belphegor," La Fontaine envisions accompanying Mlle de Champmeslé after death as the Ephesian Matron envisioned accompanying her husband.

Significant Alteration

In Petronius, the source for "The Ephesian Matron," the criminal was crucified, not hanged. By having him hanged—on a "*potence*" [gallows] (5.1, line 84)—La Fontaine sets up another parallel with "Belpheghor," for when Matteo confesses he cannot make the devil come out of the princess, "On vous le happe, et mène à la *potence*" [He is grabbed and taken to the *gallows*] (5.2, line 252).

Words Unique to This Tale and the One Before

(1) "prudes" in the plural
(2) "ombre" connected to death

5.3 "The Little Bell" ("La Clochette")

Source: Unknown

Belphegor disguises himself as a mortal to entice a woman to marry him; the young man in "The Little Bell" disguises himself as a heifer to seduce a girl. The young man wants the girl to follow him; by contrast, Belphegor later tries to prevent his wife from following him. The sound of the cowbell is all that constitutes the young man's disguise; the sound of the drum makes Belphegor abandon his.

When Honnesta yelled at her husband, it woke the neighbors; "Plus d'une fois on *courut* à la noise" [More than once they *ran* to the disturbance] (5.2, line 133). But when the girl cried out in her distress, no one came running: she "Remplit de cris ces lieux peu fréquentés; / Nul n'*accourut*" [Filled with her cries this deserted place. No one *came running*] (5.3, lines 67–68). This continues a thread begun in "The Ephesian Matron," noted above.

Words Unique to This Fable and the One Before

The young man is able, thanks to his disguise, to fulfill the desire that arises when he "*lorgne*" [ogles] (5.3, line 30) the girl. The only other time that verb appears in the *Tales* is when Matheo "*lorgne*" [ogles] (5.2, line 344) the pile of money he will earn if he manages to get Belphegor to abandon his disguise by coming out of the King of Naples's daughter.

5.4 "The River Scamander" ("Le Fleuve Scamandre")

Source: Aeschines, letter 10

Cimon disguises himself as a river god to seduce a girl, as the young man in "The Little Bell" pretends to be a heifer for the same motive. Both first cast eyes on the girl in question by a riverbank: "sur le bord d'un ruisseau" [on the edge of a stream] (5.3, line 25); "sur ces bords" [on these banks] (5.4, line 41). Both girls are remarkably naive. La Fontaine calls one of them a "*bergère*" [shepherdess] (5.3, line 41), even though she herds cows, not sheep; the other has an "air de *bergère*" [shepherdess's air] (5.4, line 39).

In both, La Fontaine begins by excusing himself for writing yet another erotic tale. "J'ouvre l'esprit, et rends le sexe *habile*" [I open the mind, and make the female sex *capable*] (5.4, line 14) of seeing through men's stratagems, he says in "The River Scamander"; echoing what he wrote in "The Cowbell," in a discussion of the age of marital consent for girls: "Non qu'à treize ans on y soit *inhabile*" [Not that at thirteen a girl is legally *incapable*] (5.3, line 34).

The thread of the woman's "cry" continues, in a wholly new context. In the streets of the city, when she spots Cimon in a crowd, she "*crie* en ce moment: / Ah! voilà le fleuve Scamandre" [*cries out* then: 'Ah! There is the River Scamander'] (5.4, lines 95–96).

By contrast to the girl's cries in "The Little Bell," which attracted no attention, this cry drew a crowd. By contrast as well, while the other girl was crying out in alarm, this one was crying out in joy at seeing Cimon again.

5.5 "The Unwitting Go-Between" ("La Confidente sans le savoir ou le Stratagème")

Source: Boccaccio, *Decameron*,
Third Day, Third Story

In "The River Scamander" Cimon lies to the girl, and she doesn't see through the lie; thus is he able to consummate his desire. In "The Unwitting Go-Between" Amantha lies to Alis, and thus to Cleon since she knows that Alis will relay to him everything she says, but Cleon sees through the lie; thus are both able to consummate their desire. Cimon flees the crowd's violence: "aucuns à coups de pierre / Poursuivirent le dieu qui *s'enfuit* à grand'erre" [some, throwing stones, pursued the god, who *fled* as fast as he could] (5.4, lines 99–100); Amantha pretends that Cleon will have to flee from her bodyguards' violence: "Je poserais tantôt un si bon guet / Qu'il serait pris ainsi qu'au trébuchet, / Ou *s'enfuirait* avec sa courte honte" [I would soon post such a good watch that he would be caught as if in a trap, or would *flee* in shame] (5.5, lines 158–60). *Significant alteration:* This threat of an ambush does not appear in the source for 5.5; he evidently added it to set up this parallel with 5.4.

5.6 "The Remedy" ("Le Remède")

Source: Unknown

It is thanks to her remarkable "*esprit*" [wit] (5.5, line 197) that Amantha cooks up the fiction about the likelihood of Cleon's being attacked if he comes to her house, in which fiction she supplies all the details he will need to complete the assignation. It is "En fille sotte et n'ayant point d'*esprit*" [As a silly girl having no *wit*] (5.6, line 101) that the young woman in "The Remedy" actually does expose the young man to a physical attack of sorts. Had the governess not been fooled into thinking he was the girl, she would have considered him an intruder in the house, as she was not in on the secret of his nightly visits; neither were her parents. Both men come surrpetitiously; both arrive at midnight.

In the prologue, La Fontaine claims that "The Remedy" is based on a true story, "Mais quant aux *noms*, il faut au moins les *taire*" [But as for the *names*, they at least must be *kept quiet*] (5.6, line 9). This strangely echoes two passages in which Amantha speaks of keeping quiet the name of the person who she claims brought her love notes and gifts from Cleon: "une dont le *nom* / Vous est connu; je le *tais* pour raison" [one whose *name* is known to you; I *keep it quiet* for good reason] (5.5, line 70); "cette personne honnête / Que vous savez, et dont je *tais* le *nom*" [this upright person whom you know, and whose *name* I *keep quiet*] (5.5, lines 143–44). This verbal clue points us to the possibility that La Fontaine as narrator in "The Remedy" may be likening himself to Amantha. Why? Perhaps because the tale he tells in "The Remedy," despite his claim, is as fictional as hers.

5.7 "Indiscreet Confessions" ("Les Aveux indiscrets")

Source: Various, including
Les Cent Nouvelles Nouvelles, 8

In "The Remedy" a woman doesn't expose herself when she should; in "Indiscreet Confessions," she exposes herself, in another sense, when she shouldn't have. Yet both happen because she is "sotte"; the one "The Remedy" is a "fille *sotte*" [silly girl] (5.6, line 101), as is the daughter in the opinion of her mother (5.7, line 60) and the narrator (5.7, line 102).

In both tales, La Fontaine anticipates doubts from his readers. In "The Remedy," he imagines them saying, "Nous avons lieu d'en *douter*" [We have reason to *doubt*] (5.6, line 104) that the girl could have been as foolish as she was; that the son and the father would put on the saddle and the girth to proclaim their shame to the neighbors is likewise something of which "On *doutera*" [One *will doubt*] (5.7, line 84). In the last lines of each, he hints at a connection between the events just recounted and his own experience: "Chacun ne peut en dire autant que moi" [No one can say as much as I] (5.6, line 133) about the veracity of the tale told in "The Remedy"; in "Indiscreet Confessions," he concludes that he has given good advice, but "Les ai-je pris pour moi-même? hélas! non" [Did I take it myself? Alas, no!] (5.7, line 117).

5.8 "Mixed Up in the Dark" ("Les Quiproquos")

Source: Marguerite de Navarre,
Heptameron, Story 8

The two women in "Mixed Up in the Dark" are remarkably alike physically: "De même taille et de pareil maintien.... [S]ous le masque on n'eût su bonnement / Laquelle élire entre ces créatures" [Of the same size and the demeanor.... If they were wearing a mask one would not have known which to choose] (5.8, lines 55, 59–60). The two women in "Indiscreet Confessions" are remarkably alike in that they both have had a child out of wedlock, and that neither of their husbands knew this until they revealed it. Their two husbands are remarkably alike in that both have the same reaction to the news, standing on the same street corner, one wearing a saddle and the other its girth, yelling at the top of their voices, "*Je suis bâté, sanglé*, car il n'importe, / Tous deux sont bons" [*I am saddled, girded*—for it doesn't matter: both are good] (5.7, lines 94–95). It "doesn't matter" because both convey the same meaning. The two men in "Mixed Up in the Dark" become very alike in the scene in the cellar. They conspire to make the maid think that when each makes love to her they are the same man; when the wife, instead of the maid, arrives at the rendezvous they do not "lui donner le temps de reconnaître / Ceci, cela, l'erreur, le changement, / la différence enfin qui pouvait être / Entre l'époux et son associé" [give her the time to recognize this, that, the error, the switch, what difference there might in fact be between the husband and his friend] (5.8, lines 147–50). Both men in "Indiscreet Confessions" make their cuckoldry public knowledge, though they needn't have; both men in "Mixed Up in the Dark" make this husband a cuckold, the husband by agreeing to share the maid with his friend, the friend by making love to the husband's wife.

BIBLIOGRAPHY

Ariosto. *Orlando Furioso*. Translated by Guido Waldman, Oxford: Oxford University Press / Oxford World's Classics, 1983.

Athenaeus. *The Deipnosophists*. Translated by Charles Burton Gulick. Cambridge: Harvard University Press / Loeb Library, 1980, vol. 5.

Boccaccio. *Decameron*. Edited by Vittore Branca. Turin: Einaudi, 1992.

_____. _____. Translated by G. H. McWilliam, New York: Penguin, 1995.

_____. *Les Cent Nouvelles Nouvelles*. In *Conteurs français du seizième siècle*. Edited by Pierre Jourda. Gallimard / Pléiade, Paris: 1965: 1–358.

Dandrey, Patrick. "Le cordeau et le hasard: réflexions sur l'agencement du recueil des *Fables*." *Papers on French Seventeenth Century Literature* 23.44 (1996): 73–85.

_____. *Poétique de La Fontaine. 1. La fabrique des fables*. Paris: Presses Universitaires de France, 1996.

Danner, Richard. "La Fontaine's *Fables*, Book X: The Labyrinth Hypothesis." *L'Esprit Créateur* 21.4 (Winter 1981): 90–98.

Gross, Nathan. "Order and Theme in La Fontaine's *Fables*, Book VI." *L'Esprit Créateur* 21.4 (Winter 1981): 78–89.

La Fontaine, Jean de. *Contes et Nouvelles en vers*. Edited by Georges Couton. Paris: Garnier, 1961.

_____. *Contes et Nouvelles en vers*. Edited by Alain-Marie Bassy. Paris: Gallimard / Folio, 1982.

_____. *Fables*. Edited by Alain-Marie Bassy. Paris: GF Flammarion, 2007.

_____. *Oeuvres complètes. I. Fables, Contes et Nouvelles*. Edited by Jean-Pierre Collinet. Paris: Gallimard / Pléiade, 1991.

Le Pestipon, Yves. "Note sur cette édition" and "Notes," in: La Fontaine, *Fables*, ed. Alain-Marie Bassy: 35–37, 413–514.

Lindner, Hermann. *Didaktische Gattungsstruktur und Narratives Spiel: Studien zur Erzähltechnik in La Fontaines Fabeln*. Munich: Wilhelm Fink Verlag, 1975.

The New Princeton Encylopedia of Poetry and Poetics. Edited by Preminger, Alex and T. V. F. Brogan. Princeton: Princeton University Press, 1993.

Ovid. *Metamorphoses*. Translated by Mary M. Innes. New York: Penguin Books, 1955.

Rubin, David Lee. "Triple Calculus: Notes Toward a Poetic and Rhetoric of La Fontaine's *Fables*, Book 7. *The Ladder of High Designs: Structure and Interpretation of the French Lyric Sequence*. Edited by Doranne Fenoaltea and David Lee Rubin. Charlottesvile: University Press of Virginia, 1991: 91–109.

Runyon, Randolph Paul. *In La Fontaine's Labyrinth: A Thread through the Fables*. Charlottesville, Va.: Rookwood Press, 2000.

Scaglione, Aldo D. "Shahrar, Giocondo, Kote'rviky: Three Versions of the Motif of the Faithless Woman," *Oriens* 11.1/2 (Dec. 11, 1958): 151–61.

Slater, Maya. "La Fontaine's *Fables*, Book VII: The Problem of Order." *Modern Language Review* 82.3 (July 1987): 573–86.

Tyler, J. Allen. *A Concordance to the Fables and Contes of Jean de La Fontaine*. Ithaca: Cornell University Press, 1974.

INDEX